D1809047

A PLAGUE OF DISSENT

A Political Thriller

NIC TAYLOR

This book is dedicated to all those that have put up with me over the years, but in particular to my three beautiful children, Adam, Dan and Shakira.

Chapter 1

Rosie sat all night alone in the dark, not daring to turn on a light and far too frightened to sleep. Fear crept through every pore of her body. How could she sleep when she knew that there were men outside who were waiting for her to leave the house. Knowledge of that terrified her. The men banged on the front door, shouting through her letterbox and checking every accessible window.

All night she'd huddled up on the couch, fearful of every sound outside. Each creak of the old house filled her with panic.

Had the men somehow got inside?

She saw them arrive outside the front of her apartment, only minutes after arriving home. She'd parked her car in the car park just around the corner, rather than outside the apartment. She didn't want to advertise her presence. She was uncertain if they knew she was home, but convinced they wouldn't leave until they'd found her.

Rosie's heartbeat pounded in her ears; her breath caught in her throat, acid rose in her stomach, and the urge to be sick consumed her. She needed to focus and clear her mind, but the fear of being captured overshadowed all her thoughts.

The events of the past week churned through her mind. How had they discovered what she'd done? Everything had been arranged by text. No one could have overheard a thing, but evidently someone had. And the news of that; how had it spread so quickly? One second she was committing the act, and the next these men were everywhere.

Over the past hour, her thoughts gradually turned from fear to the desperate need to escape. Weighing her options, he paced her small living room in an attempt to calm her thoughts. The front door was out of the question. She could climb out of her bathroom window, sneak out through the rear garden of the apartment below and into the back lane, and then get to her car before it got light. That was her best option. No, it was her only option. Dawn was an hour away, and she was nearly out of time. It was now or never. She had to make a decision.

She slipped on a pair of trainers and packed a small bag. Necessities only, her car keys, a pair of pants, and the cash she'd frantically scraped out of a drawer, her passport and credit cards were the only items she carried in the bag. Her only coherent thought was to get the hell out of town before the shit truly hit the fan.

Opening the bathroom window she slid out with her bag in tow, and dropped the few feet into the garden, trembling as she did. It was dark, very dark, and what little light the moon would have provided was soaked up by the thick black rain clouds that hung overhead. Cautiously, she made her way down the garden path, taking care not to kick one of the numerous potted plants that lined it, towards the gate and the back lane.

She checked; the lane was clear, and she could see the

car where she had left it the night before. None of the men were in sight.

It's now or never.

They would spot her soon enough, and the chase would begin.

With all the strength, she could muster Rosie took a deep breath, steeling herself for what she had to do before she slowly eased open the gate, hoping it didn't creak and give her escape away. She entered the lane. The street lights at each end of the short lane, normally welcome, would tonight spotlight her to anybody at either end. She took her first steps as two men appeared under the street light at the far end. Too late now, they'd seen her. The shout went up

"There she is! She's going for the car park."

These words were quickly replaced by the sounds of running feet, as close to a dozen men appeared around the corner, illuminated under the street light.

She had no choice now, running was her only option. Rosie froze, but only for a moment. Then she ran.

Only three hundred meters to the car park. Get into the car, and get away.

I can do this.

Rosie ran, heedless of the numerous potholes brimming with water from the overnight rain that contrived to bring her to her knees, and dodged the randomly placed waste collection bins overflowing with rubbish. She crossed the road at the end; the car park and her car was close now, just on the other side of the road. She could hear her pursuers' feet splash through the puddles, getting closer with every second. Venturing a glance over her shoulder, she could see they were gaining on her. She saw the double-decker bus when it was far too late.

When she turned her head back, the bus was on top of

her, the shock on the driver's face clearly visible as he tried to brake and steer away. Rosie screamed. The scream was followed by a sickening crunch, as the number six bus flung her ten meters through the air, to crumple like a rag doll onto a parked car.

Rosie lay over the front of the car, crumpled and broken on this wet forlorn morning, with her dying thoughts.

Why?

The seduction that started it had been going on from the moment she first began to temp in his office. Yes, of course she had known Alex Great was married, but his power and all that money he controlled as Chief Secretary to the Treasury seriously pressed her buttons. After all, all the politicians did it, didn't they? The more senior they were, the more they slept around, and the office temps seemed to be the nature of the game. At least that was what her friend Jonathan had told her.

For the past five years, ever since her divorce, she'd had a succession of temp jobs. The first, in the International's office, where she had met and had a brief fling with Jonathan Mason, and then one Fleet Street office or another followed. None being quite what she truly wanted; all of them left her unfulfilled, her true worth never recognised. The men she worked for saw only one thing, her stunning figure, which if truth be told, she'd always displayed and used to her advantage. But she craved more, much more; one day the right job or man, perhaps both, would come along, but until then she would make the most of her situation and her assets.

When she ran into Jonathan at a party, she'd told him quite innocently of her new job and the attentions she was getting from her new boss. She'd jumped at the offer Jonathan had made.

For several weeks, the Chief Secretary had been pleading with Rosie to have dinner with him. Following Jonathan's suggestions she had capitulated, accepting an invitation to dine at the penthouse he kept at the Soho Hotel. He didn't want to be seen out in public with her, she assumed. The thoughts of the eventual, generous pay day that Jonathan had promised removed any residual doubt she might have had.

That fateful night, Rosie knew she looked exceptionally good, she always did. Her office attire was revealing enough, but the dress she wore tonight, was little more than a spray- on. A sheath of red, clinging to her every ample curve, revealing more than it concealed. She'd expected that they would eat before she got her clothes off, but it hadn't happened that way. No sooner was the door closed, than Alex began to pull off that tantalising dress, quickly revealing her stupendous body.

Later, lying back on the bed, she thought that, for an old, fat and balding guy, he was quite an attentive lover. It had been far better sex than she had anticipated. He certainly talked a lot in the office, and she had just discovered that his tongue was quite skilled in several other things as well.

There was a knock on the suite door.

"Room service."

Alex opened the door and invited in the waiter with a service trolley.

"Over there," he said.

Ah yes, the hotel does like to look after their distinguished guests; I wonder what they have sent me?

The waiter pushed the trolley through the doors and into the center of the lounge of the hotel suite, and then proceeded to remove one of the silver domed lids covering the plates.

As he did so, it struck against a metallic object underneath, and the sound of metal upon metal caught Alex's attention. As the lid cleared the plate, Alex was perplexed to see not a plate of food, but a camera. This the waiter-playing paparazzi quickly picked up, shooting five frames per second before he even had his eye to the viewfinder. It captured the balding, fat politician wrapped only in a towel, with his pretty blonde temp in bed behind him, clearly visible through the wide open double bedroom doors.

"What do you think, ah..?"

As soon as the paparazzi had picked up the camera, Alex Great raised his hands to try to cover his face, letting go of the towel around his waist, which had quickly slipped to the floor. The final shots captured Alex naked, red faced and screaming obscenities.

"No, stop! Get out, get out!"

It was over before they knew what had hit them; a precursor of the double-decker bus that would take her life twelve hours later. The paparazzi was gone within a minute, his memory card full and containing over a hundred compromising shots of them. It undoubtedly was far too late to panic, but that is precisely what the politician had done. He was still screaming obscenities at Rosie, accusing her of setting him up; that his career was over and his life in ruins.

It had all seemed like such a brilliant idea at the start. The plan, as suggested to her by Jonathan, had been exceedingly simple. Sleep with him for a few months and get something on him which Jonathan could use. The affair in itself would probably be enough; she would also be amply rewarded, the five figure sum Jonathan mentioned would have been very useful indeed.

She hadn't bothered to think what Jonathan was getting out of the arrangement, or why he was prepared to pay so much for it. She'd worked with Jonathan as his secretary at the International, and should have been aware of his unorthodox methods. Unfortunately, like most dead certainties, it really wasn't turning out the way she expected, although this was precisely what Jonathan had planned. It never crossed her mind he wanted the dirt on Alex Great now, not in a few months.

Rosie hadn't anticipated this result at all. Lying in bed with a hysterical and profusely sweating politician, who was standing naked in front of her screaming obscenities at her, was not what she'd had in mind. Definitely this was the time to leave town for a while. One thing was for sure, he was not going to be a minister much longer, and he was no use to her anymore.

Grabbing her things, she'd slipped back into her dress. It wasn't the sort of thing she would wear underwear with, so there was no need to search for them. Then she'd run as fast as she possibly could, pulling on her shoes as she ran down the hotel corridor and arrived home minutes before the hordes of press arrived at her door.

The bus driver had not seen the men chasing Rosie, and so hadn't realised quite how the accident had happened. Nor did it occur to him to think how the press had arrived so quickly.

Rosie was splayed and motionless over the bonnet of the parked car, her head sagging down over the front, her neck broken. She was clearly dead, having taken the full impact of the bus as it accelerated away from the bus stop.

The driver immediately phoned for an ambulance before jumping out of his cab, and then checked for a pulse, which he felt sure was not going to be there. He grimaced as he did, trying to look away. Streams of blood ran down the bonnet and over the front of the car, pooling on the street. The tips of her long blonde hair, already beginning to stain the color of her blood, nestled in the widening red pool.

Her eyes were wide open and her crimson blood ran from both her mouth and nose, clearly illuminated by the cameras' flashes. The paparazzi had arrived.

The first two, surprisingly, did not go for their cameras immediately, but as the rest arrived with their flashes blazing, Carl turned to his associate Fred and said:

"Stupid bitch! We might as well get something for our trouble".

They, too, pulled up their cameras and recorded the scene, in all its gore.

Chapter 2

Several hours after Rosie's death, Carl and Fred were in their office at The International's HQ, or what used to be their office until recently. The office was hardly recognisable to what it had been only a week before. The four interconnecting rooms that made up the office space had been crammed with electronic monitoring equipment. It looked more like mission control for a space flight than a typical media office. Banks of flat screen computer monitors lined each workspace and a touch screen commanded the majority of most desks, with more monitors hung from a metal lattice work attached to the ceiling.

There wasn't a communication device, computer or data network in the UK, even those that didn't officially exist, that couldn't have been accessed from here. Now all that remained was the metal framework hung from the ceiling, along with a few desks and hundreds of cables that sprouted from every conceivable point or coiled up upon the remaining desks.

A TV on in the corner of one of these rooms, the boss's office, showed the Secretary of the Treasury getting out of his limo, outside No 10. The scene was a complete free for all; every TV crew in the western world seemed to be there, all jostling for the best position to record the action. They had only one theme to their shouted questions.

"Did he have any comments on the news stories that morning? Did he think the girl had committed suicide by running in front of the bus? And had he been summoned to No 10 to hand in his resignation?"

Carl, Fred and their boss Jonathan sat in his office, watching the breaking news. Through the glazed wall at the rear of the office, in an adjacent suite of rooms, three others could be seen packing the last of their delicate and expensive equipment away. When the breaking news bulletin finished, Jonathan turned to Fred and angrily spat:

"What the hell went wrong?"

"I sent the two of you to get the damn photos, not to instigate this shit fest. What were you doing?"

He certainly hadn't intended it to be all over the airwaves that day, if ever. Carl handed over the shots on the memory card to his boss. They were even better than expected, the last few he'd taken captured the politician naked, the dropped towel at his feet, his hands attempting to cover his face, screaming at the top of his lungs.

"Look, I'm sorry, boss, the guy just wouldn't shut up; he screamed louder than my teenage daughter does when I say no. I was no sooner out the damn door before every fucker on the floor was poking his head around the door to see what was going on. The security guys were there in seconds, and I thought they worked for us. It'll be one of those bastards that sold the story to that lot." Carl explained whilst pointing at the TV, still on in the corner.

"They've all got it, every bloody one of them", he

added, referring to the International's competitor news networks.

This certainly did not please Jonathan; he had plans for the Chief Secretary of the Treasury, Alex Great. Or more to the point, his private clients, Roseau and De Costa, had plans and were willing to pay a great deal of money to ensure they came to fruition. The pair had approached him a little over a year ago and, on the surface, both seemed like successful businessmen, although they seemed prepared to do whatever it took to keep ahead of the competition.

Their business was that of contract services, and they now wished to acquire government contracts. Jonathan could easily help with that, with the right introductions and a little insider information. He had so far supplied everything they asked for and more, doing exceptionally well out of it himself. But there was something about them that worried him. It was nothing that he could actually put his finger on, but he was now beginning to suspect they were involved in organised crime. Not that it bothered Jonathan, their money was as good as anyone else's, but he would need to tread carefully with them.

It wasn't so much the business with the Treasury Secretary; he could easily understand how they might fit him into their plans, but there were two other pieces of information that he had supplied as requested, without considering what they were to be used for. One was on a company CEO involved in an insider trading scam. He had committed suicide by taking a swan dive from the roof of the bank where he was CEO into Canary Wharf, within a week of this info being delivered. Another was the name of a gun-runner who'd been in the witness protection scheme. He was about to provide evidence on the people he worked for, and then, he had just disappeared.

Considering the business he was in, Jonathan knew that it was wise to take precautions and had always done so. His insurance policy was a list of all those he had business transactions with, including names, dates, amounts of money paid and information supplied. And, as a consequence of his suspicions, he was also in the process of trying to discover more about these particular clients, both as further insurance and as a potential future revenue generator.

He would need to find another way of gaining the leverage Roseau and De Costa wanted. Jonathan prided himself on always delivering, and this business with Alex Great would be no different. Fortunately, he and his colleagues were the best in the business, and Roseau and De Costa were well aware of it. He had demonstrated that, with the information, his informants had supplied about the gun-runner, information that could only have come from high up within the Metropolitan Police Force.

For over four years, Jonathan had been running a project for Dandelion, the International's owner. Their brief was to collect data, every conceivable piece of data they could obtain, from every source open to them, legality notwithstanding. Initially this was limited to data that they could intercept electronically, but was soon expanded to include information supplied by the police and public officials, at a hefty price.

Dubious methods of information gathering had always been employed within news organisations. They needed to obtain information for their stories from somewhere. Now, with the prevalence of electronic communications these days, that's where the bulk of information came from. Dandelion, always wanting to be one step ahead of the game, centralised those that knew how to get this and provided them with all the tools available to excel at it.

This created an immensely powerful information gathering machine. A tool Dandelion wanted total control of, hence the reason to run it from the International Building.

Jonathan and his five colleagues supplied phone inter-cepts, text messages, voice mail, e-mails and computer files as well as the human intelligence to reporters and TV crews of the International group on anybody of interest. From Prime Ministers to murder victims, if it was in an electronic form or on the airwaves and they wanted it, they had everything they needed at their disposal right here in these rooms to gather it. For several years, they built this capability with state of the art equipment and employed the best in the business to run it.

That was until public scrutiny began to examine how media organisations, particularly the International Group, obtained their information.

The scrutiny their methods were now receiving made it necessary for Dandelion to be able to deny all knowledge of his enterprise. Therefore, as of two years ago, to all intents and purposes Jonathan and the group were no longer employed by the International Group although, in reality, they continued with their work from the same office space, just as they had done before. The costs of the project, including all the wages, had gone down in the International's budget as entertainment, which in some sense of the word it was. It certainly entertained the general public, every day.

Really, they had been too good at their job, and the International Group was now under intense investigation. For years, the International's editions published story after story, exposing which footballer had yet again been caught with his pants down, which public officials had been taking bribes, which pop star had been caught taking drugs or caught soliciting for sex in public toilets or which actress had confided intimate sexual details to a friend. Many complained about the International's tactics, but all too often, these complaints fell on deaf ears.

Then, two years ago, official complaints were made by Buckingham Palace. It was claimed that stories containing private conversations between Prince William and his girlfriend, and between him and his brother Prince Harry, had been published by the International. The content of these conversations could only have been known through the interception of their texts. The police had no choice but to investigate these claims. So far only one reporter had been charged and convicted, but that was about to change.

The police investigations revealed the editor at the royal desk had intercepted these messages with the help of a private investigator; both were prosecuted and eventually jailed. Or that was the official story. In truth, the information had been supplied by Jonathan and his group. The private investigator had been implicated by Jonathan hacking into his computer and planting incriminating evidence for the police to find. Both the editor and the investigator were paid handsomely by Dandelion for their silence.

For a year or so, with the help of certain police officers, that ruse had held. But politicians, footballers and show business celebrities began to make claims that they had been targeted by eavesdroppers. That their phones were being bugged and their texts intercepted, as stories appeared about them in the International's papers and news channels. The police investigation resumed, and a government appointed committee had been formed to investigate the claims.

Jonathan was aware of the investigations, and that the committee appointed by the Prime Minister would soon be calling the owner of the International Group, Dandelion, or Dandy as they all called him behind his back, to testify. Naturally, Dandelion was also aware of this, and decided it would be wise to cover the tracks.

The Surveillance Group, as he called them, and all their equipment needed to be removed from the International Building. He instructed the only two others that actually knew of the project, his two vice presidents; print and electronic media, who had disseminated the information throughout his news network, to get the Surveillance Group dismantled and covered up.

Although many at the International knew the information from texts and e-mails were being collected, none knew the specific details or the extent of it, other than nine of them. Those were the six members of the Surveillance Group, Carl and Fred, who looked after the physical surveillance, the eyes on stuff, and the three electronics experts, Jonathan and Dandelion of course, along with his two VPs.

The members of the Surveillance Group were given exceedingly generous bonuses, told their services were no longer required, and that they had two weeks to get out of the building. This was nearly two weeks ago, and today they were packing up the last of their equipment.

The fact that Dandelion wanted to distance himself from their operation came as no surprise to Jonathan. He had always suspected that there was a finite time limit on how long they could remain secreted away within a news group before drawing attention to themselves. But more importantly, he had for some time wanted to expand their enterprise, and herein came the opportunity. Thus far, whilst based at the International, he had been unable to do that for other than his single very private group of clients, and this was the perfect opportunity. He had already acquired the premises that they needed; all their equipment was being packed away, ready to be moved through a series of cut-outs so it couldn't be traced. It would be installed not five miles away from the present location.

Once the installation was complete, in about a week, he would be ready to begin again, but this time their endeavors would be far more profitable. Blackmail and corporate espionage paid much better than news stories. Perhaps his last voyage into that field hadn't gone exactly as planned, but he had got the girl into the Treasury Secretary's bed, and he had got the photos he wanted. If the stupid man hadn't screamed the place down, it all would have gone as planned. He would have kept the evidence to himself and his clients. It was a shame about Rosie, but now she couldn't say anything to incriminate him and there were plenty more around like her.

As Jonathan and his team packed away the remainder of their equipment, the rest of the International Media Group were experiencing an unusually busy news day. On top of the drama occurring around Alex Great, another demonstration had erupted. This one, an impromptu affair, was likely to have the same side effects as the other demonstrations earlier in the year.

Certain groups were hijacking the demonstrations to further their own ends. Their goals had not been revealed, but their methods were clear. Small bands were using the peaceful demonstrations to conduct riots and lootings in several large cities around the UK, whilst the police were distracted at the demonstrations.

It was also the first day of the committee hearing, with Dandelion the first to be brought before them. With this flurry of activity in the news rooms, nobody would notice what was going on in their remote corner of the International building.

Before Jonathan had his team up and running in their new offices, he had two problems to deal with. His private clients wouldn't be happy with the way the business with the Secretary of the Treasury had turned out. He had received an e-mail from them, saying that they would be back in London in a few days and wanted to have a meeting. Then there was a problem of a more private nature to deal with: his wife.

Chapter 3

"Will there be any other guests accompanying us today, sir?" She said with her radiant smile.

"No," he replied, "Just get this thing off the ground and bring me some coffee".

The stewardess hoped that coffee would be all he wanted on this flight to London today; some of his demands on previous flights that the agency has sent her on, had been far more onerous.

With all that he had achieved, one would have expected Dandelion to be a happy man; today, he wasn't. Within minutes of him settling into his seat, the G5 took off. The wheels left the tarmac and rotated into their bays, his coffee arrived and he began ranting to himself.

"How dare they summon me like this? It was me who put them into power in the first place. If I hadn't shifted my support from the Labour Party to the Conservatives four weeks before the election, Labour would still be in power, and the Conservatives would still be the opposition. Perhaps some compromises had to be made, but that's no reason to humiliate me like this."

In Dandelion's opinion, the compromises were the real reason he was being summoned to the House of Commons, to be grilled by this damnable Robertson Inquiry committee.

"Blain should be kissing my arse, not humiliating me; it was Blain's policies that were in place, not that of Labour or the bloody Liberal Democrats."

Dandelion knew the Robertson Inquiry was toothless, nothing more than a political maneuver so he would deny all knowledge, keep it limited to a rogue reporter, and it would all blow over. But the audacity of having called him in to testify would be remembered, along with those who had done it.

"They will pay for this, every one of them."

Dandelion had been in the news business all his working life. At the age of 16, he joined his uncle's newspaper. He had worked his way up through assistant editor to where he was now, the sole owner of one of the largest and probably most powerful media companies, and had built this empire on the knowledge that information and how it was disseminated or not, was the key to everything. Any slant could be put on any story and made to convey precisely what you wanted it to.

"Sir, would you like some more coffee?"

Disturbed from his thoughts by the stewardess, Dandelion noted that he had already been in the air for over three hours.

"No.

What do you want? Leave me alone, can't you see I'm busy?"

. . .

Dandelion settled back into his plush leather seat of his G5, contemplating the questions he would be asked by the inquiry panel and the answers he would give, but events upon the ground in London were taking a turn that even he could never have anticipated.

Over the past year, there had been four large demonstrations and numerous smaller ones across the UK, many of which had turned into riots. The reasons for the peaceful strikes and demonstrations were multi-faceted; much of the dissent had been in response to the present government's policies of fiscal control. There was hardly a segment of the population that hadn't been adversely affected and wasn't extremely unhappy with what the Government was doing, and yet more segments of society that would take full advantage of the fire that was beginning to rage amongst the populace. For each peaceful demonstrator, another had joined in, and some were simply looking for either the short term gain they could achieve by looting shops or for the enjoyment they seemed to derive from it, but there were others that were far more organised.

The demonstrations and particularly, the riots, created great headline for Dandelion's media companies, but it was also creating problems, one of which was about to get right into his face. About half an hour out from Heathrow, his musings were again interrupted by the stewardess,

"Excuse me, sir, but we are half an hour out of Heathrow and the pilot asked me to tell you that there is a demonstration happening in the center of London, around Oxford Street. He says it shouldn't affect your drive in, but he wanted you to know."

"The shooting, no doubt."

"Yes sir, more of what happened yesterday."

Unperturbed by this news, he decided it was time to get ready for the hearing, due to take place at the Palace of Westminster in two hours or so. He was exiting the bathroom just as the stewardess announced they were landing. Within ten minutes of touching down, he was exiting his private jet past the smiling stewardess.

Thank you, God, for getting me through another flight with him without him touching me, and I hope he runs straight into the riots.

Minutes later, Dandelion was in his limo, passing through security gates at the airport and toward the M5. Near the M5 approach road, the driver said through the intercom:

"Sir, the demonstration has escalated into a riot and has spread through the center of London, toward Piccadilly and Green Park. I have the radio on, sir, do you want to listen?"

"No, I don't, just don't get stuck in traffic."

The day before, after the shooting of the young man, several small, seemingly insignificant incidents happened around the UK, all of which petered out quite quickly. But that morning, following the start of the demonstration at Broad Water Farm, they took hold again, all in the form of looting. Not in the immediate areas of the day before where the police still had a large presence, but a few miles down the road.

This feat of instant and secure communications had taken a lot to achieve but had worked spectacularly, both in its reaction to the first event of the killing and then anticipating the events that would follow. Those that had achieved this act now had control of large bunches of mostly men but quite a few women as well, from no particular affiliation, which could be organised into a mindless horde, intent on larceny and destruction and with only a few hours' notice.

One such element had been sent to Oxford Street, the shopping heart of London's West End, believing it would make an excellent target. They worked on the knowledge that there would be large numbers of police required at Broad Water Farm, thus depleting the West End of London. Their game plan was to split the several large groups along the route that they intended to loot.

Groups of up to a dozen strong gang members, all wearing dark clothing with their faces covered in ski masks and armed with pepper spray and baseball bats, stormed into shops and department stores. What appeared random on the surface was far from that; each store had been identified in advance, and each group had been supplied with a sketch of the positions of the tills and counters, displaying goods they were targeting.

As the gangs entered each store, the first reaction of shoppers and the staff was that of incredulity, but that quickly changed to panic as shop employees were savagely beaten to open their tills, display counters smashed with baseball bats with their contents shoveled into bags and any that the gang encountered were sprayed with pepper spray.

"Two minutes, one minute, thirty. One minute, thirty seconds. Go."

Working with military-like precession, two of the gang members remained by the main doors through which they entered, one of whom held a stopwatch shouting out to the others what remained of the time each store had been allotted. The other sprayed any shopper or store employee that came near with pepper spray, forcing shoppers toward the back of the shop rather than blocking the entrance and the gang's means of escape.

Within thirty seconds, they were gone, and on to the next set of targets. Within another thirty, the panicked shoppers who had for the most part kept relatively quiet during the robbery, huddled in the back, now ran for the exit. As they did so, display stands of goods were knocked over, glass cabinets broken, and the shops' remaining merchandise spread all over the floor.

As the rest followed the initial exodus, some slipped on the glass or fell as their feet became entangled by clothes on the floor, and were then being trampled by others still trying to escape the chaos.

Within five minutes of the start of each robbery, each store was almost deserted. Of those that remained inside most were injured in the flight, some remained to help the injured but most now milled about in the streets, in shock. The buses and taxis that were allowed to drive along this stretch of Oxford Street were soon brought to a standstill, blocking the roads and any immediate possible police response.

This tsunami of destruction rolled along Oxford Street and down Regent Street before turning right along Piccadilly, allowing fresh rioters to enter the fray from the Mayfair direction, where they had initially gathered. As fresh rioters joined in, others left with their spoils moving toward the Strand and the Embankment and to the minibuses that had been laid on to aid their escape.

The entire process had taken this particular crew only ninety minutes from the start of the looting spree in Oxford Street, where they hit a high-end jeweler, the first of many stores robbed that day, to sitting on a minibus.

The minibus, driven by the leader, had picked them up on the Mall. They were now nearly over the river and into South London. Home was no more than an hour away.

"Joe, come here; have a look what Simon has."

"Yeah, that jewelry store we hit first was the best of the lot, thanks Mr. Wayne or whatever it was. You two must have got something good, let's have a look?"

"No! You keep your hands to yourself."

"Fucking shut up, you lot, there's flashing blue lights on the bridge. I ain't going that way. I'm going straight on, Lambeth Bridge it is boys."

The driver of the minibus accelerated through the junction and looked left over his shoulder toward the police car stationary on the bridge, and crashed straight into the back of Dandelion's limo as it slowed to go through St Stevens Gate and into the Houses Of Parliament on his way to sit before the inquiry.

The impact spun the limo. As the back end came around it clipped a man, Charlie Parker, who was just passing St Stevens Gate to access the pedestrian gate a few meters further along. Flinging him through the air to collide with one of the concrete barriers, the car completed a 360, coming to rest a few feet from Charlie. The minibus, now stationary at an acute angle over the two carriageways of St Margaret's, its bonnet knocked open during the impact and now clouds of steam erupted from under it, hissing as it escaped.

The young men, who a few minutes before were jubilant, already taking stock of their stolen goods and estimating what they would fetch once they got home, now exited the bus like a pack of rabid dogs, on the hunt for whomever they could take vengeance on.

The first six, spotting the driver's door of the limo open, charged toward it, screaming. They grabbed the driver, dragged him out of the car and knocked him to the ground, raining in kicks and punches. The driver never had a chance. Within two minutes, he was unconscious, and from this he would never regain.

As the six men put in the last of their kicks to the driver's limp body, the remainder were exiting the bus. Some bleeding from head wounds gained in the crash; they looked about for others to punish. Spying Dandelion in the rear of the limo, they moved toward the right hand side rear door.

Fortunately for Dandelion, the spin the limo took during the collision had pushed both the front and rear against the concrete bollards, blocking off the left hand side passenger door. That forced the men to try to drag Dandelion out of the car to the right and over the vacant rear passenger seat.

Hauling the door open, one of the men dived into the back seat, punching Dandelion in the face as he grabbed his collar to pull him out of the car. Just as a shocked and now panicking Dandelion felt himself being dragged out of the car, the man stopped and jumped back out, hearing his friend's shouts.

"Police! Run!"

As the man stood up he saw several officers from the Palace of Westminster division of the Met that were trapped by the car at the gates, begin to climb over the back of the limo. Conscious that it is now time to leave, he began to run toward Abingdon St Gardens after his accomplices.

As he came level with the front of the car, he saw Charlie who was trying to make it up onto his knees. Side-stepping left the man attempted to kick Charlie, aiming at his head with all his might. At the last second, Charlie looked up, saw the man coming at him and dived to the right with the man's lower leg and foot hitting his chest and shoulder.

Instead of Charlie's head snapping back with the kick and allowing him to keep on running, the impact found him tumbling over Charlie, to collide head first into one of the concrete barriers. That was enough to stun him, but he was soon rising to his feet, alternating between looking at Charlie and at his avenue of escape.

Before he had time to make up his mind whether to kill the old fool or run, he was tackled by three officers and once more knocked to the ground. This time with two large policemen sitting on his back and the third fitting him to handcuffs.

Within minutes, more police arrived, then the ambulances. As the paramedics attended the driver and Charlie, police officers helped Dandelion from the car. Because of the confines of the back of it, even a limo, it is not easy to get a powerful punch in. As a result, although Dandelion's face was going to swell, there was no real physical damage, but he was certainly in shock.

The unconscious driver was rushed to the hospital, but would never regain consciousness. Apart from several broken bones, he had massive internal injuries and was pronounced dead upon reaching hospital.

Another team of paramedics worked on Charlie. In reality he had been lucky with the car, it had spun from the collision to the rear and had only clipped Charlie's right calf, removing large chunks of skin but not breaking anything. The impact with the concrete barrier had broken several ribs and severely concussed him, but his worst injury had come from the kick, which had shattered his collar bone. If that had connected with his head as intended, his neck would surely have been broken.

The inevitable media crews arrived very quickly,

having already been present in the vicinity as they normally were during the days when something was going down at the palace.

So they were in plenty of time to capture footage of Charlie and the driver being put into ambulances, the arrested man put into the back of a police car, and Dandelion helped through the adjacent gate, as St Stevens was still being blocked by the limo. They took their cameras into the wrecked minibus, revealing most of the stolen goods strewn over the floor. It didn't take them long to piece the visible facts together and begin broadcasting the story live from outside the Houses of Parliament.

No one was certain, but there seemed to be about a dozen men in the minibus at the time of the accident. All had made their escape before the police officers could get to them with the exception of the man arrested after kicking Charlie. This man would eventually provide limited information to the police, in that his crew had received messages over the Blackberry Messenger service early that morning, directing them to Mayfair and Hyde Park where they would assemble before the riot and looting spree. He told them that they had been given specific targets to hit and had also been supplied with the minibus to make good their escape. Although he didn't know whom these instructions and arrangements had come from, he did supply the names of four of his companions who would eventually be arrested.

Over the next few days, several more would be arrested, some charged with the murder of the driver and others with a variety of offences. Their identities would come to light after the police appealed for videos taken by the public witnessing the events that day, many of which were appearing on social networking sites, only minutes after each incident.

Officers of the Palace Division had helped Dandelion out of the battered limo, who despite his ordeal and bruised face was keen to get away from the spectacle. Media may have been the backbone of his business empire, but he didn't like being under the spotlight of it, particularly now as he was being dragged in front of a committee investigating his misdoings. With two officers guiding him, Dandelion was soon through the pedestrian gate into the courtyard in front of the palace. They left him with a paramedic, saying that they would soon return for his statement.

The paramedic examined him and after a minute or two, said:

"You may have a mild concussion; I'd suggest you go to a hospital, so they can have a better look at you and do something for that bruising."

Dandelion, forever the strategist, decided that he could get mileage from the incident. Firstly, he wanted to get the testimony over with, and secondly, realising that should he say something now which was later contradicted, he could blame the concussion for his mistake.

"I think I will be okay. I really don't want to be late. I will be fine for now, and perhaps go later."

Dandelion turned, and before hurrying off, added:

"I know the way; I will be fine. Could you tell the officers I've gone to the Chambers? If they return, that is."

He was gone before the officers could return and delay him further.

The ambulance carrying Charlie arrived at St Thomas hospital some ten minutes after the one carrying the driver, and Charlie was quickly ushered through for treatment.

It was not many minutes later that TV crews began to

arrive, although they hadn't actually witnessed the crash, only the following mayhem. They had pieced a story together of how a long term employee at the palace and former paratrooper Charlie had foiled a murderous attack on Dandelion, receiving severe wounds in the process.

The story, being broadcast live from outside the hospital, went on to describe the hero, Charlie. He was employed as chief engineer at the palace and was on his way into work as the incident unfolded around him. And, how he intervened as men intent on killing Dandelion were dragging him from the car.

They hadn't actually gotten the facts right, not mentioning that he was first knocked down by Dandelion's limo, but that didn't seem to matter. They had a terrific story here and would milk every ounce from it. It wouldn't be until the next day the whole story would become clear.

Charlie had, in fact, had been the chief engineer at the palace for over 20 years, until two years ago, and was about to retire at the end of next year. He had loved his job keeping everything running there. He knew more about the building than anyone else alive, and because of that he had been kept on to assist and familiarise the new contractors with the vast building.

Up until that point, all maintenance work had been carried out in-house. Then some bright spark within the government had an idea. That, as the palace was an asset to the country, bringing in hundreds of thousands of tourists every year, why not expand on that concept and open up areas within the palace as hirable function rooms, to offset the running costs?

As this was a departure from how the palace had been used and run for hundreds of years, the PM had decided that this service should be independently run. The reason given for this was that the company, who would take on this contract, would pay for the refurbishment themselves, which was estimated at running into millions.

On the surface, this seemed like a sensible suggestion. In reality, it was just another political stunt. The company awarded with the contract expected to make a great deal of money out of it, and just happened to be owned by a businessman who had contributed a large sum of money to the Conservative Party. It was nothing more than the privatization of another economic asset, just as profitable sections of the NHS were being privatised.

Charlie was now little more than a guide to these new contractors, but he did know far more about the building than anyone else. Still, Charlie had a job and was thankful for that, which was more than could be said for the majority that had looked after the building up until that point. Most of them had lost their jobs in the government's cost-cutting measures and the awarding of these new contracts.

Although Charlie was relegated to a guide and wasn't particularly friendly with the contractors who tended to keep to themselves, he couldn't complain about the work that was getting done. It was all of the highest quality, many of the antiquated systems had been upgraded or totally replaced, with each discipline having its own workshops in the cavernous underground bowels of the building.

As these events were being televised around the world, two men sitting in Charles De Gaulle Airport on the outskirts of Paris were paying particular attention. They were immediately responsible for many of the organised elements of the riots, and were extremely happy with most of the results.

The fact that some of the attention surrounded the Palace of Westminster had them a little concerned. Nevertheless, the majority of the news centered upon the riots, particularly those happening in the West End of London, and with that they couldn't be more pleased.

Chapter 4

"No, don't do that," came the voice through the fog, and a little later, "No, leave that alone."

As his senses gradually returned, Adam felt the mask being removed and his drugged stupor gradually subsiding. His first coherent thoughts were how much he hated coming out of a general anesthetic, unable to think clearly, unable to move. He really ought to make sure this was the last time. He has been in this situation far too often for such a fit young man, with the vast majority of the occasions of his own making.

The problem had started early, or at least made itself known early the previous evening. As he walked off the pitch after a two hour training session, the pain was already creeping up his abdomen, which was really nothing unusual. The core sessions he did as part of his daily workout routine in the gym always left him a little, sore as they should. No Pain, No Gain being the gym rats' universal by-line. On top of that, his brother Dan always managed to get some decent punches into his ribs during their rucks and mauls, so he thought nothing of it.

That evening's events went on much as usual. After they had showered and removed the mud, it was down to the Barbican. The Barbican, the hub of the entertainment area of Plymouth was always busy during the summer months with its numerous pubs and restaurants along the harbor walls, perhaps too busy for hungry, thirsty rugby players after training. But winter was perfect: plenty of space for something to eat and a couple of beers with the squad.

The brothers had almost been inseparable since Adam's return to England a few months earlier. Dan had convinced the head coach at Albion that he would recover from his knee injury that had plagued him for the last year far quicker, if Adam was allowed to train with them. Nobody ever said no to Dan; his nickname was Bear, but it wasn't just the 120 kilos of muscle which was daunting in itself. He had a way of charming everyone around him and always got his own way. Ever since he was a baby, all he had to do was look at you with his big brown eyes and that cheeky grin, to get exactly what he wanted or get away with whatever he had done this time. One look and girls lost their knickers in every country he had played in during his international career as a wing forward for England; at home in Plymouth he was legendary.

Adam hadn't initially been sure that training with Albion would be a smart idea, but had allowed himself to be talked into it. It wasn't that he too hadn't been a very talented rugby player, but he hadn't played seriously for several years since the boys were at university together. And then it hadn't been with a Premiership winning team. As a ninety kilo winger, having a pack of forwards topping a thousand kilos running at you was a daunting experience.

The boys, or men as they were by now, were the product of an English father and a Singaporean mother.

Nobody was sure where the size came from. Many of the couples' friends joked that they must have uncommonly large milkmen in Singapore. Their mother was tiny, with classic South-East Asian looks which the boys had inherited; their father a marine biologist, by no means small, had topped out at a fraction under 6 foot. And had been exceptionally fit until the day that bomb took both their lives.

Ironically, it was the terrorist bombings in Bali where they lived until the boys' early teens that had brought them back to the UK, only for their parents to get on a tube train in London a few years later and run into another suicide bomber.

Dan's team mates at Albion had heard all about his brother. In fact, he was famous for his exploits throughout the local rugby community, mostly through Dan's tales. So he was very welcome within the group both on and off the pitch, and constantly harassed for more stories. A particular favorite was one of Jamaica.

Dan had gone to Jamaica to visit Adam, and after a nights' drinking at Pier One, Adam had suggested they go and score some weed from some friends of his that lived on a beach in a ramshackle hotel beside the airport.

It was situated just outside Montego Bay, on an old road that was no longer used since the building of a new one at the other side of the airport. After being dropped off by a bewildered taxi driver, who had tried to tell them the place was closed, Dan was led along the beach to a series of tented cabanas.

It was a classic Jamaican evening with a light breeze blowing off the sea; the enormous full moon hanging so low in the sky it appeared to touch the water, with the sound of waves gently breaking over the white sand beach.

A setting from paradise, with a surprise Dan was not expecting.

As they got closer, they could hear voices and music playing softly. Pulling the billowing curtains aside, Adam ushered Dan through to where he witnessed four stunning girls, three dark skinned and the fourth fair with long blonde hair. The girls, upon seeing Adam, rushed forward to plaster him with kisses.

What Adam hadn't told his brother was that his friends, these four girls, were the most exclusive escorts in Jamaica. They had bought this place as their private retreat when it had closed down as a place to relax and meet with friends when they weren't out working. Adam, being a good friend of the girls, regularly visited them after a night's partying in Montego Bay. He had told them of his brother's forth-coming visit, prearranging the evening many days before.

Dan could never remember if he was given their names or not. He did remember being led away by two of the girls, the leggy blonde, and a small exquisite dark skinned girl, to a more secluded part of the cabana arrangement, which he realised at some point during the night was made from parachutes.

The brothers spent the rest of the night there, eventu-ally kissing their goodbyes as the sun rose, to head off for an ackee and salt fish breakfast. Of course, nobody ever believed this story; nevertheless it was greatly enjoyed by all the players with frequent requests for retelling by those that hadn't heard it firsthand.

Part way through the second beer that evening, Adam decided to go home. By then they had the company of several pretty girls, but he wasn't interested. In fact, he had recently met a girl whom he was very interested in. And his abs were seriously hurting by now, so it really was time to go home. Bidding goodnight to his brother, he got a cab and headed home.

They lived together in a house in Wembury, a couple of miles from Plymouth, which their parents had left them. His dad had built it years before, just outside the village, on the headland overlooking the sea.

So typical of his dad, it wasn't quite finished, and the brothers had left it that way. Not through being lazy or lack of money, neither of the boys had to work, the IP's their dad had created left them very well off. But this way, it reminded them of their dad.

The house was a large, modern-looking structure with full height windows on both floors and a terrace on the first floor extending the full width of the house. With its unfinished garages and workshops behind, the house sat alone on the rocky headland with breathtaking views out to sea and across Wembury Bay itself.

As the taxi approached the house, the first signs of the coming storm were in the air. Lightning flickered out to sea. The trees beside the unfinished workshop swayed in the wind, their overgrown branches scraping along the roof.

The weather reflected the general talk that winter, which was gloomy, of a severe cold winter ahead, stock market declines, unemployment, the looming general strike and a triple-dip recession in the air. It was all the news channels talked about at the moment.

Getting out of the cab, Adam walked around to the front of the house, noticing the gravel drive already covered in dead leaves from the early autumn. His mood was dropping. Thinking of his dad, Adam sat on a bench beside the porch, looking out over the leaden grey sea, the crest of the waves flecked in white, illuminated by the lightning as they broke upon the rocky shore. The storm was going to be a big one; rain was coming in at 45 degrees already, and the wind was picking up.

Despite that it had been many years since his parents had been murdered by a suicide bomber, he still thought about his father a great deal. In good moods, which they were for the most part, his thoughts were about all the good times.

Although his father was a workaholic, they had spent a lot of time together. He coached their rugby team, taught them to dive and to sail when they were still young boys living in Bali, as well as talking about his work and beliefs in a more sustainable future. His passions, particularly in the oceans, had rubbed off on Adam.

In his darker moods, as he was by now, he thought how things would have been different if his dad hadn't gone to London that day. If he hadn't got on that tube to go to the conference, or if he hadn't on this very rare occasion taken the boys' mother with him, with a promise of a shopping trip after his presentation.

Up until that fateful day, things had been very different. He had been due to go to the University of Bath that September to study marine biology or, more importantly to him, to play rugby. He and his brother were in the West England Rugby Academy; both were destined for exceptional rugby careers. Dan had achieved his, although his present knee injury had plagued him for the last year. He was now finally on the mend and set to reclaim his No 6 England shirt.

Adam had not. Not that he regretted his choices at all, but instead of going to Bath University, he was too distraught about the death of his parents at the hands of a terrorist who neither knew nor cared whom they were. Desperate for some sort of payback, Adam had joined the Naval Intelligence Services.

He may not have regretted this choice. Like his dad he knew there was no point in that, you learn from it and move on, but he did realise what a stupid decision it was. Adam was not well suited for an army career, being extremely opinionated and possessing a big mouth that he could never learn to keep shut. He got himself into trouble at every turn. Not that, at times, he hadn't enjoyed some of it. He'd made lifelong friends and perhaps enemies, and learnt skills that at that moment, he never thought he would need again. After six years, he left, knowing how pissed his dad would have been with him for wasting his talents, and he reapplied to Bath.

As luck would have it, his brother was also still at Bath University, finishing a Master's in marine engineering. Not that he had been captured by the marine bug of his dad, but he was smart enough to know that even if he did earn a place as a professional rugby player, an education was still important; an injury could end his career in seconds.

Adam, his mood lightening a little, with memories of the two of them terrorising Bath for that year, went into the house. Dropping his soaking wet clothes on the hallway floor, he grabbed himself a protein shake and a handful of pain killers, stuck his feet up on the couch and clicked on the TV.

The lounge was warm as it always was in winter; a large room with little clusters of seating areas, the main one beside the fire where Adam now sat. The blinds to the full-height windows remained open and the lightning out to sea briefly illuminated the darkened room, with its intense flashes of cold blue light.

By midnight, the pain had eased slightly. Dan still wasn't home, which wasn't unusual; he'd probably turn up in the morning and be rather worse for wear. Adam decided bed was the best option; maybe sleep would help, not that he slept at all in the end. The pain in his abs got worse.

What have I broken this time and God, why did I let Dan talk me into training with them.

And the pain rose in waves.

No, this can't be right, I need to do something about it now.

Deciding to take the Pajero, as it was the most comfortable to drive and as it was an automatic, he reckoned that he could manage to drive it despite his present doubled up stature. He pulled on a reasonably clean set of trackies and a hoodie, and made his way gingerly down the stairs, making judicious use of the banister for support. He paused at the door.

Maybe I should call an ambulance.

Those 20 meters to the car and the 8 mile drive to the hospital were not enticing, but the alternative! Call an ambulance, wait for an hour, get to the hospital and then get sent home with bruised ribs. No, his brother would never forget that, nor would any of the Albion players, and Dan was sure to tell them all about it. They would all have a field day rubbing that in.

Once in the car the plan seemed achievable. By leaning forward, the pain seemed to subside enough to be able to drive. Fortunately, the traffic was light, but arriving at the hospital Adam discovered the holes in his plan. The trackies he was wearing had no money in them, nor did there seem to be any change in the car for parking in the usual places he kept it.

After a once around the car park closest to the A&E, only to discover no empty spaces, there seemed to be only one thing to do, dump the car by the fence. If he got onto the grass, it wouldn't block anyone in. Yes, he would get tickets, but they wouldn't be able to tow it from there. So, in the words of the numerous coaches he had throughout the years, it was time to "suck it up and get on with it".

Later, in recollection, this was going to seem very funny, not that it was at the time.

Open the door, swing out your legs, fall over, grab the fence, pull yourself up and use it as support as far as the crossing. 20 meters to go, hobble over the road, 10 meters to go and make the door. Done, now it should be easy.

Chapter 5

Having navigated the car park, Adam then pushed his way through the two sets of double doors and all but fell through the last.

A queue, now that was to be expected, but there were only two people in it. The first was already at the counter, and the other a policewoman. He had obviously attracted her attention as he stumbled through the door. She looked him up and down for a minute or two, obviously deciding he wasn't deranged and likely to run amuck in the hospital. She spoke in the usual authoritarian manner that all policewomen seem to have.

"You look as if you're in pain. Why don't you sit down?"

"Yes, I am in a lot of pain, but if I sit down, I doubt I would be able to stand up again," Adam said as he leaned on the wall for support.

At this, she turned her back, moved as if to guard her place in the queue, waiting for a few minutes until the receptionist beckoned her forward. Just as she approached the desk, her phone rang, which she proceeded to take out and answer, indicating to the receptionist to wait by holding up her hand.

After a minute or so of conversation, to what was obviously a female friend, she finished the call, walking up to the counter to proclaim that she had come to pick up a sling for her son's arm. By this time, several of the patients sitting in the waiting area who had heard the original exchange between her and Adam were giving her really dirty looks.

Had this been any of the other numerous occasions that Adam was in this A&E, he most certainly would have told her what he thought, but this morning he hurt far too much. Fortunately, by now the receptionist had also heard the exchange as well as the comments and gestures being made by others in the waiting room.

"Would you mind waiting over there, please? I think the patient behind you needs to be taken care of first."

"But I was here first. I'm in a hurry and need to get back to work."

The receptionist ignored the policewoman and waved her out of the way, much to the amusement of those sitting in the waiting area, and beckoned Adam forward. The receptionist asked him what the problem was and after a few seconds, picked up the phone to call for a nurse and wheelchair. Much to his relief, as by this time another step would have been the last. The nurse pushed him past the policewoman, whose face was now a vivid shade of scarlet. She was clearly very embarrassed.

Once secreted away behind a closed curtain, the nurse produced a paper gown.

"Could you put this on, please?"

Adam attempted to stand but didn't get far; his arse lifted an inch or two from the wheelchair and slumped back in agony.

"Here, let me help you."

The nurse helped Adam up and pulled off his hoodie, then pushed down his trackies, managing deftly to keep his boxers in place. As she did so, she tried not to smile and think about the body she was revealing.

Shame I'm undressing him here. No, bad girl, stop that. But what would I love to do to that body.

She helped him slide his right then left arm into the gown, and then maneuvered him over to the bed.

"Sit down, and I will help you swing your legs around."

With Adam lying on the bed, she slipped her arms around him and under the paper gown, and removed his boxers. Trying to regain her composure and get her mind on the job at hand and not think what she would rather be doing with her hands, her mouth.

Stop it!

The nurse wiped the sweat from her brow; she began to examine him, whilst listening to his explanation of the pain and prodding his abdomen through the gown.

"Does this hurt?"

"Uh, yes, rather a lot."

Oh God. I like his body, that's not a six pack; it's an eight pack I can feel under there. I wonder how many times a week he works out.

"I think you have a ruptured appendix," she said as she stoked his abs subconsciously "And I need to get one of the doctors to see you now."

She picked up Adam's discarded clothes and put them on the chair. Adam's car keys clattered to the floor.

"Shit! I am going to get so many tickets" Adam said to the nurse, as she put the keys back in one of his pockets before hurrying off to get the doctor.

A doctor arrived and things went from there as they usually do: needles, pressure cuffs and blipping monitors.

One of those needles, thankfully enough, was connected to a syringe and a dose of morphine.

The Conservative Party might well have been castrating the NHS, but Adam certainly hadn't any complaints. He was visited within an hour by the surgeon and his gang and told that they would be removing his appendix, that he was at the front of the list and would be in theatre as soon as they had finished the kidney transplant that they were about to perform. That was followed soon after by another shot of morphine that had Adam feeling much better. Even to the extent that at one point, he asked if he might go outside for a while.

He knew there was half a joint in the ash tray of the car which he had spied earlier and, in his drugged-up stupor, this seemed like a sound plan to him. Not as much so to the rather annoyed nurse.

"No, of course you can't do that, and anyway, you are about to have several holes made in you. If I were you, I would try to go to sleep for a while." She replied, rather more sternly than she meant to compensate for the lust she was actually feeling.

This he promptly proceeded to do, or was in the process of doing so, as orderlies arrived to whisk him off to the men in gowns. Adam later would tell that it seemed like a very expedient service: in, out, stitched up, a vague recollection of being in a recovery room and then waking up to somebody's bloody mobile ringing.

What time is it? Don't know. It's still dark! Why can't I move? My legs are all tangled up! Shit, where's the damn call button? Don't know, it's dark!

The ringing had now gone from intermittent, waking him every 10 minutes or so, to constant.

That is the strangest ring tone I have ever heard. Ah! Ring tone that gives me an idea.

If he could find his trackies, which in theory should be on a seat beside the bed, he could then find his mobile phone. Which should again, in theory, give him enough light to see the call button. If not, bung a pillow at the offending phone owner.

The first part of the plan went quite well and indeed the trackies were on the chair, which he found remarkably quickly in the dark, and unable to move anything below his belly. The mobile was in his pocket too, as he had hoped.

The next bit didn't come along quite as planned. The meagre illumination the mobile provided was enough to see the edges of the bed and a table beside it, on which was a paper piss bottle and some paper bowls, presumably for something else.

He could turn enough to see the chair with the remainder of his clothes at one side and a little cabinet at the other, but no call button. Attached to the rail running along the side of the bed were two plastic bags, both with a smattering of something that looked like cat's vomit inside them. They had tubes attached to them, which ran underneath the blanket which was wrapped tightly around him.

He wondered where the other ends of the tubes went.

That might explain the pain when I move.

The rest of the plan wasn't so hot either. A curtain surrounded the bed preventing him flinging a pillow, not that he thought he would get it very far anyway. The phone was still ringing or beeping or whatever. And whoever it was kept on ringing back, or so it seemed in the aftermath of a general anesthetic and morphine.

The offending noise was actually not that of a mobile, but an alarm on one of the many instruments attached to the patient opposite. He, as Adam discovered later, was not well at all, making him feel rather guilty for his thoughts at that time.

But now a more pressing issue had to come to hand, or rather to his bladder. He really did need a piss.

The question was: should he wait until a nurse turned up and help him unwrap himself, but by then would be so desperate he would end up pissing everywhere or should he do it himself? Really there was no option. He gradually managed to un-wrap the blanket from around his torso and thighs, leaving his lower legs and feet entangled to reveal a very fashionable paper gown, which naturally was fastened at the back.

God, I hate these things, why are they tied down the back?

After a great deal of messing around in the dark, he eventfully reached over for the piss bottle, which wasn't actually made of paper, but more of a cardboard. But now came the tricky bit, getting the neck of that bottle between his legs into the hole in his boxers, around his dick and pee, without wetting himself.

He did think later that it was a shame that there wasn't a camera recording the scene. The tape would have made for some very funny viewing and a number one You Tube video. Eventually, he did get his dick into the bottle in time and was mighty relieved to empty his bladder and get the bottle back on the table, with all but a small fraction of his urine in it. He had found out it is really hard to shake when inside a piss bottle.

Adam was wondering what to do about the incessant noise coming from across the ward, when he heard a door opening and in came a nurse. At least now he could go back to sleep, but no such luck, and, after 20 minutes of footfalls, the lights came on.

It was about half an hour later before the curtains

around his bed finally opened, during which time he had a good look around and took stock of the state he was in. The tubes from the bags did seem to enter him, as just above his groin was a large plaster into which the tubes disappeared and above that seemed to be dollops of super-glue, which in fact it was. His navel was covered in a large blob of it, as well as patches of glue lower down.

Enquiring later from a nurse, he was told that they go in through the navel with a thing to cut and remove the appendix, with a camera and manipulator arm stuck through the holes to the left: keyhole surgery apparently, and then stick it back together with superglue. He still had his feet wrapped in the blanket and only the remnants of the paper gown, but he did have his boxers on which were more or less covering him up.

So, when the nurse finally did open the curtains, the choice words that were going through his head wouldn't be delivered by a man totally lacking in dignity, even if his boxers were a little stained.

As the curtains opened, they revealed an exceptionally pretty, tall blonde nurse. If there was ever anything to make Adam's mood brighten it was the sight of a pretty girl, so instead of the tirade she was going to get, it turned into a weak smile.

"Hi, I'm in a lot of pain. Do you think you could get me something?"

Pathetic, he knew, but it worked well. Just to make sure he left the right impression, he managed to tell her about the full piss bottle before she moved the wheeled table beside the bed, getting a smile from her and words of appreciation.

Adam really did like to flirt. It didn't have to be serious or lead to anything. It was just an enjoyable thing to do with a pretty girl. So, despite the fact that he was lying there, nearly naked with piss-stained boxers, a couple of tubes and a wad of superglue over his belly, the opportunity to flirt was irresistible to him.

The nurse soon had him cocooned again in the blanket, and departed.

"I'll be right back with your pain killers," and true to her words, she was.

Chapter 6

Lying around in a hospital bed is a really boring thing to do once the drugs wear off; at least Adam always found it so. So when the man in the bed beside him offered Adam his prepaid TV card as he was about to be discharged, Adam accepted and turned on the news.

He was greeted by images of shops burning in Tottenham, black balaclava wearing youths smashing shop windows in Manchester, and looters running out of shops with bags full of stolen goods in the West End of London.

Of which Adam had heard nothing.

The shot cut to the anchor as she commentated upon the riots.

"It appears that these riots are in response to the shooting of a young man in London by the police yesterday, but how and why they had spread across the UK and why so many who would never have known of the existence of this young man until a few hours before, are involved in such wanton destruction, no one seems to be able to explain," said the pretty blonde anchor.

"So far the police have only confirmed that riots have been reported in the city centers of London, Manchester, Birmingham and Bristol, all of which started less than an hour ago but have given no further statement other than that they are responding as quickly as possible."

The image on the TV cut back to the violence and looting on the streets; the first a shot of several wheelie bins piled high with flammable material, covered in sheets of flame with thick black smoke billowing into the sky. They were being pushed down the street by gangs of rioters and into shops and cars.

"We have Bruce Dickinson reporting from a helicopter over Tottenham. Can you tell us what is happening there, Bruce?

"Yes, Sarah Jane. There seems to be a lady standing in the middle of the street, shouting something at the rioters. There are a few police standing behind her, about 100 meters further up the street, as yet they don't appear to be moving and are by the looks of things completely outnumbered by the rioters. Wait!

"The rioters are getting closer to the lady who is still shouting something at them and doesn't appear to be moving out of their way. My God! This is awful. They have pushed her into a burning car and are now closing on the police line. There must be at least 200 of them."

The commentary was suddenly lost as the helicopter shot pulled back, revealing more and more rioters moving toward the police, some armed with Molotov cocktails, machetes and homemade spears made from knives taped to lengths of wood. As the rioters passed the lady whose clothes were now beginning to burn, several people ran out of a shop doorway and pulled her away from the burning car.

The shot continued to pull back, revealing the police holding position at the end of the street with their riot shields raised, steeling themselves for first contact with the rioters. It was painfully obvious that they were completely outnumbered. The shot continued to widen, revealing fires sweeping across the city behind them, as the first of the rioters hit the police lines, hurling their spears and Molotov cocktails.

The TV then cut back to a shocked and somewhat distracted anchor, as she explained that they had lost the live feed.

Adam watched the images of similar incidents in cities across the country for several more minutes, as shocked as the anchor seemed to be. He then switched the TV off; this wasn't what he needed right now. It was far too depressing. He then began to think about events in his own life over the past few weeks.

Despite that he had flirted with the nurse; he had recently become very interested in a girl he had just met, so his thoughts soon turned to her. He had first seen her in the steam room at the gym. Shrouded in steam, all he could see was a pair of athletic legs, a great backside and a slender tattooed back, as she was lying face down. But it was definitely that bum that grabbed his attention. It had taken a minute or two to realise that he was staring, it was that good. The tiny bikini wasn't helping either. She would soon turn around and catch him, he had thought, so he'd gone to the sauna to cool down.

After 10 minutes in the sauna, it was time to get a cold

shower, his mind still on that great bum, and then a dip in the jacuzzi, much as he did regularly, as a workout recovery routine.

As he immersed himself in the hot bubbling water, he discovered much to his pleasure that the girl was now in the jacuzzi; there was no mistaking the bikini, and she was as pretty as she was sexy. She made room for him to sit beside her, said hello with an enticing smile and then turned to another older lady sitting to the other side, speaking to her in what sounded like Spanish.

As they talked, Adam thought as he relaxed into the bubbles.

Spanish, I wonder where she's from. South or Central America, perhaps?

When they stopped talking, he decided that it would be easier to ask than to keep guessing.

"That's Spanish you are speaking, isn't it? Where are you from?

"I'm from Cuba, but I live in Plymouth now. This is my mother who is visiting me. Do you speak Spanish?"

"No, not really, just enough to order a beer and get by with the basics."

The smile and the knowing look he received told him that she understood exactly what he meant by the basics.

"That's okay; I like to practice my English as much as possible, anyway."

Adam noted that she wore no wedding ring, but had a ring on her right hand. There was also no white mark of a wedding ring on her finger, and she did have a tan.

Adam had spent a lot of his time sailing in the Caribbean and had stopped off at a Cuban island once, so getting the girl into conversation wasn't difficult at all. He occasionally brought in the mother as well, making sure she didn't get bored and drag her daughter away.

After nearly 20 minutes of conversation, the mother and her daughter said their goodbyes, but not without an introduction.

"Hopefully I'll see you again, we come here around this time several times a week."

As she rose, Adam again had sight of that gorgeous backside and the best set of legs he had ever seen attached to it. Beads of water trickled down her bronzed back, over her tiny bikini and down her legs as she walked up the steps and out of the water. If that wasn't enough to ensure that he would be there every day at that time for the rest of the month if he had to, the look she gave him over her shoulder surely was. Not that it had taken that long; a few days later they met again and again a few after that, all the time in the presence of her mother, who spoke no English at all.

It was during their fourth meeting in the bubbling jacuzzi, when the subject of the forthcoming America's Cup came into the conversation. The two, Isobel, it had turned out was her name, and her mother wanted to watch it but were wondering where would be the best vantage points. Adam happily suggested various places for them to watch the races.

"It's a shame I don't know more about yacht racing. I've heard it is fun, but I don't understand the rules at all," Said Isobel with what Adam thought she intended as coy smile, but there was nothing coy about Isobel; she had him wrapped around her little finger and knew it, as did he.

"That's okay, I can explain what's going on as we watch the races."

Although Adam's favorite sport was definitely rugby, growing up by the sea particularly in a place like Bali, instils a love of water sports in many, and Adam was no exception. He was a very good surfer, he'd dived all over the world and spent a lot of time sailing, even competing several times in the King's Cup, an annual event which took place in Phuket, Thailand every year.

Spending an afternoon with Isobel and explaining the rules of the America's Cup seemed like a great idea, even though she probably wouldn't be wearing one of her tiny bikinis. Upon leaving he offered his mobile number, arranging to meet the following Sunday.

Lying there in the hospital bed he thought that, at that point, everything seemed to be going very nicely, he had a tentative date with the cutest no sexiest girl he had met for a long time. It didn't seem to be all about her looks or her body, there was something else there as well, although her body was the primary interest at that time. His research work at the Plymouth University and others in Europe certainly brought him into contact with lots of girls, but this one was definitely something special, not that he could quantify what that was.

It had all looked good until he got that first text from her.

I will be on the Hoe on Sunday with my mother and my husband, and I hope to see you there. Isobel xx

Husband! That had been a devastating blow, he couldn't believe it.

On that Sunday afternoon, the sun was out and a good racing wind was blowing across the Sound. It promised to be a good day to watch the first race, and he decided he might as well go up to the Hoe which overlooked the whole of the Sound; it was the best vantage point to watch the races, after all.

Leaving his car in the car park of a friend's hotel, figuring that he might as well stop there for dinner later, he walked up the hill towards the Hoe. As he rounded a corner, he almost collided with a man cursing into a mobile phone, catching the words:

"He wants me where, tomorrow? Jesus Christ! Can't you handle it?"

And after a pause, "OK, OK. I'll be there".

He was about to apologise to the man for almost colliding with him but before the words rolled off his tongue, the man launched into a tirade.

"Why don't you look where you are going? Get out of my way, you fool!"

Adam, not really in the mood for that, decided to keep on walking and ignore the rude fool. A few minutes later, he arrived by the big screen that had been installed on the Hoe to display the races, and began to watch as a shot taken from a helicopter tightened on the yachts as they crossed the line to begin the first race.

He was right with his initial assessment of the day, it was perfect sailing weather. The wind, coming in from the southwest, was strong enough to get the yachts moving very quickly, but not too strong to prohibit the use of their enormous spinnakers. As they were pulled up the mast, they popped open, accelerating the yachts forward, skipping over the white crested waves.

After watching for maybe 5 minutes, he heard that unmistakable voice again. This time instead of shouting into a mobile phone, he was shouting at somebody obscured from his view. Adam decided he really didn't like this guy and moved slightly to his left to get a better view of whoever he was chastising this time, only to discover it was Isobel, standing there with her mother.

That was enough, he thought, and began to walk

towards them. As he did so, Isobel looked up, catching sight of Adam as he walked toward them, realising his intent; she shook her head before turning to the man and saying.

"But we have only just got here."

"I don't care; I have to be back in London in the morning. I need you to pack my bags, now!"

By now, many others in the crowd had heard the argument and had turned to look and stare. The man, who Adam now realised must be the husband, grabbed Isobel's arm and began walking away, pulling her after him. Isobel turned to look at Adam, whose face by now was like thunder, and shook her head, cast her eyes down and followed the man, calling her mother to do the same.

Adam watched as they walked away, thinking. That explained quite a lot. Isobel, it would seem, was not very happy, perhaps trapped in a marriage to a man far older than she and one obviously without an ounce of manners.

But what could he or should he do about it?

She had his mobile number, so if she wanted to contact him she could, and he certainly wouldn't be feeling guilty about it if she did, with that prick of man she was married to.

What to do now?

Well he was here, the sun was out and apart from the performance he had just witnessed it was a lovely day. So why not make the most of it and watch the rest of the day's races? Perhaps he would stop off for a drink and a meal at his friend's hotel, where he had left his car earlier.

That was what he did, and part way through his meal he received a text from Isobel.

She told him she was very sorry about what he had seen earlier, that she really wanted to see him again, and that she would be going to the gym alone the day after next, if he would like to meet her there. He texted in reply, that he would like to see her as well and that he would be there at his usual time, mid-afternoon as it was the quietest.

As arranged, they met on Tuesday. Adam had just finished his daily workout and was already in the jacuzzi, as Isobel slid in beside him. He wasn't angry with her; he had no right to be, but he was confused. He sat there without saying a word for several minutes until he felt her hand move over his fingertips to grasp his hand. He turned to her and was about to speak as she said:

"I'm sorry. I should have told you I was married when we first met, but couldn't. I liked you; I still do, and want to see more of you"

They talked for a long time, Isobel told him how she had met her husband in Cuba when she was still a teenager, how he had swept her off her feet and brought her to the UK with promises of a great life. And how subsequently he had left her alone most of the time for the past two years, he living in London and her in Plymouth. She had been ready to leave him and the UK and go back to Cuba, when her mother came over for a visit, realising how alone and desperate her daughter was becoming.

She also told him that her mother had realised what was happening between Isobel and Adam over the past couple of weeks and actually approved of it, thinking her daughter would be much happier with him than with her husband.

As luck would have it, just as Adam was about to kiss her, which was all he had wanted to do for the past half an hour whilst they talked, they received company. By this time, the gym always started to get busy. As others stepped into the jacuzzi, Isobel stood, gave him a quick peck on the cheek and left, leaving him even more confused than before. He knew he wanted her badly, but not as another man's wife and a casual fling. That really wasn't his style at all.

Chapter 7

The next morning Adam woke with his head full of Isobel and in a playful mood. He made some coffee and opened his bedroom blinds with their spectacular view out to sea. Particularly on such a day as this, with the early morning sun streaming into the room, he couldn't imagine living anywhere else in England.

The design of the house might have been rather too modern for some tastes, with its full height glazing on both floors, but that did allow spectacular views, particularly from this room, with its glazing wrapped along the front and around one side of the room looking across Wembury Bay.

The bedroom stretched the full width of the house; it could have easily housed two equally master bedrooms and really was more of a hotel suite. It had a split level with a lowered seating area, an espresso machine to one side and a high-tech glass and stainless steel desk along with a computer to the other and an enormous en-suite further on. A pleasant room to spend the morning in, making himself comfortable back on his bed, Adam picked up his mobile and sent a text

to Isobel.

I woke up this morning thinking of you, and how badly I want to kiss you

He didn't have to wait long for a reply.

I woke up this morning thinking about you too, but my dream went much further than just kissing you.

Spurred on by Isobel's text, he decided it would be a lot of fun to text her and tell her exactly what he was thinking about.

After each explicit text, she sent a simple message of 'tell me more' which he did, each more explicit than the last. Before he knew it, it was late afternoon, and Dan was arriving home after the day's training. He sent her a final text for the day, asking when he would see her again.

To which she replied that she could come over to his house for a couple of hours the following evening, and was he really capable of performing all the actions he had been promising all day?

As promised, the next evening the doorbell rang. He had managed to get rid of his brother, so he had the house to himself, exactly what he wanted. He opened the door, quickly ushering Isobel in. No sooner was the door closed, than she smothered him in kisses. He led her to the lounge. There, standing in front of the roaring fire, which he thought would be a nice touch, he slowly removed her clothes pulling her onto the couch, to kneel over him.

Then, enthusiastically, he went about fulfilling the promises he had made on the texts the day before. Starting by kissing her mouth, he slowly worked his way down her neck, along her shoulders, down to the tip of her fingers on both arms then across her chest to her stunning breasts.

There he lingered for a long while, just as he had

promised. Continuing, he kissed and licked her hard belly, around both hips and made his way down. Where, he again remained for quite a while, just as promised.

She had said nothing up until now, but then she said somewhat breathlessly,

"What was it you promised me now?"

Without a verbal reply, he slipped his fingers inside her, searching for her G spot whilst still playing with her, with his lips and tongue. He was soon rewarded with her nails raking his back. Her breathing becoming faster, she moaned softly, as he completed what he promised would be only the start of their lovemaking.

Adam picked her up and carried her up to his bedroom, stripping off what clothes remained on his body as he went. Once in his bed they made love enthusiastically for over an hour until collapsing, exhausted. He apologised for his exhaustion, to which she laughed.

"I will remember in the future not to take your promises too literally; it was all night you promised me, wasn't it?"

Much to his reluctance, he let her get out of bed to fetch her phone that they could hear ringing downstairs, and watched the way her spectacular body moved as she walked across his bedroom and out of the door. Isobel soon returned, smiling like a Cheshire cat.

Crawling back up the bed, she took hold of him, cradling him with her fingers, and then took him into her mouth, so deep he could feel the back of her throat against his rock hard cock. She licked and sucked him; playing with him and feeling his whole body stiffen, knowing he was about to come. Adam could hear her breathing hard; she obviously enjoyed this as much as he did. By the time he came, she was moaning more than he was. Isobel wiped her mouth with the back of her hand, kissed him deeply and announced that she had to leave.

Then she was gone. They had barely exchanged two dozen words in the two hours she was there; he knew he had his hands full with her but reckoned it would be worth every bit of it.

Over the next two weeks, they met in his bed almost every day, usually in the afternoon when Dan was out. Adam felt great, better than he had for a long time, and was probably in love, which might have been a problem, but he would deal with that as and when he had to.

Then on one afternoon, Isobel announced that she would be going to Cuba at the weekend to take her mother home, and that she would be there for two weeks.

That came as a bit of a surprise, but over the past couple of weeks he had got to know her quite well, realising she was a complicated girl and rather unpredictable. Anyhow, it really was time to get some work done. If he got two weeks solid in his lab, he would be able to take a few days off when she returned.

That seemed like a solid plan. Unfortunately, as it often happens, his plans didn't go at all to plan.

Now, here he was lying in a hospital bed, thinking about what was going to happen next. He knew Isobel wanted to leave her husband; they had discussed this before she left and again via text whilst she was in Cuba. They had also discussed the fact that her husband treated her as a possession, rolling her out to impress when required, and would put up a fight to retain his trophy.

As he pondered this, the curtains opened to reveal his

brother Dan standing there, with the normal stupid grin on his face, which was quickly replaced by a look of concern.

"You are such an arsehole. You know that, don't you?"

"Why didn't you call me, an ambulance, something? I can't believe you drove yourself here?"

"And you look like crap."

"I don't feel any better than I look" Adam replied sheepishly, once he could get a word in.

The boys talked for a while, and as they did so Adam began to feel better. The painkillers were working, and thoughts of Isobel's return bolstered his spirits.

Whilst they talked the surgeon visited, gave the normal checks and checked the drain bags connected to the tubes protruding from Adam's belly. All the time talking to the myriad of assistants that clung to his scrubs. Not a word to Adam, until he finally turned to him.

"I think we got that just in time, there doesn't appear to be any inflection. You were lucky, Mr. Young, any longer and we would have had a serious problem here. I will send someone to remove the drain tubes in a few hours."

"Any idea when I might go home?"

"Tomorrow I should think, all going well."

With that the surgeon was gone, followed by his entourage, all furiously making notes on their pads as they went.

"Doesn't look too good, that, does it mate?"

said Dan, indicating the food that had just been plonked down in front of Adam.

"Would you like me to get something for you from the shop downstairs? And how about a toothbrush and paste, I don't suppose you brought any with you? Did you?"

"Don't be daft, little brother, I didn't bring change for the car park, so what do you think?

"I think you are an idiot, but then again that is a universally held opinion of you. I will get you some stuff and check your truck, if it's still there."

Within a few minutes he was back. Dan deposited a salad and a sandwich, along with a plastic spoon, a toothbrush and paste on Adam's tray, and pushed aside the untouched meal the nurse left earlier, all the time with a big grin on his face, shaking his head, and laughing quietly to himself.

"What's up with you?"

Dan replied through his laughter "You never lose that touch, do you?"

"Why, what's up?"

"I went to the parking office, assuming your truck had either been towed or was covered in tickets. But they said a nurse had come over to the office several times, to tell them that you were having an emergency operation and would they please not tow or ticket your truck; she seemed very struck with you, by all accounts."

"I really don't remember much after they banged me up with painkillers, it's all a bit hazy."

"Yeah, sure" Said Dan, still cackling to himself.

"You never could resist a pretty girl."

Dan chatted as Adam gulped down his salad and sandwich.

"Right, I need a piss."

"Let me move that," said Dan as he jumped up from his seat to help Adam swing the tray away from the bed; he then pulled down the blanket covering Adam, to help his brother up.

Taking a step back, Dan started to laugh.

"What have you been doing?" he said, gesturing at the remnants of the paper gown Adam was still wearing.

"Oh, that! Yes, well when I woke up I needed a piss and the bloody blankets were wrapped around me, so I couldn't move. I had to peel them from around me and then come across this bloody gown, of course tied at the back. So I had to tear it off and piss in one of those bottles. Why the fuck do they tie them at the back?

"I had to use my mobile to see what I was doing, but every bloody thirty seconds the damn thing would shut off. Then I had to get one of those bottles between my legs and not get piss everywhere, it was a bloody nightmare."

Adam's recounting his morning's adventures having a piss had Dan in stitches.

"Come on, help me up before I piss myself again."

Dan helped his brother to his feet.

"No, I have it from here; you can carry one with your laughter, dickhead."

Dan watched Adam painfully shuffle the 20 meters to the toilet. In one hand, he had the bags connected to the tubes which in turn disappeared inside him, these he held up in the air and in the other his toothbrush and paste, with the remnants of the tattered green gown flapping against him.

What a sight.

Five minutes later Adam reappeared, looking a little fresher.

"I see what you mean about the boxers", the staining still obvious as Adam shuffled back.

"Yes, dickhead, I'm sure I remember a nurse taking them off when she undressed me. What was that, yesterday? I haven't the foggiest how I managed to wake up wearing them."

"Some prude of a surgeon, perhaps, couldn't stand the sight of it flapping around?"

"Fuck off."

"And I thought you didn't remember anything about a nurse."

"It's all coming back mate, and she was hot."

Dan could see his brother was feeling better. His sense of humor was returning, a good sign. He soon took his leave, saying that he would be back in the morning to take him home.

"And get some sleep."

That was far easier to say than do, the tubes in his stomach hurt with every tiny movement, so what sleep that did come was quickly disturbed.

Fortunately, within two hours a nurse turned up to remove the tubes and their connected bags. After that the pain almost disappeared, allowing him to sleep until early the next morning. His brother turned up shortly after breakfast, and he was allowed to go home, with explicit instructions to take two weeks off and rest.

With an arm over Dan's shoulder, the two of them approached the main door of the hospital as they slid open to reveal a pretty brunette walking towards them. She smiled.

"Hi Adam, uh, Mr. Young, I hope you are feeling better. Do you remember me? I helped you in and examined you when you were admitted."

"Of course," Adam said, smiling in return.

"You didn't look well at all. I don't think I have ever seen anyone that green before."

"That bad, huh?"

"You know, that horrible green liquor you get in some bars?"

"Chartreuse, they call it" Dan put in,

to receive a withering look from his brother.

"Yes, exactly that color."

Adam hadn't thought he looked too bad, not that he checked his reflection before leaving the house or in the car for that matter. But he knew Dan was loving this.

"You know," the nurse carried on "It was a good thing for you to look that bad, I was able to immediate tell that you had a burst appendix. If I had only suspected you had a problem with it, then I would have run more tests. One of them would have involved me sticking my finger up your bum; it's the best test, you know."

I bet it is, you naughty girl, I think you are probably an expert at it, as well. Better than when Jane tried it, shame about that. If she'd told what she was about to do, I might have gotten into it, but all of sudden, out of the blue like that! She didn't half make me jump, shame she was sitting on me. Never did see her again, did I? But you, perhaps!

Dan spoke up, disturbing Adam's thoughts.

"I assume it was you that told the parking wardens about his truck. Thank you for that."

Um, two of them and he's very cute, a big boy too.

With a look at her watch, she realised she was going to be late again.

"You're welcome, but I'm late, got to get moving. It's good to see you looking better, I hope the next time we see each other you're fit and strong. Bye."

With that, she turned and hurried off into the hospital.

"What?"

He remarked about the look of mirth over Dan's face.

"You have to be sick, you didn't get her number. Come on, let's get you home."

Chapter 8

Ensconced in the lounge, Adam had definitely had enough of beds for a while, and made comfortable in front of the TV by his brother while Dan went to fix something to eat. He clicked through the channels of nondescript nonsense, mostly reality TV shows, until deciding upon the news. After watching for a minute or two, Adam shouted to his brother.

"Have you seen all this shit? What's it all about?"

"The riots, you mean?" Dan replied, returning from the kitchen

"Yeah, I caught a little in the ward."

"While I was waiting to pick you up, they were talking about it on TV. I caught it between games, of course. This guy was wanted in connection with a fire extinguisher thrown from the top of a building during a riot earlier in the year, during the student protests."

"Yeah, I remember, during that protest a group had invaded a government building in the center of London and were up on the roof. When the police tried to get them off, that dropped fire extinguisher killed a policeman. But still, why the armed response and why shoot the guy?"

"Seems as though these guys are neo-Nazi's and believed to be armed, hence the armed response at the arrest. They shot him whilst attempting to escape."

"Yeah, well okay, but why the riots?"

"Well, I'll be fucked if I know, turn it up, let's see what they are saying."

The crime correspondent for Star, standing outside the metropolitan police station, was in mid flow of his answer to Sarah Jane's question from back at the broadcast center,

"Earlier I interviewed three young men that told me they were part of the riots; they refused to be caught on camera but agreed to answer certain questions.

"I asked firstly, how and why did they get involved, and this is what they told me.", said the correspondent as he consulted his notes.

"They said it was the best days of their lives that they saw the police as the face of the privileged minority, and were taking this as an opportunity for revenge. That they had no jobs and could never see that they might get one; that they have no future and had nothing to lose. They went on to say that they were happy the government were cutting police numbers, and that the next time this happened, which they were convinced it would, there would be even less police available to mount a response."

Sarah Jane then turned to one of her guests.

"What is your response to that?"

"We have an excellent record in decreasing unemployment; just look at our revolutionary back to work program," responded Mark Cobalt, the employment minister.

"But that has been described as an abject failure, as it has only delivered temporary unpaid jobs and only one in four people has found a job afterwards, and then for only for six months. So how can that be described as a success?"

"But it was revolutionary, we are only paying the companies involved by results, when they have found someone a job and removed them from the unemployment register"

"Yes, but only for six months, during which they've learnt nothing."

"Exactly," put in another of Sarah Jane's guests. "What we need are proper training schemes and apprenticeships, where young people can learn a skill and have something to offer employers. At the moment, it is cheaper for employers to hire from abroad than to train up our own apprentices. The government has to do something about this."

"And quickly, too," put in another of the show's guests. "This recession the UK is enduring has seen many businesses go under, some huge household names, with unemployment on the rise all over the UK. The Government has promised economic stimulus and said that the worst was over, that the UK was recovering, and have published their unemployment figures as proof. Yet what have they actually done, other than send us into a triple dip recession?

"The only thing I can see is this back to work scheme, which is just a way of manipulating the numbers whilst people lose their livelihoods and their homes."

Becoming more agitated by the second, the speaker carried on.

"Whilst the National Health Service is being decimated with funding cuts, Government Ministers are lining their pockets with falsified expense claims. And now a recent study has shown that 12 million children are living in poverty in the UK: that's one in three, and yet, dinner at the Prime Minister's table sold for tens of thousands of pounds, the price demanded to gain the man's ear.

"Just look at the police cuts. They weren't been able to quell the riots before they became serious, and yet their numbers are to be reduced, which you claim will not affect their ability to prevent crime. That is ridiculous, and you know it. It's the same with the military; they've laid their lives on the line on a daily basis, only to receive a simple letter upon returning from deployment, stating their regiment was to be cut."

Before he could carry on or the employment minister could respond, the presenter said:

"Thank you. Do you have anything you would like to say Dr. Logan?"

"In my opinion, almost every one of the government's cost cutting initiatives seemed to be disproportionally affecting the less well-off elements of society, making that age-old adage, "the rich get richer as the poor get poorer", ring even truer.

"Do you know it is estimated that up to half a million young people within today's society are so disenfranchised that they see no future for themselves. They are so malleable, and will take whatever short term gain came their way or could be used as tools of others' agendas, as we are now seeing. I can't understand why the government hasn't recognised this and started to do something about it, before it's too late."

"Who's this guy? Obviously not a politician; he seems to know what he is talking about." asked Dan, carrying a plate load of steaming pasta which was plonked on Adam's knee. "Get it eaten."

"Some psychiatrist. But yes he does, not like those bloody politicians, they haven't got a clue, they live in a world of their own and will never understand the responses to their crazy fiscal measures. They are the real cause of the demonstrations and the strikes. He's also right, any group could use these peaceful demonstrations to advance their own agendas."

Adam forked in mouthfuls of salmon and pasta, realising he was far hungrier than he had originally thought and continued to watch the news show, as Sarah Jane said:

"But it's not only the government that's unpopular, is it? The banks and the bankers that ran them are equally well despised. They've lost fortunes, rewarded themselves with million pound bonuses, and the general public are struggling to pay for their weekly groceries as a result of this greed and incompetence. In addition, they have now been shown to have been working together to manipulate interest rates. This manipulation and the illegal fixing of LIBOR rates, the rates at which banks lend to each other, has again allowed them to make billions at the expense of the man in the street as it has increased the cost of nearly everything he or she purchases."

Adam couldn't but agree with what was being said, but his attention was beginning to waver as he reached for the remote his mobile beeped.

Just about to get on the plane, can't wait till tomorrow. Going to go shopping in London and pick up something I know you will enjoy removing. Should be there about 6. Iss XXX

His thoughts were on Isobel, she would be back tomorrow and there were several things he very much wanted to do with her. He hoped his condition wouldn't hinder him too much, but she was definitely going to need to be far gentler with him than she normally was, for a week or so.

"Who's that texting you. If I were you I wouldn't be arranging any dates for a while. Not in the state you're in."

Ignoring his brother, Adam switched off the TV as the discussion continued; how the general strike, which had been called towards the end of the year, promised to bring out hundreds of thousands of demonstrators, at demonstrations across the country. This, finally, had the government worried, and they were at last beginning to realise how unpopular they were.

From doctors to company professionals to the unskilled work-force, the support for demonstrations and strikes was unanimously and overwhelmingly given. The day of the general strike would see an almost complete walkout of the UK's labour force. No public transport would operate; schools and universities would shut, hardly a shop, factory or office would open, doctor's surgeries and hospitals would be for emergencies only, and construction sites would shut down. The doors would be firmly closed in all government buildings and, although the police couldn't strike by law, they had taken a ballot in support of the industrial action and had pledged their support for the strikes.

If this general strike escalated the way others had, the whole of the UK was going to look more like Beirut in the 1970's.

Chapter 9

Isobel made her way through customs; it was slow today, but knowing she soon would be in Adam's bed made it easily bearable.

As she came through baggage and out the doors, Isobel thought about her shopping trip and the underwear she would buy that she knew Adam would love to remove. As she looked around for the best route to a taxi stand, she was surprised to see her husband standing there.

He hadn't called or texted whilst she was away and she hadn't expected him to be meeting her. Trying not to look worried, she smiled walking up to him, kissing his cheek as he liked her to do in public.

He didn't look in a good mood, but then he never did these days, always far too preoccupied with his work. She wished she knew what he was really like when she first met him; she certainly wouldn't have married him and probably wouldn't have gone out to dinner with him on that first date. But had she taken that course, she would never have met Adam, a man she knew she loved and would happily spend the rest of her life with.

"I have the car in Short Term so hurry up, otherwise there will be another hour on it. We will be going to the Park Lane apartment."

"But I had plans to go shopping and then back to Devon."

"Well, change them. You are staying in London, that's what you keep telling me you want, isn't it?"

A jolt of despair shot through her; all she could think about was getting back to Adam, assuming that her husband would be staying alone in London as he always did.

The drive to London was done in silence; she knew something was wrong. She thought that he couldn't possibly know about Adam. Nobody except her mother knew, whose blessing she knew she had.

Once in the apartment she noticed suitcases everywhere, her suitcases. On closer examination, she saw that they were full of her clothes. In fact, it seemed that almost all her clothes were there. She looked at Jonathan questioningly; he turned to her.

"Do you really think I'm that stupid? I know all about him. I have received every text he has sent you whilst you've been in Cuba."

Isobel replied angrily "But how can you know that? You don't have my phone."

"I don't need your phone. What do you think I do, that pays for all this? And everything else I give you?" waving his hand around the apartment, he continued.

"If I can read every one of the Prime Minister's texts, listen to his calls and read his e-mails, don't you think I can just as easily do the same to you? We will be staying in London for the foreseeable future, and I have closed down the house in Plymouth."

Isobel didn't know what to do or say; all she could do was burst into tears at which her husband sneered.

"Get into the bedroom, have a shower and get dressed. We're going out to dinner," he said, pointing toward a door off the hallway.

"And before you can text him," he said, "give me your phone."

She had no choice but to comply with his demands.

Whilst Jonathan had no problems meeting his disgruntled clients on his own, he thought that by bringing Isobel along, as a little eye candy, would make the meeting go smoother; he knew the effect she had on men. The previous day he had booked a table at Le Gavroche. Normally, one would expect to book weeks in advance, but he was a regular customer there, with his apartment a five minute walk away on Park Lane.

Arriving precisely on time rather than his normally fashionable 15 minutes late, the maitre'd took Isobel's coat, revealing her in a low cut backless dress. She, as always, had the desired effect. He doubted that there was a male head that didn't turn to stare at her, and many female ones, as well. He had expected two of them to be there, both Roseau and De Costa, they were at Le Gavroche after all, but only one man, Roseau, sat at the table they were shown to.

They ordered and ate with only the minimum of polite conversation. Jonathan, his normal public jovial self, but Isobel sullen, pushing her food around her plate more than eating. Across from them sat a man Isobel had never seen before; one not looking particularly happy to be here. After the meal, Jonathan suggested that Isobel use the ladies' room whilst they had a business discussion in private. As soon as she left Roseau leant forward, speaking very quickly and quietly.

"We are very disappointed in the outcome of our recent transaction, and should you want the whereabouts of your recent move and the extents of your involvement in the hacking scandal to remain secret, you had better deliver as promised." At this, he finished his drink, got up and left the restaurant.

To say this shocked Jonathan was the understatement of the year. Nobody knew of his move other than the six of them, and exceedingly few knew of his work for The International Group.

Who are these people?

Isobel returned a few minutes later to find Jonathan ashen-faced, enquiring:

"What's the matter?"

She was dismissed with "Get your coat, we are leaving."

Leaving the restaurant, Isobel followed Jonathan back to the apartment. She, having just flown back from Cuba was very tired by now, and as soon as she got into the apartment she went straight to her bedroom. She undressed quickly; dropping her dress to the floor, all she could think about was Adam and her hatred of her husband. Isobel sat on her bed and the tears quickly came; within a minute her face was soaked with them and her eyes bloodshot. She was desperately tired, badly needing some sleep to clear her head and decide what to do. She stood and walked naked to the bathroom and into the shower.

As she turned the shower on she heard her bedroom door open and the sound of footsteps on the hardwood floor.

No, I can't handle this.

She shuddered and stifled a sob, preparing herself for what she thought was about to happen. Sex with Jonathan had never been very good, and over the last year, when they did make love it was more of a feral mating act than anything with any real affection.

She'd had no choice, just bend over and get it over with. Jonathan certainly didn't have Adam's finesse, his nimble fingers and seeking tongue.

Thank God.

Her relief was palpable as she heard the sound of suitcases being thrown onto the bedroom floor, followed by a slamming of the bedroom door. She had escaped for now, but that couldn't last for long. Sitting in the shower she let the hot water run all over her body for a long time before eventually getting out, drying herself and falling into her bed.

Despite the tiredness, it was some time before she finally dropped off to sleep. She should have been ecstatic about to see Adam again, but it now appeared that she was a prisoner.

Whilst Isobel was in the shower, Jonathan thought firstly about the meeting that had just happened. There was no way his client should have been able to know about his new office; they didn't know where the last one was and certainly didn't know where he lived, or at least they shouldn't. He'd known for some time that he needed to find out a lot more about them, although he didn't believe they represented any danger to him, should he be able to supply the information they wanted.

Next, his thoughts turned toward Isobel. He was not going to take Isobel's unfaithfulness without extracting revenge. She belonged to him, but he was limited with his options of what he could do to her. Killing her wasn't in the cards, although he would dearly love to strangle her right now. Divorce, no. Too embarrassing and costly. It would have to be constant humiliation. That he could do well. Maybe after a few months of that, the bitch would cut her own wrists. But that bastard Adam, he certainly would get what was coming to him. As of yet, he knew little about him, but that was no problem. He had spent many years getting dirt on hundreds of people and Adam would be no exception.

Over the years, online security had become a great deal more difficult to circumvent, which was why he employed the best to do the job. Stella was still away on holiday; she was the best by far, but she would also want to know why he was doing this. Jonathan picked up his mobile and rang Carl to find out if Dave had all their systems up and running yet.

"Sorry boss. He says no, it won't be finished until Thursday evening."

"Why?"

"Because you told us we had this week to sort it out."

This was not what Jonathan wanted to hear.

"Carl! Tell Dave this. Go somewhere he can get online and find out about a guy from Plymouth, called Adam something or other. All I have is his mobile number, but that's all he needs."

"07853638994, you got that? And tell him I want it in two hours."

"Look, it can't be that important. That won't be secure, and you know that." Carl replied, alarmed at his boss's demands.

Today was not a day to say no to Jonathan, who was never one to be patient. He repeated what he wanted done and hung up the phone.

It wasn't a good idea, Carl knew that, but he was without a lot of choice in the matter. He relayed the instructions and something of their boss's mood to Dave, who was up to his eyeballs in cabling. A job that he didn't enjoy, but which needed to be done carefully and correctly. He also needed a break from it.

"Okay, but there is a wireless network at the King's Arms I can use, a damn site closer than the West End."

He got into his car and drove around the corner to park outside a small hotel, taking his laptop with him. This was far preferable to a West End Cybercafé, all that would be open this time of the night, and he could do it from his car. He spent approximately an hour setting up a new e-mail address to have the requested data sent to, and begin searching into Adam's life. His probing soon bore fruit; he discovered that Adam, Young being his surname, worked at the University of Plymouth and had a website dedicated to the research he did there. On the website, there was a contact page tab which he clicked on, hoping it listed the man's address.

Within another hour, he had everything he wanted and shut down his laptop. What he was not aware of was a mistake in the script of the contact page form. If no data were entered it should have simply closed, but instead it sent an enquiry to Adam's e-mail address. This enquiry contained no information other than the IP address it had come from.

On his return to the office, Dave rang Jonathan.

"Okay boss, this is what I've got. His surname is Young, and he presently works at the University of Plymouth doing research, and apparently a PhD. He got a Master's degree from Bath a couple of years or so ago, and before that was in the navy for a little while. I couldn't find out much about that but,"

"That's not relevant, you have his address?"

"Yes, I have his address and will text that over as soon

as I'm through here. I have gotten a very interesting bit of info. Apparently, it seems as though his parents were killed in the London Tube bombings."

"Yes. Interesting, what else?"

"Not a deal. I have his IP and can get into his computer, I think. Other than that not much. He's into rugby and used to be a very useful player, and still coaches kids locally."

"Wait, what's that? Coaches kids' rugby, did you say?"

"Yeah"

"Send me all the info, now."

Armed with this information, Jonathan got down to work. He had made up incriminating stories many times in his work for the International Group, and was very good at it. Recently, he had implicated the parents of a missing girl in the little girl's death, leaving enough convincing data that the police had charged the parents with her murder. He had also planted evidence on an actress's computer, implicating her in an orgy ring, even doctoring photographs so she appeared in them.

If all went well, Young would be found guilty and sent to prison, and if by some chance he didn't go to jail, it didn't really matter as the press frenzy he could create would ruin Young anyway. The fact that he was the son of victims from the tube bombing would attract massive media attention, a nice bonus.

Early the following morning Jonathan began the data gather to use against Young. He created a file which he uploaded to their secure FTP server, and then phoned Dave to give him instructions. Dave was still sorting out his cabling; routing all the computer systems through several hardware firewall systems, as the call came in.

. . .

"Right, I've put a file on the FTP, named Young, you can't miss it but you will obviously need to rename it. I'll leave that to you. You have the IP, right?"

"Yes, but,"

"Shut up and listen."

"Yeah, okay boss."

"Just get that file on his computer, and do it now."

"Look boss, I can't do it on an unsecured line, not until we have everything sorted here. Your instructions, remem…"

"Shut the fuck up, Dave. Go back to where you were yesterday and do this, and don't say anything to anybody about it, you hear me?"

"Okay, whatever you say."

Dave again got into his car to drive and park close to the hotel, whose internet service he planned to piggyback on again. The night before when borrowing some of the hotel's bandwidth, there had been lots of available parking spaces. Now, being the middle of the morning, there wasn't any legal parking spaces to be had.

He needed to be within 50 meters of the hotel's wireless router so had no choice but to park on a double yellow. Breaking yet another of their normally inflexible rules, not to do anything that would draw attention whilst performing this type of work.

Still, he had a good view both in front and behind which would give him enough time, should a traffic warden appear. He did consider going into the cafe that was two or three doors up from the hotel, but this time of the day it was usually filled with people. In addition, it was pouring with rain and didn't want to get himself or his laptop wet.

After booting his laptop, he checked the signal strength which showed 3 bars, about half strength, which should have been enough. The night before he had easily gained access to Adam Young's local area network (LAN) and noted there was an active computer on the network. He hoped the situation today would be the same but if not, there was a Boot on LAN feature that he could use. Five minutes later he was browsing through Young's files. Young obviously wasn't very security conscious; all Dave had to do was get past a simple firewall.

He then logged into the company's secure FTP site. He instantly groaned at the size of the file.

Well over five gigabytes, that was going to take ten perhaps twenty minutes to transfer, judging by the speed of the hotel's system. He would need to transfer the file via the hotel's computer but once initiated, he could shut down his laptop if necessary. As long as nobody shut Young's system down before the transfer completed, there wouldn't be a problem. He needed to rename the folder, and he'd noticed Young wrote a lot about seaweed. He chose Sea Lettuce as the folder name, having noticed an article that Young was working on that, mentioned that.

He then initiated the transfer, just as a traffic warden appeared around the corner, heading in his direction. Shutting the laptop immediately after checking that the transfer had started, he started the car and was in the process of pulling away from the curb as the traffic warden closed on him. As he passed her, she gave him one of those looks as if to say you lucky bastard; two more minutes and I would have had you. Relieved that he had got away with it, Dave drove back to their office to finish his cabling.

Within a few minutes of Dave arriving back at their office, Jonathan received a text with a single word.

Done.

Now he knew the evidence was on Young's computer, the next task was whom he should give the information about Young to.

Chapter 10

Isobel remained in bed all the next day. It was one of those bleak, wet winter days, and she was as depressed and unhappy as she thought it was possible to be. She thought she would never see Adam again, a man she knew she was truly in love with. She thought she had loved him the first time they had made love; by the time she went back to Cuba she knew she did. But, at that point the realisation of what was happening hadn't actually sunk in.

For the first time in over a year, she had actually been happy, and that happiness had glossed over the practical details and what the future might hold.

She had met Jonathan almost three years ago, when she worked as a receptionist at the Hotel Nacional De Cuba. She'd worked there for a year after finishing her diploma in hotel management. It was her dream to one day go to London, Paris or New York, and eventually become manager of a luxury hotel. Jonathan had completely swept her off her feet, despite him being far older than her. He'd been so charming and so different from other men she knew, that she became immensely attracted to him.

Jonathan had only stayed at the hotel for a few days before flying off somewhere else in the Caribbean. He asked Isobel to have dinner with him at the hotel the night before he left, to which she agreed. But rather than head back to England he returned to Cuba and the Hotel Nacional, within a week.

On that second trip to Havana, he told her whilst checking in that he hadn't planned to return to Cuba but had thought of her all the time since leaving. Consequently, he had decided to stop off there on the way back to the UK, he had to see her again.

Would she like to go out with him somewhere that night and show him some of Cuba's nightlife?

Isobel was thrilled that someone as obviously wealthy as him would to fly to Cuba, just to see her, and she readily accepted the offer. He stayed for another week and on the last night, Isobel had slept with him.

Before he left to return to the UK, he promised he would stay in touch and would return, very soon. A promise he kept, ringing her every second or third day, and after a month he returned.

On his return, Jonathan told Isobel that he couldn't get her out of his head, and intended to stay in Cuba for three weeks.

Would it be possible for her to get some time off, so they might explore the Island together?

For the next three weeks, they explored Cuba. She had shown him her home town and the idyllic beaches that surrounded it, learning to scuba dive in the marine reserve. He might not be one of the usual hard-bodied young men she normally favored, but there was something safe and solid about him. He exuded confidence, and she adored that.

So when on the penultimate night, sitting in a cabana watching the sun dip below the horizon and the blaze of color that spread across the sky, he asked her to marry him, she accepted. They discussed plans the following day, deciding that they should get married in her home town in two months' time. After the wedding, she would go to London with him and hopefully get a job in some fancy hotel. He told her not to worry about getting a job for a while; he certainly had enough money, so that she wouldn't have to. But if she seriously wanted to work, he would talk to some of his contacts and easily find her something.

They were married as planned in Cuba, spending a two week honeymoon on a private yacht cruising around the Caribbean. Her life had changed so much during the past 3 months. From a receptionist in what was Cuba's best hotel, to lazing on a private yacht, catered for hand and foot, she thought she could easily get used to this lifestyle. Still, her goals, always having been an ambitious girl, hadn't changed. After a few months in London, she would find herself a great job; she knew she would get excellent references from the Nacional which was world renowned and, helped by Jonathan's contacts, it would be a breeze.

Those two weeks flew by, and they were soon boarding a plane to London. She had never felt so excited. Like many Cubans, she had never left the Island before, with the exception of the cruise for her honeymoon. It seemed like a fairytale; all her dreams were coming true. It was early April when they arrived and although extremely excited initially, she was still a little apprehensive about living in London.

Although she had lived in Havana for several years, quite a large city itself, she thought it might be difficult living in such an enormous city, surrounded by buildings, and without the parks and beaches she was used to. But once she arrived to find that their apartment overlooked Hyde Park, with that amazing pink blossom that seemed to cover every tree. Then to discover the theatres and museums that seemed to be everywhere, she felt more at home than she would have dared to believe possible.

Their first month in London had gone in an instant, dining out every night after first going to the theatre or the first run of a movie. Jonathan seemed always at her side, only going to his office for a few hours a day. She still wasn't absolutely certain what he did; she knew it had to do with a newspaper, but it certainly seemed to pay well.

By mid-May, it was already surprisingly warm. Jonathan suggested that they go down to Devon for a while. He had some family there, his aging mother and two girls from his first marriage, both of whom were about Isobel's age. He told her that he had a house a few miles from Plymouth, and that with the summer coming she could spend time there with his daughters. He assured her she would get on great with them, whilst he caught up on some work.

They could explore the Devonshire coast and the moors which were spectacular in the summer, Devon being England's premier holiday destination. Isobel still wanted to eventually get a job in London and had come to love what she knew so far of the city, but she thought that there was plenty of time for that.

In reality, this was part of her education. You had to know the country you were living in well to be successful in the hotel business, right?

Within a week, they moved to Jonathan's house at Newton Ferrer's, a very pretty English coastal village overlooking the Yealm Estuary, a few miles East of Plymouth.

The house sat at the end of a drive running along the estuary, at the far end of the village, with four bedrooms above and kitchen, dining room, lounge and more below, on the ground floor. The rooms to the west side faced a long garden which led down to a small jetty, to which was moored a small sailing yacht, much in need of a little TLC.

For May in England, the weather was excellent, with long sunny days and hardly a cloud in the bright blue sky. It made Isobel feel far more at home than she ever thought possible. She, as Jonathan had predicted, got on very well with both his daughters; one a year older than her and the other two years younger. They spent a great deal of time together that summer, so much so that she didn't actually notice how much time Jonathan was spending in London, for a while at least.

It began with him spending two or three days away from her, then the whole week, coming back at weekends. He explained this: he had spent a lot of time with her in the preceding few months and needed to catch up with his work and once he did, he would only be a few days here and there. If she wanted, he would find her a job in the autumn, and then she could go back to London.

The summer seemed to be gone in a flash, and as the weeks flew by as they do exceedingly quickly when you are having fun, Jonathan's visits to Devon became less and less frequent, sometimes spending two or three weeks away at a time.

By late September, the weather was changing. There was a chill in the air, particularly in the morning, and Isobel had not experienced an English winter yet. She had heard from Jonathan's daughters that it could get pretty bleak here especially if it snowed, when the roads around the village froze, making it almost impossible to get around. So, when Jonathan appeared after another three week stint in London, Isobel told him that she wanted to return to there and get a job.

Jonathan immediately became angry, shouting at her about how well she was taken care of. He had treated her like a lady of leisure, given her everything she could possibly want and that he'd taken her away from a boring job with no prospects, but a dreary existence in Cuba.

Yes, it was true, he had given her so much, but her life in Cuba had been far from dreary. It had been very good, surrounded by friends and family. Here she felt cut off, and was beginning to get lonely. The argument continued throughout that weekend, until Jonathan went back to London alone, giving Isobel no resolution to her predicament.

The weeks now seemed to drag. As Jonathan's daughters had predicted, it was different here in the winter. As December arrived, she felt as though she was confined to the house, no more walks along the beach or strolls over the moors, it was too cold for her for that, and she was bitterly unhappy.

Over Christmas that year, the situation improved somewhat. Jonathan took her to London for the seasonal festivities; party after party with his friends. She found that she could bear the winter weather in London and even found snow fun, when it was possible to get out of it and into the warmth quickly. But when the New Year arrived, she was sent back to Newton Ferrer's. Any discussion of her staying in London was met with an outright no. And as to getting a job, she was told that it wouldn't do for a man of his position to have his wife to perform menial work.

The weeks dragged by, then months. Jonathan's visits became less frequent with each month that went by. He did turn up for their anniversary to stay with her for almost a week, before heading back off to London again. She had almost stopped asking Jonathan about going to live in London and find a job, as every time she brought it up, the result was just another argument.

In May, she got Jonathan's permission to go and to see her family in Cuba. It seemed to her as though whatever she wanted to do, she would need to get his permission to do so. Her mother soon detected that Isobel was not happy in England, although she could not get her to tell her what the problem was. She asked Isobel if she would like her to come to England with her on her return. An offer Isobel immediately accepted, much to Jonathan's chagrin when he met the pair of them at Heathrow a few days later.

After spending a couple of days at the London apartment, Isobel and her mother went down to Newton Ferrer's. With the summer clearly on its way, Isobel actually looked forward to a summer here with her mother, whom she knew would stay as long as Isobel wanted her to. Now, Jonathan's appearances became even less frequent having only visited on three occasions by September. In late September, she met Adam.

During her most recent stay in Cuba, she thought long and hard about her future. Knowing that her life with Jonathan, as he had shown it to be, was not what she had anticipated. She also knew that she wouldn't be able to keep on living like this for long. She wanted to leave him, and was planning to discuss this with Adam as soon as she got home, but now she was to all intents and purposes a prisoner in the London apartment.

She spent all that day thinking about what she could do; only venturing out to the kitchen to make some coffee when she heard Jonathan go out. He had her passport, her purse with her credit cards in it and whilst briefly venturing out of her bedroom, she noticed that there was no key to the front door. The door was locked with a mortise bolt, preventing her from leaving even if she knew where to go.

She thought Adam loved her. He would be expecting her today, but how would she get down to Plymouth with no money and what would he think when she didn't arrive? She couldn't ring him as his number, as with all her contacts were on her mobile, which Jonathan now had. There was also no landline at the apartment, and no computer; only a wireless system which Jonathan used for his laptop.

A slamming of the front door stopped her musing. The sound of footsteps striking the hardwood floor got louder and then suddenly stopped outside her bedroom door. As she looked up she saw the door handle turning, and felt the dread start to crawl up her belly.

Jonathan, now in a better mood, having decided how he was going to destroy Adam Young's life for sleeping with his wife, had now decided it was time she really knew who was boss. Upon entering the bedroom, he looked at Isobel with a smirk. She sat up on the bed, wearing only a large baggy tee shirt. As he walked toward her, he started to remove his jacket, then unbutton his shirt.

With a realisation of his intent, Isobel began to tell him that she didn't want to and was not feeling well, but before these words come out of her mouth, he said:

"You will do what I say, when I say and do exactly as I say, do you understand? Now get that thing off and come here."

She understood all too well what he wanted her to do and was not about to do so willingly. She tried to crawl across the bed, but he quickly grabbed an ankle and pulled her toward him. He was a big man, not fit and muscled like Adam, just tall and fat, but he was much stronger than her.

With little difficultly, he dragged her to the edge of the bed, face down, whilst she kicked and screamed at him. With one hand pushing all his weight into the middle of Isobel's back, he used the other hand to unbuckle his trousers. Moving forward and kneeling on the bed he pushed Isobel's thighs apart with his knees, punching her hard across the back and shoulders as she tried to resist.

His punches soon knocked the wind out of her. All his weight pinned her down; she knew that she couldn't stop him but still continued to struggle as much as she could, as Jonathan forced himself inside her.

Knowing that it was useless to continue to fight, Isobel tried to force better images into her mind, to deflect the act of violence that was happening to her. She thought back to the last time she made love to Adam. He had started kissing her on the mouth and worked his way down her body, covering every inch of her skin in kisses, stopping to suck and lick the more sensitive parts as he worked his way down her torso, then down her legs.

At her feet, he sucked each of her toes as she watched him, her back arching in pleasure. He then gently reached up to her hips and turned her over, working his way back up her legs, then gently biting her bum. Sliding his fingers inside her he soon brought forth her second orgasm; he then raised her hips and slid inside her. Holding her by the hips, he pushed deep into her, eliciting moans of pleasure.

But this wasn't Adam making love to her. It was her husband raping her, making her not only experience considerable pain but making her feel ashamed and dirty. Fortunately it didn't last long, and after a minute or two, Jonathan got off her and quickly left the bedroom, leaving her in tears as he closed the bedroom door.

Chapter 11

As Isobel was being beaten and raped by her husband, Adam stood naked in front of the mirrored wardrobe in his bedroom, appraising the scars the surgeon's scalpel had left behind. It was his first decent shower since the operation, had lasted nearly half an hour, and was as hot as he could stand it to be.

Not too bad, and most of that bloody superglue has come off at last.

Only a large blob of the surgeon's glue remained in his navel, which he now picked at.

My abs aren't looking too bad, almost as good as they had before the op. Isobel will like that.

Happy about that and more importantly, happy about Isobel's imminent visit that evening, he put on a bathrobe.

He had teased her a few weeks before. Telling her about how he had answered the door naked, thinking it was Isobel but discovered an old woman instead. Of course, Isobel didn't believe it, but she told him the next time he knew it was definitely her, he should answer the door naked, she would enjoy it.

Maybe I should today; it would be a good way to welcome her home.

Yes, food time, what's in the fridge? I'm starving.

He walked down the stairs and made his way toward the kitchen, just as his doorbell rang.

It can't be Isobel, she would have texted earlier.

Adam hesitated, debating with himself whether to put some clothes on, but before he could make up his mind there was a second knock, then a continued banging, followed by a shout of:

"Police! Open the door. You have one minute before we break it down."

Rather than have his door broken down, and wearing nothing but his toweling robe, he opened the door to reveal five police officers. They immediately pushed past him; one of them thrust a piece of paper into his face.

"This is a warrant to search your property, Mr. Young; you are Mr. Adam Young, aren't you?"

Adam mutely agreed that he was, with a nod of his head.

He was stunned. Speechless, in fact.

This has to be a mistake, what's going on?

As his thoughts cleared a little he noticed a TV crew standing behind the officers still outside; they had their cameras trained upon him, and if he was correct there was a red light on the front of the camera.

The fucking TV's here as well, sod that.

Adam tried to close the front door but was pushed against the wall by two of the officers. He pushed back against the men who had just invaded his house and two more joined in, the second spraying CS gas directly into his face; the TV cameras recorded the whole scene.

Adam was dragged with streaming eyes, coughing and choking from the gas, and nearly doubled up in pain from the surgery into the lounge. Then he was roughly pulled around by one policeman as another handcuffed his hands behind his back and pushed him into a chair.

"You are under arrest, son."

"Fuck you, I haven't done anything. How dare you come into my house?"

Adam managed to get in between bouts of coughing.

As his eyes began to clear and his coughing subsided, his confused mind cleared a little, enough to say:

"Would you mind telling me what I am under arrest for, and what you think you are doing here?"

To this, he was told that he was under arrest on suspicion of providing child pornography, and that they were about to search his house, removing any computer equipment that they found.

At this Adam would have laughed, had he not hurt so much. He also doubted that laughing would go down well with the policemen, who were already tearing his house apart looking for something he knew they wouldn't find.

Nevertheless, those words 'under arrest on suspicion of providing child pornography' scared the shit out of him.

Adam shut his eyes to try to clear the mental paralysis running through his brain and the sickening churning of his stomach that accompanied it. Keeping quiet was probably the best plan, but not before telling them that they were wrong, he had not been or would he ever be, involved in anything like that.

Another thought caught him a little later.

I'm glad that Dan isn't at home; he would have fought for all he was worth; that would have gotten messy.

For a little over two hours, he watched as the police searched his house. He couldn't exactly say that they had trashed it, but it wasn't far short of that. His books and papers were strewn all over the floor of the lounge, and he doubted whether it was any better in the rest of the house. The first thing they had done was to remove his PC and take his laptop, which he assumed they had put in one of their vehicles.

As the activity around him slowed, two officers approached. With one grabbing each arm, they pulled him up and out of the chair. His hands and arms were numb and he was still in considerable pain, a result of the rough treatment and the pepper spray.

"You are under arrest, sir, on charges of resisting arrest and the suspicion of distributing child pornography. You will be taken down to the Plymouth Police Station and questioned further on these charges. Do you understand?"

one of them announced rather officiously.

"Yes, I understand your ridiculous charges, both of which are a load of bollocks. Do you think I might get dressed and make a call to inform someone of them?"

He was told no, he couldn't get dressed. He was handcuffed and told that he could make a call from the police station later, once he had made a statement.

"My only statement to you is this: I haven't gotten the faintest idea what you are talking about, and as far as resisting arrest, I was simply trying to close the door to that TV crew you have outside."

Adam was led to the front door as he felt a towel thrown over his head, making him look the part for the TV cameras. He was then pulled through the waiting throng and pushed into the back of a waiting police car.

Adam noticed with immense relief that there did not appear to be an outside broadcast vehicle yet; these pictures would not be going out live, but soon enough they would be broadcast and he could guarantee that outside broadcast vehicles would be on their way.

His greatest fear was that Isobel would see it; she surely wouldn't believe it.

But still.

There didn't seem much point in saying anything at all during the short drive into Plymouth. As Adam arrived at the police station and the car was ushered through the security gates, he could see a BBC van with a satellite dish on the roof. He sighed to himself.

Yes! I will be making the evening news.

The gates shut with a foreboding clang; he was pulled from the car and guided toward the open door of the station as the reporters shouted questions at him through the fence, irritating Adam even further. Once inside the station he was led to an interview room, his handcuffs were removed and the door shut behind him. The coughing fit brought on by the pepper spray hadn't done him any good at all. He tried to tell the officers at the house about his recent operation as they left, but they would have none of it.

To be honest the surgeons had done such a fantastic job, little evidence of their scalpels was visible, his navel was full of super glue and the holes below were so small they could have been anything.

Adam looked around him. The ubiquitous mirror was there as is always depicted in the movies, from behind which he assumed he was being watched, and that only infuriated him further. The walls were bare concrete blocks, and in the center of the room stood a table with chairs either side. They looked as though it was bolted to the floor which was just as well as the temptation was to pick one of the chairs up and put it through that damn mirror.

Fuck, it's cold in here.

He shivered as he paced up and down the towel that

had been put over his head earlier, wrapped around his shoulders in an effort to keep warm. It was only about this point, now alone, that he started to think about what just happened. While he was still in his house, he was too shocked to think properly but now, after recovering a little, he started to replay the events in his head.

Adam struggled to collect his thoughts, the police had mentioned child pornography; he knew that he never had anything to do with that and that they would find no evidence of it. But still, as he thought over what had just happened, the floor seemed to pitch under his feet.

Someone has made a serious mistake somewhere, but they seem certain enough of their information. It must have come from somewhere.

But where and more importantly, why?

His brain was still refusing to function, and those thoughts were making him feel sick; he was more shaken than he had ever been in his life. This was impossible; he'd been situations where is life was in danger but where he stood now was eminently worse.

The situation was unreal and at the moment he had absolutely no way of answering these questions. All he could do was try to remain calm and wait for someone to tell him what the hell was going on. Adam sat, thought about Isobel, trying to take his mind off it.

He didn't have long to wait as within a few minutes, two officers entered the room, one taking a seat opposite him and the other standing behind. If he hadn't been in an English Police Station, this maneuver might have worried him.

It didn't.

Whilst in the services there had been a short course on interrogation techniques, which this seemed to fit that bill a wrong answer often resulted in a blow to the back of the head.

The officer in front of Adam opened his notebook, and after spending a few minutes seemingly reading its contents, he looked up, staring at Adam briefly.

"It appears that you and several of your university colleagues in London like to look at pictures of naked children. Is that correct?"

"No, I don't, and as far as I am aware I have no colleagues in any London university", Adam replied.

"Where did you obtain this information?", Adam then asked.

This was ignored by the officer. Several more questions were asked which pertained to his name, where he worked, what he did there, how long he had been there. All of which Adam answered.

"Do you know a Professor Braun?", was the next question.

"Never heard of him."

At this, the officer stood, he and the other who had been standing behind him in silence the whole time, turned and left the room. As they did so, Adam demanded to make a phone call, which was again ignored.

Within a few minutes, the door opened again. This time Adam did not look up, but as the officer took the seat opposite Adam, he was surprised to see it was a friend of his, Clive Gooding, from his rugby club. He had known Clive for several years, and they both served as committee members at the club. Adam immediately asked him what the hell was going on. Clive began to tell him what appeared to have happened.

"Adam, we have had a tip off that you are involved with a convicted pedophile, a Professor Braun, and that you have been supplying pornographic images to this professor and others in a ring, in London."

"And, before you say anything, I have only just been advised of this, had it been earlier I would have handled it differently."

As they talked, Clive told Adam that something certainly didn't feel right; he had handled many of these cases, not necessarily in Plymouth, and they relied heavily on tips from the public. But, an anonymous tip passed down from the Metropolitan Police Force as this had, just didn't gel with him, particularly as he knew Adam well.

"This is not a case of mistaken identity, I'm sure of that. Is it possible you have upset someone that would do this?"

"Look mate, I just don't know. Had you asked me that yesterday I would have said no, but I'm sitting here, aren't I? What more can I say? I haven't got a clue whom it could be."

They talked a little more until Clive said he had to leave, but would soon be back with some clothes for him to wear.

Before he left, Adam asked:

"Do you think you could get me some pain killers?"

Clive asked him, why and what was the matter? Adam explained the operation and the pepper spray.

"I will look into this, but first I will get you a doctor", Clive replied.

"Don't get a doctor, pain killers will do just fine."

Chapter 12

Dan Young, just returning home, was perplexed to find not one but three TV crews camped upon his doorstep. The initial crew from the BBC was still inside the property, with others just outside the gates, leaving just enough room for his car to get through.

As Dan drove through the gates, he wondered if they'd come to the wrong house. There was nothing going on at the club or in the England camp that would warrant such attention, and he was sure that there was nothing in Adam's work that would warrant it either. He parked and got out of his car. As soon as he did, a camera was pushed into his face, a reporter standing next to the cameraman asking him questions.

"Do you know that your brother has been arrested on charges of child pornography? Do you have any comments?"

Dan had comments alright, not that any would be broadcastable; he knew his brother would never be involved in that. He had briefly seen a woman leaving the house a few weeks ago, and thought her his brother's latest girlfriend. She was absolutely stunning, and certainly no child. Dan began cursing the reporter as he grabbed the camera, smashing it against the side of the van and throwing the remains into the back through the open side door.

He snarled "Get off my property before I throw you all off."

They knew whom he was, Bear being a very appropriate nickname. The crew piled into the van as fast as they could possible manage, which was reversing before the doors shut. Far too quickly; it crashed into the Sky van and became stuck against it and the granite gate post on the other side, much to the amusement of the Sky crew who, within minutes, were broadcasting the mayhem live as the BBC crew tried to free their vehicle.

Walking around to the front of the house, out of view from the gate, Dan tore the blue and white tape that was over the front door. On entering he grabbed the phone and rang directory enquiries to get the phone number of the Police Station in Plymouth. Assuming that's where they would have taken his brother.

By now Adam was getting very cold and very angry. Fortunately Clive, good to his word, arrived with a glass of water and some painkillers before Adam really started to lose his temper. He was also carrying a pair of boxer shorts, a tee-shirt and a pair of dark blue overalls, which Adam hurriedly put on. As Clive sat down in front of him, he told Adam that his brother had just been on the phone. Despite what he had been told, there was no point coming to the station tonight, he was apparently on the way.

Clive was very much aware of Dan's reputation, and had made sure that as soon as he arrived that the officers on the desk would inform him that he would be allowed to see his brother soon, and to please wait. He also told Adam, that he really shouldn't be letting anyone see him yet, with the exception of a lawyer, whom Adam hadn't asked for yet, but he would let Dan see him for a few minutes, to calm him down.

He also asked Adam if he wanted to call his lawyer if he had one. Adam replied that at the moment, he didn't, and he would like to talk to his brother first.

Whilst they waited for Dan to arrive, Clive told Adam that he would be there at least overnight, and that his colleagues had no choice but to go to the university in the morning to seize his work computer. The computer experts would search all of Adam's computers for anything that would confirm the tip off.

"Is there anything in there?"

Although his anger had dampened a little, it wasn't enough to stop him angrily replying,

"Of course there are things in there, what the hell use was a computer if there weren't? And if you mean are there any pornographic images, no, there aren't any".

As he finished, he turned away in an attempt to calm down. Clive was a friend, he thought, and seemed to be trying to help, but at that moment he desperately wanted to hit somebody. Dan may be the one that had the reputation, but that came from the rugby pitch where he was known to be a beast. It was Adam who was the more aggressive of the two, and presently it was taking all his will not to lose control.

The door to the room suddenly opened and an officer appeared with a somewhat worried look on his face, beckoning Clive to come out. Dan had arrived. He was pacing up and down the waiting room, appropriately looking like a bear with a sore head. The desk sergeant was frantically making calls to get more officers there, as he thought Dan was about to find Adam himself.

The reception area was no more than 100 meters away. Clive could already hear the heated conversation between the desk sergeant and several officers gathered in the corridor. He was aware that he needed to get a firm grip on the situation quickly. He didn't know Dan well, only having met him a few times with Adam, but he did know his reputation on the pitch. He doubted very much whether the six of them gathered there would be able to stop Dan, short of stun gunning him. That was one thing he really didn't want to do. Firstly he liked him, and secondly he was England's wing forward, and the press feast that would follow stun gunning him would be hell itself.

He pushed past the officers, pulling the desk sergeant with him into the reception, where he witnessed a bear of man, aptly named, pacing up and down and looking as though he would explode at any moment.

He approached Dan with an outstretched hand, hoping that he would recognise him and take it, whispering a prayer of thanks as he did. He sat down, eventually getting Dan to do likewise, and began to tell him everything he knew.

As the story came out, Dan first began to shout with rage, slowly calming down as Clive told him that personally he didn't believe the accusations, certain elements of which rang untrue to him. He told Dan what would happen next.

"As accusations have been made, we have no choice but to investigate them. I don't believe we will find anything at all, and hopefully we will release Adam tomorrow."

Whilst taking Dan down to the interview room, Clive informed Dan about his suspicion.

"There are lots of things wrong with this, and something stinks. The anonymous tip to start with, coming via the Met, on top of that I know Adam well and have met several of his girlfriends. It doesn't gel for me. Do you think that Adam upset anybody enough so that they might go to this extreme?"

Dan stopped briefly, looking at Clive searchingly, deciding whether he should tell Clive about Adam's most recent flame. Upon reflection, this was definitely the better of the alternatives. It was an easy choice.

"Well, perhaps the husband of the lady Adam's sleeping with!"

Clive gave him a questioning look, and Dan carried on.

"A few weeks ago, I came home just as a stunning blonde was getting into a car parked in our drive. I know she's been at the house with Adam for a while as I had seen the car three hours earlier coming toward the house, as I was going out."

He continued "Going in that direction she could only have been going to our place, the Bennett's or the Jacob's. But seeing it was out of our drive she came several hours later, I'm sure she had been with Adam all that time."

"She's married, you say, how do you do that? And who to?"

"Last year there was one of those corporate does at the club. You know, the deal sponsorship and all that, and some of us were asked or told to attend. Well, there we are at the bar and then get introduced to some fat old dude in a very sharp suit that looked like a lawyer, but turns out worked for the International Group, one of the club's sponsors. The guy really had his head up his own ass, that was for sure, telling us how he used to play rugby. Then a few minutes later, this girl comes up to him, gives him and peck on the cheek and takes his arm."

"If you'd seen this girl you would never forget her, not

ever. The dress she was wearing to start with, completely backless, revealing the top of her ass the like you have never seen before and the rest of her, well, that dress didn't cover much."

"How do you know she was married?"

"Ah well, as they walked off, Rob turned to me and he'd had a few, and said 'I wonder how much she costs a night?' Which the bloke heard, you could see him straighten a bit, he definitely heard. But then Nigel puts in that they are married and have a house up at Newton Ferrer's, he's a local or used to be, that's why they sponsor the club."

Dan finished with "If I were this guy I wouldn't let my wife anywhere near Adam, that's for sure, and if anyone were out to fuck with Adam he would be my first and probably only candidate."

He then added, "The way Adam has been behaving for the last few weeks, I know he's in love with her. I suppose she could have told her husband that she was leaving him for Adam, which would be more than enough for many guys to seek revenge."

With a little laugh, Clive replied "Strange, it's you who has the reputation, you know. Adam always comes across as lily white."

"If you even knew", said Dan, "When we were kids, he used to whine to Dad all the time about how, as the elder brother, he was the one that got all the blame, but in reality he caused most of the bloody trouble."

"I knew your dad. You know, I arrested him one time and got to know him quite well after that, bloody shame what happened to him and your mum."

"Yes, it was. What did he do?"

"It's a story for another day. It's quite funny, actually."

By now they had reached the interview room door. As they stopped, Clive said:

"You've got 5 minutes, and please, would you cooperate when told your time is up? There isn't a copper in the station that isn't terrified of you."

For the first time since he had been in the station, Dan laughed.

"You don't have to worry about me. I wouldn't hurt a fly, well that is unless he wants my rugby ball. Adam is the one with the temper. If he believes he is being set up, it'll be him you need to worry about."

As Dan was shown into the room, Adam jumped to his feet, coming over to wrap his arms around his brother. Dan looked at his brother and asked "What have you done this time?"

After a pause, and witnessing the red mist appear in his brother's eyes, he said:

"OK, OK. I was only trying to lighten the situation. Your copper friend Clive gave me the story; he also says that when they don't find any evidence, they will let you go tomorrow."

Adam immediately said, "No, I have to get out tonight; there is something I have to do." Dan held his gaze for a while and then continued.

"You mean you want to see that girl you have been fucking, and you're horny as hell; you haven't seen her for over a week."

After a short pause, Adam replied "Well, yes, and it's been over two weeks, and how the hell do you know about her?"

"I know far more than you think. Firstly, she's married, then she is the best looking girl I've ever seen, so I can't blame you for that, and you've also been acting like a love sick twat."

Momentarily silenced, Adam then carried on. "Her name is Isobel and yes, it's been going on for a while. You are also right, she is married to a right pig of a man."

"That's not really an excuse, you know. Pig or not, she's still married, but I wouldn't have said no either."

Adam then sat down, with his brother taking the chair across the table.

"Still, that has nothing to do with this. I can't believe what is going on, who would tell the police that I am into kid porn? It's fucking unreal!"

"Have you stopped to think about this for a minute? Of course, her husband could be involved. You, by the sound of things, have taken his trophy wife away from him. A woman some men might kill for. Don't you think that he might do something? If it were me, I'd rip your balls off, brother or not."

Adam, who obviously hadn't thought about this eventuality, thought about it for a while before replying. "Yeah, good point, but what now?"

"Where's your mobile?" Dan asked.

"Home, I left it when they arrested me."

"I presume her phone number is in it, yes?"

"It is, she was going to text when on the way over this evening about nine, but don't know if she did or not, she may have seen something on the TV. Did you?"

"No, I haven't seen the TV, but I've seen them, hordes of them around our house. How does it work with you two? What? Texts only? There must be some sort of system?"

"Not really, her husband is away for weeks at a time. In London mostly, I think."

Dan knew he had been in there a lot longer than five minutes, so he was aware he needed to hurry this up.

"When I get home, I could send her a text asking her to ring back urgently. Would Isobel know whom I am?"

Adam was sure she would, and that she would ring back if asked. They decided that for now this was their best option, or more to the point, their only option.

Dan quickly added "She does know your surname, doesn't she?" to which Adam looked down before replying. "No, I'm not sure she does."

"Ok, I will think of something, do you know hers?" Dan asked as the door opened. Clive appeared in the doorway.

"OK guys, the time's up."

Dan turned to his brother; Adam shook his head in answer to Dan's last question. As they both rose to their feet, he gave him a hug, turned and walked to the door, where he stopped.

"You need to tell Clive about her. I'll see you tomorrow when I pick you up." He followed Clive through the door, leaving Adam alone.

Clive escorted Dan out of the station, walking in silence and aware that Dan was deep in thought. As they went through the main doors, Clive extended his hand again to Dan.

"I will see you tomorrow then, but don't come before late afternoon. I will take care of Adam, but don't you do anything stupid. I don't want both of you in here" Dan shook his hand, nodding at the last comment and walked off to find his car.

It was only a 20 minute drive back to Wembury at that time of the night, all of which Dan was deep in thought. So far they only had the Isobel idea to work on, but in his opinion, it felt right. If this man is some sort of big shot in the press, he could easily pull this off and certainly had reason to do so. Losing your wife was a big motivation to seek revenge and she certainly was a stunner and probably trouble, as all the guys at the event a while back agreed to.

Arriving back at their house and navigating the media vehicles still camped outside, he went in search of Adam's mobile and looked at the incoming texts. There was nothing from Isobel. He grabbed his own and sent a text:

Isobel could you please ring me on a matter of urgency, Dan the Bear Young.

If Adam had talked to Isobel about me, he was sure to have mentioned my nickname, he always does that. He was very proud and protective of his little brother, but now it was Dan's turn to look after him. He would wait until the morning; see if there was a reply before working out the next best move.

Chapter 13

Dan had always been big, and had always acted the fool from a little boy. Always wanting to make people laugh so everyone thought, not that he was stupid, but that he wasn't particularly smart. They were dead wrong. He had a very sharp mind, just as sharp as his brother's and maybe more so. He had caused his father years of worry as a teenager; all one needed to do was suggest something silly to Dan and he would do it, purely for the amusement value.

He had always underestimated him in that regard, which was fine by him. He preferred to keep his talents hidden, surprising them when he let them glimpse his true potential.

There was no reply to his text to Isobel the next morning, so deciding to give her a few hours, he got his gear on and set out for his morning training run. The house was located on the edge of the rocky outcrop between Wembury and Heybrook Bays; it was perfect for his morning run. He started along the footpath beside the rocky outcrop in front of the house, and then dropped down to sprint along the sandy stretch of beach. Next, a long climb up the hill past the Langdon Court Hotel, through Heybrook Bay and back home. It was almost four miles. Dan did this run every morning, rain or shine, hangovers notwithstanding.

On hot summer mornings, he would often continue past the house and back along the beach, stopping at the café and sitting outside for his breakfast, followed by a little sunbathing and a swim.

That wasn't going to be the case today. It was a wet morning with low grey clouds hanging over the bay, obscuring the headlands either side. He was also in a hurry to get back, have a little breakfast before he rang Isobel, hoping that she would be able and willing to answer, particularly to a number she wouldn't recognise.

Unfortunately, Isobel didn't answer the phone. It went straight to her answering machine without a ring, indicating that it was switched off. Dan wouldn't be going to the club today to train. Firstly, he wanted to be able to pick up Adam as soon as he was released, and secondly, he really didn't want to have to explain what had happened to his teammates and coaches, not until Adam was released with no charges. To save any discussion at all, he texted the head coach, saying simply he wouldn't be there.

With that done, his thoughts turned to the problem in hand. It would be useful indeed to get some information on Isobel's husband. He decided to spend the rest of the morning doing a little research. He made a cup of coffee, grabbed his laptop, his mobile, and began.

All he had to go on was what they both looked like, that they were at the event several months ago at the Albion ground, and had a house at Newton Ferrer's. It would have been useful to have their surname; so typical of

Adam not to ask the full name of a girl he was sleeping with.

Meanwhile, officers from the police station holding Adam were at his lab at the university, armed with their search warrant. They had been shown to the area where Adam kept his computer, books and papers. This was a section of a large room adjacent to the lab, which several researchers and technicians shared. The officers removed his computer, placing it in a plastic evidence box and began going through his books and other printed material in the vicinity.

Finding nothing of interest, most of it was technical, discussing alternative energy production and its use; they were then shown to a locked cupboard to which there seemed to be no key available. Nevertheless, it took the police less than a minute to force it open discovering again, nothing of interest. Only hundreds of samples of dried seaweed ground up and stored in plastic containers, along with bits of laboratory equipment. Satisfied that there was nothing else to discover, they left saying that they would return the computer once its files had been searched.

Upon returning to the station and now armed with both Adam's work and home computers, the police technicians began to remove the hard drives. They then connected them into their own systems in preparation to search the contents of the drives. Between the three computers, there was nearly 500 gigabytes of data consisting of some 120,000 folders and nearly 500,000 files. Many of these were fairly easy to dismiss as operating system and program files.

The technicians used their proprietary software to search for any files of the many image formats. This was then narrowed down further, eliminating images that were the standard part of programs and the operating system, anything from the multitude of desktop theme images to hundreds of small gifs used by websites.

Up until this point the search was automatically conducted by their program. What was left after this initial search was approximately 100 folders containing over 5000 files. From this point forward, the search would be much slower. Each file had to be individually opened, examined and either eliminated or marked as suspicious.

For nearly four hours, the technicians pored through the remaining files until there was only one folder remaining, named Sea Lettuce. This contained only two files under their suspicious heading. And this folder, they noted, was created only two days before. The two files were jpegs, one which wouldn't open whatever they did to it, it was definitely corrupted and beyond repair, the second a high resolution pornographic image.

Adam could not have been said to be lucky in any part of this debacle, but here an element of it stayed in his favor. He actually had a traffic warden to thank for it as well, but he was never going to know whom to thank. The day before as Dave initiated the transfer, several guests at the hotel, the receptionist and the hotel's accountant put demands upon the fairly basic system, overtaxing it. It froze and then crashed the FTP transfer. In itself not too bad; Dave could have restarted the process but for the timely arrival of the traffic warden.

The technicians, having discovered as much as they were going to, phoned through to the officers investigating the case. They also called Inspector Gooding. Once the investigating officers and Gooding arrived at the technician's lab, the lead tech summarised their findings. Out of the over half a million files contained on the hard drives;

only one could be considered pornographic. This image was contained in a folder with the creation date of two days ago. This folder also contained one other image file, but it appeared to be badly corrupted and was unreadable by their systems.

He clicked on the image which opened up in Windows Photo Viewer. The image was clearly pornographic. It showed a female upon her knees performing oral sex on a male who was standing in front her. It had been shot at a three quarter angle from behind the female, so didn't show her face. She also seemed well developed. The man's face could be seen, he appeared to be in his teens or perhaps early twenties.

After studying the image the lead investigator thanked the technicians, asking them to send a copy of the image to his computer and to reassemble the confiscated computers for their return to the owners.

Back in their office, Inspector Clive Gooding began the conversation.

"From what I can see and in my opinion, that image cannot be classified as child pornography. If that is all we have, we have no choice but to let Young go with no charges against him."

At this, the lead investigator replied "I agree that neither of them look as though they are under 16, but we had a reliable tip that must be correctly followed up."

"Have you considered that the tip might not be as reliable as you think? You said the tip came from an officer of the Met, whom I've spoken to. He claims that tip came from another officer who got it from a newspaper reporter. I don't like it. Look at what is happening in London at the moment with the Robertson Enquiry; reporters are making up stories right, left and center.

"Perhaps a connection here is worth our looking into,

and I certainly don't see anything to be gained by further investigating Adam Young, not with what we have at the moment."

"OK, I can see where you are coming from, but why Adam Young? What does anyone gain from framing Young?"

"I am working on a theory and will discuss it with you later once I have talked to Young again", Clive replied.

"Fair enough, we will let him go for the time being and return the computers, but I am going to keep the investigation open until we have either further evidence to arrest Young again or evidence that false accusations have been made, which will be investigated."

Adam had been sitting alone in a cell since late last night. He had received something that represented breakfast, and later lunch, each time asking the officer delivering the food what was happening and when were they going to let him out of here. His pleas had fallen on deaf ears.

Eventually the door opened again, and he was told to get off the bed and come with one of the officers that had originally interviewed him. He was led back to the interview room and asked to sit down.

The officer began with "We have been to your work place this morning, impounding your computer, which was then searched along with the two computers we took from your home yesterday."

When Adam simply looked at him, he continued.

"So, what do you think we have discovered?"

"Sod all" he said, looking directly into the officers eyes as if daring him to tell him they had found evidence.

"Do you like pornography, Mr. Young? Most men do."

"I guess as much as the next man; if you mean do I

look at porn regularly, then no is the answer. I find that I get plenty of female company, which I find suits me far better. Maybe you are not so lucky."

"That attitude won't help you, Mr. Young. So do you deny that there are images of a pornographic nature on your computer?"

"Too bloody right I do!"

"In that case you might be surprised to find out that we did find a pornographic image in one of your files."

"Bullshit" was Adam's only reply.

"Again, that attitude is not helping, and I would ask you not to swear at me again."

"You have invaded and trashed my home, pepper sprayed me, dragged me here in the middle of the night, locked me up for hours with no information at all. How the hell do you expect me to react?"

"Fortunately for you, the image we found cannot positively be shown to be that of child porn."

"I know. There is no porn on my computer, whatever you may claim."

"You are not exactly cooperating, are you Mr. Young? Do you always have such an attitude?"

"Perhaps I have an attitude, particularly in a situation such as this, but it pales into insignificance compared to yours," replied Adam as he continued to stare at the officer.

Neither man said anything for perhaps a minute or more, their eyes firmly locked on each other in a contest to see which would be first to concede defeat. The policeman eventually did.

"For now, you are free to leave, but I believe we will be discussing this again."

He rose from his seat and left the room just as Clive entered.

Clive told him that his brother, whom he had just spoken to, was on the way and would be bringing some of Adam's clothes with him. He then sat down and asked Adam to tell him all about this present girlfriend, explaining that there may well be a connection. To this Adam agreed, he wanted to get out of there, contact Isobel and try to explain to her what had happened. Perhaps she had already replied to Dan's text.

As he told Clive all about Isobel, or at least as much as he knew, it began to dawn on him as he told the story that he actually didn't know that much about her at all.

On arrival at the Police Station, Dan found parking quite close, surprisingly enough within a two minute walk. As he rounded the corner to the front of the station, he came face to face with a TV crew waiting outside. There appeared to be only one plus a few lone individuals whom he guessed were press reporters. He made his way past them and was almost through the front doors before he was recognised, suddenly hearing from behind.

"Do you have any comments on your brother's arrest?" This he just ignored and continued through the doors without turning around.

Clive informed Adam that he was free to go, but warned him that there would be reporters outside, and his best course of action would be to ignore them. They were likely to follow them to the car and perhaps follow them home, about which he could do nothing. But, should a press presence continue at the house, then they should ring him and he would try to do something about that.

Clive doubted that the press would follow Adam for long. They had very short attention spans for stories, particularly those that seemed to be dying rapidly.

Doing exactly as instructed, the two of them walked straight out of the station and towards Dan's car, ignoring the calls from the press for comments. The night before, Adam did make the late evening news when brought into the police station, as he feared. He had also made the front page of the Herald that morning, but fortunately for him the media attention would die almost immediately.

The media were given a much larger story to get their teeth into.

He actually had the Iranians and some Somali pirates to thank for this small mercy. Within the last 24 hours, it had been revealed that two ships had been hijacked in the Indian Ocean, an oil tanker by the pirates, presumably from Somalia, and a British Naval ship, by the Iranian Navy. This was now making headlines across the world. The media were full of speculations about the ramifications of the Iranian action, relegating Adam to minor local coverage only.

It had been a long term goal of the Iranian Government to be both a nuclear power and the dominant power in the Middle East and Africa. To accomplish this goal, they had to be able to manufacture their own nuclear weapons as nobody, not even secretly, would be selling them theirs. For many years, sanctions had been in place to discourage the Iranians from continuing with their nuclear weapons programme. These included financial, import and export embargos. Nevertheless, the Iranians continued with their clandestine nuclear weapon development.

This was done under the guise of developing nuclear power stations. To achieve this they needed to be able to produce their own nuclear fission rods along with all the refinement equipment that was required to produce enriched uranium 235. In early 2010, the Iranian scientists produced their first uranium oxide rod bundles and completed construction of their first light water reactor. From there it was only a simple step to being able to produce plutonium 239, a fission product of uranium 235, and necessary for high yield nuclear weapons.

The Iranians had also recently declared that they would shut the Straits of Hormuz, should the sanctions not be lifted. As a large percentage of the world's crude oil supplies transited the Straits of Hormuz, this was becoming a major international concern.

Throughout the first decade of the 21st Century, the Iranians continued to test the resolve of the West. In 2004, eight British servicemen on a training exercise with the Iraqi navy were captured and detained. They were kept bound and blindfolded and put through a mock execution on Iranian TV, before being eventually released.

In 2007, fifteen service personnel were captured whilst searching an Iranian merchant vessel suspected of weapons smuggling to the insurgents in Iraq. Again in 2009, another vessel was detained and her crew was kidnapped. This time, whilst they were British service personnel, they were on a civilian racing yacht registered in Dubai. After each of these events, the British Government did little but make demands for their return.

Now it seemed it was time to test the new conservative government, with a much larger incident.

HMS Enterprise had been conducting a survey into climate change north of the Maldives in the Indian Ocean and was sailing toward Muscat after a brief layover in Karachi. Now close to Muscat, she was scheduled to rendezvous with HMS Ranger, who would escort her home through the Suez Canal when she received a mayday from an oil tanker. The tanker approximately 50 nautical miles to her north had been attacked and boarded by pirates.

It had become a common event over the past few years for Somali pirates to hijack ships for ransom. Although this was out of their normal operating range, several hijackings had occurred around Muscat. Therefore, it was assumed that they were the ones responsible for the hijacking.

The ships belonging to the Combined Task Force 150, based out of Bahrain, were too far away to reach the tanker in time. So despite that the Enterprise was only lightly armed with a single 20mm cannon, four general purpose machine guns and two miniguns, the captain was ordered to interdict the tanker.

With the tanker on her radar approximately twenty miles outside Iranian territorial waters and steaming west, the captain ordered a change of course to the northwest to intercept her.

As the Enterprise neared the tanker, the Captain ordered her complement of two RIBS to be launched. They quickly closed on the tanker, which now appeared to have heaved to. As the RIB's approached the tanker, five fast attack vessels darted out from the far side of the tanker to close in on the Enterprise, surrounding her within minutes. A message was broadcast to the Enterprise in that they were in Iranian territorial waters and that they must prepare to be boarded, to which the captain replied that they were responding to a mayday from the tanker and still ten nautical miles outside the Iranian territorial waters.

The only response this elicited was a repeat of the demand to be boarded, to which they added that the Enterprise was being targeted by medium range anti-ship cruise missiles based in Chabahar. The previous week, the Iranians had conducted naval exercises during which they had test fired several such missiles.

The Captain of the Enterprise was aware that this was a possibility. His reaction was to contact his superiors in the

UK with the secure communications his ship carried. He was told to comply with the demands of the Iranians. As they were boarded, the Captain was arrested and charged with spying on the Iranian naval training maneuvers.

Over the next few days, demands were made by the Iranian Government. The demands were threefold. Firstly, all sanctions against them would be lifted. Secondly, the UK Government would admit to spying on the Iranian naval maneuvers, and finally, that the West would recognise the Iranian's sovereignty over the Straits of Hormuz.

Chapter 14

The inside of the enormous warehouse looked more like a medical research lab than the storage facility it was registered to be. Part of the warehouse had been converted into an environmentally controlled unit. This contained a laboratory equipped with its own environmental controls, inside of which white suited and helmeted figures could be seen. A large air handling and sterilization unit stood to the rear. Although they had all been inoculated against the virus, they were still taking every possible precaution. The rest of the warehouse was empty, with the exception of piles of large packing crates in one corner and several vehicles. The warehouse had been fitted out just under a year ago and had been running experiments ever since.

Acquisition of the virus they were experimenting with had been relatively simple. Although the general consensus was that the virus had been eradicated worldwide, many countries still maintained stocks for experimental purposes. It had, in fact, been the first biological weapon ever used.

During the French and Indian wars in the 1754, it had been used by the British and again in the American

Revolutionary War, by infecting blankets, which were then given to the Native American Indians. During World War II, serious researches into its use began and by the early 1990's stockpiles of more than 20 tons of the weaponised Variola virus were held by the Soviet Union, with specialised refrigerated warheads to deliver it.

With the breakup of the Soviet Union and the unemployment of hundreds of weapons program's scientists, it became readily available for anyone with the funds and expertise to use it. The weaponised virus had been purchased by several Middle Eastern governments in large quantities and was one of the reasons behind the invasion of Iraq.

Those that now experimented with the virus in their secret facility had acquired a small amount of the virus. This had been sent inside diplomatic pouches to the Iranian Embassy in Austria and from there in a circuitous route to the warehouse via train, ferry and car. Once there, it had then been cultured, and several men now watched a video of an experiment that their scientists had been running.

The cultured Variola virus, which caused the Smallpox disease, had been diluted with high purity water, which was in turn placed into a sealed container and pressurised with a carbon dioxide propellant. There were many choices of propellant available; some instantly killed the virus whilst, in others, the virus had a lifespan varying from hours to days. Eventually carbon dioxide was chosen, this kept the virus alive longer than all the others but gave the worst dispersion distance, and this was considered the best trade-off. This could be easily accommodated for by increasing the amount dispersed. An additional benefit came with this propellant as it was heavier than air; the carbon dioxide would sink taking the virus with it, enabling distribution from above.

The video began by showing a room within the laboratory. It looked much like a normal hospital ward containing ten beds, each individually screened. On one of these beds, an unconscious naked man lay, connected to medical monitoring equipment. The video then cut to a white suited and helmeted figure holding a spray can, which he then sprayed for two seconds over the unconscious man.

The next scene consisted of several close-ups of the man's body, where a faint rash could be seen on his face, under his arms and over his groin. A further cut then showed the man walking around wearing a hospital type gown. Although he had obviously contracted the disease as the last shot had shown, he was still mobile, with the only outward signs the rash on his face and an unpleasant cough. The lead scientist showing the video pressed the pause button.

"This last clip was shot sixty hours after the initial exposure, at which time the second set of test subjects were exposed", he said.

The tape was restarted. This time it showed the first man back in the bed, strapped down with intravenous tubes in his arm and again connected to medical monitoring equipment. Through the double doors at the end of the unit, white suited figures began pushing nine more beds, each with a man strapped to them. Like the first, all had intravenous tubes in their arms.

Each of the beds was placed within a screened enclosure the screens were pulled back, and each was then connected to the monitoring equipment fixed to the wall.

Again the scientist stopped the video, going on to explain.

"The air circulation was turned off at this point for fifteen minutes, after which time it was turned on again, and each of the beds was then screened to prevent further cross contamination."

He asked if there were any questions at this point.

The scientist, taking the silence as an instruction to continue, pressed the play button again.

The first man was now completely covered in large, angry red lumps, each of which had a dimple in the middle.

Six of the second set of men had the rashes the first man showed in the earlier shot. Again the scientist paused the video and explained. This shot was taken five days after the initial exposure and that six of the second set of nine test subjects had been infected only by proximity to the first. The play button was pushed for the last time, and the men watched the video to its conclusion.

When it finished the scientist continued.

"At eight days after exposure the first man died, followed by the four of the second set between three and four days later. The second set took an additional day to two days to succumb to the disease, a result of the intensity of the exposure the first man received via the aerosol."

"Of the remaining five, three had contracted the disease, but started to show improvements in their condition after a few days. The other two, who were furthest away from the initial test subject at the time of exposure, showed no sign or symptoms whatsoever."

Again the scientist asked if there were questions,

"Does proximity exposure work as well as you predicted? Or are there any complications we need to be aware of?"

"Yes, the proximity exposure works as expected. The two that didn't catch the disease were each at least ten meters away from the first, outside the range we predicted for airborne cross infection. It seems that for a period of between three and six days, after initial exposure to the aerosol, the infection from the test subject became airborne, and all those within ten meters will catch the disease. It only seems to last that long, as the subject of the initial infection was so inundated by the disease that most of his bodily functions were beginning to shut down. At the three day mark the test subjects were still mobile, with minimal outward showing of the infection."

"So, we can expect an approximate 45% cross infection mortality rate from every subject that is infected from the initial exposure. Then each of these will in turn infect many more, of which half will ultimately succumb to the disease."

"Essentially our calculation is this; for every hundred exposed to the aerosol, we would expect eighty to contract it, out of which forty four should die. Should each of the infected be in close proximity with say, ten others within the airborne window stage, they will pass on the virus to eight hundred others, of which four hundred and forty should die. In other words, there is over a 500% increase in mortality rate from first infection. This is exponential, of course."

"The most crucial phase for us is immediately after the initial infection. At the three day point, the cross contamination is already underway with no way to stop it. Essentially, it's become a plague."

Chapter 15

The drive back home from the police station was done in silence, Adam deep in thought about the events of the last few hours, his brow furrowed; he stared straight ahead through the windscreen at the road. Dan couldn't help but notice his brother's countenance and respected his brother's silence. The only sound in the car was a rumbling of the tires on the rough tarmac, left scarred and potholed from neglect.

Once at the house, which seemed to have lost its complement of press vehicles, Dan turned to his brother and suggested that they go into the kitchen, make something to eat and discuss what had occurred. Then, perhaps, they could decide what course of action they should take.

As with many homes the kitchen had become the focal point of the house. Again, it was a large room like every other in this house. As high tech as the building's facade; the polished black lacquer doors of the kitchen units were set off with large stainless steel hardware. The worktop, a black slab of granite, extended around and over the units. An island section near the center of the room, its worktop also black granite, housed the cooker hob with a stainless steel cowling above. The far side of the island unit formed a breakfast bar and beyond that sat a huge dark oak table, surrounded by chairs.

The kitchen was separated from a more formal dining room by a closed set of dark oak doors; that room rarely used as it was their preference to cook, eat and partially live in this very comfortable and well-appointed kitchen.

The only compromise in the high tech look was an oil-fired Rayburn, its hinged and domed lids covering the hotplates stood open, at which Dan stood preparing some food. The Rayburn served as their main cooking appliance during the winter months, as well as heating the house and providing all their hot water. The solid black of the kitchen units was set off by a pale limed light oak wooden floor and a huge window facing east flooded the room with light during daylight hours. Dark now, the light from a dozen or more down lighters illuminated the area.

Adam went to the fridge, pulled out two beers, popped the tops and handed one to his brother. He then sat at the breakfast bar, sipping his own while he checked his mobile for calls or texts from Isobel. There were plenty of missed calls and many texts, some of which pertained to the arrest, but nothing from Isobel.

"Did you get a reply from your text to Isobel?" Adam asked.

"No," said Dan with a shake of his head "I texted and called her twice, neither of the texts was answered and the calls went directly to the machine". I do have some information, though."

Adam looked up from his mobile enquiringly.

After his morning run, Dan had spent the rest of the day before going to the police station to collect Adam, trying to discover as much about Isobel and her husband as possible. Firstly, he had been able to find out their surname by back tracking records of functions at the Albion ground. The name was Mason. Armed with a surname, he discovered where their house was located in Newton Ferrer's and that her husband, Jonathan, had two daughters from a previous marriage.

Both were now married; one living in Plympton and the other in Brixham. For both, he had full names and addresses. There were also several records of properties in London belonging to Jonathan Mason. Searches on Mason had confirmed that until two or three years ago he worked for the International Media Group. Although they didn't explain what he did there, he seemed to have been highly placed within the organisation; unfortunately there was no information on what he had been doing since.

Dan recounted what he had been able to find out as he finished plating up the scrambled eggs and salmon he'd just finished cooking, which they both ate as they digested that information.

"The last time I spoke to Isobel she was about to board the plane in Cuba, and she promised to ring as soon as she landed at Heathrow, she couldn't possibly of heard that I had been arrested, so why didn't she call?"

"Perhaps she couldn't, maybe her husband picked her up at the airport?", Dan replied around mouthfuls of food.

Adam agreed that this was a possibility with a nod of his head

He still couldn't understand why she hadn't contacted him? She may have seen something on the news but still he thought, that if she were able to text him she would have, so why isn't she able to?

The tentative link between the accusations, his arrest and Isobel's nonappearance was all he had to go on. Adam decided that he should begin by eliminating the unknowns.

The first of which was whether or not Isobel had come back to her house. Newton Ferrer's was no more than a twenty minute drive, so a visit there might tell him something.

"I'm going to take a drive over to their house, just to see if she ever arrived back, you coming?"

There was no way he was letting Adam out on his own, so he agreed to the plan saying,

"Let's get some suitable clothes on and have a look"

It was yet another wet and stormy night as they drove toward Newton Ferrer's. The trees along the lanes were beating each other to death as the wind tore at them, not a pleasant evening to be out. But that would also go for anyone else; they should be able to snoop around without being seen.

The address that Dan had uncovered was, The Foundry, Court Wood Road. Googling the address before they left, they discovered that the house was located at the far end of the village. It appeared to be a large property, surrounded by trees with a garden leading down to the estuary. There also appeared to be a car park beside the estuary, about three hundred meters before the house they decided that this would be the best place to park unnoticed.

Newton Ferrer's a smallish and exceedingly picturesque village that sits beside the Yealm Estuary, it is immensely popular in summer with holiday makers, but in winter, it's quiet. They parked at the car park they noted earlier, which contained only one other car, nobody seemed to be about. Hardly surprising, as it was now pouring with rain and the wind was hammering up the estuary from the sea.

Dressed in dark waterproof tracks and jackets, they left the car and walked the three hundred meters or so towards the house. The road finished at the front gates.

The house was set back approximately a hundred meters; it was a large property, perhaps four, or maybe five bedrooms. Some of it was a single story, the other comprised of two, with what appeared to be a garage to the right hand side. There was not a light showing anywhere.

The gate stood open swaying to and fro in the wind. They took a good look around, and no one was in sight. They hadn't seen a soul during the walk from the car park.

They cautiously walked through the gateway towards the house, keeping off the drive, under cover of the trees growing along it. The wind whipped the branches back and forth, and the noise it created would cover the advance of an army, never mind two lone men. The gate too swung in the wind, and looked as though it would be ripped off its hinges very soon if not secured properly.

Approaching the house, they skirted to the right and under the trees keeping away from the garden leading to the estuary, which was in clear view from the house. They could hear the sounds of metal striking upon metal, coming from the bottom of the garden. Keeping to the cover of the trees, they made their way around to the back of the house looking for any lights seeing nothing.

With the driving rain, it was almost impossible to see each other, even only a few meters apart. They decided to have a look around the garden and at what was making all the noise down there, before venturing closer to the house. They made their way down the garden, still keeping to the cover of the trees, toward the estuary.

The noise got louder with every step; they were no more than five meters away when they saw a wooden jetty, to which was moored a small sailing yacht. It was from the boat that the noise was coming. The halyards were beating against the side of the mast, and the boat itself was grinding back and forth along the jetty. Whoever had tied her up had made a bad job of it.

Very soon she would either break free or smash herself to pieces against the jetty.

They huddled close together, squatting on the edge of the jetty and looked back at the darkened house, just visible through the driving rain.

"Deserted. I don't think anyone is home, they would have to hear this." Dan gestured over his shoulder at the yacht behind them.

"Yeah I agree. Did you see the door leading into the garage?"

"Yes, let's have a look"

Surprising both of them, they found the door unlocked. Cautiously they opened it and made their way inside. It contained only a single car, although there seemed to be room for at least two more. The car looked like Isobel's, but Adam couldn't be absolutely certain. There was also another door, apart from the several double doors at the front; this was glazed, and should lead into the house. Adam looked at this and then his brother, who shook his head.

"Not yet, let's go around to the front door, ring the bell, we still don't know that this is definitely their house. If anyone answers, we could say that we had heard all the noise coming from the dock and ask if they need a hand in securing the yacht."

Agreeing this was the best course of action; they made their way to the front door and rang the doorbell, waiting for an answer. After a few minutes, they rang the bell again, no reply. Putting their heads close together to talk as it is by now almost impossible to hear each other talk more than a meter apart without shouting,

"You go around that way I will go in this, look out for alarm boxes"

They met back at the back door to the garage. Neither of them had seen anything indicating an alarm, but with this weather they could have easily missed it.

Having already been arrested within the last 24 hours or so, Adam was definitely not keen to repeat the performance.

"I'm going to break the glass, hand me that rag."

Dan picked up the rag from the floor and handed it to his brother.

Adam wrapped the rag around his hand and smashed the glass the sound of it hitting the floor momentarily startling the two of them.

Taking the small torch from his pocket and directing it through the broken glass he could see the door led into a kitchen.

"Okay, let's back off into the trees for a while and see if anybody comes."

Nodding to his brother, they made their way back into the trees, to begin their vigil.

They waited for half an hour, and no one appeared. They decided to give it a while longer and waited for another thirty minutes, and still there was no response. Deciding they had waited long enough, they made their way back to the garage and into the kitchen, where they waited in silence for another ten minutes. As they still heard nothing, they began searching the ground floor.

A hallway led off the kitchen toward the front door with several doors on either side. Making their way toward the front door Dan immediately spotted a security alarm box, but all the lights on it were green. It seemed as though whoever was last in the house, had forgotten to set it.

The doors off the hall revealed, first a dining room and

the second a large lounge with French doors leading to the garden, through which they could still hear the sounds of the yacht striking the jetty and halyards against the mast. Shining his torch around the lounge, Adam spied a large fireplace with several photos on the mantel piece.

Taking a closer look he saw one depicting Isobel, her husband and two other women. Beckoning Dan over, he showed him the photo, pointing out Isobel. At least now they knew they were in the right place. On a whim, Adam pulled out his mobile taking a picture of the photo.

I miss you so much, where the hell are you?

A quick search through the rest of the house revealed nothing much of interest. They made their way back into the kitchen. Just as Adam was about to enter the kitchen, he noticed a door at the end of the hallway, which as yet they hadn't looked in.

Opening the door revealed a small office. There was a desk with a computer on it and several opened and unopened letters. Picking up the letters, he looked at the address of each in turn. They were all to this address mostly to Jonathan, Isobel's husband. As he shuffled through them one caught his attention.

An electricity bill made out to Jonathan Mason for an address in London. Quickly making a note of this address, he put down the letters and joined his brother in the kitchen. They had been there long enough and had never meant to break into the place. It was time to leave before they were discovered.

By the time they were back at the car, the brothers were completely soaked and freezing cold, neither had realised this, both being energised by the adrenalin flowing through their bodies.

The drive back home was uneventful arriving a little after 1 AM, although both constantly looked over the shoulders until they were clear of the village. They both went up to their respective bedrooms to shower and change, before meeting back down stairs to consider their night's foray. Showered and clean, dressed in bath robes, they sat in front of the dying embers of the fire Dan had lit earlier in the day.

Neither had said much during the drive but were now somewhat shocked by what they'd done, not being the type for, or well versed at, breaking and entering. Nevertheless, and despite the considerable risks, they had made useful discoveries. One, the house was definitely the Mason's place, and two, that nobody had been there for at least two weeks. A check on the fridge contents revealed milk which had passed its use by date, two weeks ago. Three, that the Masons seemed to be well off, and four, they now had another address in London.

The address on the electricity bill was for a property on Clerkenwell Road. Adam asked Dan for a list of the properties that he had found for Mason in London. None of them matched all of them in West London, one in Kensington; yes, Mason did seem to have money. Of the others, two were in Notting Hill and one in Hammersmith.

"Can you get your laptop mate?"

Booting Dan's laptop and launching Google Maps, he looked at each address in turn.

"Look, all these seem to be in residential areas but not the one in Clerkenwell, that's all commercial. A new office perhaps? The bill is recent, only £56 and for a recent installation by the looks of it"

Dan agreed that this was possible and asked what Adam was thinking, knowing full well he was thinking of going to London to find Isobel.

"I have to know what happened. She isn't in Plymouth so I'll have to go to London."

"Yeah, and how do you think you're going to do that? There are five places to check, you could be checking one as she walks into another, if I come with you the chances get better but still it's such a long shot mate!"

Adam thought about it for a while. Dan was correct, but there was the bill at the house in Newton Ferrer's, which would seem to indicate that Mason had been there recently. That would be the best place to start. Also, he really didn't want to go into work at the moment, not with all this hanging over his head.

He would ring them in the morning; try to explain that the arrest was a mistake and that he needed a few days off. If they didn't like it, then screw them. He hadn't been told by the police not to leave town, and sitting around doing nothing would just drive him mad, but more than anything else, he wanted to see Isobel.

Even should they be wrong about Mason; he needed to know she was safe even if she didn't want to see him anymore. He told Dan what he had decided and that Dan couldn't go with him as he had a match on Saturday. He promised not to do anything stupid, and would be back in a few days. He would ring him regularly.

It was getting late nearly 3 AM so they decided to go to bed. Adam knew that sleep was unlikely, but although he loved his brother dearly, he needed to be on his own. He felt very guilty about dragging Dan into this. If they had been caught earlier it would have been the end of Dan's career, and he couldn't let that happen. Surprisingly enough, he did sleep. Within a few minutes of his head touching the pillow he was out. By now the stress was outweighed by the exhaustion and several painkillers.

Waking the next morning at 8.00 and feeling a little better, after a few hours' sleep in his own bed his mind was clearer than it had been for several days. Adam, now with renewed purpose, his mind set on what he had to do packed some clothes put them into his 4x4, along with a sleeping bag and some bottles of water.

That complete he had a huge breakfast of bacon and eggs, making the same for his brother whom he could hear moving about upstairs. He delivered Dan's breakfast to his bedroom, something he realised he very rarely did. Adam's view on food was that it was purely a necessity as fuel for his body, whereas Dan loved his food and did most of the cooking in the house.

He told Dan he would be away for a few days, and that he would ring every day, leaving a message should Dan answer. Adam thanked him for the night before and told him he loved him and not to worry about him, he would be fine. Before Dan could argue he left, jumping into his car and beginning to make his way through the back lanes to the A38 and off toward London.

Chapter 16

As Adam was beginning his drive to London, Jonathan was walking back into his apartment holding a copy of the Herald, the local Plymouth newspaper, published the day before. Several times during the previous day he had checked the news channels for any coverage of Young's arrest. He hadn't seen anything; the media's attention was firmly focused on events in the Persian Gulf. There seemed to be hundreds of experts giving their opinion on the events there, on which surprisingly enough as yet there had been no official statement from No 10.

His intention had been to drag Isobel out of her room, thrust her in front of the TV, showing her the arrest of her lover. That plan hadn't worked, so he arranged to get a copy of the Herald delivered that morning and now carried it purposefully, towards Isobel's bedroom.

Opening the bedroom door and finding Isobel still sleeping, he crossed to the bed as quietly as possible. Depositing the paper on the vacant pillow, to greet her as she woke up and then slammed the door to make sure she did, straight away. The slamming door had the desired effect. Isobel awoke to find the paper next to her and instantly saw Adam's picture under the headline. 'Local Man Arrested in Pedophile Ring Round Up'. The photo showed Adam being led into the police station wearing nothing but a bathrobe and a towel, partially covering his head but revealing his face clearly to the camera.

Upon seeing this, Isobel screamed, flinging the offending thing across the room. Hearing Isobel's screams Jonathan smiled with satisfaction, clearly not expecting what was about to happen next.

Isobel flew out of her bedroom, screaming at him.

"These filthy lies are all your doing; I know you've done this, you bastard!"

She knew he was capable of it; she had learned more about him in the last two days than she had in the previous two years. Before he had time to deny his involvement; she was on him like a tigress defending her cubs. Digging her nails into his face and teeth into his shoulder, the severity of her attack knocked him over the coffee table, whilst she hit, bit and kicked every part of him she could reach.

Eventually, Jonathan recovered from the initial shock of the attack. And, with his much greater size, managed to push her off him, but not before blood was running freely down his face. Pushing Isobel away he punched her hard in the face, sending her reeling back over the couch, to crash onto the floor.

Before Isobel could get to her feet, he kicked her hard in the stomach twice, knocking the fight out of her. As Isobel crawled back into her room, she shouted abuse at him before wedging the door shut with a chair under the handle to prevent him from opening it as he beat on the other side.

Jonathan had not expected the attack. He hadn't really known what to expect at all. He just wanted revenge and the satisfaction that would give him, but that had certainly backfired. He had some nasty gouges on his face; his left eye was swelling and the bitch had kicked him in the balls, which hurt like hell. He knew he would need to get his face seen to.

Not being a NHS man, Jonathan had a private doctor whose practice was based in Mayfair. He rang and was told that he could come straight over; grabbing his coat and umbrella, he left the apartment as quickly as his aching balls would let him.

Having not read the paper, being far too keen on Isobel reading it, Jonathan hadn't noticed that his plan was not as successful as he had hoped. The story went on to say that although Young had been arrested, he hadn't been charged, and that the police statement said that they had found no evidence to charge him with. His plan had really backfired. Adam would certainly feel ramifications of the arrest in later weeks, but not the life ruining outcome Jonathan had intended.

The net effect of the setup was to unleash the tigress in Isobel and to have an extremely pissed off young man driving to London to find both Isobel, and him. If he had known this or had the benefit of hindsight, rather than going to see his doctor he would have been packing his bags and getting the hell out of Dodge. He didn't know he was blindly walking into events that would soon spiral out of all control.

As Jonathan was locking the door, Isobel was reading the Herald, no longer crying but as angry as she had ever been in her life. She read how Adam had been arrested and released without charges and although she hadn't known him that long, she knew he loved her and that he would march into the gates of hell to find her. Knowing this, she too began to make plans.

. . .

The weather for Adam's drive had improved slightly although it was still lightly raining, but the wind had died down somewhat. Still it was slow going on the M5 and then the M4 into London. He reached the outskirts of London just after 2 PM, deciding to take the M25 to the south rather than forcing his way through the inner London traffic. It was nearly 4.00 by the time he found the Clerkenwell address, which as he had predicted turned out to be a commercial building.

It looked as though it had been recently been refurbished, and Adam noted two white transit vans parked in the street. They had the look of contractor's vehicles neither was sign written, but as he parked in a small car park thirty perhaps forty meters up the road, he could see workmen loading their tools into one of them and driving away.

The car park he was sitting in appeared to belong to an office building adjoining to the left as he waited several people had got into their cars and had driven away, shortly after five. One had given Adam's 4x4 a curious look, but he had still got into their car and driven off. He had a good view from where he was, back down the street, and could easily see the front door of the building he was interested in. A couple of people had come out within the last half an hour, but no one had gone in.

Inside the first floor of the building, Jonathan sat in his new office nursing a headache. It still stank of paint, which was not helping his head. He had thought the contractors would have been finished days ago, but no, they were still there. Dave had managed to finish the installation of the computers and all the electronics equipment and was busily deflecting the contractors' interest in what they did here. It was now at little after five in the afternoon and the contractors were packing up for the day, after promising to have all the work finished in the morning.

Jonathan had arrived at the office mid-morning, after being tended to by his doctor; he had taken a taxi there not wanting to go back to the apartment for his car keys. When he arrived he went straight to his office, avoiding any contact with the contractors for fear that they might think his injuries suspicious. He had called his team in for a meeting a few minutes later.

As Carl, Fred, Dave and Nigel sat around the large conference table with him they brought him up to speed upon the completion of the work to the office and on several pieces of ongoing work they had on.

None had mentioned the state of his face, and he wasn't volunteering information. Despite this, they had all guessed correctly his beauty queen of a wife had finally snapped, but all assumed that this was due to the various mistresses Jonathan had had during his short marriage to her.

They had all joked amongst themselves shortly after he got married that he had better watch out. That Latin temperament all the South American girls were supposed to have was going to bite him one day. In that they were correct, but the circumstances were wide of the mark. After the rest left, Carl remained behind. Jonathan knew of their gossip and used it to his advantage, covering the real situation. He told Carl that yes, his wife had found out about the girlfriend he had staying in his Notting Hill flat.

For the rest of the day Jonathan stayed in his office, catching up with various pieces of work, and wondering what series of events he had set in motion. Isobel was not reacting as he had expected. He was also waiting for the contractors to leave, and as soon they did he took a look around the suite of offices, and was relatively satisfied with them. He then checked with Dave to make sure they had everything up and running and told him he would see him in the morning.

During the drive, Adam had stopped once at the motorway services along the M4 to fill up his car, grab some coffee, a sandwich and take a leak, but he was now bursting for a piss again. He'd packed several bottles of water upon leaving his house, figuring he might be sitting in his car for a long time, and thinking it smarter to have some water for his wait. He took one of the bottles, drank most of it before emptying the rest out of the window, so he could relieve himself into it.

Just as he finished, a man exited the doors of the building across the road. He waited there for several minutes as if looking for something, then began walking in Adam's direction.

As the man closed the gap, Adam could see it was Jonathan Mason, and did not believe his luck. Perhaps it was changing for the better. Mason was still looking around, perhaps in search of a taxi. He obviously didn't spot whatever he was looking for, and carried on walking. Not about to let this bit of fresh fortune get away from him, Adam got out his car, locked it and followed him.

Mason turned right into Farringdon St, and after a few minutes it looked as though he was going toward the underground. Adam could see a sign for the underground in the distance. He turned out to be correct. Mason approached the entrance, turned to go down the steps into the station. It appeared that Mason was not a regular user, he had no season ticket or whatever it is they use these days. He stopped at the queue for a ticket machine, rumbling through his pockets looking for change.

Adam did likewise, picking a queue a few of meters up, looking away from Mason in case he recognised him. He purchased the most expensive ticket he could find, just to be on the safe side and headed through the barriers just in front of Mason.

Adam stopped to look at the underground map briefly, letting Mason pass him and then followed. If he'd read the map correctly there are only two platforms here, Mason took the stairs to the west bound platform, with Adam twenty meters behind him. Several trains were due through within the next ten minutes, when the first arrived; Mason boarded it. Adam followed him.

Now with a closer view of Mason, he noticed the marks on Mason's face. He couldn't tell if they were fresh or not as Mason stood at an oblique angle to him. But he was sure where not there when he first saw him in Plymouth, on the Hoe the first day of the Americas Cup, and they certainly weren't there in the photo he saw at the house.

Wondering how they got there, he tried not to let his imagination run wild, but already felt his anger rapidly rising. He needed to keep a clear head to follow Mason without being seen.

If you have hurt Isobel, those marks will pale in comparison to what I will do to you.

Mason didn't look for a seat as the train pulled into the next station, King's Cross, and he got off. Walking along the platform, he seemed to be following signs pointing to the Piccadilly line. Adam followed in his wake, trying to stay far enough back not be noticed but close enough, not wanting to lose Mason now, after such a lucky first strike.

Mason made for the Piccadilly Line and was soon waiting on the platform for his train. Within five minutes, a train arrived it was already bursting with people in the rush hour traffic. Adam got on at the next set of doors to the ones that Mason had used.

There was standing room only, but he could easily see Mason. His only problem would be guessing the right side of the train to be on as it reached whatever station Mason was headed for.

The train passed through Russell Square, then Holborn, then Covent Garden, Leicester Square, Piccadilly, and then Green Park. As the train neared the next stop, which according to the map was Hyde Park Corner, Mason eased toward the left hand side door. The train slid into Hyde Park Corner, and the doors hissed open; Mason got off. More people seemed to be getting on than getting off, which Adam wasn't sure how they managed to accomplish, full as it was when he was on there, but it made it easy to follow Mason.

There were no interconnecting lines here, so this has to be his destination.

Adam felt his pulse quicken in anticipation.

He followed Mason up the escalator. Keeping his distance now, once at street level Mason walked off down Park Lane. Stopping, he entered what appeared to be a large apartment building. He approached the building No 55 Park Lane; it was named Hype Park Residence, and was overlooking the park.

I bet that doesn't come cheap.

As Adam walked past, he caught a glimpse of the entrance, it looked more like a five star hotel than a block of flats. He could see Mason as he walked up to the manned reception, the uniformed receptionist or perhaps concierge was his title seemed to saying something to Mason, and then handed what looked like some letters.

Perhaps he does live here. Adam's pulse quickened further.

Taking stock of his surroundings, Adam could see Hype Park across the road and thought that it would be a far better place to keep watch, than in the street. He made his way over to the park and settled against a tree directly opposite the entrance to the apartment building.

The building was six stories tall and must have had upwards of twenty or maybe thirty apartments. Mason did seem to be known, perhaps he lived here, but this wasn't on the list Dan gave him the night before.

On entering the apartment, Mason couldn't help but remember how Isobel caught him unawares earlier that day. Isobel was not the demure little thing he thought she was. He didn't think she would be standing behind the door waiting to smash him over the head with something solid, but was taking no chances.

Latin girls always had a reputation for fiery behavior, though not as nefarious as Thai girls, who were rumored to have cut their husbands' balls off, whilst they slept in a drugged stupor.

He opened the door as quietly as he could before pushing it open forcibly; the door hit the wall hard and bounced back. It would have caught him in the face had he stepped forward. Hearing nothing but the slam of the door, he pushed it open again and walked into the apartment.

It was all quiet; Isobel must still be in her bedroom, and he knew she had no key, so couldn't get out. He didn't want to see her, so quickly went to his bedroom.

He wasn't planning to stay there tonight, just in case

she had heard what some Thai girls did and got ideas. So, after packing a bag with enough to last for a couple of days, he left again, this time remembering to take his car keys. He wasn't planning to take his car; he intended to go to the Notting Hill flat, but that had no secure parking and he didn't want to leave his new DB9 on the street close to Portobello Road. Taxis should be easy to find by now, the concierge would go out and get him one anyway while he waited in the lobby.

Adam had been standing beside the tree, opposite the entrance to the apartment building for about forty minutes. It was still raining and he was cold and very wet, not dressed for an all-night surveillance of the building. Not that he thought he could get away with it; sooner or later a policeman would come along. That could only lead to more trouble. The longer he stood there, the angrier and more worried he became. The marks on Mason's face looked as though they might have been caused by nails.

What if he had hurt Isobel?

He didn't have to wait much longer, as within a few minutes the concierge came out, walked to the pavement edge and stood there with a hand on each hip, looking in the direction of the oncoming traffic.

The guy looked so camp it almost gave Adam cause to laugh, which he would have done if in a laughing mood. Finally, the concierge saw what he was looking for and hastily stuck out his arm, flagging down a passing cab. Mason appeared a minute or so later with a bag over his shoulder, jumped into the back of the cab and was gone down Park Lane.

Adam briefly thought about hailing a cab himself and doing the movie trick of 'follow that cab and I will give you a hundred'. Not that he thought that would ever work, and even if he did get a cab he was on the wrong side of Park Lane, which had two lanes in each direction. Basically, there was no chance.

The bag worried him; it looked like a reasonable size which might mean he was going away for a few days. When Mason had gone in to the building, he looked for any lights being turned on, but hadn't seen anything.

Does he live there, and is Isobel in there?

He had to find out, but not tonight. He could hardly enter the place looking like he did, and would have to come up with some sort of plan before attempting it.

The question was what to do now, standing here was pointless. He'd lost Mason, but maybe, just maybe, he'd found where he lived. He was tired and hungry, having had only a sandwich since his monster breakfast this morning. He would also need to check his car at some point. Not having noticed whether or not there was a lockable gate on the car park where he had left it was definitely a mistake.

Still, he had been far luckier than he imagined he would be during the drive up, he had found what he thought was Mason's apartment and that the electricity bill seemed to be for his office. There also appeared to be contractors there.

That might present an avenue.

What he needed now was some food and some rest, and then he could plan his next move.

Now he hailed a cab, giving the driver the Clerkenwell address. When he got back to the car park, he was relieved to discover, it hadn't been locked up for the night. Climbing into the back seats of the car, he stripped off his wet clothes, throwing them into the back, and pulled on some dry ones from his bag.

Now it was time to find something to eat. A few

minutes before in the cab, he had seen a kebab place a couple of minutes' walk up the road. That would do nicely. He enjoyed a decent kebab, as long as they weren't the after pub variety, which inevitably led to a bad gut in the morning.

Now with food in his stomach and dry clothes on his back, he thought about what to do next. It was only 9.30 and although he was tired he was far too wound-up to sleep. He still had Dan's list, so he might as well check those addresses.

Before driving out of the car park, he first checked for a sign indicating if it belonged to a specific building or several. He thought if it were for several then parking here again and grabbing a few hours' sleep later, would be an option. Sure enough attached to the wire of the fence was a notice saying Private Parking and had a list of building numbers either side of the car park, for whose use it was.

The first address he checked was the Kensington one. As he arrived outside the terraced house, he noticed a man letting himself in. The man looked of Mediterranean origin or perhaps Middle Eastern, and carried an overnight bag over his shoulder.

He found a parking space a little way down the road, and then walked back to check if it was a single house or several flats. As he neared the place, he saw another man draw the curtains, who looked curiously at Adam as he inspected the front door, much as one would expect. The door had a single letter box and a lone door bell, for now he would cross that one of his list.

That left three more, one in Hammersmith and two in Notting Hill. Putting the Hammersmith address into his iPhone and following its directions, he soon found the place but nowhere to park. Eventually, he did find something, walking back a mile or so before standing in front of the door. The door had four bells to the side of it and the whole building looked shabby, to say the least. He couldn't see Mason living there and crossed another from his list.

By the time he had got back to his car, it was nearly 1 AM. Still too wired for sleep, Adam thought he might as well check the remaining two addresses. Using his iPhone again, he tapped in one of the Notting Hill addresses and then the next, noticing that they were only half a mile apart and both close to Portobello Road. He had been to Portobello a few times, on each occasion for the carnival, and he soon found a suitable spot to park, within a short walking distance of each address.

As he approached the first he could hear some seriously loud reggae emanating from the building. Another one down, he thought.

Mason doesn't live there.

One to go. Within a few minutes he was standing outside the last address.

Again, the door had several bells, but the building was far smarter than the last two and there were lights on, on the first floor. As he stood there, a silhouette appeared at the window, looked out for a second or two, and then pulled the half opened curtains fully closed. The lights went out seconds later.

It was definitely a man's silhouette, a man with Mason's build, as well. Perhaps Isobel was there with him, but he was grabbing at straws. There was no way he could be sure that was Mason, there were thousands of men in London with that size and build, but still, it was a decent start. He now had two places to look for her.

It was by now approaching three in the morning. He needed sleep badly, and he also hasn't phoned his brother, as he promised. He would park up, get some sleep and ring first thing in the morning. Debating with himself where to park, he decided he might as well go back to the car park in Clerkenwell. There, he would be ready to keep watch in the morning without having to deal with the rush hour traffic.

Once back at the car park, which to his surprise still had two cars in it, he parked, climbed into the back of his car and into his sleeping bag, with his phone set for a 7 AM alarm. He was asleep within a few minutes.

It's was still dark when the alarm woke him. As usual, he was busting for a piss first thing in the morning. He grabbed the bottle he used the day before, which fortunately he had already emptied. Once relieved, his thoughts turned to breakfast, remembering that he normally had a few tracker bars in his gym bag. He searched the back of the car until he found it and was rewarded with two bars. Breakfasting on those and some bottled water, he settled back to wait.

The rear windows of the Pajero were tinted, so if he remained in the back he could only be seen if someone were to peer directly through the front wind screen, he would be fine there for as long as it took.

By 8.00, people began to arrive at the building across the road. First a lone man, and within a few minutes the lights were switched on in the first floor offices. This was shortly followed by the arrival of one of the white vans Adam had seen the day before. Three men got out, unloaded some tools from the back, locked the van and rang the doorbell, which was answered by the man whom Adam had seen arrive earlier. Soon several more arrived with lights going on all over the building. It still was overcast and gloomy outside, although it had finally stopped raining.

Adam continued to watch the front door, and at 9.15, a taxi arrived, out of which climbed Mason. He produced a key from his pocket, letting himself in, and thirty seconds later lights went on in a section of the first floor.

Perhaps that is his office.

Just then his phone began to vibrate. Picking it up, he looked at the incoming number which he didn't recognise after briefly wondering whom it was; he thought he may as well answer it anyway. Discovering it was his policeman friend, Inspector Clive Gooding.

He first asked Adam where he was, to which Adam answered that he was at home. After a slight pause, Clive told him he had just tried his landline.

Is he not answering it? Adam told him that he is out the back and didn't hear it. "Not to worry," said Clive. "But I do have some information for you."

He went on to tell Adam that he'd had his technicians looking at his home computer again, and they had found something a little strange. It appeared that his computer was remotely accessed the day before he was arrested. He went on to say that there was also an automatic inquiry made through his website, which resulted in an e-mail being sent to his server. But the most interesting part of this was that both of these anomalies originated from the same source, a hotel on Clerkenwell Road.

Did he know anybody that might have done this? Adam replied that he didn't, although Clive seemed to hear a change in his voice as he did so.

"OK," said Clive. "Please let me know when you get back" and hung up.

OK, Clive knows I'm up to something; how, I wonder?

But, more importantly, a hotel on Clerkenwell Road.

He was sitting on Clerkenwell Road right now. He really wanted to get a look inside the building he'd been watching; he was convinced now that Mason was behind the anonymous tip.

He noticed whilst sitting there that the contractors frequently came out to their van, and when they did so, they would jam the door open so they could get back in again without ringing the bell. He still had no way of knowing whether or not if they were working for Mason, but that didn't particularly matter. He could follow them back in the next time they came out to the van.

He left his car, noticing that the car park was now full, which worried him a little. His car might stand out as not belonging there, but sod it; he wanted to have a look inside that building.

He took up a position some 20 meters down Clerkenwell Road, close enough to get to the door before it closed but not so close that he would be noticed hanging about outside. There he waited for no more than half an hour before the contractors came out to the van again.

They jammed the front door, opening the back of the van and pulled out a door wrapped in plastic. By the time they had it in their hands and were about to carry it inside, Adam was at the door entering, just before they did.

He stood out of their way allowing them to carry the door up the stairs following them up to the first floor landing. Rather than ascend to the floor above they turned down the corridor stopping before a set of double fully glazed doors. They were about to put the door down, to open the glazed door as Adam said,

"Let me get that for you"

Nodding, one of them thanked Adam.

He opened one of the doors, holding it open for the men to maneuver the door they were carrying through.

The whole floor seemed to be a single suite of offices. He could see what he thought was Mason's office in the far corner, with perhaps Mason sitting at his desk with his back toward him, talking on the phone. He didn't want to stay there for long, but took a few of steps inside, which gave him a good view of the entire floor.

He could see several offices, a small reception in which he was standing, it was all newly renovated and pretty well too, with hardwood doors and skirting, new expensive looking office furniture and the smell of fresh paint in the air.

Immediately to his left was a large room with fully glazed walls, containing rack upon rack of computer and electronics equipment. Somebody had spent a great deal of money here. A man sitting at a desk in the room suddenly looked up, noticing Adam at the door; he quickly got up and walked out of the room toward him.

Adam was instantly on edge.

Should he turn and walk away now or front it out?

Fortunately for him, the contractors suddenly dropped the door they were carrying, cursing loudly, followed closely by the sounds of a computer monitor hitting the floor. The man, momentarily distracted, looked away, which gave Adam a few seconds to turn and leave the office. Deciding to get out of the building as quick as possible, he returned to his car before he was noticed by anybody else.

Adam sat in his car for a while until another car entered the car park.

I'm pushing my luck here; it is time to leave.

He reversed and then swung his car out into Clerkenwell Road, but not before he was photographed doing so.

Chapter 17

At about the same time Isobel was hatching her second plan, her initial one hadn't worked.

She'd ground up a packet of strong sleeping pills that Jonathan kept in the bathroom cabinet and mixed the resulting powder with the sugar in the bowl beside the coffee machine. Knowing how much Jonathan liked his coffee, this would make a perfect sleeping tonic. She hoped the strong taste of the Blue Mountain he liked, along with the sweetness of the sugar would mask the taste of the pills.

She liked coffee herself and had done so from childhood. Although not as well-known as the Blue Mountain Coffee, some excellent beans were grown in Cuba. She could never figure out why he ruined the taste with sugar, but in this instance it was just, as well.

He was bound to have several cups that evening after returning to the apartment, once he was asleep she would sneak into his room take the keys and what money she could find, and get out of the apartment. What she hadn't counted on; was that Jonathan wouldn't stay there that night.

The priority now was to get a key to the front door; she knew that the apartment was meant to be serviced. This meant that there had to be a key somewhere she hoped that the concierge might have it. There was no phone in the apartment, but there was an intercom unit to the reception desk by the front door.

That she picked it up which was quickly answered with,

"Good morning Mrs. Mason. How can I help you?"

"Hi, good morning Derek, I hope you can help, I have stupidly lost my key, do you think you could bring the spare one up you keep down there?"

"Certainly madam," was the reply "I will be up in a few minutes."

As promised, within two minutes there was a knock at the door followed by the sound of a key being inserted and the door opened. Isobel stood beside the door waiting for him, trying to look as casual as possible. She had applied as much makeup as she thought she could get away with, to cover the marks on her face.

Taking the key from him and thanking him again, she asked him not to tell her husband. He would be very annoyed with her for losing the key. Derek agreed that he didn't have to say anything and left. Now she had a key, no money, but at least she could get out of her prison.

Whilst Adam had been watching the office building he was slowly hatching a plan of his own. He had two addresses to look for Isobel. He thought the Notting Hill address was the easiest, and would start there. He didn't think that simply knocking on the door and asking if Jonathan lived there would work, so he decided a different ruse might gain him more information.

He stopped off at a motor bike shop he had seen the day before, along the Bayswater Road, where he bought a motor bike helmet and a leather bike jacket.

He then drove a little further, stopping at a post office where he bought an empty cardboard box, some tape and a marker pen. He then went back to his car, drove around to Portobello until he found a parking space. He then taped up the box and wrote Mason's name on it along with the Notting Hill address. Then putting on the jacket, with the box under one arm and the helmet in his hand, he walked to the final flat he had checked out the day before. Hoping someone was in, it could be Isobel, if so the ruse was a waste of time, and rang the doorbell.

The intercom was answered by a woman, who certainly wasn't Isobel; she didn't have her Cuban accent. He said he was a courier with a package for Jonathan Mason.

Knowing he was being watched through the camera that he could see was part of the intercom, he put on his best smile, holding the parcel toward the camera lens. A tall attractive woman in her early thirties opened the door. Initially she was hesitant but warmed by Adam's friendly smile; she told him that Jonathan didn't live there he actually lived in Park Lane, but he did spend a lot of time there and she was expecting him that evening. She would take the parcel and give it to him later.

He thanked her, leaving quickly, suddenly realising he hadn't thought of taking anything to sign as a receipt. He didn't worry too much as she was evidently eyeing him up and down, appraising the cut of him, which she seemed to approve of.

It may have cost him a few hundred pounds for the

jacket and helmet, but he now knew Mason lived in Park Lane. That must be the building he followed him to the night before. He didn't think the same ploy would work at the Park Lane address. For that, he needed something different.

Stopping at a florist, he bought the biggest most expensive bouquet of flowers he could imagine. He then went into a Boots a few doors down, bought some black eye liner and a pack of make-up remover tissues.

It took quite some time to find anywhere to park close to the apartment building, but he eventually found an underground parking place some way down Park Lane. Sitting in the car, he pulled his gym bag out again, from which he took a tight vest he used to work out in. Noticing how badly it smelt, he also pulled out a can of Lynx Fever deodorant.

Taking off the leather jacket he was still wearing, and the sweat shirt that was underneath it he put on the vest. Liberally spraying himself with the Lynx he replaced the leather jacket.

He then positioned the rear view mirror where he could see his face and began to apply the eye liner. It took several goes to get it looking half right he had never worn makeup before. But after the fourth attempt he thought it would pass.

Now hoping he looked suitably camp, he took the bouquet of flowers form off the back seat, got out and locked his car. He hoped the makeup would soften his image enough for the concierge to let him in with the flowers he couldn't help notice how camp the man looked the day before, that didn't mean he was gay, but it was all Adam could come up with in the time he had.

Walking up Park Lane he practiced a little sashay that he thought would be a suitable and entered No 55 Park

Lane. As the automatic doors opened Adam was rewarded with a big smile from the seated concierge, to whom he walked up to, announcing that he had a delivery for Mrs. Mason. The concierge said he would take them up until Adam then told him he had a little poem to go with the flowers which needed to be delivered in person and that it was Mrs. Mason's birthday.

The concierge agreed after thinking this over, but not before telling Adam that he would need to check with Mrs. Mason first and that he would also need to accompany him up to the apartment. To this Adam easily agreed, his heart already skipping a beat as he realised that the concierge had just confirmed Isobel's presence.

The concierge used the intercom to get through to the apartment, Isobel answered. She was told there was a flower delivery and that he would escort the delivery man up.

Isobel was instantly suspicious. If Jonathan thought he could make amends after raping her and beating her up he had another think coming, hesitantly she agreed.

Adam followed the concierge into the lift with his heart beating almost out of his chest. During the short ride up, Adam's pulse began to race and could feel beads of sweat form on his forehead.

Maybe I'm not doing the right thing. Perhaps she didn't want to see me anymore, and all this business with Mason is in my imagination.

The fleeting heat Adam felt then turned to a shiver down his spine.

He wasn't poor but certainly didn't have the money, power and influence that Mason obviously had. Let's face it he could never afford anything like this apartment nor could he keep Isobel in the lifestyle she was used to,

Perhaps she had decided she didn't want to give it up!

The lift stopped at the top floor.

Adam nervously followed the concierge as he walked down the corridor stopping to knock on the door.

A minute later the door opened to reveal a slightly suspicious but still smiling Isobel. Seeing her through the flowers Adam could hardly restrain himself the bouquet was so large it took Isobel a second or two to realise it was Adam hidden behind it. As she did, she thanked the concierge, inviting Adam in with the flowers.

As soon as the door closed she leapt into his arms. Adam dropped the flowers to the floor. She held him as tight as she could, and then slowly released him, holding him at arm's length, to peer at him.

"What took you so long and why the fuck are you wearing makeup?"

Adam hadn't heard Isobel swear before, other than the things she whispered into his ear when they were in bed together. He laughed at what she'd said. Instantly he felt the weight of the last few days lift from his shoulders.

She did want him.

It took a while, but over the next two hours, Isobel and Adam told each other what had happened to each of them over the last few days.

Isobel's main concern was the operation that Adam had just had although he tried to dispel her concerns by telling her it was routine, and he was fine. Nevertheless she insisted on inspecting the damage but only after cleaning that ridiculous makeup off his face.

Adam was far more concerned about the state of Isobel her black eye and the bruising down the side of her face was still plainly visible despite the makeup. She also had what he thought might be cracked ribs and Adam wanted to get her to a doctor as soon as possible.

Isobel decided not to tell Adam about Jonathan raping her, worried predominantly that Adam might kill him as soon as he saw him.

Adam was torn between extracting revenge on Jonathan and getting Isobel out of the apartment as quickly as possible. In the end it was Isobel who made the decision, she went into her bedroom packed a bag announcing that they were leaving.

Derek, the concierge liked his job and so after half an hour of the delivery man not having left the building, he decided he should call Mr. Mason. He had previously rung through on the intercom again and had been assured that everything was fine, but he knew he shouldn't have left the man with Mrs. Mason.

He told Mason both of the flower delivery and Mrs. Mason's request about the key. He asked whether he should call the police, to which, Mason said would not be necessary and he would be straight over. Mason immediately told Fred to get his car and with Carl accompanying the two of them, they drove to Mason's apartment, to arrive in the lobby just as Isobel and Adam were coming out of the lift.

When Adam saw them, he made a move forward, in an obvious attempt to hit Mason, only to be restrained by Isobel holding even more firmly to his hand.

"Let me" was all she said.

Striding forward she kicked Mason hard in the groin. Mason having no time to react took the full force of the blow upon his already swollen balls. Immediately falling to his knees then crumbling over on to his side in agony. Carl and Fred reacted, trying to grab Isobel only to be flattened by Adam, both receiving vicious punches to the face.

With the three of them out for the count, Adam picked

up Isobel's bags, she picking up Jonathan's laptop bag, which he had foolish brought with him. Isobel's parting words to Jonathan were,

"I hope I never see you again, if I do, that is only a small sample of what you will receive. I'm also taking your laptop as I'm sure there is stuff on here you don't want known, so don't try anything, or it will be"

With that, they both walked out of the building's lobby down Park Lane to retrieve Adam's car.

As the automatic doors closed behind the couple, the concierge popped up from behind the desk, where he had been hiding for the last minute. He asked whether he should now call the police and was again told no.

Both Carl and Fred helped Jonathan to his feet. Carl's nose was broken having taken the initial punch. Fred had fared better only taking the punch to the left side of his face; still he would be sporting a nice black eye, as a result. They helped Jonathan to the lift and into his apartment. Once inside they were both told to leave and not to say anything about what had happened.

"Before you go," said Jonathan. "Make me a pot of coffee, use the Blue Mountain beans, and make it strong, put some milk in a jug and bring the sugar."

Adam drove the car out of the underground car park and down Park Lane. As they stopped at the lights at the bottom, he turned to Isobel and with a big grin said,

"Remind me never to piss you off."

"The only things I have planned for you are very nice indeed," she said demurely. "In fact, would you like some now?"

This made Adam laugh so much he nearly choked. When he regained his composure, he said:

"You know what honey, can I have a rain check on that and wait till we get home. I don't think my battered body could take it right now, well, not and drive at the same time. In any case, we would probably get arrested for indecent behavior."

They turned onto Cromwell Road, which in turn would take them onto The Great West Road to the M4 and hopefully within four hours, home to Wembury.

"What do you plan to do now?"

"Well, If you've changed you mind about me, I could always go to my house at Newton Ferrer's, I'm sure there are lots of other fit men I could meet in the steam room" she said teasingly.

"You are a bad girl. You know that, don't you? If you don't stop teasing me, I will put you over my knee and spank your backside."

"Um, promises, promises."

"You know what I mean. Your husband?"

"I plan to divorce the fat bastard, and with everything I have on him, I plan to take him to the cleaners too."

She continued, "I should be very well off by the time I've finished with him."

"We didn't meet in the steam room anyway, it was in the jacuzzi."

"No, it was in the jacuzzi where you plucked up the courage to talk to me. You had been watching me for ages in the steam room before that; I could feel your eyes all over me I was waiting for you to say something."

"Those tiny bikinis you wear are very hard to keep your eyes off."

"Was it only my bikini you were looking at or was there something else that caught your attention?"

"You know it was something else, your spectacular backside, which is going to get spanked when we get home."

"Yes please," she said. "I like that."

So it went on, all the way back to Plymouth. An observer would never have guessed what the pair had been through over the past few days; all they would have seen, was a happy couple on the way home.

Chapter 18

Jonathan was woken by the ringing of his mobile; he had fallen asleep on the couch after drinking the coffee laced with sleeping pills. On answering the phone, he was told by Fred that two people were in the office looking for him, by the name of Roseau and De Costa. He told Fred to ask them to wait in the conference room he would be there as soon as he could.

Finishing the call, he realised much to his amazement and displeasure that he must have been asleep on the couch all night. He hurt all over, particularly his balls, which hurt even more as he tried to get up. Ringing the concierge, he told the man to get him a taxi straight away he would be down in ten minutes.

The two men were sitting at the expansive conference table briefcases and papers arrayed before them in the newly finished conference room as Jonathan arrived. He hadn't had time to shower or change, so was still in the clothes he was wearing the day before, whilst his head remained thick from the large dose of sleeping pills from Isobel's laced sugar. He was also having a great deal of trouble walking, and the side of his face was showing the damage Isobel inflicted.

This didn't go unnoticed by either Roseau or De Costa who had also witnessed Carl's broken nose and Fred's black eye.

After a minute or so Roseau began,

"It appears you have a problem, which also means we have a problem."

Jonathan thought he was referring to Isobel and Adam.

"It isn't a problem anymore, and it's a private issue that has nothing to do with our work together."

"Please explain."

"This is a personal issue concerning my wife."

Both Roseau and De Costa exchanged looks, with De Costa continuing,

"Are you aware that you have been under surveillance?"

"What do you mean under surveillance? By whom, from where and how do you know about it?"

Now Roseau said, "We know because we have been watching you, and this person has been sitting in the car park opposite, he has also been in this office, at least once to our knowledge"

"When and who is this person? And why are you watching me? Jonathan said with alarm.

"Whom he is, is what we want to find out and why he was in your office yesterday morning."

"You mentioned a problem with your wife; does this have a connection?"

"I can't see how. As I said it is a personal matter, what's this person look like?" thinking perhaps Young had followed him, whist looking for Isobel.

Roseau then described the man and his car asking if it sounded like anybody Jonathan knew.

Jonathan pondered this for a while. It did sound like Young, and these two, who he originally thought were just businessmen were far more, as his investigations the day before had begun to show.

They also just confirmed that they too had been watching him, for how long he wondered, perhaps he should come clean. So, somewhat ashamedly he told them about Isobel, the affair with Young and that she had left him, adding that he still didn't see how it affected his business with them.

"This man appears to know you quite well, he has been watching you and has gained access to your office; he is also intimate with your wife. I think this could have a great bearing on our business together," Said Roseau.

"Tell us everything you know about this Adam Young?"

Jonathan told them all that he knew, including where he lived and also revealing the pedophilia setup that had backfired.

"So you are telling us in the last few days this Young has found your address including your office, which you say, nobody knew about including your wife. He has been in your office, but you maintain that he knows nothing of your business, is that correct?"

"Yes," replied Jonathan hesitantly, he had clearly underestimated Young.

Roseau and De Costa exchanged a glance with a small nod coming from De Costa, who got out of his seat and walked toward the conference room door before he turned to say.

"I think we have made a grave mistake using your services, which I think, we need to rectify immediately before further damage is done to our enterprise"

After a pause, Jonathan replied with as much attitude as he could muster.

"We have supplied you very valuable information on several occasions. I don't think there is any danger from Young; after all you have already taken over the contracts our information pertains to, it is impossible for Young to know of those transactions. I am also about to finalise arrangements to gather the leverage you require on the Treasury Secretary, which I should have before the end of the week. I'm sure we can work out these issues to everyone's mutual gain."

"I don't think we will be requiring your services any longer," said Roseau as De Costa left the room.

Roseau placed the folder that was in his hand in front of him and swiveled the briefcase around to face him. Clicking both locks he opened the case as if to put in the folder. But rather than doing so, he produced a silenced pistol which he aimed at Jonathan.

Jonathan's jaw dropped, his face one of disbelief before he could utter a word he was shot twice in the head. His body initially rocked back hard against his chair before falling forward, his shattered head resting on the tinted glass of the conference room table. A pool of blood slowly spread out as Roseau replaced the pistol in his briefcase.

Roseau then took out a cloth and began wiping every surface that either he or De Costa had touched.

Meanwhile, De Costa went from office to office and similarly put two rounds in the heads of all the others before any had time to understand what was happening. With the exception of one man, the last, who tried to escape and was shot several times in the back, and again in the back of the head to make sure.

"Are we sure this was a good idea? We have a great deal of money being held by the British Government without the right leverage at the Treasury we might never see it again" De Costa said as he returned to the conference room.

"Agreed" replied Roseau "but we cannot risk having this lot, or this Young getting in the way of our main objectives here."

"So we will need to take care of Young then?"

"Perhaps but first I want to find out what he knows, and who he has talked to I don't want to do anything unnecessary that will bring undue attention onto us."

Taking his mobile from his pocket, Roseau pressed his speed dial and said,

"Bring them in now."

Within a few minutes, three men arrived at the office main doors while De Costa let the men in, Roseau again wiped down the conference room, to ensure they have left no prints.

For over an hour, the five men removed every hard disk from every computer in the suite of offices. They removed every address book they could find and searched through any papers that were on and in the various desks, to see if there was any mention of them.

Once complete, they turned off all the lights, checked that none of the bodies would be visible through the glazed offices doors, then locked the doors and left with the drives and papers.

As they left Roseau said to De Costa,

"I also want any computer that is in Mason's apartment. I doubt he has been stupid enough to have used it for our work, but I am not prepared to take that risk, send some men there tonight."

. . .

The following morning the same three men who assisted Roseau and De Costa in the Clerkenwell office, pulled into the Wembury Beach car park in a Range Rover.

It wasn't actually raining for once, but the air was thick with fine droplets of water, the moisture soaking everything it touched within minutes. The three, dressed in wet weather walking gear exited and locked the car.

There were several other cars in the car park, all seemingly belonging to surfers, who could be seen pulling on wet suits or walking along the beach with surf boards under their arms. The wind, which had been blowing hard for several days, was much gentler today and was coming from the northwest nearly parallel to the beach and slightly offshore. As a result, there was a perfect two meter swell with white breakers crashing up the sandy beach. As the waves retreated a white foam was left behind which hissed as it soaked into the sand.

The house, in which the Young's and now Isobel lived, was a little over a mile from the car park. A foot path wound along the top of the beach and along the rocky foreshore as the cove that formed Wembury beach gave way to the headland.

As they walked, they chatted amiably amongst themselves. It was not uncommon for walkers to use this path even in the middle of winter, although one would normally see either middle aged couples or families doing so. Approaching the headland where the Young's house sat a jogger came toward them. As he passed them, they gave friendly nods, continuing with their walk discussing the state of the surf.

Dan, out on his normal run, ran past the men who had momentarily stopped to let him by, he acknowledged their friendly nods with one of his own. He rarely passed walkers this time of year, particular at this time of the morning. He thought they had to be out of town surfers waiting for the high tide, although they were not dressed like surfers. Certainly not the ones he knew around here, who like Adam, whilst waiting to get in the water almost always wore their ubiquitous hoodies.

Within ten minutes, the men passed the Young's house, which was set back from the path about 200 meters or so. With only a cursory glance, they continued by.

All three, experts in surveillance amongst their other talents had captured the scene accurately in their heads. The large house was set back from the path; the property was surrounded by either a low stone wall or a wooden fence. The two story elevation that faced the foot path and the sea was mostly glazed, with full height windows and a front door in the middle on the ground floor and a terrace above.

To the left of the house there was a gravel drive that ran along that side and around the front, with a gateway to the road approximately fifty meters beyond the house. There was also a single story building attached to the rear of the house which appeared to be a large garage.

The house sat on approximately two acres of land; the men continued their walk having absorbed this information. Three hundred meters further on, the footpath met a small road running from Heybrook to their left and back toward the Wembury Road to their right.

They turned right along the road which skirted the back of the property, providing access to the drive and house through a set of double gates, set into granite posts on either side. Walking past the rear of the house along the road, they could see that the single story building to the rear extended the full width of the rear of the house, with the property line some hundred meters further on.

The men had most of this information before leaving

London, courtesy of Google Earth, but wanted to have a proper look at the house itself, before deciding their best method of approach.

Once past, the property line was marked by a wooden fence. The small road then turned north running away from the coast; they could see the coast footpath no more than two hundred meters away across a field. Halfway across the field there was a small copse of trees, which they now made for.

This was the only spot that provided real cover from which they could see the house, along with a spot at the front of the house behind rocks on the foreshore, which was in direct sight of the front rooms. Stopping briefly at the copse, they then made their way back to the coast foot-path and walked back to their car.

Rather than sit in the car, which still had a few surfers milling around it, to discuss what they seen, the men drove off toward Plymouth, intending to check into the hotel at which they had made reservations the night before. And they discussed their options as they drove.

They were at somewhat of a disadvantage. Normally they would have had both landline and mobile monitoring in place, but because of the haste in getting here and the fact that Jonathan now dead provided these services to them, these they didn't have.

Before directly, and only if absolutely necessary inter-rogating Young they would like to listen to any conversa-tions made both in the house and over the phone. To do this they needed to get some equipment in place, in or around the house.

There had been a 4x4 and a small Mercedes sports car in the drive indicating, probably, that somebody was in as they had anticipated at that time in the morning. They had also noticed a burglar alarm system, of the variety that had both landline and mobile monitoring, which would need to be circumvented if they were to get inside.

They also needed to get their surveillance equipment in place. This was something, they would normally want to do under the cover of darkness, but rather than wait for night, they decided to check into the hotel, and then revisit the house in a few hours hoping that at some point, the inhabitants would go out.

At that time, they could attach microphones to the ground floor windows, which would at least provide coverage to the ground floor. The small copse of trees would provide night time cover for physical surveillance and provide a monitoring position for the microphones. But, it would only provide cover for a person hiding there at night; it was too exposed during the day. They could also pick up the broadcast from the voice activated microphones from the road, and would do so if necessary.

This, they decided was their best course of action and a few hours later they returned, this time by road.

They drove slowly along the small lanes that wove around the immediate countryside, passing the house every half hour or so. At the third pass, the 4x4 was no longer in the drive; they parked the car at the entrance to the drive. One of them exited the car, walked through the now open gates and up to the front door and rang the bell. Should anybody be at home he would simply ask for directions. Having had no reply within the first minute he tried again and waited for a further three minutes, before making his way around the house. There, he attached a tiny microphone and transmitter near each of the ground floor windows. That completed he returned to the car.

Certainly these microphones would be discovered in time. But for the week they needed them to be in place, which was all the internal batteries would last for, the man was convinced they would remain undiscovered. They would provide a base cover, which would then be augmented with laser listening devices, operated by the watchers from the rocks at the front of the house and the copse of trees to the east side. Happy with their progress so far, the men returned to the hotel to get some rest before that night's surveillance activities.

Adam and Isobel had arrived home late the day of the murders at Jonathan's office, slept in late and then went into Plymouth in the afternoon to pick up some clothes for Isobel.

That evening Adam and Isobel had talked about their future, rather than revisit the events over the last few days. So it wasn't until late the following evening, once Dan had returned from training at the club that the three of them begin to talk about the events of the last few days.

By then, the listeners were well in place. One was concealed in the copse of trees, another at the rocky outcrop to the front of the house, not as well concealed as the man in the trees but hidden well enough, given the pitch blackness that surrounded him. The other man was in the car a mile away in the village of Heybrook Bay.

The three of them sat around the fire, sharing a bottle of Rioja after the dinner that Adam, for once, had cooked. Adam told Dan all about the events in London with Isobel injecting comments and filling in the gaps from her perspective as he went along. They ended with the confrontation with Jonathan, at his Hype Park apartment and the removal of the man's laptop.

Adam hoped the laptop would contain evidence tying Mason to the attempted pedophile frame up. It came as quite a shock to both Adam and Dan when Isobel revealed that Jonathan had been able to hack into her mobile text messages revealing her affair with Adam. And an even greater shock came when she told them that he had boasted of hacking into the Prime Minister's phones.

This inevitably brought up conversations about what he did. Isobel had told Adam when they first became lovers that Jonathan was an executive with The International Media group. From what Adam had seen of his office he had seemingly set up on his own recently. They concluded, quite rightly, that Jonathan was in the corporate spying business providing information for newspapers and who knew who else. Talk turned to whether he was involved with the hacking scandal which again, they rightly agreed, he probably was.

All this was clearly received by the listener hidden in the rocky outcrop no more than two hundred and fifty meters away, with his laser microphone which he had supported on a small tripod in front of him, trained on the windows as he lay there. So far he hadn't needed the microphones that he stuck to the huge front windows of the room in which Isobel, Adam and Dan sat. They were so small they would seem no more than a piece of dirt until examined very closely. Which would reveal a tiny wire, super glued to the frame leading away to a transmitter hidden in a flower pot, beside the window.

There was a similar device fitted to the ceiling height windows the other side of the front door the dining room, with yet another applied to the kitchen window. Although the present conversation was picked up using the laser microphone, they would be very useful for continued monitoring when the team could not be there during daylight hours, with a hard disk recording device hidden in the copse of trees where his colleague now hid.

The conversation in the house continued with more speculation about Jonathan and his business until Dan brought up the laptop.

He asked "Have you had a look at the contents of the laptop?"

"Not yet, let's have a look at it." He returned a few minutes later with the laptop after retrieving it from the back of his car.

Adam plugged in the mains adapter and proceeded to boot the laptop, which after a few seconds asked for a password. Adam tried a few times, followed by Dan, but the thing just told them no and shut down. After looking at it for a minute or two, Dan then asked Adam if he had spoken to Officer Gooding at all.

Adam told him that he had briefly, whilst in the car park outside Mason's office and that Clive had sounded a little suspicious on the phone as if the policeman knew where he was.

"I really think you should ring him tomorrow and fill him in with all this information and you still need to make sure that you are completely cleared of these allegations."

Adam agreed he would do it first thing in the morning.

The conversation kept on for an hour or more until Isobel confessed to still being tired after the ordeal and would like to go to bed. In reality, she thought the boys would like to talk in private for a while and wanted to give them that privacy. So after kissing them both good night, Adam's kiss being much longer, biting his lip as she did so, an aperitif of what was coming later. She bid them both good night.

"Well brother," Dan began once he thought Isobel was out of hearing range "I can see why, she is absolutely stunning and a nice girl to boot, any idea of what you are going to do now?"

"What do you mean, right now or now in general" Adam replied in a playful manner.

"No, not right now, I know what you are going to do right now. I meant future."

"Well, I would like her to stay here if that's Okay with you and then take it as it comes."

"Of course that's Okay it will be nice to have a woman in the house, I'm sure she can cook far better than you and I'm fed up with looking out for you, and I'll know where you are."

"What do you mean?"

"In bed with her as any sane man would be."

They talked for a while, about nothing in particular, both deciding they had talked enough about the last few days. Just before Adam went to bed, Dan asked him if he was still coming up with him to London next weekend to watch the game. Adam thought that he would and asked Dan if Isobel could too? It was about time she learnt about rugby.

"Yes, of course. Good night mate." at which both went off to bed.

Dan thought to himself as he climbed the stairs; I'm glad my bedroom is at the back of the house. He also thought that neither Adam nor Isobel had mentioned the bruises on Isobel's face. He assumed they had been given to her by Mason and had decided not to mention them. Isobel also hadn't told Adam about the rape either, knowing his reaction, fearing that he might kill Jonathan, the worry, not for Jonathan but what might happen to Adam if he did.

As Adam opened the bedroom door, he was very happy to see Isobel still awake waiting for him. That captivating look appearing on her face as she looked up at him was all it took for his heart to race. They had made love the day before, but Isobel had not been her usual enthusiastic self, which had worried him. She had told him of the beatings Mason had given her, her face testament to that, but he knew she wasn't telling him something. He had seen the bruises on her thighs, which told him all he needed to know.

His blood boiled when he had seen them, wanting to make Mason feel some of the pain he had inflicted on her.

Yet, he could understand why she had said nothing of their making, hoping that soon she would confide in him. But she would do that when she was ready. Now that the look he so adored had returned, he felt that she would recover from the trauma.

A simple "come here" had his clothes off in seconds.

The listener at the front of the house had picked up the entire conversation that night and had a recording on a hard disk in his pocket. He now listened to the sound of their love making, which he thought they were going about with considerable enthusiasm before eventually the lights went out.

For a further hour, the listeners stayed in place before the one at the front texted both to rendezvous near the gates to the house. Once in the car on the way back to their hotel, the second listener confirmed that all the recording equipment had checked out. It had plenty of space on the disk and charge in the battery to record all data coming from the microphones they had in place until the following evening, when all three would return to repeat the process again. Once back in the hotel, the listeners went to bed as the driver transcribed and encrypted their nights take, and e-mailed it back to their boss.

Back in the house, in Kensington, that Roseau and De Costa shared, Roseau had been waiting for the e-mail.

First, he decoded the encrypted message and then began to go through the transcript of the various conversations. He didn't like what he was reading. It appeared as though Young knew nothing of their operation, unaware that they existed at all, but he had by chance discovered their address in Kensington and had even seen him at the window.

This was a revelation; they had not picked up Adam's surveillance until the second day of his watch on the Clerkenwell office. So, they were not aware that he had checked their house whilst searching for Isobel. He also had the laptop, and although he couldn't access the data himself, he would, at some point, tell the police of its existence. They surely would have the tech to crack the password.

Still, he was sure that Jonathan would not have had any data on the laptop pertaining to them. He might have messed up in the end, but he was smart enough not to have incriminating material on an unsecure system.

The options, as he saw them, were; he could order his men back tonight and shoot the three of them, but that would alert the suspicions of the police. Or, he could hope that the police would listen to what Young and the girl had to say about Jonathan Mason and be satisfied that Young had nothing to do with the pedophile ring in which Mason had implicated him. That would, in turn, put an end to that, requiring no further action on his part.

Alternatively he could arrange for something to happen to both the Young men and the girl when they were in London the following weekend. It would be far easier for him to control events here making their deaths appear as an accident. He could monitor them until then, and then decide if it would be safer for the operation for them to die in an accident in London.

The latter seem to be the safest course of action.

Chapter 19

Early the next day, Adam did ring Clive Gooding asking him to meet him but not at the police station. He didn't want to be seen going in there as it would be interpreted as him being called in by the police; he wanted to avoid that speculation. Gooding agreed that this was a good idea and, given the sensitivity of the case, would meet him at his house later that day. He called Adam back around midday confirming that he would be there about 3.00.

When he arrived, Adam introduced him to Isobel; they sat beside the crackling fire which seemed to be constantly lit during this exceptionally cold and wet winter.

Adam and Isobel told him everything they knew, starting with how and where they had met. They continued for more than two hours, uninterrupted by Gooding, with only a couple of breaks for more coffee. Upon finishing Gooding remained quiet for a few minutes thinking about what he had been told, then asked a few questions to clarify certain points.

Firstly he enquired about Isobel's bruising and whether or not the assault had been sexual, as well? After looking at

Adam for a second or two, she confirmed that there had been a sexual assault.

He then asked if she would like to press charges against her husband. She confirmed that she would. After that, he told the two of them that he would like to take the laptop to his computer experts, to see if there was any evidence of the setup Mason tried to pull. He also asked for a list of the addresses that Dan had discovered, including the address of the office in Clerkenwell.

Whilst saying his goodbyes, he told Isobel that if she were to press charges against her husband she would need to come into the station to make a formal statement.

Once back at his office, Inspector Gooding sat at his desk with his chair pushed back and his fingers clasped together at the back of his head and pondered what he been told.

After several minutes of quiet contemplation and many more minutes checking his copious notes, he called the computer staff to pick up the laptop, asking them to have a look at the contents and then he called his boss.

Many of the things he had been told bothered him greatly. This man Mason was obviously involved in illegal activities, the rape and assault notwithstanding. The hacking and his boasts of tapping the Prime Minister's phone had serious implications, with implications tied into the Robertson enquiry that was currently underway in London.

The description of his office that Adam had given him and the fact that he had worked for The International Group compounded this. The shit was about to hit the fan of that he was sure. He wanted to go to London to question Mason, but first he would need to enlighten his boss, who would surely inform the Met. His boss told him to come straight up.

Once sitting in front of his boss, Chief Inspector Blyth, he went through all he had learned that day. When Gooding finished, Blyth looked at him with a mixture of incredulity and annoyance, at this being landed upon his desk. Then, he asked Clive to go through it one more time? After listening for a second time, he said to the officer in front of him,

"This is a bloody minefield, and so far above my pay grade, I need to refer this to our Assistant Chief Constable who is bound to refer it one of the Chief Inspectors at the Met. Get ready to go to London, I will tell you when as soon as I have talked to him tomorrow"

Realising he was dismissed; Clive rose from his seat and was leaving the door as their boss added "I don't think I need to remind you to keep all of this to yourself, do I?"

"No, sir" was the only reply.

For several days, the listeners had very little to report other than the visit of the police inspector and his removal of the laptop. It was now the weekend, the conversations in the Young household had turned to different matters.

There was a rugby match at the Albion ground on Sunday afternoon, prior to which Isobel had her first lesson in the delicate arts of the game. This entailed watching video recordings; most of the Saturday, of what both Adam and Dan told her were great games. But really all she saw were men covered in mud and a fair bit of blood, fighting for an odd shaped ball.

As Chief Inspector Blyth had predicted he and the Inspector Gooding where asked to visit the Metropolitan Police in London. An appointment had been arranged with Deputy Assistant Commissioner Layton on Tuesday afternoon. In the interim Gooding put together a briefing package containing everything they had learnt to date. He also included some information that the computer boys had been able to glean from the laptop.

Much of the data it contained was encrypted with a sophisticated encryption system, which would take some time to unravel, but a folder named Young had been discovered. This contained over 500 pornographic images of a pedophilic nature, with one image identical to that of the one that had been found on Young's computer.

Upon arrival at New Scotland Yard, both officers were met by Layton who escorted them to a lounge area. They were told to help themselves to coffee and asked to wait there while he went through the document Gooding had prepared. Some forty minutes later Layton reappeared, he told them that he could certainly understand their concern and asked whether they were requesting a formal visit and interview with Jonathan Mason at his office in Clerken-well? To which the officers replied that they were.

"Yes that's what I believed you would say and I have asked Assistant Commissioner Bates to join us. He is more intimately involved in ongoing investigations into phone hacking than I am. I would like his input before we visit Mason" he then added "Assistant Commissioner Bates is engaged right now but should be free in about half an hour, could you please wait here and I will call you when he is free?"

Assistant Commissioner Bates, after receiving the call from Layton told his secretary that he was slipping out for a moment and wouldn't be long. His secretary took this to mean that he was going outside for a cigarette which he often did, particularly when stressed as he was looking right now.

She was correct in that assumption, but there was a far more pressing reason for him to get out of the office. When he had taken the call from Layton, he had said to him that the name Jonathan Mason meant little to him, but that was far from the truth. Although Mason wouldn't have been counted as a friend and wasn't on his Christmas card list, he knew Mason very well indeed and had for many years.

Bates had been one of the several senior officers inside the Met that were Mason sources. Sometimes this would have been passing along information that had just come to light. At others, it was details of cases already under investigation, most of which made great headlines and copy for the International Group. It had also worked as a reciprocal; Mason had on occasions supplied information back to officers of the Met, when they were unable to get it themselves.

That Mason had set up on his own was unknown to Bates but was hardly surprising. Dandelion would be moving heaven and earth to distance himself from anyone that could implicate him in the hacking scandal, the ongoing Robertson Inquiry and other Police investigations that were being instigated at the Met.

Jonathan and his crew moving out of the International building made a great deal of sense to Bates. And So far he'd managed to keep the lid on those enquiries, at least as far as the he and the Met were concerned. This was proving more and more difficult as the weeks went by and the claims of hacking and police involvement increased.

He needed to talk to Mason immediately. He would not be able to stop the visit to Mason's office, but he could give him a heads up delaying it until they had time to deal with the problem.

Pulling out his mobile once outside and out of earshot of others officers that had nipped out for a quick cigarette. He dialed Mason's mobile, to which he got no response. Undeterred by this, he walked out of compound, hailed a passing cab and gave the driver Mason's Park Lane address. He asked the driver to wait for him once the cab arrived at the apartment building, which wasn't long as he was soon told that Mason wasn't in and he hadn't been seen for several days.

He knew that he would have to delay the Plymouth policemen until he could talk to Mason; unfortunately for him events were already spiraling out of control. Mason would never be interviewed, it's difficult to get a corpse to talk, but his equipment could and eventually would.

At 3.00 PM, a call came into the Islington Police Station from an officer that had responded to a call from a property agent, who had in turn been called by a tenant of the building. The officer informed his dispatcher that he had met the agent at the property, who had taken him to the floor where the office in question was situated. He had no keys to gain access to the offices but could smell what he thought was a decomposing body. He needed a lock smith to be sent to the address.

A little more than thirty minutes later a lock smith, contracted to the police for such situations arrived, gaining access to the offices in a few minutes. As soon as the doors opened, it was obvious to the officer that there was a dead body in there.

He asked both the agent and the locksmith to wait outside whilst he investigated the office. It took no more than a minute to discover a body in the conference room, after a cursory look in each of the offices contained in the suite; he rejoined the agent and the locksmith at the entrance. Thanking the locksmith for his time, he said he could now leave, he then asked the agent to remain while he called in his discovery?

Some twenty minutes later six senior officers arrived at the address. They told the responding officer to wait outside and get as much information on the tenants as he could while they fully checked the offices. After an initial look into the conference room, the lead officer called the crime scene investigators based at New Scotland Yard and the coroner's office informing them both of the situation. It took a further thirty minutes for the coroner and the investigators to arrive.

At 5.00 PM, Inspector Layton opened the door to the lounge in which Gooding and Blyth had been sitting for the last three hours. What Layton was about to tell them was probably the last thing they expected.

He informed them that bodies had been discovered at the address they were interested in they had apparently had been there for several days. It appeared that all were the victims of gunshot wounds and that teams of investigators were either already there or on their way. He thought perhaps Gooding and Blyth would like to accompany him over there. They instantly agreed they would, following Layton to a waiting car. During the thirty minute journey, Layton filled them in with everything he knew so far.

As the three officers arrived, the police machine was already in motion; one team laid out a barricade across the street while another was erecting a white tent over the building's entrance.

The rest of the building had already been evacuated, and TV crews were beginning to arrive. They were allowed through the barricades and parked in the same car park Adam had spent two days in the week before, where a mobile command unit already sat. Layton asked Gooding and Blyth to wait there while he found the senior officer on the scene.

He soon returned with an inspector, introducing the three of them. The inspector briefed them on what they had found, he then went on to tell them that the crime scene people where inside at the moment looking at the bodies. All of which had at least two bullet holes in them. Gooding then informed the inspector of their interest

"That complicates matters," said the inspector with a glance over his shoulder at the camera crews at the end of the street, "You think they are involved in phone hacking? Um well, there are certainly a lot of computers in there; one room is dedicated to them. I have already called in some computer experts, but they are going to have to wait until the crime scene people let them in, which I'm afraid also includes you" looking at Gooding and Blyth.

"We'll wait; we're used to it," said Blyth.

"You are welcome to use the mobile unit" gesturing over his shoulder "I will call as soon as I can" He left them there, crossing the road and entering the white tent.

The scene inside the office suite would have seemed chaotic to the untrained eye, but in reality it was exceptionally well choreographed.

Every inch of the conference room was being photographed; every surface throughout the suite was being checked for fingerprints and every conceivable piece of trace evidence. Once satisfied, they had the scene recorded, and the immediate surroundings of the bodies searched for the smallest detail, the bodies were released to the coroner.

The coroner and his assistants initially checked and

photographed the bodies in situ before calling for gurneys to take the bodies away. Everyone inside the office suite wore white paper suits, gloves, boots and hoods, travelling only along pre-described routes along the floor that had been previously been checked for evidence.

It was 3 AM before Gooding and Blyth were allowed in to the suite by this time the computer experts were in full flow, all wearing the ubiquitous white paper overalls and accoutrements, as were Gooding and Blyth.

They were shown around the offices by the lead inspector with Layton in tow. Gooding said "This does seem a little extreme for a case of phone hacking don't you think" to nobody in particular, he went on "Have you found anything on the computers?" This last was addressed to Layton.

"Difficult," Layton said. "None of the computers have any hard drives in them we think they were removed after the killings, perhaps by those that did it" the latter a seemingly an obvious statement to Gooding.

For two hours, they looked around the office until satisfied they could glean no more. Blyth suggested they go to the hotel they had booked whilst waiting earlier. Once outside they saw teams of like clothed officers were combing the street and the car park opposite, under a blaze of lights they had erected in the street.

In the car that was taking them to the hotel, they discussed what they had seen and agreed there was little point in speculating the reasons behind the shootings until they had further information. Which may well be some time coming.

Agreeing that sleep was in order they decided to meet at midday in the restaurant of the hotel, which would allow them five or six hours sleep.

Chapter 20

Rounding the corner onto Clerkenwell Road, after a very packed tube ride from her home in Ruislip, Stella wasn't happy to be going back to work. She had just returned from the Seychelles. Two weeks of lying in the sun and dining on seafood had refreshed her, but still she was uncomfortable with the job. Yes, it paid very well indeed; she was moving into her new office today decorated and furnished to her taste, but it was the nature of the new work that disturbed her.

She had worked with Jonathan at the International for many years. She had been an up and coming investigative reporter before accepting a change of job roles to work directly with Jonathan. It was the money that tempted her, a more than a doubling of her salary. Initially the work she was doing was similar; she was extremely good at teasing interesting data from others' electronic forms of communication. This used to result in articles that she wrote, but now, the data just seemed to be used by others or stored for later use.

In her early years as an investigative reporter what she

did to acquire her information didn't worry her. In her opinion, those that she wrote about needed to be exposed for what they were so the means met the ends. Over the past few years, it had become more of a challenge to her to acquire the data, than write about her discoveries. It was a challenge she relished and still she knew that her work had a purpose; exposing those that had wronged others.

But over the past few months, particularly with the complete separation from the International Group and the new office, her hard won dirt on those that she researched seemed to be more stored or sold than used, something that bothered her.

The company she worked for seemed to be becoming more about corporate espionage and money making than it did about reporting facts. Even, if it where facts as she and those she worked for saw them.

She had always been close to Jonathan who confided in her she had worked with him longer than any of the others. Jonathan had confided in her, all his plans for the company after the move, before she went on holiday. As a consequence of what she had been told, she spent a good proportion of the holiday worrying about what he had told her.

She was still divided on whether or not she was going to quit; she had given herself a week to make the decision. She was loath to leave Jonathan's employment the money was very good. So good, that she had put quite a lot away and could now afford to take on a new challenge of writing the book she had in her head for a while. But Jonathan had said Isobel was moving back to London, whom she was looking forward to seeing. That would be difficult if she quit Jonathan would not be happy.

She liked the fiery little Cuban and was glad Jonathan had taken the advice she had given him, about patching up his marriage with her. She was far too good a catch for him to ruin it again. It would be a lot of fun to be around her again.

As she approached the office, she could see that the road was blocked off ahead, pedestrians were still moving forward, but all cars were being diverted. Still deep in thought about the week ahead, it wasn't until she was right on top of the barrier before she noticed it was manned by police.

Stella stopped beside several people standing beside a barrier that extended from the building next to her destination, to the building beyond. The barrier cut off the whole road with the exception of the footpath. On the opposite side of the barrier, several TV crews had their cameras trained on a building's entrance covered in a white tent.

Her new office.

She had only been there once; several weeks ago. She looked at it when Jonathan first divulged that they would have to move soon. It seemed suitable as far as she was concerned and had picked out color and furniture for her office, before going on holiday.

She was sure she was in the right place

That's odd

"Excuse me; do you know what has happened?"

"Several people had apparently been killed in there, that's what they are saying at least"

Replied the man standing next to Stella "Four or five, so they say, all in the same office on the first floor apparently"

That was her office; they had the entire first floor.

It was only a second or two until the shock hit. Her knees began to buckle, the individual voices, the sounds of cars, the noise of the TV crews across the street all blended in one, a cacophony of sound, all contrived to bring her to her knees. She put her hand on the man next to her for support.

"Uh, sorry"

The people they were referring to could only be Jonathan, Fred and the rest.

But why, who would want to kill them?

She was going to be sick and needed to find somewhere quick.

Turning she spotted the car park that Adam sat in a week ago which now held a large van, she just managed to get to the fence between the van in the car park and the footpath before she was sick. As Stella wiped her face and looked up there was a policeman standing next to her,

"Sorry madam, can I help you?" Unsure of whether to be angry at the fact that she had just thrown up all over the incident vehicle or whether to be concerned for her.

"Morning sickness she replied" adding "I'm so sorry, all of a sudden it just."

The policeman held up his hand and said "Don't worry, I understand my wife made my life hell, but please not on my van again."

Stella mumbled a reply and began walking away from the scene; at the first right she turned down it, stopping just around the corner to catch her breath and then burst into tears.

It must have been a built in instinct to protect oneself that kicked in to take her the next half mile as she remembered none of it. She was in Charterhouse St, a few minutes away from Barbican underground station before she realised where she was. She headed towards it to find a place to sit down and think.

Within a few minutes, she was sitting on the first west bound train that came along. Slowly, as her head cleared of the anxiety that had been running through it and the panic subsided a little, she began to think.

First thing I have to find out if it really is them and if it is what am I going to do about it?

There was no point asking herself why at this moment as she hadn't got a clue on that. During the thirty minute train ride that followed a few ideas had come into her head.

What they were doing there was technically illegal. Well, maybe completely illegal. Going straight to the police before she had considered outcomes, was not an option. Certainly it wouldn't take the police long to find out that she also worked for Jonathan. There were no personal mementos in her office as she had never used it. But sooner or later the computer files would be dredged through, and they would discover her. So, at some point she would have to go to them.

This has to be connected to something we have been doing there is no other explanation. It can only be about something we have done or maybe know about. It makes no sense otherwise, why kill everyone in the office. Evidence, that's the only thing that makes any sense.

Certainly over the past few years she had uncovered some very incriminating material on a lot of high profile people, even her ultimate boss, Dandelion, up until recently. Some of the stuff could easily send some to prison, and to be honest, there were more than one or two; she had facts on that may be capable of something like this.

They have to be looking for me as well but who is it and what is it we've done?

It was only a short walk to her present boyfriends place. As soon as she had seen the destination of the train, she had decided to go there rather than home. He boyfriend's place was much closer than her house in Ruislip, and she wanted to get onto the internet as soon as possible, somewhere quiet, not an internet cafe.

Undoubtedly, her boyfriend would still be in bed they had only just got back from the Seychelles early evening of the day before. He still had a few more days off, and had suggested she take a few more. But work had been nagging at her. Both the decision of whether or not to quit and the immediate task as she saw it yesterday, the checking of all their data and then deleting the cloud copy that had been made to secure the data for the move.

As she neared the flat she was glad of that instant decision, going back to her place might not be such a good idea at the moment.

She let herself in. Sure enough he was still in bed, he claimed to be about to get up, but Stella thought she had woken him, not that that mattered. She told him through the open bedroom door that the commute into work had made her mind up for her, and she was going to quit, effective immediately. She needed to check something on the computer and would bring him a cup of tea in bed in a few minutes.

The laptop in front of her soon confirmed that she had the right office and that five people had been found dead there. They were presumed by the media, to be workers in that particular office suite and the police, who would give a news conference in the afternoon.

There was nothing she could do for now she needed to get her mind off it for a few hours until she had more info and perhaps could even think straight. So bed sounded like a good option, sex might distract her for a while.

By 4.00 pm, she was back on the computer, only a few minutes after stories appeared on the net, reporting on the police news announcement that had just been released.

Steeling herself for what she might find, she read several. All reporting the same basic information, that five men had been found in the offices, all dead from gunshot wounds. The names of three had been released by the Police, hopeful, that this would enlist information from the general public. The three men were Carl, Dave and Fred. There was no mention of Jonathan and Nigel, but it did say two others were unidentified.

I have to keep calm, have to think. My God what shall I do? Where do I go? I can't go home. I suppose I'm safest here, how knows about this place, no one from the office. I'm in serious trouble.

Going to the police with her suspicions was certainly a possibility, but they were only suspicions. To justify those suspicions she would need to tell them all she knew about their business. That included the purchase of information from senior police officers so that avenue was also dangerous. Finding out whether Jonathan was one of the victims was crucial right now.

She had, of course, considered ringing him earlier in the day, but something had stopped her. If the police or someone else had Jonathan's phone, ringing it might not be such a good idea but,

Isobel, why didn't I think of that earlier? Jonathan could be with her she is supposed to be in London.

As Stella's boyfriend had gone out to the shops, being short of basic necessities due to the holiday, she used her personal mobile to ring Isobel.

At the cottage in Wembury Isobel's mobile rang. She had taken it back from Jonathan upon leaving the London apartment. That, her credit cards and her passport were in the laptop bag she had taken from him.

Looking at the display and noting that it was Stella, she almost didn't answer it. She was reluctant to talk about

Jonathan and what had happened. She knew he and Stella had been close but would he tell her the truth? Isobel doubted that. After a second or two hesitation she answered the phone with,

"Hello Stella how are you?"

"OK, I'm just got back from holiday and wondered if Jonathan was with you?"

Isobel faltered a second before responding, she didn't want to lie to Stella, who seemed to be unaware of the problems over the past few days.

"I saw him four days ago in London but then had to come down to Devon. Since then I haven't heard from him"

Followed by "Why is it important, don't you have his number?"

Now it was Stella's turn to hesitate, Isobel seemingly knew nothing about the murders, what she should say? Eventually she decided that Isobel would know soon enough, so she might as well tell her what she knew, she began.

"Do you know of the new office we have moved into?"

"No."

"Ah well," said Stella "in that case I have a little story to tell you, can we talk?"

"Yes" was Isobel's response, a little hesitantly, quickly even subconsciously checking the battery level of her mobile.

Stella told her about the company move, her holiday, her return to work that day and the horrifying situation she returned to. When she finished Isobel asked,

"But what sort of business could you have been doing, that would cause this? I suppose that you think Jonathan is one of the other dead men?"

"Yes I think he might be"

Adam who was not sitting far away picked up on the last, stood and walked toward Isobel, with a concerned look on his face. Other ears outside picked it up as well; instantly alert.

Stella told Isobel something of the nature of their business finishing with "You wouldn't believe some of the stuff we have on some very important people. I would never have imagined anything at all like this could happen, but I don't know what else to think or what to do next"

Isobel then asked Stella if she would mind going through it all again with a friend listening in, someone she knew she could trust and that he might have an idea of what to do.

After listening once, Adam asked her to repeat various bits of the story. He then asked more about what they did. Stella replied that it was basically information gathering she didn't want to say too much on the phone, but if they could meet she could tell him more, when she had finished he asked,

"Where are you now, are you safe?"

"At a friend's"

"Good, stay there. Don't go home or out if you can help it. We were planning to come to London the day after tomorrow but could come tomorrow instead?"

"Okay, we can meet when you get here, text me where and when, I have to go, see you tomorrow."

Adam looked at Isobel with "Shit" being his only comment.

"You didn't lie to me, did you brother, and off them all before you came home? The timing is about right. The police seem to think this may have happened 4 or 5 days ago. I've got a few reports online here."

"It does seem a little extreme, even for you" Dan continued.

Adam's only reply to this was his middle finger vertical the rest forming a fist with his right hand.

"I bet there will be some that make that accusation, but no I don't think anyone would seriously think I killed all these guys, not even over you honey."

"What would he be involved with that got him killed?"

"I really don't know. I didn't know anything about his business. You've just heard more than I have ever known. All I knew, it was to do with newspapers" said Isobel testily.

"Sorry honey, this isn't good. Shit."

"It's Okay. We don't know if he's dead, but what do we do now? Do you really want to go and see her, if someone wants her dead?" Dan put in whilst browsing through the story breaking on the internet.

"Yeah, I know what you mean but we seem to getting dragged into some serious shit anyway, and I would like to know what we are getting into before we get dragged in too deep. It should be safe enough; talk to her, get a bit more of the truth and decide what to do."

"She doesn't appear to be keen to go to the police; otherwise she would have done so already. But if it looks that bad we just go to the police, we have nothing to hide" said Adam, mostly looking in the direction of his brother.

Dan merely nodded, then added a shrug for good measure.

Outside, the man that was listening had summoned the second watcher with a preset message by text,

"Come here now."

As soon as the three way telephone conversation in the house had begun.

They had been lucky. He had only arrived at his station some fifteen minutes before. Had this call happened before then, it would have been recorded but they might not have listened to the recordings until back at the hotel early tomorrow morning.

The second watcher arrived a minute or two before and was now beside the first, under cover and listening to the continued conversation in the house. The first had begun making notes shortly after hearing the word 'Jonathan' for the first time. Instinct told him this was going to be crucial and needed to be delivered now.

He signaled to the second watcher to remain while he went off along the path to meet the car, whose driver he had also texted a few minutes before.

He knew this had to get back to his boss quickly, but his boss liked it concise and accurate. So he always went through his notes before reporting in by e-mail and would do so the same now. Before the car moved off, with him in the passenger seat he was going through his notes. Once back in the hotel it would only take him ten minutes to send the encrypted e-mail.

Chapter 21

No more than thirty minutes later Roseau began reading the decrypted e-mail, after being alerted by text that he had an incoming report.

Again, he wasn't happy with what he read, but he wasn't overly surprised either. Their operation had been in motion for over a year without a single hiccup. Now, as the day got closer problems were beginning to rear their ugly heads. As yet there was nothing that specifically jeopardised his mission, but these problems could easily get out of control, and needed to be nipped in the bud and now. He had worked toward this day for too many years for it to be undone by simple mistakes.

Thinking back to Mason's office and in retrospect there had been an empty office that looked as though it might be awaiting a late arrival. He really shouldn't have missed that, nor should have De Costa.

He often wondered why De Costa been put on this mission he seemed to have his own agenda much of the time.

Factions within factions; wasn't it always the way?

Certainly that was the case with his superiors.

His computer guys looking at the data they had taken from Jonathan's office would have found trace of this woman soon enough. He would need to deal with her, and the three in Devon, but now they were all coming to him which made things a lot easier, and would probably be a lot more fun.

The killing of those fools in the office had reminded him of how much he enjoyed killing his enemies. Discovering this Adam Young wandering around under his nose had embarrassed him. De Costa was sure to have mentioned that in his report as he had in their barbed conversation earlier today. Taking care of Young now had become personal and needed to be done before his next communiqué home.

There would be a status update from Plymouth in the morning he would wait until then before deciding on the best method of achieving the Young's demise, without drawing undue attention. An accident would be best, but that was such a coincidence that no one would believe it. A quick and simple in and out with ample distractions should be all that was required.

Those in the Young household had decided much the same. Little could be achieved by speculation which was about all they had been doing for the past few hours since Stella's call. They would get some rest, Isobel and Adam starting for London at daylight, and Dan would follow as planned the next day. If the hotel they had reservations in couldn't get them in a day early, then they would find something else.

· · ·

The watchers hadn't had much time to prepare; they would need to follow them to London. Although the trip to watch the game that Saturday had been mentioned several times over the past few days, no reference to where they were staying had been made. Following them now was crucial.

They had rented a second car as back up a few days before, and now both vehicles would be needed to follow the Young's to London. One man would stay behind he could rent another hire car the next day, and then monitor the recordings as the other two tracked the Young's.

As Adam and Isobel had begun their drive to London just after 7.15, the watchers each in a separate vehicle waited half a mile apart on the back lanes. They knew the Young's must use these to get to the main road, and now had been following them for a little under two hours. The two watchers had swapped the leading car several times, being very careful not to be detected. They too were good at their jobs; equipped with state of the art communication equipment it had all been easy so far.

Just after they swapped the lead for the fourth time Adam pulled into the services and was followed in. As the lead watcher followed Adam's truck into the service's car park, he radioed his colleague using the voice activated throat mics both wore. He told him that they had stopped and that he should stop at the next junction, wait, and then follow again as they passed.

Both Adam and Isobel wanted coffee, but little else in the end they took a Danish with it. As with all motorway service stations there was little difference in any of them, plastic tables secured in front of plastic chairs, in a seating area surrounded by fast food outlets. Not a place to spend any quality time, but the coffee was good although not strong enough for either of their tastes, and the Danish was edible.

Adam's primary reason for stopping was to ring the hotel, both to see if they could get in a day early, and whether they could park there. Initially the idea was to go by train, but the Pajero allowed more room to take stuff they might need, so they had packed it with loads of "may be useful to have along" stuff that morning.

After the coffee and the call to the Carlton Towers confirming both a room and parking were to be had they were soon heading back to the car.

All morning, the motorway had been relatively quiet, as Adam had signaled, checked his mirrors and pulled into the services he noted they were followed in by a single black car which parked several rows back at the back of the car park.

As he and Isobel walked back to the car he could see that the man was still sitting there; he hadn't gone into the services, and didn't appear to be on the phone; he just sat there looking out the car window. He also noticed that the car, a late model Audi A6, followed them away from the services although it soon overtook just after the next junction. Probably a coincidence, but subconsciously it took hold, and after seeing the car again thirty minutes later, he started to pay more attention.

As a Naval Intelligence Officer, he wouldn't have been expected to be an expert in covert surveillance. His fields included data mining, predictions of aggressor's movements and producing counter movements to intercede them. It included liaison with Special Forces personnel, notably the Special Boat Squadron or SBS as it was more commonly referred to, but he also worked with human intelligence, the man on the ground, so he had attended several courses in this art. He knew what to look for if he thought someone was following him.

In the next hour and a half, driving just slightly slower than normal he saw the Audi twice more. When it was not in sight in his rear mirrors, there was a choice of perhaps four or five, which had consistently been in them.

Just after Heathrow, the Audi passed him again so if he was correct the other car should have taken up position behind him. There was a services coming up, into which he turned late. There was no one directly behind him that followed, but a few cars back a dark green Range Rover also pulled into the service's slip road. He'd seen the same Range Rover several times over the last few hours.

As he parked, Adam told Isobel to walk like she was in a hurry for a piss, to which she replied,

"How is that supposed to look?" Adding with a shake of head, "I'll think of something"

True to form, she really did look like she needed to go as she walked across the car park followed by Adam. This time the driver didn't repeat the earlier mistake of his colleague, he came into the services. Adam waited close to the ladies and kept a good eye on the guy. When Isobel came out he asked her to pick up some stuff from the Marks and Sparks they had there, giving him some time to make a few calls.

This made it easy for the watcher who had got himself a cup of coffee, and was adding sugar at the stand next to the counter. It was easy to watch Adam from there, but it also made it easier for Adam to study the man while he made a call or two.

The man appeared relaxed, by all intent and purpose a traveler needing coffee, but his eyes never strayed very far from either the shop door, or where Adam was standing. Once Adam knew what he was looking for it was obvious.

He was scanning every ten seconds or so never letting his gaze linger, just make sure you were still there. He was definitely watching something; Adam's bet was it was them.

The watcher got his timing spot on. He was heading out of the door just as Isobel came out of the shop allowing Adam and Isobel to follow him back to the their car, parked behind his. The watcher must have thought he had got away with it, Adam pulled into the slip road and then the motorway, behind him. Obviously content to let Adam follow him for a while until he eventually indicated left and pulled off.

Sure enough after ten minutes, the black Audi appeared behind; these guys were obviously following him. But by now they were only thirty minutes from the hotel.

Adam told Isobel of both his suspicions that they were being followed and that he had made some more reservations at another hotel. The Roof Gardens, no more than a five minute walk away from the first. His plan was to check into the first and be seen doing so. Leave through the car park, walk over to the Roof Gardens, check in and stay there.

He thought that there were only two cars with one man in each, whom he would recognise, so getting out of the first and into the second hotel unseen by them, should be easy enough. When Isobel asked why where people following them and how? Adam replied that he would rather concentrate on what he had to do now and could they talk about that once securely in the second hotel.

They managed the deception quite easily, leaving the car with most of the stuff in it, at the Carlton Towers, with their followers watching that hotel and presumably for their next moves. The car was accessible when needed. For now everything they needed was with them and they could meet Stella without being followed.

Once in the rooms Adam had reserved at the Roof Gardens the conversation turned to who was following them. They had again spotted the drivers from both cars standing near the hotel entrance as they left via the car park.

It could be the police that were following them. Either in connection with Adam's arrest, although that was very unlikely, or in connection with the deaths, again unlikely as they would surely have tried to question them. That left only the people that seemed to be looking for Stella and had perhaps killed Jonathan.

It also appeared that they had been followed from home, which implied they were being watched before Stella's call last night. It was conceivable that Isobel's mobile signal had been traced to Wembury and that these men had got there before they left this morning and then followed them to London. But the time constraints made that most unlikely.

If they were being watched in Wembury, it was worrying he would need to let Dan know as soon as he could. For now though, they could meet Stella in the restaurant, the address of which he just texted her, and find out what was going on, or at least part of it.

As Adam and Isobel walked to the restaurant to meet Stella, the watchers reinforcements arrived at the Carlton Towers. The four men took up positions in and around the hotel and waited for their prey's next move.

Chapter 22

Stella arrived five minutes after Adam and Isobel. Adam knew it was her by the furtive look she gave all as she walked in.

It was an early booking, and at that time of the evening there was only one other table occupied, by a couple. Nevertheless, Stella had a good look round appearing very nervous. If Adam hadn't already known she had just returned from the Seychelles, she appeared so pale he would have thought she had been in a basement office for the last few months.

Isobel rose and beckoned her over; Stella sat but still looked around. She appeared very frightened; the realisation of what was going on had obviously hit her, and it was easy to see she needed to talk about it.

Isobel introduced Adam but didn't explain his presence. She asked Stella to tell them again what happened and what she saw, with as much detail as she remembered. Stella told the story again, this time adding bits of detail as she remembered them. Once finished, she had told Isobel and Adam not much more really than she had the night before. She then said that she had kept abreast of the story as it came out over the net and speculation was rife amongst the media.

The Police had said no more on the identity of the remaining two bodies since their last statement, but both Jonathan's name and Nigel's had been mentioned as possible victims by the media as they worked with Carl, Fred and Dave, who had already been positively identified. There was also a great deal of speculation as to the nature of their work and whether that had got them killed. It had been reported that these five men worked together in a department at the International until recently along with a sixth, a woman. Stella had been named as this woman.

No wonder she's looking pale

The term "Information Gathering" had been used to describe what the six did at the International. It was very doubtful that any of the reporters, reporting on the murders, believed that it wasn't tied to the phone hacking. None had yet made that specific allegation. They stated that their sources informed them that the group had moved out of the International Building no more than three weeks ago. No mention of moving to a new location had been made, and this didn't seem to be directly connected to the International Group. It appeared as though the six had just set up a business on their own, doing much the same thing as before.

The fact that the police had not as yet mentioned Stella by name was reassuring to her, but they soon would. Passport records would soon be found indicating that she was back in the country; the police would be looking for her within a day at most.

It had finally sunk in to Stella that her she was with the wife of a colleague, with livid bruises down the side of her face. Who was sitting very close to a man she hadn't met before, and there was a very large possibility that this woman's husband was dead. Yet they had made no mention of it,

Something definitely isn't right here

She began to feel the panic rising again.

Isobel noticed her friend straighten in her chair, the look of fear creeping into her features; eyes becoming large and staring at the two of them before Stella could get up, she said quickly.

"There are some things I need to tell you but here really isn't the place. It's about Jonathan, and suffice to say, these bruises" gesturing to the bruises that were still visible on her face "he was responsible for them"

She added "The hotel we are staying at is just around the corner we should eat our food" which was just arriving "then go back there, talk in private and in a bit more comfort, along with a drink or ten, which I think we could all do with."

Stella relaxed a little as they ate, although still suspicious of everything; a couple opening the door almost gave her a heart attack. With food done, Stella knew she had to talk to them, tell them the truth about Jonathan, their work and what she had done. The weight of it all was almost too much she needed to talk about it and get some help. Isobel, she trusted as a friend and this guy with her; he looked as though he could handle himself, so going to the hotel seemed a sensible option, or perhaps the only option.

Adam went out first, casually checking the street out front, followed shortly by Isobel with Stella on her arm. It was still raining and the street was nearly deserted, one or two walking quickly by with their heads down. Some parked cars but empty and nobody hovering in a doorway. It felt safe enough, and it was; their ruse had left the two men who had followed them sitting in cars close to the Carlton Towers.

Their watchers had immediately called in for two new cars just in case they had been spotted at any time during the drive from Plymouth. The two new men were sitting in the lobby of The Carlton Towers, hoping to catch sight of Adam and Isobel and their meeting with Stella.

These new men didn't work for Roseau directly per se but were contractors hired to do specific jobs and knew very little. The present task was to keep tabs on Adam and Isobel, who had checked in and gone to their rooms, so far not to reappear.

Adam, Isobel and Stella, arrived back at the Roof Gardens within minutes and were soon finding what they needed from the mini bar. Adam had done well with his impromptu booking. A quick Google search on his mobile whilst standing in the service station, turned it up as the closest hotel to the Carlton Towers, and although there was little information, he had booked the only suite available. The suite had a large lounge with several large comfortable leather sofas, facing glazed patio doors and a terrace beyond.

Sitting on one of the sofas, opposite Isobel and Stella, Adam began by telling Stella about the drive up here, how they were followed but managed to lose them by switching hotels. He thought it may be easier for Isobel to tell Stella about the last few days if he weren't there, so suggested they talk while he phoned Dan from the next room. Dan needed to know they had been followed anyway.

Isobel sat next to Stella and told her everything from

the problems with her marriage, being stuck on her own in Plymouth, meeting Adam and then her return from Cuba last week.

After a minute to absorb what she just been told Stella said,

"Sorry honey, I know what an asshole of man he could be toward women. But when he brought you back from Cuba I really thought that nonsense was all over that he would never risk losing you. Evidently I was wrong."

After giving each other a hug and peck on the check Stella added "You seem to have traded up though," flicking her head to her right in the direction that Adam had just gone,

"True," Isobel conceded "But I am very concerned about what has happened to Jonathan, I wouldn't wish that on anybody."

When Adam returned to the room he asked Stella, who seemed to be warming to him a little at least she didn't seem as frightened of him as she had half an hour before in the restaurant.

"If this really is about some piece of information that your firm knew about, and considering the organisation of these people; they seem to have found us and followed us from Plymouth very easily, whatever it is you have, must be very valuable to someone. But, from what you have told us so far about the type of people you were for the want of a better word, spying on, they just don't seem to fit the bill, do you know what I mean?"

"Yes," said Stella "I know exactly what you mean there is also a lot more I haven't told you, and it's going to take a while, so you might want to get another drink first."

They all took that sound advice and once seated again, Stella began,

"I have to go back a way, to when I first met Jonathan

for you to really understand. I would have been about 23 or 4 when I first met him. I had just had my big break I got a job with the International Group as an Investigative Reporter and was given an assignment and leads to get going on my first piece.

"After spending a couple of weeks chasing down leads, I had almost everything, but I needed one thing more, which was proving impossible. I knew to get it someone would need to do something that I thought wasn't entirely legal or ethical. Someone in the press room introduced me to Jonathan. I told him what I needed and what I needed it for, never really expecting a positive outcome, but in no more than two hours there it was, the confirmation for my article

"It turned out to be really big news. My article was about the House of Lords and how peerages were being sold. I had discovered that the then Prime Minister had arranged for seven of his friends all successful businessmen to be awarded lifetime seats in the House of Lords and the titles that went with them, in return for huge donations to the Labour Party. It was illegal and a massive story.

"The piece of information I needed as final confirmation, was the cash trail, which I got from Jonathan. These guys should really have been sent to prison or at least stripped of their Peerages and the PM should have made to resign. I don't know if you remember it, but the investigation at the Met was handled by Assistant Commissioner Bates. I will tell you more about him later but suffice to say that the investigation was dropped. The Met came to the conclusion that these businessmen had made loans, not gifts to the Labour Party. And, that there had been no prior arrangement for their Peerages. This was blatantly untrue as I had already proved, but with Bates at the helm, that was the end result.

"Nevertheless I'd had a huge scoop, so one night there was a little party thrown in my honor at the local pub. Jonathan obviously thought he had helped me enough to get into my knickers and tried it on quite strongly, only to find himself flat on his back with me snarling something very crude into his face, I was rather drunk. After that, surprisingly enough, we got on very well, becoming close friends but I think he thought I was a dyke for a while.

"That experience taught me a lot and all I wanted to do in those early days was get the truth out, exposing those people that would otherwise get away with it. I was very passionate about my work. I saw myself as a crusader exposing those who deserved it. This always required a great deal of information and confirmations that were difficult to access. So I saw a lot of Jonathan he never exactly had a title, and it was just him you went to find something out.

"As time went by, it just seemed to be one more crooked businessman, corrupt politician or homosexual priest. I began to find that writing the stories no longer excited me. There is only so many ways you could write about them, and in truth these people sicken me. It was just another in the thousands of arseholes out there. But what I did enjoy was digging out the dirt on them, which no one else could find, and let others do the actual exposure articles. So I began to work more and more with Jonathan, he taught me all he knew of electronic surveillance, which I mastered quickly and improved upon. He taught me about eyes on surveillance and eventually even shared his informant list with me, at least I thought he had but recently I discovered several others that weren't on the list.

"There were also the other exposés, I think you know the ones I mean, which footballer was being unfaithful to his wife, which pop star had been caught soliciting for sex in public toilets or which celebrity was taking drugs. I personally found these stories a waste of time and discussed my issues with the management. But I was told that this type of story sold huge quantities of newspapers and without those and the methods that had been developed to gain the information, then I wouldn't be able to do what I considered was the important work. I can't say I was ever very happy with that, but had no choice.

"Obviously I was not the only person involved in this at the International; loads of reporters were digging up dirt for their articles. We even used private investigators for our physical surveillance. Then four, maybe five years ago came a major change in the way we operated. Dandelion, the owner of the International Group decided rather than have reporters gathering their own information; it should be done by a dedicated group.

"Jonathan was chosen to head this group, and he offered me a place in it. To be honest, it was the money that attracted me more than anything. There were six of us; Carl and Fred had been PI's and did all the physical surveillance work. Then there was Dave who worked with me and Nigel that looked after all our equipment. The setup we put together was impressive, to say the least. We were moved into a section separate from the news rooms, and had four large interconnected rooms absolutely crammed with gear. It almost felt as if I was working on the set of 24"

Throughout Stella's dialogue, Adam sat opposite Stella with Isobel next to her on the couch, holding her hand in support. He'd quietly listened as he sipped a Corona and lime. This now depleted he rose went to the minibar for another and grabbed the bottle of white wine the girls had been drinking from and topped up their glasses. Once seated again and Stella had refreshed herself with a big glug of wine, she carried on with her story.

"As the means of electronic communication surveillance widened it became a specialist field, one that I eventually specialised in. There isn't a phone call, text message or a computer I can't access with the right equipment. I still saw my primary goal as an investigative reporter, to bring people to account for what they had done. Somewhere down the road, the data I gathered would be used for this purpose, or, so I let myself believe.

"There were always those that had big enough teeth or enough money for the best lawyers in town that could get away with anything. These guys scared the media which is why I thought they are often left alone. But more recently I've found it is a bit more than that, they also have some very high level protection

"On top of the new hardware we had there was also a brand new source of information. Every text and phone call made inside or into the UK is sent to Thames House and monitored by automated systems and operators, and we suddenly had access to that. I have no idea how that happened, and you wouldn't believe what information is out there and how easy it can be to get hold of with the right equipment"

Adam would, but he let her carry on uninterrupted. Much of the work he used to do for Naval Intelligence had many similarities in its intelligence gathering, to what Stella did. He knew exactly what happened in Thames House and had used that data almost on a daily basis to search for terrorist threats.

Stella continued with her story; she told them about the types of people she had data on, these ranged through past and present prime ministers, leaders of parties, banks and the stock exchange, Buckingham Palace officials even her old boss, Dandelion himself.

"On top of that," she said "we were buying a lot of information from the police, not for small amounts of money any more from lower ranks but for large sums from some of the most senior of ranks, including officers that I already knew were protecting others.

She told them about information she had on present and past prime ministers and letters between our secret service and those that many think are our enemies collaborating on action. About bribes to government officials for planning, access to government contracts, even alterations to policy. About officials at the Inland Revenue office rubber stamping multi-national's accounts that claim their principal revenue comes from abroad. Which banks have been laundering drug money and the massive amount of collusion between banks, governments and the civil service.

Stella hesitated before continuing

"Then, and the most sickening of all; the sex rings, underage girls and boys from both the UK and abroad. Some vulnerable or disabled, some kidnapped, some sold to syndicates but all used by sick individuals.

"More and more of the stories never saw the light of day particularly those of the rich and powerful able either to conceal what they were doing or of such notoriety that it wouldn't seem credible."

"Recently," she told Adam and Isobel "they had begun taking on private clients which all seemed to her to be more corporate espionage than news.

"Over the past two years I have become increasing disillusioned with what we do, but the pay checks were the allure. I am paid an obscene amount of money for my talents."

The more she told them the more they became

appalled at what they heard. With that came the realisation that there were many from the list of names she was reciting that would kill to protect themselves.

Adam stopped her at this point he said

"So what you are telling us is that over the past, say few years you have been collecting dirt on a lot of very bad and extremely powerful people who would do anything to protect themselves; there are so many possible candidates.

"What do we do? Go round to their offices and inquire whether it was you, Mr. Pedophile the Vice President of some billion pound corporation, who wants us dead simply to conceal what you consider entertainment? I don't think so.

"I don't suppose you have fucked around with a few terrorists as well just to widen the pool some more."

Stella could see what he was getting at, she had never before verbalised what she and the team did. She was becoming disgusted with herself for having participated.

"No, we haven't dealt with any terrorists, and yes there are quite a few to choose from, really I had no idea it would be so many"

"But the thing is," said Adam a little more calmly, "It may not be about someone trying to hide information; it may be about trying to get hold of it. I'm sure it's worth a great deal of money to the right people, which only adds to the numbers"

After a pause "Earlier you said you still had the data where is it precisely?"

"A secure cloud store."

"Wherever it is, it may be the only thing we have to use. Is it something that can be accessed from any computer?"

"Yes, any computer on the net but only with the right access codes which only Jonathan and I know."

Over the next hour, the three of them continued their discussion, mostly with Stella revealing more about her and Jonathan's work. Adam was astounded at how stupid they had been it was plainly fire they were juggling with, and they hadn't a clue about what they were doing.

He was freed from hearing any more by the ringing of his phone in his pocket. Pulling it out, he looked at the display to see if he knew whom it was. A mobile number, but no he didn't, and answering anyway, the voice at the other end asked,

"Is this Adam Young?"

Yes, can I help you?"

"This is Inspector Morris from Devon and Cornwall Constabulary, we have been trying to contact Isobel Mason, is she with you?"

"She is yes, what's it about?"

"Well um, Okay, have you seen the news and anything about the shootings in London?"

"A little, caught something about it briefly, why?"

"Well we need to speak to Mrs. Mason, could I now, please?"

Adam replied "She's in the bath; I will get her to ring you as soon as she is done"

"Okay. But please make it quickly?"

After hanging up on the policeman, Adam walked over to the two women still sitting side by side. Isobel was trying to give Stella as much support as she could. Adam told her about the phone call and that an Inspector Morris wanted her to call urgently and that it was about Jonathan, or so it thought. They agreed that she should say she was in London at The Carlton Towers but not say anything about Stella, and all she knew of the shooting was from the news.

Isobel called the policeman, the trepidation in her voice easily discernible after a three minute conversation she hung up. She had been told that they thought it was Jonathan and needed a family member to ID the body. She had said she would do that tomorrow and would call first thing in the morning to make the arrangements.

Isobel sat down heavily opposite him with another glass of wine in her hand. Adam thought she didn't look good,

I guess that's how you look and feel after the police has just told you they think your husband is dead.

They all looked tired; he knew he felt it, rather scared too.

In the past few hours, he heard more about the operations of the establishment than he ever wanted to hear. Had he been able to forget what he'd heard he may well have taken that route, but it was too late for that.

Stella, in revealing her long held secrets, had dragged both him and Isobel so deep into the dirt that no amount of cleansing would remove it. Walking into the middle of a mine field was hardy an appropriate metaphor, more apt would be standing under a howitzer barrage. The mere fact that they had met and talked to Stella would promote them to the top of some extremely powerful people's hit list, no matter what they did or said.

By now Adam's brain was so addled with facts and the thoughts of the consequence of those facts he was finding it very hard to think coherently. It was well after midnight, so he suggested that Stella stay in one of the other rooms. He had intended to get a two bed suite at the hotel, assuming Dan would stay with them, but all they had was a three bed suite on the top floor, which was rather pleasant if you had a minute to look around or cared right now. Showing Stella the room, he then took Isobel's hand and led her to bed.

It was quite a while before they fell asleep, the ramifications of all they had heard and all that had occurred, running through their heads. Stella to was also having trouble sleeping, her last thoughts before finally drifting off were,

Well it didn't get any clearer talking about it as it was supposed to do. All I've done is highlighted how complex the situation really is but at least I'm not alone in it now.

By now the men staking out the Carlton Towers had realised a mistake had been made. They weren't sure how but the two they had been following, had checked in but had not stayed there, seemingly having walked out as soon as they checked in. The only explanation was they were spotted during the drive up here, and they got out of the hotel, in the time it took to them to get out of the car, shut it and turn around.

One of the watchers had seen them at the desk from his car all the time whilst Adam and Isobel were checking in the only time they were out of view was as he got out the car. They had eventually found an employee that would check the room for £100.00. It revealed nothing at all of the Young's, not even any luggage. They were now sitting in the cars waiting for orders.

Chapter 23

The next morning, things didn't seem any clearer or brighter. The weather outside was wet, grey and nasty, and inside the atmosphere was little better.

There were potentially a dozen or more individuals, outfits, or groups that had the motive for the killings it was an impossible job to determine which, if any, it was. The only thing they could do was to wait, and perhaps use the data as leverage.

There was also the police, and how much to tell them? By now they must be actively looking for Stella. The police were also presumably going to interrogate both Isobel and Adam about their whereabouts at the time of the deaths. The news reports had indicated the killings happened during the day, presumably the day after Isobel and Adam had last seen Jonathan in Park Lane. By then they were already at home in Wembury with motorway fuel bills as evidence of their drive to Plymouth that night. Adam had previously given all that information to Clive, but not as an official statement in connection with these murders.

Adam wasn't looking forward to another interrogation

that would certainly soon be on the cards. The last was bad enough this time he knew that several members of the police force had a vested interested in keeping the information contained in Stella's cloud hidden. They would need to tell the truth, but leave out Stella, and all she had told. In addition, they should tell the police that they were staying at the Carlton Towers just to be on the safe side. He would go over it with Isobel before they went to ID the body.

By 10.00 AM, they were on the way to the mortuary at Hammersmith Hospital. Arriving 20 minutes later, they had discussed what to say, and were both prepared for the worst.

Isobel was led into a room alone returning several minutes later; she looked ashen and shaken as she had last night, and had been crying. That answered the question then, no doubt it was Jonathan. The words,

"It's him," drifted from her tongue as final confirmation.

Seconds later the door opening admitting Inspector Clive Gooding and another officer, they first went to Isobel and offered their condolences, and then Clive introduced the other man as Deputy Assistant Commissioner Layton to both Isobel and Adam. Adam was at first surprised that Clive was here and working on this case, but after considering it, he did say he would check Jonathan out, which may have resulted in a trip to London, and a walk into this mess. At the moment, he was glad he was here, but that could quickly change, he was a policeman after all. The police involvement with Jonathan and their vested interests in the case, particularly that of senior officers, meant that as a result, Adam felt he really couldn't trust any of them.

Layton began with,

"Again, we are very sorry for your loss, but we need to ask you a few questions."

"Please go ahead."

"We need to talk to both of you separately could you please come with us?"

It was going down as Adam had predicted, Clive looked at him gesturing him to follow him into another room, next to the one Isobel had gone into. He obliged Clive by walking in, shutting the door, and sitting down before anything at all was said.

"I can imagine you must have realised that the Metropolitan Police is looking at you very carefully, the time line fits so far. But as yet they haven't been given an official time of death, on account of the condition of the bodies. I personally don't see you connected with this and have told them what I know of you. As a result, we are talking now, which I think is better than you talking to another Met man."

Adam replied he understood that, and as he had nothing to hide his statement would be identical to the account of events he originally gave. The only thing he could add was what he had done since, which was to hang around the house in Wembury and the trip up to London yesterday. Isobel would give the same answer, and whilst he didn't like Mason, he was sorry he was dead. There wasn't anything more he could add. After almost an hour answering Clive's questions he was ushered out, joining Isobel in the corridor.

They were both free to leave, for now!

It was still before 12.00 as Clive watched them get into a cab outside the hospital. He had been in London three days now and whatever was going on was getting stranger by the minute. He'd come to talk to this Jonathan Mason, who subsequently had turned up murdered. Mason seemed well known around here, particularly amongst the senior officers but some seemed very anxious over events, particularly Assistant Commissioner Bates.

He didn't like what he was seeing or more accurately feeling.

What was it about Mason that had them so worried?

He was dead so posed no obvious threat, but these missing disks, perhaps they did? Much had been made of corruption in the Met, particularly in connection with newspapers.

Could that be it and would their names be in those files on those disks?

He had a great many questions to answer, if he could.

Assistant Chief Inspector Blyth, who had accompanied Gooding to London three days ago, had left him alone, and returned to Plymouth. Gooding was left on the periphery of the investigation into the deaths, essentially following Inspector Layton around, allowing him a great deal of time to observe. He was very good at this. The name Mason enlisted interesting reactions. With his suspicions aroused Gooding knew it was time to talk to someone about them, but precisely who, was the question right now.

Adam had a similar problem, although he hadn't seen the information gathered by Jonathan and Co he had no reason not to believe of its existence. It seemed to be having a profound effect on his life.

The day had turned out better, weather wise than the early morning rain had led them to believe it would be. Rather than go straight back to the hotel and possibly be followed, a walk through Hyde Park seemed like a good idea. It was certainly possible that those that had followed them yesterday were working with or for the police, or had sources of information within the ranks at the Met.

As they walked hand in hand, Adam was again, deep in thought. For half an hour or more they had walked with hardly a word spoken, but they were being very careful to make sure they weren't being followed. Sitting every few minutes on one of the innumerable benches around the park and scanning the vicinity and any surrounding people.

As he saw it, he, Isobel, Stella and perhaps Dan were being pursued by several men who believed that they knew secrets about them or others. The forces against could potentially be from elements of the Met, some corporate executive with secrets, or a company itself, trying to hide what is up to. They could even be from the government, a truly daunting prospect, whatever the direction of the threat.

He, like Gooding, needed to talk to someone. The police were out, certainly the Met policemen, possibly Gooding but once he did that he would have to mention Stella. Again, her name had not come up at the hospital as they had expected, so what did that mean? He did have friends from his old days with military intelligence he hadn't kept in touch with many; there really was only one place to go.

Deputy Assistant Commissioner Layton, now in charge of the case at Clerkenwell was also not having a good time. His investigation kept turning into dead ends. The brass were being evasive and, as for records, there didn't seem to be any less than two years old. He had all the names of the victims now the first identified were Fred Green, Carl Morris and Dave Sumner.

All three were married men having been reported missing by their wives, before the discovery of the bodies. The second two had taken a while; first there was Nigel Brown a single man in his late twenties. He was identified later the same day from records and the final one to Jonathan Mason. Formally identified earlier today, although they had been certain it was him for the past couple of days.

None of them with the exception of Nigel Brown had any criminal record; there was something on Nigel, an arrest for marijuana possession as a teenager, so his prints and mug shots were in the system. But, that was about all they had.

Up until approximately two years ago all of them worked for the International Group, a media conglomerate owned by a Mr. Dandelion. Then two years ago, they all quit on the same day and none had an employment record since, with the exception of Mason who filed his tax returns last year, as a self-employed surveillance contractor.

But, all five were seen at the International's HQ two weeks ago, in the company of a woman, Stella Ward. They were all together packing away several offices worth of equipment and documents.

But, if they quit the International two years ago, what were they doing there?

Stella Ward apparently worked with the rest, or at least that is what was presumed as her employment at the International ended on the same date as the others. But where was she? What they knew was she left the country two weeks ago for the Seychelles and returned the day before yesterday after the killings took place but hadn't been seen since. She filed a tax return as a freelance communications consultant last year and had been an investigative reporter when she worked for International.

All of them had either been investigative reporters or surveillance and communications experts. That certainly fit with the equipment in the office and the dedicated fiber optics cable that they had installed. It also fit with the theory that the Met had, and the media were speculating about. That they had been killed as a result of information they possessed, whether to cover it up or use it for other purposes was unknown. There was also speculation that they were heavily involved in computer and phone hacking, perhaps even corporate espionage, which also seemed to fit.

It seemed a much more plausible than the theory that some held; that Adam Young and Isobel Mason were involved in the killings. Although initially the time line did fit with this theory, a more accurate time of death had now been given by the pathologist. This now indicated that the deaths of Mason and Co happened after Adam and Isobel arrived in Plymouth. It was an outside chance that they could have returned to London, but the nature of the incident would seem to preclude them from the investigation, at least as suspects in the killings. But he would be interviewing them again officially this time, as he was sure they knew more than they told.

So basically he had nothing to go on. All his attempts to get some up to date records on Mason, whom even he knew by reputation, had proved fruitless. There was no current address either. He owned several properties but lived in none of them. He had to have a residence in London somewhere, and Layton thought that several of his colleagues knew exactly where it was, but his request for information had hit a brick wall, or perhaps evasion.

Now, why would that be?

For several months, now it had become glaringly obvious that there was corruption in the upper echelons of the Met. The speculations had been that senior officers were being paid for information. Which officers was unknown, and supplied to whom was as well.

Could this be the who?

Mason was certainly a candidate for that. Did he have a cache of information somewhere? All the hard disks had been removed from the office in Clerkenwell but surely there would have been a backup. That data would be worth a fortune to a great many people. He wanted this information and before anyone else. He needed to find Stella Ward;

She could be the key to this.

Chapter 24

Lorenzo De Costa and Paul Roseau at least those were the names Jonathan Mason knew them by had a couple of days to decide what to do about Adam, Isobel and Stella. They would have liked an accident, but that wasn't practical, and their deaths were going to ring bells anyway. So the plan was to grab them, ask a few questions and then dump the bodies somewhere they wouldn't be found at least for several weeks, by which time it wouldn't matter.

None of that was going to be difficult; they had a dozen men available for the grab, and many more for the distraction. This distraction would be supplied by an impromptu riot and looting spree. This could be in place within four hours of a go and a location. The location was the only problem.

They knew that Isobel and Adam had planned to come to London to watch a rugby match in which the brother was playing, and they had come up a day early to meet with Stella Ward the empty office owner. Unfortunately, their men had lost them. Apparently they had been spotted somewhere during the drive, that would be dealt with later. But, after checking into a hotel, where they had a booking made over a week ago they disappeared. They had probably checked into another hotel and gone there meet Ward. But what did this mean?

The recorded conversations made at Wembury didn't indicate the Young's had any idea of their existence. So was it merely a precautionary measure or had their men been spotted? All Roseau could do was guess, and he knew there was little point in that. All that really mattered was that they were disposed of and with what he had planned, they would never see them coming.

They had been picked up again at a hospital earlier today after being asked to identify Mason's body. The information on their whereabouts came from an informant in the police department, but their men got there too late to pick them up outside, and follow them back to whatever hotel they were staying in.

In all other departments, everything was going well.

Once the Young's and Ward were out of the way, that backup destroyed if, it existed at all, and Mason along with his people dead, there was nothing to stop the operation succeeding. In two weeks' time, no one would be able to recognise this country.

Roseau's associate, De Costa, was of the opinion they should forget about the Young's and Ward, even if they had access to these files. Mason knew nothing of their mission. As far as he was concerned they were businessmen who liked to tilt the advantage in their favor.

Yes, there was probably a record of the houses they rented from him, but it would take detectives so long to go through the data there was no chance that they could stop them. Just let the speculations continue about who was after the data. Let the police chase the suspects there was going to be quite a few of them.

De Costa was all about smoke and mirrors. Roseau preferred direct action and his gut instinct was direct action against Adam Young. The tenacity of the man did bother him.

Adam had decided to talk to an old friend whom he believed still worked in the military. He taught Adam most of what he knew, or used to know about the job. He was also a maverick and would talk to Adam, of that he was sure. But not on the phone, this had to done in person. It was only an hour's taxi ride away and well worth the effort.

They walked out of the park confident that they were not being followed and into a taxi which dropped them back at the hotel. Stella was still in the room waiting for them. Adam outlined his plan whilst they ate some food. He explained that he thought it better if he went alone, making it easier for him to talk to his friend.

Soon after finishing his food Adam showered, dressed for the weather forecast which was wet and cold again, leaving the ladies still sitting in front of the news. He asked them not to go out, nor order from room service again, and keep their mobiles switched on and set to vibrate not ring. In explanation to that, he said someone outside the room door, could ring the mobile if he heard it ringing inside the room, there was a good chance you were in there. He cautioned them not to open the door and keep the chain on it until he returned, which they promised they would.

Once in the hotel lobby he asked the concierge to find him a cab rather than order a minicab, he didn't want to mention his destination. And once in the cab he told the driver to go to a village called Groombridge, three miles west of Royal Tunbridge Wells. To take the Streatham High Road to Eastbourne Road then toward East Grinstead and he would direct him from there. Forty five minutes later the driver said,

"East Grinstead Sir, which way do we go?"

Adam directed the driver for the next ten miles, arriving at an isolated house. He paid the driver but asked him to wait a minute, he wanted to check someone was in and that they still lived there before letting the cab go.

The house's nearest neighbors were a little less than half a mile away, and the house itself was a sprawling affair. It had originally been part of a farm and had, over the years, been added to many times. As a consequence, it was a bizarre mixture of styles. The main house, itself well over two hundred years old, was built from oak, a brickwork extension on one side, with another of rendered blockwork on the opposite side. Barns and workshops littered the area. It was no architectural masterpiece, but it was a great place to live.

Knocking on the door he was rewarded by the smile that appeared on the face of his friend's wife as she opened it, followed by,

"Adam, my god, how are you honey?" she turned and shouted "Ron, come look who's here!"

That told Adam all he needed to know, his friend was indeed there. He turned waved at the driver who started his cab and drove away.

Adam was more or less dragged into the kitchen of the farmhouse. He could hear kids in the background, sounding much younger than they should be. Maybe the old devil has had some more, the two he had should be at University by now. Ron bustled into the room, saw Adam, picked him up and spun him around like a rag doll, Adam wasn't small, but his friend Ron was huge, far bigger than even Dan.

"Where have you been, you dog?" his first words "bout bloody time you came to visit" his second.

A mug of fresh coffee was quickly thrust into his hands. Gloria still remembered his likes she should, this had been more or less his home when he worked with Ron. After fifteen minutes of chat, whilst he drank his excellent bean, Ron turned to Adam and said,

"So, we had better go down to the Crown for a couple of pints so you can tell me what trouble you are in now."

"That obvious?"

"Afraid so mate."

The Crown has about half a mile away on the outskirts of the village; it had been a regular waterhole for them when not away working for DIS.

The DIS, or simply DI as it is now known, was the intelligence arm of the military. Staffed by both military and civilian personnel, they worked very closely with the SBS, or Special Boat Squadron, who are often referred to as the SAS's poorer brothers. The SAS certainly got more publicity, but that was part of who they were, and their deterrent value. You tried to avoid kidnapping the British because everyone knew the SAS would come for you.

Whereas the SBS with little or no publicity did a lot more than they were credited for; again all part of the design. Ron was a member of the SBS and was seconded to the DIS when Adam worked for them. Both worked out of Thames House when in the UK, the home of the Security Services or MI5 as it was more commonly known. MI5 and MI6 were both civilian led, although members of all the services worked with both agencies. DIS provided a crossover between both MI5 and MI6 with the MOD as well as providing military intelligence, where they used SBS as their operative personnel.

Adam had gone through the University route with the Navy, studying counter terrorism, thinking he would become a Royal. Instead, when offered a position at the DIS upon graduation he took it and was ranked as Sub-Lieutenant, later making Lieutenant. He had always outranked Ron, who had been a color sergeant in the Royals and made it to Warrant Officer in the SBS before Adam left.

Not that that had ever mattered to them. Ron was keeping Adam out of trouble and in a job from day one. Ron had already been working with DIS for a couple of years before Adam arrived. They liaised with the SBS squads for missions required by DIS and vice versa, seeking intelligence that the SBS required for tasks allotted by their immediate superiors, the Navy.

Adam was immediately assigned to work with Ron on his arrival, which was the only job he had for the five years there. In Ron's opinion, he was still a kid, but bright and very perceptive, as he demonstrated in the first year of his arrival, potentially keeping him and some of his SBS mates out of harm's way. Ron decided to make a real marine out of the lad, which to a great extent he had.

The pub was not the same as it used to be, new decor and obviously new owners. He remembered it as a dark, somewhat dingy and definitely very smoky but a highly entertaining pub, particularly during the real ale festivals. It was still okay, far more comfortable in its seat-ing, bright and airy even on a wet winter's night. The food smelled good too, but Adam doubted that they would still be smoking a bit of weed out the back anymore. It was definitely not that type of establishment any longer.

Part way into the first pint Adam started talking. Ron could see as soon as he saw Adam in the kitchen that he was troubled. More so than he had ever seen him before, he looked desperate for advice and the opportunity to talk. So he let him.

As Adam finished his first pint, rather rapidly, Ron signaled for another to the barman, getting a nod as reply. Adam hadn't stopped talking for a second, but Ron could see he was beginning to relax; another couple of pints were what he needed.

Adam talked for nearly an hour nonstop, with the exception of taking more mouthfuls of beer, without a word from Ron, by which time he was just finishing his third and had visibly relaxed. He had told Ron everything he knew and all that he speculated upon. It was now Ron's turn; he had a great memory and took Adam back to the beginning with questions and seeking confirmations.

Their drinking had slowed, the first three pints in a little over half an hour, the next pint lasted an hour or more, both men knowing instinctively, that they needed to keep reasonably clear heads. After the two hour discussion, Ron felt as he understood what had happened, but as yet couldn't offer a better hypothesis than Adam already had.

During the drive over Adam was finally alone to think. He had concluded by the end of the drive that they really only had two options. Trying to find out whom these people were wasn't going to work, there were too many possibilities. Going to the police was also out. This left them the first option; to wait for an encounter with these people, which conceivably could be arranged, so at least they weren't killed on sight. Perhaps that would give them time to barter their way out of this situation with the data they possessed.

That would only work if either their desire was to buy and use it for their own gain, or if the desire was to conceal and a believed safeguard had been installed i.e. they had a copy; don't kill me or it will be released, kind of thing.

The other option would be to publish everything they had, as per the wiki leaks; a dangerous ploy which would only work on certain types, many would still seek vengeance. The first was the better option, but there was also the shot on sight part. On the plus side, they might be able to identify these people and take action themselves. The path Adam had decided upon before even reaching Ron's place was a combination of the two. This was the only approach where he rated the success above zero, just, which was better than none.

If he could engineer a way to get them a message and find out whom they were, he could then arrange to put all the data on to a website. But that presumed that they could glean enough information from the data to establish which policemen they could talk to and keep hidden away for a while. If they could pull off the impossible, they might just survive this.

Adam's talk with Ron had helped him sort through all the data that was clogging his head. Now, realising this was the only option, it was easier to begin the actions required. He hoped Ron would see it similarly. Either that or produce a magic bullet to cure it all, which was never going to happen.

The talk had stopped barely a minute when Ron said,

"It would be time to go then."

"I think so" was Adam's reply far more cheerily than he could have managed a few hours ago.

The two walked back the half mile to Ron's house. Whilst they walked Ron told him what he thought,

No, to going to the police and no, to finding out whom they were even with the resources at DI it would be difficult which they didn't have. He just hoped they wanted to buy it; that would be the easiest solution.

"I thought about that but, you know I really don't want them to have it."

"Yes, I thought you might say that and I agree; so?"

"I think I can get them a message to meet or hope I can; there is also data on the police which is useful. A long shot but I don't see much else."

"You could always just walk away."

"I've thought about that as well, I can't and even if I could it would mean looking over my shoulder for a long time to come."

"Don't suppose you are armed at all?"

"No, I don't have a license and with all these policemen around and with a high likelihood of being searched I'm not sure it's clever."

"Um, I have one."

"What you want to come with, you sure?"

"Yes, I am."

"You know I'm not going to say no, don't you?"

"Shut up boy let's get started." said Ron as they walked into the kitchen.

There was a bag sitting on the kitchen with a note saying I've taken the girls to bed, see you in a few days. Love you.

Ron picked up the note, scribbled on it Love You Too and put it back on the table, picking up the phone by the door he ordered a taxi to take them to London.

The ride back was mostly quiet, both men dozing with the effects of the strong real ale they'd drunk. Adam rang Isobel as they approached London. She was already in bed, as was Stella. He told her they would be there in twenty minutes and to expect their knock on the door.

It was just after one when they got into the rooms Adam showed Ron the other bedroom, told him he would see him in the morning and went to bed himself, for once falling asleep without sex on his mind.

Chapter 25

Nothing Adam had come up with would have made the slightest difference, Roseau and De Costa didn't want the data, they wanted it gone, and all those who knew about it dead. They had been planning the next day very carefully, and had something workable on the table.

They had e-mailed their gangs' go-between with instructions. He was to provide three mini buses with eight men plus a driver in each, and to have them in central London before 10.00 AM the next day. The go-between had received a heads up message earlier in the week, so this email was all he needed to put his boys on standby. From there, it was just a question of hiring the buses, and using their blackberry messenger service, which all his guys used to give them their instructions.

One such group had just arrived at the rally point they used, the driver who acted as the boss for each group told the assembled crew that they had a job on. They were to go down to London, rob a few shops and any general public that got in the way, cause mayhem for an hour or so and be home for teatime.

He added that they had to hit very specific targets at specific times and would be waiting on the bus until given a go. They had all very done well for themselves the last time they did a job with this guy, so they should do so again.

One of the crew said, "You mean we are going to get to do our favorite pastime and get paid for it?"

"That's it," said the driver.

"Fucking bring it on," was the unanimous response.

The next stage of the plan was to locate the Young's, and Ward at the game, if Ward where there, if not they would get her whereabouts from the Young's. They would follow them back to wherever they are going and look for either an opening on the way, or once they were there, then use the diversion and take them. It hinged on spotting them at the stadium, but they had managed to get their seat numbers, so knew where they should be. Roseau had thirty nine men on this including himself and De Costa, so he was not going to miss them.

De Costa still had his doubts but was going along with the plan. His main concern was that his partner Roseau was getting too worked up by this Adam Young character. His focus seemed more on a little petty revenge than on their mission. He knew that Roseau had enjoyed killing the men at the office and wanted some more of that buzz, if Young could provide it for him all well and good. If he didn't, and if this went too far, well, he had contingencies for that.

Early the next morning, the day of the game, Adam, Isobel, Stella and Ron were up early enjoying a room service breakfast. It was served on the garden terrace that was part of the suite of rooms they now occupied. It wasn't exactly alfresco time of year, but it was a beautiful morning, the sun was up, and there was hardly a cloud in the sky. It was such a contrast to the endless rain they had endured for the past few days that an outside breakfast seemed a good idea. Whilst they ate Adam outlined the plan of action he had come up with the night before.

It was an exceedingly simple plan whose success or failure relied on getting a message to the people that had been following them. In Adam's opinion, these people were smart enough to find out that they were to attend the England v All Blacks game that day and would try to locate them there. He knew what two of these guys looked like and was hoping he could spot one and deliver a message to him.

This message was that they had the information and were prepared to deal with them on its hand over. With a message delivered and the supply of his mobile phone number, he hoped they would contact him and from there be able to identify their pursuers. Really, it was a shot in the dark but was better than to sit and wait for them to kick down the door. Whilst at the game he wanted Stella to download the data to his laptop and begin preparation for uploading the information to a website.

The plan called for Isobel not to go to the game, but to remain in the hotel with Stella. Although Isobel had no problem with the plan per se she had no intention of staying in the hotel, she had come to London to watch this game and had been looking forward to it. It was just about all Adam and Dan had talked about for the week she had been with them. They had built it up to the match of the century, and she wanted to see Dan in action.

After waiting for a minute or two, for them to finish eating she then said,

"I can see the sense in what you are suggesting, and the options are very few, but I don't want to sit around the hotel, I came to London to see this game and see it I will. Anyway if I do go it will appear more natural to these people, whoever they are"

Adam started to reply, but Ron cut in with "What happens if you don't spot either of these two men? I agree that they will be looking for you there, but that doesn't mean you are going to spot them or even if you do, be able to give them your message."

"Yes I've thought about that, and am working on the premise that they will try to follow me. So I thought I would go the Carlton Towers, assume they are following and, attempt to make the contact there"

"Assuming things again are we? You've been out of the game to long, but yes I would follow you back if I were them, and if Isobel is with you I think it will appear as though you are relaxed about the situation. Don't forget, from their point of view all you have done so far is change hotels. They don't know you have met with Stella or that there is a copy of this information, so by taking Isobel, you put out the message that you are not too concerned, which may make the opposition relax somewhat"

Isobel cut in after a little smile to Ron, with "I know you are worried honey, but I will be okay. All we have to do is give these people a message, and once that is done, you and Ron can handle the rest. They are hardly likely to try and kidnap us in broad daylight, are they?"

"No, they're not"

Adam had introduced Ron before breakfast arrived, as an old Navy buddy that was going to help them. It was obvious from Isobel and Stella's faces that they wondered how. Isobel's little smile indicated that she was definitely warming to the idea of having him around.

Stella had said almost nothing all morning but now added "So your idea is to find out whom these people are, then why would I be putting all this data on a website?"

"Okay, first the website, from what you have told me, it is safe to assume" looking at Ron before he continued "You have always wanted this information to come out and those that need exposing and prosecuting, exposed and prosecuted. By publishing it all, we do that, and it will also stop others looking for us to get it if it is no longer any value to them. Additionally if it is a cover up, rather than someone trying to get it, then we have to hope they start to run and hide rather than coming for us.

Now the 'then what'; as you've said, in your records is information about which policemen have been in Jonathan's pay. From this, we should be able to find out those that have not been, and there must be plenty we can approach. We need to find the best person to talk to, and I want you to do that first"

"Yeah, okay I can do that."

Ron then added "We also have another option here I'm not sure if he has mentioned this, but when Adam worked with me, we worked for DIS which is military intelligence. Because of the nature of the work we did, there are avenues to contact both the secret intelligence service and the security service. Therefore, there are the police, MI5 and 6 that can provide protection for you three, whilst the perpetrators are caught."

"Couldn't we go straight to them?" was Stella's reply

"We could" added Adam "But, we have no idea whom these people are, so what do we say? We think someone is looking for us, but have no idea who and can only a guess as to why. "

Ron then said "It is a long shot I know but better that waiting for them to show up. I also think it very unlikely anything would happen at the stadium there are far too many witnesses, and my bet is at the hotel"

To which Stella replied "So what happens to me if you don't come back?"

"You go through your data, reference that to senior Metropolitan Police Officers, which you will be able to find on the web. Get the address of the most senior you think you can trust and I'll bet you can do that, then you knock on his front door until he answers it and tell him or her everything you know."

This received a nod of approval from Stella. At this juncture, Isobel asked if they could go back inside. They had been out there for over an hour, and she was getting cold.

Once back inside and seated on the couches drinking the last of the coffee, Stella told them that she could see a problem with the plan. She didn't think they realised the amount of data that she had, which she said was in the order of Terabytes, and that they had a dedicated fiber optics line in the offices, both their new one and at the International. With even this ultra-fast connection, it had taken hours to upload all the data. In the hotel, they were limited to whatever the hotel provided, which might mean it could take days to download it all.

To Stella's surprise Adam had actually considered this, his suggestion was to download the index or directory first, which they must have to organise that much information. Stella agreed they did. Then the files on people taking payment from Jonathan that he hoped would be illustrated by the index. Again, Stella agreed that was feasible. He hadn't foreseen the amount of data, but that could be quickly remedied with external hard drives, which he said he would go and buy as soon as he had finished his coffee.

The Roof Garden was only a few minutes' walk from

Brompton Road. It was also in the opposite direction of the Carlton Towers, which he thought would still be watched. It took him no more than thirty minutes to return with six external hard drives of a terabyte each. Armed with these, Adam's laptop and a cable, Stella plugged in and logged into the hotels internet network and began to work.

By now it was approaching midday. The game started at 3.00 pm, so they needed to be on their way before one, it was time to get ready. Ron already was, so sat down in front of the TV and switched on the news, to see if there had been any developments.

Isobel and Adam went to their room, which as, with all good hotels, contained an en-suite bathroom. Pulling off his trackies Adam headed for the shower, only to have the door of it opened a few seconds later by a naked Isobel.

"This might be our last shower you aren't going to have it alone."

It wasn't the biggest shower in the world half the size of the one Adam had attached to his bedroom, in which the two of them spent a lot of time. But it was still big enough for Adam to scoop Isobel up into his arms. Her legs immediately fastened around him, and they made love until it was time to get dressed.

Suited and booted, Adam and Isobel climbed into the taxi which had been flagged down by the doormen, quickly departing on the drive to Twickenham. Ron watched them get in as he got into one of his own. He had gone down to the lobby and out onto Pavilion Road, on which the hotel stood, fifteen minutes before, had done a reconnaissance and phoned the room to confirm it was clear. They didn't expect the hotel to be watched, but it didn't hurt to take precautions.

Although Ron was also a big rugby fan, it would be difficult for him not to be, working with Adam all those years, he wouldn't see the game. For one, he didn't have a ticket; they had sold out weeks before but more importantly he could spend the three hours that they would be in the stadium looking for the opposition.

Whether the opposition had managed to get tickets to get into the stadium was a much debated point but, it was a foregone conclusion that they wouldn't be able to get all their men in there. Nor would they want to. If tickets were to be had, he would have had four men inside with other teams outside on foot and in cars, ready to respond. Therefore, he would do everything he could to spot those outside the ground.

He had spent many years performing covert surveillance and was very good at it. He wasn't known by the opposition and thought that would give them a big advantage in the identification of those who were looking for Adam and Isobel.

Match days at Twickenham were busy, to say the least, with eighty thousand people making their way there, mostly by tube and buses, and the streets were heaving as Adam and Isobel arrived. They got out of the cab on Whitton Road, at the junction with Rugby Road and joined the thronged masses making their way through the turnstiles, and into the stadium.

Their seats were in L6 just below the Royal Box and next to the tunnel. Police presence at Twickenham had always been light with less than eighty officers on duty in and around the ground. Those in the grounds would be around the tunnel and at the entrances with additional security staff around the royal box, which gave Adam and Isobel an extra sense of security once in their seats.

Once seated, Adam didn't want to move again until the end of the game, or if he spotted either of the two men. So whilst he was out picking up the hard drives he also bought a flask which he had filled with good coffee from the hotel, laced with a little brandy from the minibar. By 2.15, they were in their seats.

He rang Dan briefly on the way over as he had done that morning and the night before from the taxi. He hadn't wanted to go into any detail just in case their mobiles were being intercepted, which was a fair assumption, considering all that had happened. Adam reassured him that they were safe and in control of the situation and that they would see him after the match back at the Carlton Towers

At ten minutes before 3.00, the national anthems of both countries were sung and the game commenced. Dan was out there with number 6 on his shirt, chasing down the kickoff which England took. It was a great start they managed to pin the All Blacks down inside their 22 and keep the pressure on, which ten minutes later resulted in a penalty being given, and a 3 point advantage to England following the kick.

By half time England still narrowly had the lead, 10 points to 7, it was going to be a game of attrition, being decided by who tired first. As the second half began, pressure from the All Blacks forced a penalty, which squared up the game. That was followed by another twenty minutes later, with ten minutes to go England was losing 10 − 13. The game had been back and forth, a hard fought match, and as expected was extremely close.

Then a kick from the All Blacks 10 was intercepted by Dan at the half way line. He charged forward supported by a winger on his right shoulder and the outside center on his left with only three of the All Black players between him and the try line. At the 22, a dummy pass left and an offload right to the winger as an All Black player tackled him, sent the winger on to score a try under the posts. The kick was good giving the lead back to England, with a $17 - 13$ score.

The game was not dead yet, the All Blacks kept pushing forward but the England defense was outstanding, holding the All Blacks five meters out. With three minutes to go England gave away a penalty, but as the All Blacks needed a try to win, they tapped and went, the ball given to the loose head prop. Dan, as usual in the right place and the right time, hit the man so hard the ball popped loose, and was picked up by the English fly half, who kicked the ball into touch just short of the half way line.

An excellent steal at the lineout secured the ball for England which they mauled forward; all the players were exhausted by now. If England could keep the ball in the All Blacks half, they would secure the win. Keeping on their feet, the English forwards hit the maul driving it forward and infield until almost on the All Blacks 22. With less than 2 minutes to go a pocket was formed and the ball was passed back to their fly half, who kicked a drop goal, which sailed through the posts.

At this, the mostly English crowd erupted as it gave the English an almost unassailable lead of 20 -13 lead. The All Blacks could draw with a converted try but had less than 60 seconds to do so. From the restart, the ball was run back at them, but they managed to hold the All Blacks at their own 22 until the clock wound down. At an All Black fumble, the ball was retrieved and kicked into touch as the game ended.

Chapter 26

It was certainly a good a game as expected, unfortunately for Adam not one he could concentrate on, or even enjoy. Throughout the match, he had scanned the stadium looking for some clue as to who followed them but saw nothing. Fortunately Ron had more success.

He had been to Twickenham many times before so knew it well, he also knew what it's like leaving there, which predicted what the opposition would have to do to guarantee following them after the match. That would be to have men stationed at the car park to the north beside the main turnstiles, more to the west between the stadium and the school, which served as a secondary car park on match days and still more along Rugby Road, where most spectators would walk to the tubes, buses and taxi ranks.

They would need to be in communication with each other, and would be easy to spot. They would also need to be in cars, which were quick to respond, meaning they couldn't be parked because of the mass of traffic and people, and therefore would be constantly on the move. He arrived at 1.45 and wandered around until just before kickoff. By this time, the streets had quieted down, letting him discern the chaff from the wheat.

By half time, he'd spotted several potential targets; two men to the west between the stadium and the school, two men to the east on Rugby Road and a further three at the turnstiles. He also thought he had identified another man going between these three loose groups.

Using the cars in the car park to the north as cover Ron could move from one side of the car park to the other to keep them all in sight. Sure enough a little way into the second half, the last man he had identified was moving from one group to the next. As a roar erupted from the stadium with about ten minutes to go, which Ron assumed correctly was an English try; he began to notice two cars that were cruising around the stadium both of which had stopped, ever so briefly to speak to the walking man.

There would probably be a third car somewhere he thought as he watched. He had also tried to apprise the men he had seen, all of them were white, and all of them looked capable, as well. The walking man could be of a Mediterranean origin or even South American perhaps as he seemed to have slightly darker skin than the rest. That would be that he was the boss, if not of the whole enterprise, at least of this surveillance exercise.

With that amount of man power and the assumption that they had three cars, it would make following Adam and Isobel back to the hotel relatively simple. Ron had to work on the assumption that these people believed that Adam and Isobel were staying in London. As Adam's car was still in the Carlton Towers car park, the most likely mode of transport these men would expect Adam and Isobel to take back to their hotel would be either taxi or Tube.

With this in mind, Ron had told Adam to use the north

east turnstiles as point of egress from the stadium and to go toward the first taxi rank on Rugby Road. They should wait for a taxi there he would join the queue a few places behind and keep tabs on anybody he had spotted. Ron had a small digital Leica camera with him to which he had a telephoto lens attached. The thing was tiny but captured excellent high resolution images. He had taken shots of all the men and their cars and would later download them, blow them up and use them to identify these people. He thought that could be achieved quite quickly, and with relative ease by an associate or two back at his office at Thames House.

He doubted whether he would be able identify them all, but all of them he had seen looked as though they could have been ex-military, so that was a good place to start. And, of course there were also both databases they kept on known national and international criminals. And terrorists for that matter not that they had considered that option.

He was beginning to feel a lot more confident that Adam's plan might work. He had also toyed with the idea of approaching the walking man as he now called him, give him Adam's message and see what happened. He dismissed this as it would give away the big advantage they had, of him being unknown to this group.

At the end of the game, Adam and Isobel filed out along with the rest of the spectators. Adam was on edge, having had no success identifying anyone and was now looking at the people that surrounded them with unease, tensed to react at the slightest provocation. The crowd slowly moved towards the exits with every one of Adam's instincts attuned to detect a danger.

The danger hadn't yet materialised, but with every minute of exposure Adam's anxiety escalated. For fifteen minutes, they went with the tide of people exiting the stadium and making their way toward their transport home until finally they were in a queue for a taxi.

There had been a row of taxis waiting, but far more people than taxis, so they would be waiting for one for a little while. He saw Ron join the queue four places back, and whilst there was no obvious communication between them, Ron had all his fingers and thumbs spread out indicating that he had spotted ten watchers.

Ten thought Adam, more than he expected, but at least part of the plan had worked. But, that knowledge only served to spur his apprehension. Any one of them or others that Ron had not tagged could silently and stealthily slide a knife into his or Isobel's back. Or a couple of sniper's bullets from one of the innumerable windows in the buildings that surrounded them could end it all.

The rate of fresh taxi arrival had slowed, and it was another twenty five minutes before they were at the head of the queue and into a taxi. There were more arriving now as the roads around them began to clear a little. Ron would be in one too within a couple of minutes.

As Adam's taxi pulled away, Ron saw the walking man get into a black Audi A6. One that he had spotted earlier with a single driver, of whom he thought he had a good photo.

Four of the other men, then got into a Range Rover, a car he hadn't seen before, rather than pull out his camera; he made a mental note of the number plate. That left the other three whom he assumed would be in the second car he had spotted earlier. That made a total of eleven arrayed against them.

Although this was a lot to go up against, they now had

the element of surprise. What he would like to do right now was let Adam now what the situation was and wished they had bought a new mobile for Adam. He didn't want to give the game away, so couldn't risk phoning Adam's mobile in case they had an intercept running, this was definitely a mistake, but too late to remedy now.

He was two cars behind the Audi, two more behind the Range Rover and another three behind Adam's cab as they pulled away from the lights into Whitton Road. As was to be expected on a match Saturday afternoon, the roads were very busy, but Ron managed to keep them all in sight for the majority of the journey. As they entered central London, Ron did send Adam a text which said,

Saw the game today and thought of you, I bet you were there, Dan had a terrific game, and it was a success. We are now behind you on points but will catch up soon enough, and I'll bet we beat you there in the end

He hoped Adam would understand that he was being followed and that Ron would try to get to the hotel before he did. The traffic was just as bad as or even worse than Ron thought it was going to be. It was a slow going along Twickenham Road, London Road, High St and the Chiswick High Road, and when they reached Kensington, the traffic slowed to a crawl. These days it was far quicker to walk around London than drive.

Part way up Kensington, just as it turns into Knightsbridge, he told the driver to pull over and let him out. He walked past the Audi which had been directly in front of the cab and then past the Range Rover, which was about six cars behind Adam and Isobel's taxi.

He walked slowly beside the cab for a while hoping Adam would see him, and he did. As Adam looked up at him, he signaled for them to stay where they were. Ron slowly increased his speed to make it across the road and over the junction onto Sloane Street before the taxi did. He could still see both of the followers.

This was the risky part. He really didn't want to take his eyes of the taxi or the cars behind, but he needed to get to the hotel before they did. They knew that there was the possibility of being shot on sight that was the calculated gamble they'd chosen to take. One, whoever it was that wanted them wouldn't be prepared to open up on a taxi on a street in the middle of London, and, two, that Stella was the main target and to get to her, the opponents needed Adam and Isobel alive.

As all three cars moved through the junction, he sprinted ahead until he approached West Halkin St. He then walked around the corner to the front of the Carlton Towers, two minutes ahead of the rest.

As Ron neared the hotel entrance, the other car he spotted at the stadium stopped beside Cadogan Place Gardens and disgorged its three passengers. The driver stayed with the vehicle and kept the engine running. The three crossed the road and took up position close to the entrance.

A smart ploy, as they still had sufficient numbers in the cars behind. Adam's taxi was just about to pull up under the portico that covered the entrance to the hotel as screams and shouts suddenly erupted from the gardens opposite. Then more screams broke out from Sloane Street, momentarily diverting Ron's attention from the three men waiting for Adam as he looked to see what had caused the commotion.

The minibuses carrying black clad and masked men dropped their passengers off at the top and bottom of Sloane Street and beside Cadogan Place Gardens. From there, they ran into shops grabbing everything they could easily carry, attacked shoppers on the streets and those walking through the gardens with pepper spray, grabbing watches, purses, wallets, anything of value.

It was a scene of utter pandemonium as shoppers ran down Sloane Street others ran up, colliding with each other at the junction of West Halkin. More were running through the park and into the entrance of the Carlton Towers. Many ran out into Sloane Street, and traffic instantly came to a standstill, as drivers avoided pedestrians and gawked at the scene unfolding around them.

It was all part of Roseau's design he wanted Sloane Street blocked off, but left an avenue of escape open along West Halkin Street.

It was into this chaos that Adam and Isobel emerged upon leaving the confines of the black cab, now under the portico of the Carlton Towers hotel. As they did so, the three men began to move towards them. Adam looked over his shoulder to see if he could see what was causing the panic, completely unaware of the approaching men, only a few meters away.

As the three men neared Adam and Isobel, Ron ran past, his mind back on the three men, having realised that what was happening on Sloane Street was a deliberate distraction. He noticed how close they were bunched together, one slightly in front and their eyes upon their quarry, not on him.

They all had their hands under their jackets presumably on their weapons. Ron ran toward them, rugby tackling the first with as much force his bulk could muster, he took the two behind him as well, with all four of them ending up sprawled on the pavement.

The first was out for the count, having cracked his head hard against the curb, but the other two were recovering swiftly. The first to realise what had happened was getting to his knees and pulling out his gun. As Ron rose up from the tangle of bodies he kicked out, taking the man on the chin, whose head to snap back audibly.

The third, with his gun already out trained on Adam was just beginning to realise what was happening. As the synapses of the third fired beginning to evaluate the situation, and was bringing his weapon around to bear on Ron. Fortunately for Ron, he was too slow, the Glock the second man had drawn was now leaving Ron's hand flying the two meters between them and smashing into the man's forehead, right between his eyes.

Three out, thought Ron, but lots more to go.

Adam initially tried to get Isobel into the hotel lobby, but that wasn't going to work. Stunned shoppers were running up the steps, others left and yet more going right, it was like a scene from an alien invasion movie. Before he knew it, Ron was by his side thrusting one of the guns he'd taken from the fallen three into his hands.

Ron gestured back down Halkin, to four more men coming their way, all carrying 9mm automatics. The two in front, twenty meters or so from their colleagues, had their weapons levelled aiming in Ron's direction. Their instructions were to keep Adam alive until he gave them the information they wanted. Both began firing as Adam and Ron ducked behind the back of the cab, pulling Isobel to the ground with them.

They knew that people had been hit behind from the screams that followed the shots, and both wanted to prevent any more innocent bloodshed. As the assailants rounded the back of the cab Adam and Ron raised their guns, shooting a man each twice in the chest, neither had noticed or expected them to be armed.

Roseau and De Costa watched the carnage from the corner of Halkin and Sloane; they could see they were down to two men and the driver of the car on the curb, beside Cadogan Place Gardens. Screaming could still be heard from all directions, along with the smashing of shop windows as their diversionary measure took full force. The black clothed and masked men had been told not to touch any cars or get in their way unless they were police, just in case Roseau and his men were in them, but everything else was fair game.

Roseau turned to De Costa "What the fuck is happening? Who is the guy with Young?" it was more rhetorical than anything. "This shouldn't be happening; they are a complete bunch of wankers. I will finish this myself."

He began to walk quickly toward the portico, only to make it a few meters when he was stopped by a sledge hammer blow from behind, shortly followed by another as De Costa put two rounds in his back from his silenced and concealed Glock. As he walked past Roseau, he said:

"Sorry mate, but I told you to forget about Young. You gave me no choice, in times like these, sacrificing an operative can be the best way to ensure your future success."

Then he dropped a leather wallet next to the body which he kicked gently under Roseau's jacket.

As De Costa walked away most of the screams subsided with the exception of those of the injured. As the screams stopped, they were replaced by cheers, followed by,

"Come here you bastards".

The remaining two men turned to look. Behind them lay their boss, face down and further back a dozen or more burly guys in suits, were kicking the shit out of the men in black. It was definitely time to walk away from this catastrophe.

Calm slowly descended on Halkin and Sloane as the rest of the black clad men decided they had enough; shoppers on a Saturday afternoon where one thing, but these gorillas in suits where something else entirely. Those that could, ran, those that couldn't because of various broken bones didn't. The quiet didn't last long as no sooner than it began it was replaced by sirens as the police arrived.

Both Ron and Adam had been pretty much sitting on Isobel in their effort to protect her, they were only alerted to the fact by Isobel's words

"Do you think you could get off me now?"

Both stood quickly, with Adam pulling Isobel to her feet but still wary of attack. Ron went over to the three men he had initially tackled; one was attempting to get to his feet. One was unconscious, and the other he had kicked in the head was dead; from the look of his neck it was broken.

The one attempting to rise got a kick in his ribs as a reward and fell back with a grunt. Pulling some plastic cuffs from his pocket, Ron rolled both of the men that were still breathing over onto their faces and cuffed their hands behind their backs as the shout of,

"Get the fuck off me," could be heard behind him.

As he turned to look, he was stunned to see Dan Young dragging two of the black clad men by the hair toward him.

"Nice one mate," Ron said "Long time no see, how was the game?"

The bus carrying the England team had not been far behind them. As the bus turned into Sloane St, the players saw the black clad men or some of them at least jumping out of a minibus and proceeding to go on a rampage. All to a man got off and went to help; they had, in all, detained 15 of the gang members with the rest managing escape on foot.

. . .

It was going to be a long night sorting all this out. First the police along with the armed response units arrived en mass and cordoned off the area, only allowing ambulances in. There were three hundred or more people inside the cordon; most of them stunned shoppers. A line of armed Police made its way down Sloane Street with their H&K MP5's at the ready, reports of gun shots making them very cautious. Another line made its way up Sloane Street, from the Sloane Square end and yet another along Cadogan Place.

As they came across the stunned shoppers, each was told to put his or her hands on their head and was checked for weapons. Behind each line came more police, questioning anyone they encountered as the lines moved forward, nobody was released. It took more than an hour before the two lines of Police working along Sloane Street finally met at the junction of West Halkin and Sloane, the epicenter. The third was holding position 50 meters from the Carlton Towers and spreading out over Cadogan Place Gardens.

Satisfied that they had what ever had occurred contained, several armed officers came forward. Ron, Adam and Isobel, who had been helping with the wounded walked forward to meet them, all three with their hands on their heads. As they neared Ron called out

"I am with DI, I have my identity cards in my wallet in my jacket pocket" nodding down to his right, "I am also armed" nodding to his left.

One officer held his MP5 centimeters from Ron's sternum whilst another put his hand inside his jacket, firstly removing the Sig Sauer, then his wallet. After taking a step or two back he checked the identity card and then again Ron's face. Once satisfied, he said:

"Okay, you can put your hands down now. Could you

please tell us what happened here?" Beckoning Ron forward.

Ron did as requested, after a ten minute conversation with the policemen he stepped back to join Adam and Isobel, still under the steady gaze and MP5 of the other policemen.

The officer, who had spoken to Ron, told the other that it was okay, meaning he could lower his MP5, and walked back to the rest of the police gathered at the perimeter, returning almost immediately with many more of his fellow officers.

He said to Ron, "I would like you three to remain here until I have had time to talk to some of the others."

"Do you mean here, here or could we perhaps wait in the hotel?"

A frown was all he received but he did let the officer that was with them take them into the hotel to wait.

The lobby of the Carlton is big, but it was standing room only, as was the lounge next to it. Many of those inside were suffering from shock and the after effects of pepper spray. Slowly the area began to clear as the police made their way through questioning everybody.

The injured were taken to hospital, those detained by the rugby team where taken away in the backs of police cars and the dead to a mortuary somewhere. It was another two hours before room appeared in the lounge, which Adam, Ron, Isobel and Dan who had been standing together all this time, made full advantage of and were followed by the rest of the England team.

Sometime later, they had all stopped looking at their watches long ago, the accumulated bunch were addressed by yet another policemen. He told them that a picture of the incident was beginning to emerge and that he was going to do them a favor.

As they all were staying in the hotel, he would let them go to their rooms but asked they stay within the confines of the hotel. And, that there would be police on the doors to make sure they did. He then added that they would be back early tomorrow when statements would be taken from all of them and that some of them would be asked to attend the station for formal questioning. At this he left, only to return a minute later to say,

"I would appreciate it if none of you talked to the media."

There was an audible sigh of relief followed by a stifled laugh as one of players asked if they could get the bar open.

As if by magic, a bartender suddenly appeared behind the bar and was immediately inundated with orders. A couple of the players did get up to go to their rooms, but most stayed for a drink or more importantly, to talk about what had happened.

Dan began to introduce his brother, Isobel and Ron to all his teammates and gradually Ron told them of the day's events. He kept out some of the details, namely about what he did for a living, and about Stella. After a glass of wine, Isobel decided she had definitely had enough for the day and asked Adam to take her up to their room.

Chapter 27

About the same time, De Costa was finalising his immediate arrangements. The wallet he had kicked under Roseau's body had in it his driving license which had on it the address of the house they shared in Kensington. The first thing he had done upon leaving the Carlton Towers was to return there to pick up his belongings, arriving long before the police organised themselves on Sloane Street.

He had previously packed all his belongings; he knew there was nothing that would compromise his mission left there. Before leaving he placed a folder full of documents, and the hard drives taken from Jonathan's office on a table in the dining room. Then locking the door he left for good. From there, he had taken a bus then the tube train and eventually a taxi out to the Wandsworth warehouse.

The warehouse was now looking like a hostel, or more precisely a bizarre mix of hostel, medical center and warehouse. He had moved the core of his warriors as he called them, into it, after discovering that Young had been outside the house in Hammersmith. Although Young had no more than glanced at the house and continued by, unaware that twenty terrorists had been living there for several months, De Costa moved them to the warehouse immediately.

There were cots everywhere, and not all occupied as yet. Before turning in himself, he logged onto a website and left a message. Once deciphered it would instruct the rest of his warriors to make their way to the UK. As had been planned months ago, they were to check into hotels close to the airports they arrived in around the country, and wait for further instructions.

Waking the next morning, Adam knew it was going to be one of those days, not that the weather was bad; in fact it was another beautiful sunny morning. He should have been mightily relieved that whoever it was that had tried to kidnap them, had failed, and the men had been either killed or arrested.

It wasn't only the thought of talking to the police all day and again unravelling the mess he had somehow found himself in. The black cloud hadn't yet lifted; the mess with Jonathan should be at an end. But still Stella's data and the horrifying details it contained remained along with the question, of what to do about it.

The night before Ron had eventually been allowed to go to the Roof Gardens. But not until after producing the key card and explaining he was not staying at the Carlton which had no rooms left for him to do so. As a member of DI, it was difficult for the police to insist he stay and let him go as long as returned first thing in the morning. Although they had phoned Stella when the majority of the police had left, she was close to panic when Ron got there.

Overnight two bright blue incident vehicles had

appeared outside, which Adam looked at with dread from the first floor restaurant window. That's where I will be spending most of the day he thought sourly; still it was better than the cell he spent the night in recently.

Adam's trepidation was well founded, he, Isobel and Ron were separately interviewed for two hours each. There was no need for them to prepare stories, they told it exactly as they had seen it, with but a single exception, no-one mentioned Stella. Strangely enough no one asked about Stella either.

Next it was the turn of the England rugby squad; they all filed in, in groups of four. Each group was in one of the two interview rooms each of the incident vehicles provided. They were questioned for a while. It was then the turn of the hotel staff, those that were on duty in the lobby, lounge and at the hotel entrance the day before. After each interview, the interviewee was asked to go back to the lounge or their room and wait there. This whole procedure lasted ten hours, when finally they were all asked to assemble back in the lounge.

Deputy Assistant Commissioner Layton stood before the assembled throng; he first thanked everyone for their cooperation. He then told them all that they could leave, but maybe they would be called in again if new information came to light. He then said, that Adam, Isobel and Ron would be asked to attend the police station the next day for formal interviews.

As the Commissioner left, most of the crowd left soon after him, with only a few of the players staying behind for a drink. Dan, Ron, Adam and Isobel, sat together by the window overlooking the gardens opposite; none felt like drinking. After briefly discussing their options they decided as they still had the suite at the Roof Gardens, they should check out of the Carlton and go there.

. . .

Once back at the Roof Gardens they sat in the suite lounge talking. Dan was brought up to speed concerning Stella, who had spent the day trolling through her data. She had downloaded a good deal, but there was still a lot more. But she did have a list of what she thought was everyone who had been in Jonathans pay, and quite a list it was. They also discussed what they should do about it as it seemed the danger to them had passed. They couldn't reach a final decision and as they had the suite until Wednesday, Stella would continue with her work till then and from that point they would decide what should be done with it.

The decision put off for a couple days talk became a little more jovial, mostly with Dan's retelling of the moment the rugby players entered Sloane St in the coach, and their pilling out into the rioters. He described the moment their team bus turned into Sloane Street, to be confronted with what looked like the normal London traffic jam. Then the driver said to the passengers closest to him, that there appeared to be a robbery underway, after seeing several men wearing masks run out of a shop.

As the players left the bus to help, more such incidents happened further up the street. It was the looks on the rioter's faces that amused Dan more than anything. One second they were happily attacking their helpless victims, the next confronted by a not so helpless rugby player. They might have been masked, but the fear showed instantly in their eyes.

After a breakfast together next morning, Ron, Adam and Isobel caught a cab to the allotted police station, arriving a little after 10.00 AM. Before they left the hotel Ron called his office, briefly explaining his absence that day and quite possibly the next. He was damn sure they already knew of the incident and his involvement in it.

Towards the end of the conversation, he said that he had a bunch of photographs, mostly of people he wanted identified, along with three car registration number plates that he would like information on. On hanging up he caught Adam's eye, who was sitting close to him and said softly,

"Best be thorough, and our databases are much better than theirs and might turn up something they don't."

None of them had speculated on how long they would be there but after 5 hours, at 3.15pm they were allowed to leave but would need to return the next day. The priority now was clothes. None of them had expected to away from home so long, so Kensington High St seemed the obvious choice. After an afternoon's shopping Isobel was feeling far better, she had enjoyed the rugby game, although obviously not the fracas after, but her favorite sport was shopping. So she shopped for all of them, Dan and Stella included.

At the checkout of the first shop Adam pulled out his debit card to pay, only to have Isobel push a credit card into the cashiers hand, before she could take his,

"Jonathan caused this mess, so at the very least he can pay for it"

So it continued all the way back to the Roof Gardens, it was incredible the amount of shops they encountered in that half mile walk, that Isobel just had to explore. By the time they got to the hotel, they were all inundated with more bags than they could easily carry.

Stella had a good day; she was feeling much more secure and as a result had done loads of work on the files. Much of it was now ready to be published, if that was what the choice they made. Most of the files in the cloud cache were now on the external hard drives. She had even roped Dan in, who had been having a crash course on industrial espionage, which apparently he was both enjoying and was quite good at.

The TV was on in the corner as they arrived as it had been all day, tuned to BBC news at present, although they had been constantly flicking through the various news channels.

Ever since the events that Saturday afternoon, TV crews had been camped out next to the gardens opposite the Carlton Towers and had interviewed every conceivable person they could. The speculations were rife but as yet none of the presenters had made any connection with those events, and what had happened a week before in Clerkenwell, of which reporting had almost completely dropped off the air.

What continued to bother them all was the absence of any mention of Stella, but taking the positive that this represented, it allowed them all to go out for dinner.

Isobel's last visit to Le Gavroche had not been pleasant at all. It was a restaurant she liked very much, and therefore decided to see if they could get a table there that night. Giving Jonathan's name to the maitre'd might swing it, and it did; she would again charge the meal to her credit card. Although she hadn't realised it yet, Isobel now was quite a rich woman, owning several houses and apartments in London, as well as the Park Lane one which alone was worth nearly three million. She would also discover weeks later that there were several off shore bank accounts.

Buoyed up by the extravagant meal the night before, Adam, Isobel and Ron did as they were requested and turned up at the police station early next morning. This time they were not separated, but all three shepherded into a single room, in which waited Layton and Clive Gooding. They were all asked to sit before Layton began,

"We think we have a basic explanation for the events both at Clerkenwell and outside the Carlton Towers, but before I begin do any of you know a Stella Ward?" was Layton's opening statement.

Working on the principle of honesty which was basically how they had all agreed to handle the interviews that they had endured Isobel said,

"Yes I do, she works or used to work with my husband"

Layton asked if she had spoken to her lately, to which Isobel replied that she had.

"When was that?"

"She rang me and few days ago, Friday night I believe."

"Could I ask the nature of your conversation?"

"She said she had just gotten home from holiday and that she wanted to meet, I told her that I had been asked to identify a body earlier that day, it was Jonathan, who had apparently been shot."

"That was it?"

"Pretty much, I said I would ring her back and arrange to meet up but after what happened on Saturday I haven't as yet."

"Okay, you have a contact number for her I presume, could I have it?"

"Yes, absolutely, I have it at the hotel and can give it to you later."

Seemingly satisfied with this, Layton then continued.

He was looking at Ron.

"It would appear that your initial assessment of the events on Saturday afternoon was correct. The people that tried to kidnap both Mr. Young and Mrs. Mason appear to be the same that killed Jonathan Mason and his employees.

We are fairly sure that it was concerning the information that Mason kept on his hard drives, which we also believe they were after. Although we are uncertain as to whether this was for their personal gain, or to protect themselves, or another party. We have recovered certain files including the hard drives at an address discovered on one of the men that was shot, that corroborates this.

But, here it gets a little murky, this man, I will not give you his name as yet, was shot twice in the back.

You claim" still looking at Ron "that you shot one person in the chest with your own weapon and that Mr. Young here shot another, again in the chest, with the weapon that you had taken from one of your attackers. You also claim that you shot them only as they rounded the back of the cab, with the intention of shooting you, and therefore it was self-defense."

He paused before continuing "The problem here is who shot this other man? We know the gun found on him was used at Clerkenwell. But the gun that shot and killed him was discovered under a taxi fifty meters up the road there are no prints on this weapon, so we don't know who fired it."

This was new information. None of the three had even noticed another dead man in the street, but that was hardly surprising with all the confusion.

"We are still very confused as to why these people would want to kidnap Mr. Young and Mrs. Mason, and have to work on the assumption that they were still after the information on the hard drives"

Adam cut in here "I don't understand, you said that they already had the drives, so why would they be coming after us?"

"Hold on a minute please I'm about to get to that, the drives we retrieved are all corrupted, I think that was the terminology that our analysts used. They think that, when they were taken out of the computers a sophisticated piece of software scrambled all the files as a precaution, using a high powered magnet. That's our expert's opinion.

"Either that or before one of them was killed they managed to do something similar. I really can't comment upon that it is not in my area of expertise. That still begs the question as to why were they looking for you two" Layton said as he looked at Adam and Isobel, who both shrugged.

Layton waited for a little while as he searched the faces in front of him,

"The only explanation we can come up with is that, for some reason, they thought you had copies of this material."

No one said anything for a minute or so. Adam, Isobel and Ron certainly weren't going to divulge any information, unless they had to.

So Layton continued "Is there any reason you know of why they think this?"

Adam and Isobel both shook their heads.

"Okay fair enough, this brings us back to Miss Ward; she seems to be the office data guru. She didn't say anything about hard disks or backups, did she, Mrs. Mason?"

"Well no, I was very upset when I spoke to her I had just come back from identifying Jonathan's body, and we spoke only very briefly. She may have wanted to say more, or she may have wanted to talk about it when we met; I honestly don't know."

"When you give us her contact details perhaps we can get to the bottom of this."

Isobel simply nodded.

"Another area that bothers me is quite how you fit in

here Mr. James; you said you dropped into the hotel to see Mr. Young. The two of you used to work together at DI isn't that right, and were waiting for him outside when he arrived?"

"That's about it."

"But you were armed; do you normally go about armed Mr. James?"

"I do when I am working, sir, I was in London to see an informant. I knew there was an International that day as I had tried to get tickets, but they had sold out. I thought Adam might be in town so decided to ring him he was just about to go into the stadium, and we made a date for a drink after the match."

"Did you see this informant?"

"Yes."

"Can I have his or her name?"

"No."

"I see."

"I have told you about my work which is primarily antiterrorism. That as you can imagine relies heavily on informant information. These informants are confidential, should I start giving out their names and addresses I won't have them much longer."

"Okay, let's get on, there were four men killed that day, three of them we have just discussed, the fourth you Mr. George have told us that you kicked him in the head as he was drawing his weapon, that is correct, yes?"

Ron admitted it was.

"On top of these four, another four were arrested, in addition to those arrested for burglary, assault, disturbing the peace, I won't go on. But these four were accompanying the ones that were after Mr. Young. One of them is still in a coma, one under heavy sedation due to his injuries and the other two aren't saying much.

"This much we have been able to establish, the cars they came in are registered to a private security contractor, and the owner of this company is being questioned as we speak. So far, he claims to know nothing, other than he contracted out some of his guys to the gentleman we found dead in the street, shot in the back."

Layton then continued "Another puzzle is that of the other lot; I'll call them rioters for want of a more accurate description. We have no idea what sparked them off, although there are several similarities to events that occurred earlier this year. One or two of those we arrested are a little more cooperative than the rest. They don't seem to know much, but what they told us is this.

"They were being paid to terrorize, which seems very peculiar; apparently they were contacted on the Blackberry Messenger service told where to meet and what to do, which was to cause as much havoc as possible.

"It also appears this is not the first time this has happened. We have to assume they were employed by our dead man in the street, as a diversion. But have no way of knowing whether this same man instigated the riots earlier in the year, or if he did, why?

"Some of my colleagues are of the opinion that he was not involved in the earlier riots but had access to the gang through means unknown, but this asks more questions. Is there is a freelance gang of troublemakers loose in the UK? Who is behind it? And what are their aims?

"In other words the more we find out the less we seem to know. Although we are sure that you two, Mr. Young and Mrs. Mason are no longer in danger as the perpetrator is in the morgue."

"Do any of you have anything to add to this?"

They all shook their heads as one.

Layton now said "Unfortunately I have now to give a

press conference, so you are all free to go, but I daresay we will be talking about this again. Also Mrs. Mason, would you be so kind as to call me with that telephone number as soon as you get to the hotel. I am very keen to talk to Miss Ward. Here is my card with my mobile number on it, please use that."

"Do you have anything to add Inspector Gooding?"

"No, not really, other than we still believe the material found on your computer Adam, was sent from Jonathan Mason's and we have to assume with the absence of any other evidence, that it was simply revenge."

They were in a taxi before any of them spoke much, Isobel was the first, "He knows more than he is telling us, doesn't he?"

"Yes" Ron replied "I think he does, but to be honest he told us a lot more than most police officers normally would. He also thinks we know more than we are telling, that's for sure."

"So what now?" Adam interjected.

"Well I'm going home, and if I were you, I would do the same. Layton mentioned a press conference, and I will put money on it that your names get mentioned. So unless you are prepared to barricade yourselves in the hotel, I suggest you go before they find you."

"And Stella?" stuck in Isobel.

"Well, she has to make her own mind but firstly you need to give Layton the number if Stella answers it, it is up to her, but she also needs to think about all this data as do you two, I think I would destroy it."

"Would you?"

"Well, there are apparently lots of crooked policemen and politicians named there all of whom deserve to be exposed but how do we know this information is accurate. Then there is probably lots of information on others, footballers' affairs, for example, not to mention that murdered school girl's texts, you know the drill Adam, the dirt these papers dig up, it will end up wrecking people's lives and again may not be accurate."

"And these sex rings and the celebrity pedophiles; they have remained a secret for so long it has to be exposed."

After a pause Ron then added "Go home, think about it, maybe take Stella with you, she will definitely want to get out of the city. Alternatively, I suppose you could go on a spending spree with that credit card until the bank realises he's dead and cancels it."

Adam then said "That sounds like sage advice old man, don't know about the spending spree we would get arrested for fraud, with our luck. I think we should go home in the morning, and see if Stella wants to come, what do you reckon, Iss?"

"Sounds okay to me, but you had better go get your car. It's still in the Carlton garage, isn't it?" Isobel replied.

"Yes," he said "At £50.00 a day, plus two hotels, you know this has been a very expensive weekend"

"Don't worry about that," Isobel said "They haven't told me to stop using the card yet, so the parking and the hotels are on Jonathan"

With that, the decision was made. The next morning Adam retrieved the Pajero from the Carlton Towers. The media were still hanging about outside, but not at the back beside the basement car park exit.

They dropped Ron of at the train station, and drove home. The night before, after returning to their suite, they watched Layton's press conference. Their names were mentioned, or at least Adam's and Isobel's were. Stella also for the first time got a mention as a person of interest that they would like to interview. This made her mind up straight away; she would accompany them to Plymouth. Isobel, good to her word, had phoned Layton's mobile and gave him Stella's number, which rang a few minutes late. Stella decided not to answer it for now.

Chapter 28

To say Chief Superintendent Bates was relieved with the present outcome would have been the understatement of the century. He'd been deflecting all enquiries into phone hacking back toward the lone rogue theory for nearly two years. But, over the last few months, as revelation after revelation, was made on the extent of the hacking, he had known that his involvement would come to light soon.

The mention of Jonathan Mason almost sent him into a catatonic state. Then the discovery of Mason's body at his office, and the discovery of the removal of all the hard drives had nearly put him on a plane to Venezuela. He had no knowledge about the content of these disks, but the mere fact that they existed and were in somebody else's possession, was enough to tell him that they probably contained incriminating evidence that would implicate him, other Met Officers, and the people they had been protecting, as well as hundreds of others Mason had dealt with over the years.

As a British Policeman, he knew that Venezuela was one of the hardest countries in the world to find people, and they had no extradition treaty with the UK. He had enough money to do it and retire for the rest of his life, with no real ties to keep him in the UK. He was still thinking about it. He had been a career policeman, who had a law degree from University College London; a smart man with a great deal of knowledge of the both the law and the criminal justice system. This knowledge was enough for him to be certain that sooner or later some or all of his involvement would surface.

That Mason's data was gone was the first bit of good news he'd had for a long time, and that Mason's killer had also been killed in the attempted kidnapping of Isobel Mason was further good news, he could not now divulge anything he knew, which Bates supposed would have been extensive. Whom this man was baffled him, his name and ID's although seemingly genuine on the surface where soon discovered to be fake, they weren't even sure that he was British.

Finding the man's body so conveniently, with his wallet full of ID and the weapon that killed Mason was far to be good to be true. But he wasn't about to look such a gift horse in the mouth. With the governmental enquiry in full swing, fuelled by the media speculation over Mason, there still would be a great many questions to be asked and answered. He didn't think he was going to get clean away without some mention of his part in the events.

He was beginning to believe that the best way out of this situation was to come forward and confess some of his involvement voluntarily. There were events such as the influencing of the hiring of personnel and the awarding of certain maintenance contracts that were if not technically illegal; they were certainly actions not becoming an officer of the Met. He could confess to these actions and then take early retirement.

That was the way he thought he was going to play it. Shut down this investigation of Mason and then, when called before the enquiry which was due to happen next week, he would confess to his limited involvement. If he did it well enough, he might well be lauded for his courage in coming forward.

Other officers at the Met were not so happy, and neither was Inspector Gooding. Gooding may not have been a law graduate like Bates, but he had a good nose and the stink he'd noticed about the Yard hadn't gone away with the death of Roseau. In the days after the discovery of Mason's body he had noticed groups of officers huddled in whispered conversation, faces taut, heads and shoulders down. Within two days of the events in Sloane Street, a spring had returned to the step of the same officers, evidently feeling far more confident that they had been.

None more so than Chief Superintendent Bates, Gooding had neither known nor met the man before arriving at Scotland Yard, but his actions seemed evasive from the outset. There was no way at present he should allow the investigations to be wound up; there were far too many unanswered questions. The only reason that Gooding could see for this would be if Bates himself knew many of the answers to these questions and didn't want them to come to light.

But Gooding was a policeman. His job, as he saw it, was to protect the general public and investigate criminal activities, and he was going to continue to do it. He was due to go back to Plymouth the next day and once back there he planned to continue with his investigations. He couldn't trust anyone in New Scotland Yard, but there were officers within his own force that he could, and would to gain the assistance needed.

Layton's sense of apprehension was focused slightly differently; he had noticed how easily his superiors accepted that the incident was at an end. So far, he had put this down to relief that they had managed to solve several major crimes so quickly and the great PR they were getting for doing so.

His concerns were that they had put an end to it far too easily. To start with, Roseau discovered dead with his ID, and the weapon was far too easy. In addition, he had been shot in the back by an unknown person. It wasn't any of his men, and he was sure it wasn't the Young's and co, so who was it?

Lots of other things didn't fit; the hard disks that were corrupted the independent experts he consulted said it couldn't have happened as he had been told by Bates' experts. The whole kidnap attempt on the Young's was wrong, and then there were these groups of rioters which appeared to have been hired by Roseau. He had no answer to any of these riddles, and he didn't like that, at all.

Before Gooding had turned up with his questions about Mason, one of the major investigations he had been working on was on such small groups of rioters at the demonstrations earlier in the year. Several had been arrested at the time, and many more later. This investigation revealed that these men had been organised by an external party who he now believed to be Roseau the coincidences were just far too great for it not to be him.

Why?

What would a man, a seemingly ordinary man, albeit a ruthless businessman like him, gain from such a maneuver?

He was obviously no ordinary businessman. As yet

Layton hadn't had enough time to investigate this man properly and although the primary investigation was over, looking into this man's past was going to be his overarching priority. There was something that had the hairs on the back of his neck standing, and his gut feeling was that he needed to find something and quickly.

Layton's biggest issue with this man Roseau was lack of motives. In all the crimes, he had investigated over the years, and there had been many strange ones, all had an overriding motive. The motive could be hidden or compounded by others, but it was always there, and he found it. These events with the organised gangs and no doubt they were organised by someone, and very well at that, had no motive or none that he could fathom as yet.

To who was it worthwhile to expend that amount of time and money organising the riots? Is it that random that I should stop thinking about the normal motives of financial gain, concealment, or revenge and start contemplating others?

Whilst he thought about this, he jotted down notes and drew lines of interconnection between them, just to try and make some sense of many of these acts. But none of it made sense not until he started to consider the nature of the communications between the perpetrators of these crimes.

Small groups, apparently unconnected, given untraceable instructions via Blackberry Messenger, from a single controlling source, certainly they had an element of security about them. There was also the cellular nature. Again, small groups, each unknown to the next, with no motive other than destabilization.

He had never known anything like that, but there were precedents. Not in the UK, but it had been happening in the Middle East.

The revolutions in Algeria, Egypt, Libya and Syria had started that way. Could we be dealing with something of that nature? It could only mean one thing. Terrorists?

Was there a group of terrorists operating in the UK, controlling cells of British Nationals? That would be truly a nightmare scenario, but was it feasible; perhaps it was. But what could their goals be?

They surely didn't expect the British populace to rise-up and overthrow the government. That just wasn't feasible. So what was the aim, smoke screens perhaps?

There was no one at the Met he could go to with this and really it was far beyond his expertise. It was in the grounds of the Security Services.

Whom can I take this to?

Making an enquiry through the normal channels wouldn't work, no one would believe this credible, but perhaps there was one option. This friend of Adam Young who worked with them, or for them, as yet he wasn't really sure what the man did, or for whom, but this was his arena.

I'm going find out a little more about Ron James and then perhaps arrange to meet him again.

All he had to go on at the moment was Roseau; he would make enquiries about the man to see what he could discover. He didn't really think it possible that there were terrorists operating cells on that scale here, but to be on the safe side, he would run with it. If he kept it to himself for a while, then he wouldn't end up with egg all over his face when his wild suspicions turned out to be unfounded.

After being dropped at the train station by Adam, Ron had taken the train and then a taxi home. The next day he should have been in Poole with his SBS team. But as he hadn't been into his office for a couple of days and knowing there were things that he had to deal with on his desk he went back up to London. He spent the day at Thames House in meetings intending to go down to Poole the next day.

The photos he had taken at the game on Saturday and those he had taken after the events at the Carlton Towers had all been sent to an analyst he worked closely with. So, after finishing his first meeting, which had run all morning, and was on his way back to the cubicle which constituted his office, he dropped in to see the man. The analyst was just about to head off for lunch, and Ron decided to join him. The pair took a table in the canteen together and after grabbing some food, discussed the photos as they ate.

All the events over the past few days concerned Ron, on the surface it appeared as though they were over. Certainly his friend Adam, his brother and new girlfriend now seemed out of danger, which was his primary concern. But it all seemed most unusual, not that people were after this data, there was money involved there which was all the justification many needed; it was the people involved. Notably, this Roseau man concerned him. The rest, he been told by the Police, were security personnel hired by Roseau, so of no great concern.

They had in front of them a head shot or two of each of the men Ron had taken pictures of, ten in all, six of which the analyst had identified.

Ron's suspicions were correct; each of them had been soldiers having left the service within the last five years. They had all worked for one security consultant or another during that time and were at present all under contract to Harris Security Consultants, a company run by another ex-soldier.

Of the other four, three had no ID as yet, the fourth

being Roseau. These three had all been driving the cars used to transport them back from Twickenham. Two of the driver's photos were not very good their features blurred by reflections, having been taken through the windscreens. Of the third, he had taken several shots as he had stopped to pick up Roseau opposite the taxi rank. The analyst couldn't tell him much more as yet he had been unable to find anything on him in the extensive data banks they kept at Thames House.

Ron asked the analyst to run the photos of Roseau and this other man through their propriety comparison programs, against security footage taken at the major airports in the UK. This, the analyst hadn't done yet and was loath to do, due to the amount of work it involved but gave in when Ron stressed how important he thought it might be. He told him he would ring from Poole toward the end of the next day, to see if he had come up with anything.

Chapter 29

As the existence of Mason's data became public knowledge, so did the concern it arose and alarm which spread to many that had had dealings with him. One of the few left alive that knew of the extent of the evidence that the material might hold was Mason's former boss, Dandelion. Now back in New York he sat in his central park penthouse, the light of the setting sun streamed through the double height glazed windows casting a golden hue throughout the lounge in which he sat and thought.

The inquiry he was summoned to attend some week or so before had gone much the way he had predicted. He was asked questions about his knowledge of illegal phone hacking, about attitudes to information gathering generally, within his news conglomerate and of others and whether he believed it was limited to the single case.

His replies in all cases were that he had no prior knowledge to any of this and was shocked and dismayed by the single case, which had already been dealt with. He told the inquiry that there was little more he could add but was happy to provide any information that was revealed by his own internal investigation. His investigation would of course, reveal nothing. He was dismissed by the inquiry board but told his presence might be requested again. His statements might be contradicted by others, but there would be no proof or hadn't seemed to be any until now.

The spectacular view across the park and the streets below did little to improve his mood; he was clearly a very worried man. He knew that should this information come to light it would incriminate a great many people. He knew that information of his employment of Mason would be on there, and this would not only contradict the statements he had previously made to the Robertson Inquiry, but expose the depths of his dealings with the government of the UK.

For fourteen years, he had supported the Labour Party. His media outlets had been intrinsic in the shaping of New Labour's media image and that of their leader. He had also enormously benefited both by Labour's new stance to the Unions and their embracing the fiscal policies begun by Margaret Thatcher a decade before.

Many would have said he was a friend of the party's hierarchy. He spent a lot of time in their company, but to him, it was purely business. During those boom years, where further fiscal relaxation made everyone money, he put the might of his media empire behind them.

In 2010, he saw an opportunity. For three years, the country had been in the midst of a recession. A general election was due which, he felt sure; Labour would lose. The recession was not confined to the UK; it was endemic and worldwide. It was known as the Banker's Crisis, where years of relaxing the fiscal policies had brought about a highly unstable condition. The retail banking system: the consumer and commercial banks were so intertwined with the investment banks and their worth so artificially inflated that they had become vulnerable. This wasn't the first time this had happened.

After the Wall Street Crash of the 1920's, it was recognised that having institutions that did both retail banking and investment banking had a serious flaw. In that, a series of poor investments on the investment side could bring down the consumer divisions, which is precisely what caused the crash in the Twenties. Thus, after this crash, fiscal banking laws had been put in place to prevent it happening again.

But, over the past 20 years these fiscal controls had been gradually eroded, allowing the leading high street banks once again to buy up investment houses, creating mammoth institutions. Property formed the mainstay of the bank's physical assets, and as they bought, so did the general public. Facilitated with the easily available credit the banks now supplied; prices skyrocketed.

Until the inevitable happened, the bubble burst. The result: cascading property prices worldwide, followed by a run on the liquidity of the banks as the value of the bank's assets rapidly decreased. Firstly one bank was brought down, then the next, and so on, causing a domino effect worldwide.

In late March of 2010, a month before the General Election, the consumer polls still had Labour slightly ahead of the Conservatives with the Liberal Democrats showing a poor third.

Despite the Conservatives laying all the blame of the present economic worries firmly anchored at Labour's front door, they had made little gains in the polls. Dandelion expected the Conservatives to be much further ahead, but the Labour Government had responded remarkably well to the crisis. They kept economic stimulus going, and, as a result, they had hung on to a lot of public support.

Not enough support had gone to Blain, the leader of the Conservative Party, but in this Dandelion saw the opportunity.

He had on many occasions advised prime ministers how to influence public opinion, but now he could have people inside the government helping create policy: policy which benefitted him and his associates. With a new government came new ministers. These new ministers usually knew very little about what they were suddenly the minister of and then relied particularly heavily on their advisors, advisors he would have put in place, making almost anything possible. Getting the right information out to the right people was going to be the key.

In a meeting with David Blain, he outlined his plan to put the Conservatives into power. Predominantly, this relied on getting their message across and to make sure they did, he would arrange for one of his editors to become the media advisor to Blain. He would then use his media outlets from press to TV news, to denounce the Labour policies of economic stimulus, claiming they were putting the country in huge debt and would very soon bankrupt it.

Dandelion delivered as promised and swung the election to the Conservatives, maybe not quite as much as he would have liked or had led Blain to believe. Blain had been forced, in the end, to form a coalition with the Liberal Democrats to gain the required majority.

It was now 18 months after the election, and he had five senior advisors within the Conservative coalition government; there was the media secretary to the Prime Minister, senior advisors to the Treasury, Defense, National Health Service and the Ministry of Justice. Only the former was ever directly employed by him, the others, associates, he had picked up along the way, but all were directly experienced in the areas of work of the departments they were now working in, and all had agendas that complimented Dandelion's.

He and his associates were now in a superb position, to influence both policy and appointment of contracts that resulted, making them vast amounts of money. Should that agenda be the privatisation of the National Health Service or the invasion of an oil-rich foreign nation, the amount of money spent on both the health service and military appropriation contracts was astronomical, and it was all there for the taking? He was beginning similar policies of interaction with other countries' governments, all of which looked as though they would be just as fruitful. And next time no such compromises would be made.

Now this data or at least the knowledge of its existence had surfaced, and that knowledge acid etched his stomach. He had to find it before anyone else.

Lifting the phone he spoke into the receiver after dialing a local New York State number,

"Carlo, I'd like you to discuss something with you."

"Sure, when?"

"Now if possible, I'm at the Stanhope, you know the number."

"Yes, an hour."

Events of the Saturday and before hadn't gone unnoticed by the government either. There had been a cabinet meeting that morning at No 10 Downing St, after which several ministers and their senior advisors, Blain and his media secretary got together to discuss the events over coffee. Many knew Dandelion intimately; he was often at No 10 and Chequers, and whilst all of them might not have met Mason, they all knew of him by reputation at the very least.

"I think you all know why I have asked to stay behind, now what do we know and what are we to do about it?" Began Blain.

The nine men looked at each other for a minute or two before one spoke up.

"There doesn't seem much point speculating, we have had confirmation that this data exists and will contained information pertaining to us. What we need to do is find it before anyone else does"

"Agreed, we know our friend in New York will be doing the same, but there are a great deal of resources we can bring to bear form here."

"Yes, we should start Security Services operation to find it immediately," said the Secretary of Defense.

"Have then report direct to you and no one else, we have to limit knowledge of this," added Blain.

The depth of the concern didn't end with the Police, Dandelion and the Government; it was also a concern to many others. Some thought they might appear on Mason's lists; others thought that an advantage could be gained with the acquisition of the lists. Consequently several private investigators had been hired in an attempt to find it.

Charlie Parker had been discharged from hospital three days after the accident outside the palace of Westminster. His collar bone had been pinned, and his broken ribs bandaged as had his right calf, from which chunk of flesh had been removed by Dandelion's limo. Although he would need to return on several occasions to have skin grafts to his lower leg and the pins removed that wouldn't be for several more weeks.

He was now convalescing at home and watching a great deal of television to keep him busy. As a result of the amount of TV he had been watching, he had caught just about all of the media's coverage of the events in Sloane St and that of the murders in Clerkenwell.

He had seen many images of this young man Adam Young and his girlfriend that the kidnappers were after. He had also seen the press conferences given by the police, who had given their versions of the events. It was a huge story that had dominated the media for several days; consequently there had been a lot of footage on show, particularly from immediately after the kidnapping attempt.

In one shot of the couple taken outside the Carlton Towers he thought he had recognised a man with them. It hadn't been very clear footage as it had been captured on a mobile phone by an onlooker. He had managed to record the story and had looked at it several times and now was almost positive that the man with the couple had been Ron James.

He hadn't seen him for years; he had never known him particularly well but knew he was a special services trooper. He knew it could just be a coincidence, but his presence intrigued him. He didn't have a great deal to keep himself occupied at the moment, he had been pursued by the media immediately after his accident, but they had given up soon enough, as a result, he thought about Ron and why he might be there.

His recovery was going well; he was now moving around under his own steam well enough. He wanted to get back to work as soon as he could, hopefully sooner than anyone had expected. He was still a fit man despite his age. He had walked to work each morning for years and exercised regularly and certainly didn't want to be forcibly retired any earlier than was already in the cards.

He decided that he would go in the following week. He couldn't do much, but he didn't need to, all maintenance had long ago been handed over to the new contractors. So he would go, in show his face, perhaps do a little paper work. There was bound to some on his desk that needed looking at.

Stella genuinely liked the Young's house and had found a great spot to work. Just inside the sliding glazed doors in the dining room, which didn't, seem to have a great deal of use, most of their food being eaten in the kitchen. From there, she had a view of the sea which she enjoyed, and thought that she should buy a place down here to work on the book she was planning to write.

She still hadn't responded to Layton's phone messages and had not checked or even turned on her mobile since leaving London. She knew that by now her boyfriend would be very anxious. When she left his apartment, she had written him a note saying she was going back her house in Ruislip, would be tidying up loose ends at work, and would see him in a few days.

Those days were long past, but the police were bound to have questioned him by now and knowing what a straight lace he was, she didn't want to risk calling him. At some point, she was going to have to deal with this, but not just yet.

She had eventually managed to download all the data, now that she had access to a fast internet connection. She had almost finished compiling lists of all those in

Jonathan's pay but still was no clearer about what to do with it. She could always use it all in her book; the book would be an instant best seller, revealing corruption at an unprecedented scale.

It would expose an enormous cross section of society. The list of names from government, banking, media and the corporate world still frightened her, but even she was unaware of some of the ramifications that its release would have.

Stella had seen little of Isobel and Adam for the last two days. They had kept to themselves, obviously very happy to be back together and intent on making the most of it. When not in bed, they had been out, and Stella had left them alone. But now she needed to talk to them urgently and as soon as they returned she would. She needed to tell them about what she had just discovered.

After checking through all the files against the index that was attached to the data, she noticed an additional file. A file that appeared to have been uploaded by Jonathan within the last week; she read the file and its reading made her blood run cold.

What Stella hadn't noticed was that members of the security service had also managed to get their hands on the data, if not the encryption codes that Stella used. Their interest had been aroused by the murders and attempted kidnapping. They had traced all internet activity at several hotels in the vicinity of the Carlton Towers. Discovering large download rates at the Roof Garden had led them to the secure cloud where Stella had stashed it. It had also provided the IP address that Stella had just been using at the house in Wembury.

. . .

All those involved had concerns to varying degrees, and rightly so. But the fact that they didn't trust each was of far greater concern. Had they done so, they would have been able to piece together the jigsaw. With this, they may have uncovered a group of terrorists in the midst and an operation that if successful would change the face of the UK forever.

The terrorists were well ahead with their schedule. In fact, all of De Costa's men were already in the warehouse in Wandsworth, two days ahead of time. The warehouse was well stocked with everything they might require, both for the present and for after the attacks.

There were packing cases full of tinned food and bottled water that would last for many weeks, and they had a generator with ample diesel. There were vehicles too; minibuses to carry the men to their designated destinations to begin the attacks, along with several 4x4's for when they would be needed. They were all parked inside the warehouse to avoid suspicion.

There were also cases of weapons, ranging from handguns to MP5's, mortars and RPG's even portable rocket launchers. The warehouse was to remain a base for operations after the attack. All who survived were to return there to wait for the anarchy that they were sure would follow.

That was all except de Costa and the scientists. Many of the scientists had already left and those that remained would be leaving within the next few days. De Costa had a ticket booked to Paris, transferring to Istanbul for the morning of the attack from there he would fly to Tehran. If all went well it would take the authorities three or four days to work out what had happened, which would be too late to stop the subsequent infection, but he intended to be back in Tehran long before then. His standing instructions to his men were to remain in the warehouse for at least a week, and from that point to conduct attacks on a variety of targets.

Three days after the attack, those that had been infected by the virus would start showing symptoms. They would not seem alarming at first. Mostly flu-like, accompanied by a slight rash, but for the next two days everyone that had those symptoms would be infectious, inflecting nearly everyone they came into contact with.

It wouldn't be until the fourth day that people started showing up at hospitals and doctors surgeries. Still the authorities wouldn't understand what was happening; it would take them at least another day to fully comprehend the situation. By that time, many thousands would have the infection.

De Costa doubted the finger would be pointed at them and hoped that local dissident groups such as Anarchy UK would take the blame. He would ensure that the British was blamed, if not for the actual cause, but the spreading of the virus.

By this time, the airports would have closed; ferries cancelled and ports closed down. The British would effectively be quarantined, nothing in or out, and would remain so for several weeks or even months. Many would try to leave in private vessels, but the Continental Europeans would enforce the quarantine with a blockade. Eventually the authorities would get serum to everybody, but it would take the military and martial law to do so. They would probably recall their naval elements of the Combined Task force 150 from the Arabian Gulf, with any other European Ships brought back to enforce the blockade, leaving the Americans alone in the Persian Gulf.

And then their forces would move on Riyadh. Even

now Iranian forces were assembling. Many under the guise of the naval maneuvers, which had been ongoing for two weeks, others supposedly in response to HMS Enterprise and her capture. Their very secret weapons were on the move in vehicles disguised as petrol tankers from the Ural Mountains where they had been developed.

The Continental Europeans would still be trying to prevent any further spread and the British cut off, preventing any armed response from them. The Americans were still an unknown factor but De Costa doubted that they would interfere. If they did, they had an extremely nasty surprise in store for them.

Chapter 30

Ron spent the day with his sixteen man team in Poole. Arriving at 7.30, he joined them for their morning run. Despite his age and the age difference between the team members' and his, he always enjoyed these runs. Rather than the exhaustion most would feel he was recharged after his relatively inactive days in London. After the run, he had told his colleagues about his involvement in the recent events, which inevitably had been all over the news networks for days.

To a man, they congratulated Ron on his contributions in preventing the kidnapping, all offering their support should they be needed for his ongoing investigation into Roseau. It wasn't until late in the afternoon that he rang the analyst, who had a great deal to tell him.

The analyst hadn't left his desk since the lunch with Ron the day before. His marathon hadn't been planned, but with each discovery he made, new avenues opened, energising him to continue. He had initially been hesitant to start the facial recognition search on airport footage, but he had struck lucky.

The men he pursued for Ron could have used any of the dozen or more major airports in the UK or none at all. He picked Heathrow to begin his search, purely because the amount of footage made it possible to set his search parameters and simply let it run.

Within a couple of hours, he started getting hits and in another four he had established a pattern. Whilst neither of the men travelled together nor necessarily on the same flight they both travelled to the same destination within a few hours of each other. Armed with this, it was a process of cross referencing and elimination, which confirmed that the men used one of three passports each, to both leave and enter the country. And that they had done so every three or four weeks for the last year. The destinations were all within the EU, sometimes Paris other times Frankfurt or Amsterdam, all major hubs, from where he assumed they flew to another airport. First he sent enquiries to colleagues in these countries to confirm this and second, he used the names he had discovered to learn what he could of their activities in the UK.

With Ron on the phone, he told of what he knew. He began with the frequency of their travel, their initial destinations and the names they travelled under.

He told Ron that both men had normally transferred to another flight but on occasions had stayed in the city of their first stop. When they travelled onwards it was always under the same passport. From Paris they used one, Frankfurt another and from Amsterdam yet another and in each they had a serviced apartment where the analyst assumed they stayed when in that city. When travelling on, they always went to Istanbul, and he hoped he would soon hear from contacts there about their next destination.

He went on to explain some of their dealings in the UK. All of the names on the six passports, Roseau was one and De Costa another, were named as directors of various business concerns. These ranged from distribution, to warehouses, to maintenance and security companies. Each of the companies was registered at either an accountants or lawyers office; he also had various residential addresses derived from driving licenses and DVLC records.

After forty minutes of conversation Ron thanked the analyst, asking him to update him as and when he got any new information. Upon hanging up Ron looked at the notes he had made during the call, then pushed his chair back, linked his fingers behind his head, put his feet on the desk and thought about what he had just learnt.

Meanwhile, Inspector Layton was pondering discoveries of his own. Ron James had not been very forthcoming with details of his employment; only that he worked with the security services and had been in London that day to interview an informant. After several phone calls, he discovered that James had enlisted at eighteen, as a Royal Marine in the mid 1980's, immediately after completing his A-level exams.

After three years, as a Royal he applied as a candidate on a Special Boat Squadron selection course. At the end of the five week selection course, he was assigned to M Squadron, eventually promoted to command The Black Group and then M Squadron itself.

M squadron was responsible for maritime anti-terrorism operations with The Black Group specialising in helicopter assault. The Black Group were as the name suggested, a clandestine force about which there was remarkably little information forthcoming. Layton discovered James' duties were also the coordination with the newer X Squadron which was formed not only of SBS troops but that of SAS.

The name Special Boat Squadron implied that they were a maritime service, but that appeared not always to be the case. James had been involved in many missions in Afghanistan, of which there was very little specific detail, but he did find a few details of one mission that happened before the Afghan invasion. That of Operation Barras, a hostage rescue mission into Sierra Leone in 2000.

James had led the helicopter assault, consisting of two Chinook helicopters with fifty SBS and SAS troopers to rescue the eleven British soldiers, captured by a group of one hundred and fifty rebels known as the West End Boys that were being held on the northern bank of the Geberi Bana River. Another one hundred and fifty paratroopers were delivered in more Chinook helicopters supported by Lynx gunships to engage the several hundred strong rebels stationed on the southern bank of the river. To both act as a diversion and to stop them bringing their heavy weapons to bear on the troops rescuing the hostages on the northern bank.

The nickname given to the helicopter assault was 'Operation Certain Death' and would have been except for some very timely intelligence supplied by one Adam Young, who had been with an SAS observation team inserted several days before.

The observations team's original mission was to investigate the possibility of an assault by river. This was shown to be impossible after the discovery of yet another group of rebels equipped with boats mounted with mortars and heavy machine guns, making a stealthy river passage impossible. The team pressed on through the jungle toward the camp where the hostages were being held. Three days and fifteen miles later they were concealed on a slight rise between the camp and the river, with clear views of both.

From this vantage point, they were able to relay crucial intelligence on the rebel deployments back to the British forces. On the morning of the rescue, the first two Chinooks delivered the Special Forces close to the rebel's camp. They had anticipated that the noise of Chinooks, audible for several miles, would alert the rebels, to counter that, part of the observation team's mission was for their snipers to take out any rebel that approached the hut in which the hostages were held.

What wasn't anticipated was that the third contingent of rebels, equipped with boats, had moved downriver and was encamped no more than two miles away, well within the audible range of the approaching Chinooks.

The Special Forces made their way through the camp directed by the observation team. Adam, wary of an approach to the rear of their position, kept watch. The boats making their way down river kept close to the over-growth along the bank and were not seen until they were almost within range of their mortars. With only seconds to spare Adam called in the Lynx helicopters and their Hell-fire Missiles, destroying the boats before they could fire their mortars into the center of both the Special Forces and the Paratroopers.

The mission not only successfully rescued the service men but also captured the commander of the West End Boys. Sadly one member of the rescue forces was killed, and several more were wounded. But, had it not been for Young's timely intelligence, the mission would have been a complete disaster with the loss of the entire assault team.

Layton smiled as he read the last of the report, real-ising that this probably explained why James and Young were so close.

Ron James had never been decorated or even cited for any mission but then again very few Special Forces ever were, but his service seemed exemplary. So if there was one person Layton could turn to, and discuss his concerns, it should be James.

He would certainly understand his paranoia of a terrorist attack, having been involved in counter terrorism most of his working life. Layton had two contacts for James, one at Thames House and the other at the barracks in Poole. He decided to try the Poole number first, which was answered at the third ring.

As Layton was ringing James, Adam and Isobel were just returning to the house in Wembury from a day out. It had snowed a little during the night leaving a thin but crisp white coating around the house and over the rocks leading to the sea. There was never a great deal of snow around Plymouth, but Adam knew from experience that if there was a little here then there should be a lot more up on Dartmoor.

They'd grabbed a couple of old plastic sledges that had been in the garage, put them into the back of the 4X4, and spent the day up on Burrator. As expected Dartmoor was covered in snow, almost all the lanes leading to the reservoir and the Tor above were impassable except to four wheeled drive vehicles. They had parked and climbed Sheeps Tor, which towered over the reservoir.

The day was clear and crisp with a view clear into Cornwall, twenty miles away. It was breathtaking. The bright blue sky, dotted with white fluffy clouds went on forever. Although Isobel had lived in the UK for nearly two years, she had never really got into the snow. Yes, it looked nice out of the window but to roll around in it, no, that had never been her thing. But she loved doing any and everything with Adam; they tobogganed down Sheep's Tor so many times they lost count. They rolled and played in the snow like a pair of school kids, and the day had passed before she knew it and they were soaked to the skin.

On the way home, they stopped at the Dartmoor Restaurant, to warm-up and dry off, as well as sate the appetite they had built up during the day, before driving home to Wembury.

Arriving home, they had planned to have a hot shower together, and then bed to sate the other appetites they had built up during the day. That wasn't to be.

Stella had been waiting for their return most of the afternoon and was desperate to tell them what she had learnt. So after excusing themselves for ten minutes while Isobel had a quick shower and Adam dried himself thoroughly, they were back in the kitchen sipping hot tea as Stella talked.

Stella first gave them a list of names that she had found in the files. It consisted of several ministers and MPs, permanent secretaries and advisors, media personalities, and banks involved in money laundering, as well as senior policemen within the Met. The extent of the list flabbergasted them that Jonathan should have so many high ranking civil servants on his pay was astounding. And some of the huge names of media people involved in sex crimes shocked them both.

They had known for a week or more that there was a great deal of corruption in Whitehall, but this amount and the seniority of them defied belief. None of them had ever considered the workings of Whitehall before or that of any government; they just did what they did and hopefully you and the country benefited.

Therefore, they couldn't properly understand what

these people did for or with Jonathan. Obviously there was money involved, as the list of names had had amounts and dates attached to them along with specifics. After spending some time bandying about ideas with regard to how money could be made, Stella then came to the additional file she had found.

"While I was going through the index file and correlating that to the files I'd downloaded, I noticed a new file, one that I didn't put up there. It had been put together by Jonathan the day before his murder."

Letting that sink in she continued,

"It looks as though he was having second thoughts about these new clients. In addition to writing down what he had done for them he was also speculating as to what they were doing with the information he had given them. The file starts with specifics on the information he'd delivered which were all in relation to government contracts. It examines, who was in charge of them and how to make sure that they were awarded them, etcetera."

Adam cut in with "So he thought this was all about getting awarded government contracts?"

"He did initially, and that's what I think most of his dealings were about, well that and the bypassing government laws and regulations concerning monopolies, that sort of thing. That would explain why there are so many MP's involved but he goes on. These new clients, of which Roseau was one and a man named De Costa the other, were something different. They had begun to frighten Jonathan and rightly so considering the outcome. He thought they might be some sort of crime syndicate. He wasn't sure really what they were but was obviously keen to find out."

"What sort of contracts were they after?" put in Adam

"I'm just coming to that; they were for contracts for

cleaning and maintenance of government buildings, security within those buildings, others for long-time secure storage of documents and the provision of transport services."

"All very profitable I should imagine" added Isobel "but why would that make him afraid of them?"

Stella continued "I think it was because of the way they came across they seemed to be intimidating him particularly on one piece of information he hadn't been able to get for them. Do you remember a lady getting knocked down by a bus about two weeks ago?"

Neither Adam nor Isobel did.

"Well it seems that she was a friend of Jonathan's, and he had found out about an affair she was having with the Chief Secretary to the Treasury. He arranged for Carl to pose as a waiter get into a suite the man had at the Savoy and take photographs of them. Something obviously went terribly wrong, and the woman ended up getting chased down a road by several photographers until she accidentally ran in front of a bus. I can only surmise that they were going to blackmail him, but why?"

"So, on top of it all, Jonathan was involved in someone's death as well," said Isobel evidently extremely distressed by what she was hearing.

"Yes. It would seem so, but the point is that it was these men Roseau and De Costa started to put a great deal of pressure on Jonathan after that, which frightened him and started him looking into their affairs, which may have gotten them killed. He found out some things about them though. He was fairly sure that they were linked to organised crime and that they travelled a lot on several different passports. It doesn't give any names, but he did think that they travelled to the Middle East a lot."

"So let me get this straight," said Adam "These two

men are gangsters, for want of a better word, involved with corrupt politicians and perhaps police, they are into blackmail and have dealings in the Middle East. They wanted Jonathan's data to protect themselves and maybe to blackmail more of the people in Jonathan's pay. One of them, Roseau, is dead, and the other, De Costa we assume is still alive."

"And perhaps looking for us still?"

"Is there anything else?" asked Isobel

"Not much, other than a few addresses, some in London others around the country".

"Shit, I thought this was over. I need a drink."

"Girls?"

Chapter 31

Isobel and Adam had returned home without a care in the world, happy to be together, unencumbered by doubts, but now the dark cloud had descended again.

The discussion continued over two bottles of wine until nearly midnight. Just before going up to bed there was a ring on the door bell, startling them all. It was followed by a longer ring a few seconds later.

The lights were on both in the kitchen, and upstairs so there seemed little point pretending they were either out or asleep. And, as Adam doubted gangsters rang doorbells surely they would just kick them in, he decided to answer the door. But not until he had slipped an exceptionally sharp and wickedly pointed filleting knife, in its sheath, down the back of his jeans.

Opening the door he was mightily relieved to see Ron standing there, not a gangster with a gun pointed at him, but he was then perplexed by Ron's sudden appearance, so far from London. That confusion was soon replaced by greater surprise as he saw who was standing behind Ron. None other than Assistant Deputy Commissioner Layton and by the look on his face he was even more annoyed than usual.

Layton, in his opinion, had good reason to be angry. Had Young been straight with him from the outset, he wouldn't have had to drive all night to Plymouth and more importantly he would have had very valuable and urgently required information several days ago.

During his phone call to Ron James several hours before he told Ron of his concerns. Notably the continued reappearance of these organised gangs. Yes, there was a great deal of corruption going on, and whilst that did concern him, it was not of the utmost urgency. What was the possibility of terrorists controlling these gangs and that they might be planning a major attack in the UK, right now.

After explaining his concern to Ron over the phone, Ron suggested they meet. Layton agreed and was about to suggest that Ron come to London the following day. Ron stopped him, saying that Layton should come down to Poole immediately as he too had been investigating the events in London or more pointedly, the people behind them and that he had found some disturbing facts that really couldn't wait.

Layton agreed, arriving in Poole about 7.00 PM. As he was a senior policemen complete with credentials it hadn't taken Ron long to get Layton through security and into his office, a Spartan affair, where they had spent an hour discussing what each other had discovered. At about an hour in Ron decided it was time Layton knew about Jonathan's data. The more he thought about it the more certain he became that there was information contained in the files, which would be crucial to unravelling this mystery.

"There is something you haven't been told as yet

concerning the hard drives taken from Mason's office, and it could be crucial to this. Two days before the kidnapping attempt, Stella Ward phoned Isobel. That much you know, but what you don't know is that they met. All three were staying together at a hotel just around the corner form the Carlton Towers. There was a copy of the data on the disks. I think Stella now has it."

"So where is she?" Layton almost spat across the table.

"With Adam and Isobel in Plymouth, I believe."

"I see" was all Layton could manage.

After a pause for control, he continued "Then I need it now."

"Fair, then I suggest, we go there straight away."

By 10.30 PM, they were in the back of Layton's car complete with driver and heading up the A35 toward Plymouth. Unhindered by speed limits, they estimated they should reach the Young household, one hundred and twenty five miles away around midnight. Hopefully, they would still be up, but if not they could surely wake them. During the journey, they discussed what each knew with both of them arriving at a similar conclusion. It was far from certain that a terrorist group was operating in the UK, but all indications and their gut feelings pointed them in that direction. It was something neither could ignore. If they were wrong, so be it, if they were right, then time certainly was of the essence.

As Ron walked through the front door, he embraced Adam and whispered in his ear. "Just go into the kitchen mate make us some coffee, take Layton with you and make small talk nothing else, I will be there soon, Okay."

Taking his cue, Adam showed Layton into the kitchen offered him a seat at the breakfast bar and put on a pot of coffee, whilst holding his finger to his lips. The girls accepted this and joined in the small talk as Adam began discussing the weather and the day's snow as the English are wont to do.

Before Ron left the barracks in Poole, he remembered that Adam and Isobel had been followed to London. This could mean only one thing; whoever had followed them was party to the phone conversation between Isobel and Stella. So either Stella's phone was being monitored, which was unlikely, or Adam's phone and or house were bugged. He therefore had brought some detection equipment along with him.

Ron first went into the lounge he knew quite a lot about hidden microphones and their accompanying wireless equipment. As many of the newer ones only broadcast when they were picking up something, he put the stereo on and switched on his equipment. He soon discovered the tiny microphone by the window. He then turned his attention to the dining room and again found the microphone quickly. He repeated his performance upstairs and found nothing, then went outside to walk around the house. As he walked around, he noticed another attached to the kitchen window then widened his search.

It was a clear night with a high bright moon with plenty of light to look around for possible sites for physical surveillance sites. He spotted the copse of trees one hundred meters or so away in the field. Checking that, he found nothing and then walked over to the rocks by the beach. Once satisfied that they were not being watched, he returned to the house and removed each of the microphones he had found before returning inside to the kitchen and a hot cup of fresh coffee.

Once in the kitchen, he dropped the microphones onto the breakfast bar,

"Looks like somebody has been listening to you for a while."

Adam handed Ron a cup of coffee and briefly picked up the microphones, before dropping them back onto the breakfast bar. He shook head, and it in hung, in shame, he knew he should have thought about that and would have done only a few years before.

"Don't worry mate they are short range and nobody has been around them for a few days at least. I doubt that they have picked anything up since you've been back."

"That's really not the point," said Adam "I should have considered that. We also think that the people who were after us in London may still be and that they are probably a bunch of gangsters, for the want of a better word"

"Gangsters?" was Ron's reply.

"I guess you mean organised crime, and yes that is possible but we" nodding toward Layton "Have another theory, one that is eminently worse."

"Worse, what could be worse?" Adam's day after starting so well was unquestionably taking another turn for the worse.

"We need to talk, but first, I need to eat as I'm sure does Commissioner Layton."

Stella had not realised whom the other man was up until that point but now turned to stare trying not to look too guilty.

Layton turned to her holding his hand out saying "Stella Ward, I presume?"

"Yes" she mumbled.

"What would you like to eat? I can make a sandwich or fry-up perhaps?"

"It will be probably be approaching breakfast time by the time we are finished, let's have a fry up."

Whilst Adam fried up a breakfast for the three men, the girls declining the offer, they chatted amiably but once finished the chat turned serious and indeed the Sun was coming up as they concluded their discussion.

No one held anything back, and were relieved to do so for the first time, they told everything they knew and contemplated. By the time, they had done they were all exhausted and rather tetchy.

Layton was first with an angry comment,

"It's a shame that you didn't tell us all of this when we met in London a week ago, we would be in a far better position right now to stop these terrorists if that is what we are really dealing with. The days you have cost me could be the difference in these people being successful or being stopped."

To which Adam replied in a similarly angry tone "If you guys kept your house in order and your hands weren't in every body's pockets then we might have been able to trust you."

Layton stood leaning toward Adam "That is completely out of order, how dare you?"

Before he could say any more Ron stepped in,

"Now guys that really isn't helping we need to work together, not rip each other's throats out."

Isobel cut in before the argument became too heated she asked "What I don't understand is why these gangs as you've called them, would be controlled by a group of terrorists."

Calming down Layton answered "That is a very good question I have interviewed all those that we have arrested, and there is a common theme. By way of explanation all of them said they aren't aware of who hired them or why, but when hired they agreed to do it as they had nothing to lose. They have no jobs, and most have been unemployed since they left school. I think they don't see themselves as part of today's society. All of them will do whatever it takes just to make lives better for themselves.

That really isn't a valid excuse there never could be one, but that seems to be their motivation; basically they seem disaffected, essentially removed from society. In my opinion, there has been a serious breakdown in British society over the past few years, and this is a symptom of that. Many refuse to take responsibility for anything anymore, parents for their children, and politicians for their electorate, and companies for their employees. I have no idea what the cure is but really it's about time people starting doing the right thing and not taking the easy option."

"I can see what you are getting at" put in Stella "but I think it is a poor excuse, these people don't have to act that way, and it still doesn't explain much. If we accept for the moment that there are terrorists, that they are planning a strike here and that they somehow control these gangs what are they going to do with them? It's not as if they can start a revolution with them. They are a bunch of cowards that will run away at the first sign of resistance as they did on Sloane Street. With no disrespect for your brother, it was only a bunch of rugby players, not armed police that stood up to them. All they can do is smash things up, burn a few shops or rob a bunch of innocent passersby"

"I agree with that, I can't see them cooperating once they find out they are working for terrorists" Said Isobel. "I don't think they are a bunch of Jihadist suicide bombers, do you Commissioner?"

Inspector Layton thought that very unlikely, in his opinion they were a diversionary tactic, perhaps to be used as a smoke screen. As he had said so earlier, he simply shook his head.

Adam had been quiet during this exchange, still

steaming from his retort with Layton, he now said "I think we can discuss them all day as we have for the last six hours and it will still be pure conjecture. I think we need to concentrate on the remaining man, De Costa."

"He's right," said Ron "But I was just starting a ten mile run this time yesterday, and I haven't slept since, so I think we should all get a bit of shut eye and then explore what we have on him. Yes? No?"

"Yes" was the unanimous response.

"There is a spare room you two can share, come on I'll show you, don't worry it's got twin beds" Suggested Isobel with a grin. "Shall we meet again at 12.00?"

As Ron followed Isobel out of the kitchen, he turned back and asked Adam

"Where's Dan?"

"He has an away game tomorrow, no strike that, today against the Saints, so the team travelled up yesterday morning."

"I'm kind of glad he's not here, his entrance to the foray on Sloane Street was spectacular, but I doubt he would be as comfortable here."

"You would be so surprised," Said Adam with a half-hearted laugh.

None of them slept. Their brains were far too active for that, perhaps they dozed a bit, but some rest and a shower had them in much better condition than they would have been without it. By 12.00 PM, they were all sat around the oak kitchen table, which was littered with notes, trying to piece together what they had.

If they were to make some headway, they would need to look deeply into De Costa and Roseau's dealings with Jonathan they wouldn't be wasting time with these contracts unless they were useful. So they felt that had to be the key, or at least an avenue to the key.

.   .   .

Their first order of business was to find out the exact details of the contracts; Jonathan's data had been short on actual details. It had mentioned cleaners, maintenance, security and storage, thankfully not defense, but they would need to check on that too. They also had the names of several companies linked to both Roseau and De Costa as well as the aliases supplied by the analyst. It was a start.

Stella was very good at this type of work, and Adam was remembering fast although not as familiar with it as he had been. Technology moved fast and had done so rapidly over the preceding years since this had been his day job, but he was getting there. Ron and Layton were constantly on their mobiles. This was no high tech anti-terrorist operation, no cordless headsets both Ron and Layton walked up and down as far they could tethered to a third laptop, charging their phones as they talked.

Isobel was acting as a secretary to the four of them; taking notes, sticking them all over the oak kitchen table, in some sort of order and keeping their caffeine levels at optimum.

As the frantic activity continued in the kitchen overlooking Wembury Bay, minibuses were pulling out of the warehouse in Wandsworth. Each minibus contained 12 men; the back seats had been removed, and in their place sat an industrial chest freezer, filled with canisters.

Chapter 32

Meanwhile, in Iran several petrol tankers had reached their destinations. One of them adjacent a pier at the military base of Chabahar was about to unload its concealed cargo. Moored in a dry dock opposite the pier was the HMS Enterprise she had a watch on board, but they weren't British Sailors, they were members of the Republican Guard.

The ship's crew, including the captain were being held in a military prison some fifty miles south of Tehran and were due to be led into court the following morning, to face charges of spying on the Republic of Iran. The prosecutor was demanding the death sentence for both the Captain and the XO, with life sentences for the rest of the crew. This was, needless to say, of great concern to the UK government, who had been in negotiations for the release of both the servicemen and HMS Enterprise since the incident first occurred.

The back of the petrol tanker hinged open, to reveal a steel joist running the full length inside the tanker. To this was attached another section of steel extending out beyond the tanker and over a trailer that had just been parked behind it.

From inside the tanker three stainless steel cylinders were pulled along the steel rail, each a little under two meters long and half a meter wide. They were carefully placed and secured onto the trailer, which was then pulled along the pier by the tractor unit attached to the front of it.

The unit stopped one hundred meters further along between a crane and HMS Enterprise. The cylinders were then craned down into the emptied and covered dry dock and into the Enterprise through holes below the water line that had been previously cut into her hull and fuel tanks.

The British Prime Minister and the Foreign Secretary were meeting with representatives of the Iranian Government in Switzerland that evening, to conduct a face to face meeting, to negotiate their release. The Iranian representatives had an explicit set of instructions to follow.

Initially they were to demand that the British confess to sending this ship to spy on the Iranian maneuvers as had been demanded from the outset. This would never be agreed to, they were well aware of this, so the instructions were to come to a compromise, where certain sanctions emplaced upon Iran were to be removed. The ship would then be returned to the British via the American Fifth Fleet stationed in the Indian Ocean.

An hour into the meeting with no solution on the table, and the Iranians about to leave the British PM made one last bid. He offered to help lift the sanctions emplaced by the EU and return half of the frozen assets held by the Bank of England, which amounted hundreds of millions of dollars of Iranian oil money, if a compromise could be made.

Gambling might be against Muslim religious laws but these guys must have played a great deal of poker; they bluffed very well. After a brief discussion between themselves, they agreed to the PMs offer and undertook to release the Enterprise to the custody of the American 5th Fleet, within the next few days.

Prime Minister David Blain was delighted with this outcome; he had been taking a serious amount of flack in the Parliament over the last two weeks over his inability to resolve the crisis. With this agreement now in place he would be able to announce in Parliament on Monday the imminent release of the Enterprise and her crew. And, that the only concession would be that of working with other EU leaders to help lift the sanctions that they had emplaced upon Iran.

He would not need to mention the unfreezing of Iranian assets. This had never been publically requested by the Iranians. Only the Chief Secretary of Treasury, whom he had just appointed after the debacle with Alex Great and his affair with a temp, would need to be party to this. Officials of the Bank of England would also need to be in the loop, but as he already controlled them, they would manage to keep the transactions quiet.

He would look like the architect of the negotiations in the press, gaining him huge brownie points with both the general public and the military, both of which he desperately needed right now. He could give The International Group a scoop on how he had personally come up with the plan and had handled all the negotiations with the Iranians himself. This might also appease Dandelion, whom he knew was very pissed with him at present, about being summoned to the Robertson Enquiry; which he certainly couldn't afford.

All in all, a very good day he thought.

As Blain and the Foreign Secretary boarded their private jet In Bern, policemen were conducting meetings all over the country in preparation for the general strike next Tuesday.

The Trade Union Congress, or TUC as they were known, was coordinating the general strike with arrangements for demonstrations in support of the strike were well in hand. The TUC and the respective unions they represented had a membership of 7.3 million; over 5 million had balloted and had given overwhelming support for the strike action.

Those balloted came from a diverse cross section of the working populace of the UK they were teachers, nurses and doctors, fire brigade employees, government, the public sector and transport workers. They also included delivery and shop staff; in addition, students had agreed to strike action. There was hardly a section of society that hadn't been adversely affected by the cuts the government were making and by the time of the ballot deadline there were nearly 8 million people who planned to strike on the day in question.

Over the previous two months, the government had appealed to the courts to make the strike actions illegal. Every one of their appeals had been thrown out, and now there was nothing more they could do to stop the general strike. Protests in support of the strike had been planned for every major urban center across the length and breadth of the UK; demonstrators would assemble on the outskirts of each chosen city and march toward the city center, to gather at the Town Halls.

Although police officers had been balloted for industrial action and had decided to do so as they were as aggrieved as any other, the Police Act of 1966 banned them from doing so. The decision was for all off duty police employees to join the demonstrations. But, now nearly every policeman in the UK that was fit for duty had been called to the urban centers, to police the demonstrations. All leave had been postponed and rural areas left with only a few essential staff.

Barricades were already going up along the routes, and every effort was being made to ensure all the participants of the demonstrations kept within the defined routes. If they had learnt anything from the demonstrations earlier in the year, this was going to be of paramount importance if they were going to keep it peaceful. Officers would line the route with reinforcements at every major junction along the way.

The rally center for each demonstration would have a major police presence. With riot police on standby dotted along the route, these would be backed up with mounted Police and dog units. The plans had been worked on for weeks and every conceivable scenario catered for. The senior officers thought they had every contingency covered.

Back in Wembury, the ad hoc team thought they'd had a productive day although they were no clearer as to the intentions of the possible terrorists, nor any idea of what sort of attack it could be, or a timetable. But they had assembled a great deal of information on De Costa and Roseau's activities over the past few months.

They now had what they thought was a comprehensive list of the business contracts that Jonathan had helped them gain. They were all as originally thought government contracts, whether these were gained by blackmail or bribery remained unclear, but it was probably a mixture of the two.

They had cleaning, maintenance, archiving, storage and security contracts for eight Town Halls and ancillary government buildings in Bristol, Birmingham, Cambridge, Edinburgh, Glasgow, Liverpool, Manchester and Newcastle. They also had similar contracts for many buildings in London, including The Palace of Westminster. All of these had been acquired within the last 18 months.

All of these contracts would be very lucrative to the companies involved. On the surface, there was no reason to suspect anything other than corrupt business practices. But, on the other hand, this did allow unfettered access to sensitive areas, particularly that of the contracts to the palace of Westminster.

The major refurbishments underway there allowed the contractor's access to every part of the building. If Roseau and De Costa truly had intended a terrorist strike this would be the most logical place to start looking.

Despite Roseau's death, their business concerns were still up and running, so the presumption was that De Costa was now in sole charge of the operations. There were logistic centers for their operations, close to the city in which they were operating and perhaps De Costa was at one of those. The one in Wandsworth seemed most likely.

Late on Saturday afternoon Assistant Deputy Commissioner Layton put in a call to the main Plymouth Police Station, with the hope of speaking to Inspector Gooding.

Gooding wasn't on duty, but he was able to get a mobile phone number for him. Again Gooding didn't answer, but after a message and a text, he eventually rang back. Layton told him only that he was at the Young's and would like to speak to him on a matter of some urgency. Intrigued Gooding replied that he would be over as soon as possible.

By the time Gooding arrived, they had a tentative plan of action. It was all well and good collecting all this data, but at some point they needed to change from being reactive to proactive if they were ever to get to the bottom of this.

Gooding sat at the kitchen table amid the clutter of laptops, mobile phones and what seemed like reams of paper and post-it notes, whilst he listened to Layton. By the end, he was more than a little confused even perhaps bemused at the bizarreness of the story but also concerned about what he just heard.

These weren't paranoid conspiracy nuts sitting in front of him he thought. Ron James, as he just discovered, was a counter intelligence expert and a Special Forces member, Layton a senior officer of the Met and the others, well they certainly had serious expertise. He asked what they intended to do now?

Ron had formulated a rough plan which he went on to explain "We have a great deal of data here as you can see" waving his hands over the table in front of them

"But I really want to get some eyes on, hopefully to locate this De Costa individual. So this is what I think we should do. I have access to approximately twenty eight members of M and X teams; I will make some calls in a minute to find the actual number that are available. I will split them into 7 teams, sending a team to each of the locations. They will have a look around and report back what they see.

"Commissioner Layton, Adam and I will take the eighth, which will be Bristol as it's the nearest and on the way. Stella and Isobel should stay here and sift through all this" waving an arm over the ream of paper in front of them. "I would like you to stay with them, and if possible station a car outside."

Gooding considered this for several minutes whilst looking at each of the assembled throng in turn before saying,

"What you say is reasonable, I still find this very farfetched, but I don't think we can ignore it. I can stay here, although I'm not sure about the car. All my officers or nearly all have been pulled up to Bristol to police the demonstrations on Tuesday. You also mentioned you would go to Bristol on the way; on the way where?"

At the word demonstrations, all the heads went up around the table.

Layton said, "Damn it, with all this going through my head I had forgotten about the strike next week."

For several minutes, Layton shuffled through various bits of paper and post-it notes in front of him before saying "There is a planned demonstration close to each of the distribution centers. That could be significant. But, I don't think it changes our strategy."

"Yeah I'd forgotten about these strikes too, and I don't like the coincidences" said Ron "And to answer your question about where, we first go to Bristol, where I want to have a bit of a snoop around in the dark and perhaps see any comings and goings, as it gets light. I doubt it will tell us anything, but!

"Then we will go to London, meet whatever team members I have left at Wandsworth. Have a look around there and then a look at Westminster early Monday morning. If anything is happening you can bet your last dollar that's where it will be."

"Fair enough, what time do you want to leave and what time do you want me back?" asked Gooding.

"We'll leave at 3.00 AM so, say about 2.00."

"2.00 Then; I had better bid you goodnight in that case"

Isobel took his arm to show him to the door. As Gooding left he turned to Isobel to say "I'm sorry about your husband and all that you have been through I hope you are coping Okay, and if you ever need to talk to someone, you know, please let me know."

"I'm good, but I will, thanks" as she kissed him on the cheek.

She smiled thinking "He seems like a good man" as she walked back to the kitchen.

Everyone in there was ready for some sleep and already headed in that direction. Saying goodnight to them, Isobel headed off to Adam's bed. Adam was already in the en-suite brushing his teeth as she walked quietly in behind him, slipping off her jeans and top throwing them onto the chair as she passed. She put her arms around him, slipping her hands down his chest and playing with his appendix scar on the way.

"Are you sure you want to go and not stay here with me?"

Adam grinned and said between brushes of his teeth "I'd much rather stay here and play with you but…"

"But what?"

Adam rinsed his mouth and turned.

"These wankers are really starting to piss me off and I have to do something to help. I have to do the right thing here, when you look at what that lot has done, not just De Costa but all those bloody politicians. Something has to stop, and if you do just the easy thing, it never will. But right now, to get my mind of it, I need a lot of very good sex".

He lifted her up as her legs wrapped around his waist and walked into the bedroom before diving onto the bed, amid Isobel's shrieks of laughter.

Chapter 33

The alarm woke Adam at 1.30. He jumped quickly out of bed for fear of going back to sleep, momentarily looking at Isobel's bum that had revealed itself as he rose.

I could always just stay in bed.

He bent down and kissed Isobel's pert backside, before pulling back the duvet and headed towards the shower.

Fuck, I must be running on adrenalin, he thought,

turning the shower on as hot as he could stand.

I was tired the day before yesterday when I came back from Dartmoor, and I haven't really slept since. What a state to begin a spying mission. Thank god Ron's here, I really got to sleep on the drive.

He made the bottom of the stairs as Clive rang the doorbell; Adam opened it and looked at Gooding, who looked as fresh as a daisy. Adam just shook his head and beckoned Clive toward the kitchen, with thankfully had the smell of fresh coffee drifting from it.

He drank his first cup and was refilling it before he could say "Morning" to the men at the table in front of him. They all looked far better than he felt, although Layton mumbled,

"Yes I suppose it is," before returning head down, to his coffee.

Ron looked up at Adam with a laugh saying "We'd better get a decent breakfast inside us; it could be a long day, you OK mate?" he directed at Adam.

"Yeah, sure, just could do with a decent night's sleep at some point," said Adam, already walking over to the fridge. Slapping egg, bacon, sausages and cream cheese in front of Ron, he said:

"Your idea, you cook it. I'll have scrambled with the cheese."

Getting nods from the four around the table, Ron busied himself on the breakfast.

By 2.45 AM, they'd all just finished their breakfasts with only meagre words around the table as Isobel walked in carrying a bag. "You'll need some clothes" she said holding up a bag, which she then dropped on the floor.

She looks only slightly better than I feel, good, but still, now I've got that down me, I'd pick her up and fuck her on the table right now, if this lot weren't here.

Isobel, as if reading his mind, sat on his knee, wriggling her bum and pressing against him.

There was a sudden beep of a horn outside. Layton had rung his driver at the hotel he had sent him to the night before. He was now outside ready to drive Ron, Adam and him to London via an industrial estate on the outskirts of Bristol. The three of them rose and stretched out their backs as one; before Ron said,

"We are just going to have a quick look around before it gets light and then wait until day break. Have a look at any comings and goings, and then continue up to Wandsworth. I can handle that, most probably, you two get in the back, get some more sleep, I'll wake ya later."

Adam kissed Isobel, grabbed his bag as he made for the

door, followed by Ron and Layton. Stella had heard the car horn and stood at the bottom of the stairs where she kissed Layton and Ron on the cheek, she said:

"Good luck, I will let you know what I find, as and when I find it."

"Look at what they are buying," Ron added as he walked through the front door.

As they drove along the A38, forty minutes into their first leg of the journey, the last of the minibuses left the warehouse in Wandsworth. They had all been timed to arrive at their destinations, at the same time give or take an hour, so had all left incrementally through the night and early that morning.

Little was said on the drive to Bristol; Ron occasionally made small talk with the driver. He had never had much of a capacity for small talk so wasn't particularly good at it, unless he was on a mission and needed to do so. Both Layton and Adam did as instructed and were asleep within ten minutes. They arrived a five minute walk from the warehouse at 4.30 AM; the driver parked up and turned off his lights as Ron left the car heading toward the warehouse.

At 6.00, he returned. Getting back into the car with Adam and Layton still asleep but with a wide awake and vigilant driver, he told him to drive three hundred meters up the road and park in the car park opposite the warehouse. Within ten minutes of them parking up and dousing the lights, a minibus appeared, drove into the warehouse car park, parking beside the building.

Twelve men got out and walked to the front door, one of them produced a key letting them all in. Each had a small bag over his shoulder, which could have been tools or supplies for the day. A few minutes later four came out again. They opened the double doors at the back of the bus and removed a long, and what looked like aluminum, hinged top box. But Ron could see very little of it as the bus was parked rear on to a set of double doors which opened, admitting the four men and the box.

By 8.15, Ron had not detected any other activity. He turned to the two men still sleeping in the back of the car, woke them up and told them they were about to leave. They would stop twelve miles down the road for some coffee and to discuss what he had seen. At 8.30, they were all ordering coffee, ironically at a Costa coffee outlet at the Moto services just off the M4.

The four, driver included now, with coffee in hand sat at a table in the corner while Ron told them what he had seen.

"I had a good look around before it got light; it looks like a normal service or warehouse facility, with a small reception immediately inside the main front doors. There was a light on in there, but I didn't see anyone. There were the normal double loading doors along one side and to the rear. It was mostly single story but along the back was a set of offices on a mezzanine level, which also had an outside access via a set of metal stairs.

I have some low light gear here but couldn't see anything abnormal inside. Just after 6.00 a minibus turned up with twelve men on board who offloaded a metal box from the back of the bus. That could have been tools; I didn't really expect much."

"So now the plan is still to go to Wandsworth?"

"Yes, this morning I sent seven teams, of three men apiece to each of the locations. They took a helicopter up to the nearest place they could land, and cars from there, they should all have arrived about 6.00. The other five I've sent to Wandsworth, they should have got there at a similar time, and we will meet them there."

With little more to add, they finished the coffee and continued onto Wandsworth. A few minutes after 9.00, as they drove down the slip road to rejoin the M4, calls began to come into Ron's mobile. All the teams had been told to report in between 9.00 and 9.30, to give an assessment of what they had seen.

Before leaving Wembury, Ron had checked the cell coverage at each of the locations, and whilst they all looked good he told each team to bring a satellite unit and radios along. With the team going to Wandsworth bringing an additional set for him. He had also printed out maps from Google Earth showing the unit in question, in as much detail as possible and smaller scale maps of the surrounding road network, with instructions to his teams to do likewise for their own targets.

By 9.40, he had spoken to each team leader and made notes as they talked, no call had lasted longer than five minutes. Each team had reported much the same as he had witnessed; the targets were either warehouses or industrial units, on an industrial estate.

At two locations, his men had seen minibuses arriving around 6.00 AM. One of which had driven into a loading bay, so they were unable to see much but did get the impression that the buses were full. The other minibus held twelve men, and they unloaded a large chest freezer from the rear of the bus, the description they gave was much the same as Ron had observed.

All of the remaining locations had adjacent car parks, in which was at least one minibus but many contained other cars as well. By 8.30, other vehicles arrived at most sites, some were cars others vans. The vans had left soon after.

Ron told Adam and Layton of what he had just heard, and the added "There is nothing really to get excited about; it all seems to be fairly normal early morning activity. The minibus arrivals could be the early shift or perhaps the night one coming back. It wasn't obvious if any of these men left but could easily have done in other cars or perhaps the vans. I've told each team to remain in place"

For the remaining hour of the journey, they discussed the reports the freezer was mentioned, but as it could have been being replaced or repaired as part of maintenance, which is what they did, it didn't seem alarming.

On arrival in Wandsworth, they drove into the industrial estate along Armoury Way; the warehouse they wanted to look at was another hundred meters along on the right. Ron rang his men to find out exactly where they were and then instructed the driver to turn right, then left to park next to two short wheel base Land Rovers. Each had a man in the driver's seat; Ron got out of the car, and held up his hand to indicate that Layton and Adam should stay there; he went over to the Land Rovers. He spoke to the two men for a few minutes before returning to Layton's car.

He said "Not much action, a little coming and going that's all. There isn't much point in you two staying here. So I think you Adam should go and organise us a hotel, for say eight of us and you Commissioner, perhaps go home get a change of clothes or whatever and then meet us later."

"Agreed, I could do with a change of clothes, and I would like to drop into the station for a while; I will drop Adam off and catch up later."

Adam was already on his iPhone, bringing up an app for local hotels. There was a Holiday Inn Express a few minutes away which he rang and secured four twin rooms. He gave the driver the address, who quickly found the place, and deposited him outside.

As Adam checked into the hotel, Ron went to join his men watching the warehouse. The industrial estate consisted of ten buildings. Half appeared to be warehouses with the rest either manufacturing or service centers, all with small adjoining car parks. The building in question was of the latter with signage outside claiming it was maintenance and contracting company. There was nothing unusual at all, causing Ron to wonder if they were wasting their time.

After a walk about the estate, there was still little to see, all the buildings had vehicles parked outside, with some coming and going. With the exception of one of the warehouses at the end of the access road and next to the one they were watching, which seemed to be vacant, no signage on the gates nor cars in the car park.

Approaching midday; Ron could feel his stomach rumbling. Thinking that his men would be as hungry, he walked back toward one of the units that had advertised a cafe and bought an armload of sandwiches. Once back at the Land Rovers he called his men back.

Chapter 34

Just as he finished his sandwich Ron's phone rang, he looked at the display showing it was Adam,

"Hi mate, I think this might be a bit of a bust here there is nothing to see, and it's as dull as dishwater."

"OK," said Adam sounding a little disappointed "But Stella has found something that might be of interest; at least it doesn't seem to fit."

"What's that?"

"Well, you asked Stella to look at what they were buying, and she's found a load of purchase orders, god knows from where or how but all of them are what you would expect. Building, maintenance and cleaning stuff, fire extinguishers and with security equipment, some of it quite sophisticated.

"Except, one item doesn't seem to fit and that's for a consignment of medical equipment. From what she says, there seems to enough to equip a small medical center, but she has cross checked all their known contracts with nothing showing up that would require anything like that."

"Yeah, that's peculiar; I could do with a shower I'll

come over in a few minutes, ask her to send a copy of the purchase order over, what's the address of the hotel?"

Adam gave it to him along with the room number before ringing Stella.

Ron arrived just as Stella's e-mail did. They both sat in front of Adam's laptop looking at the purchase order, they didn't understand all the items but could see monitoring equipment, hospital type beds along with laboratory equipment. "Could be easily be legit, they may be selling it all on."

"Yes." agreed Ron "I'm going to grab a quick shower, keep looking at it see what you can come up with."

As Adam scrolled down through the pages, he noticed that there were a dozen items of this and twelve items of that.

Ron shouted from the shower "Where did the order originate?"

"Bristol."

"Delivery address?"

"Wandsworth, 10 Armada Way Industrial Estate"

Ron suddenly appeared with a towel wrapped around him, dripping water all over the carpet

"Number 10," he said. "The place we are watching is number. 9, and 10 looks deserted, what's the date?"

"Eleven months ago, the number could be a typo."

They both looked at the order again this time in more detail; Ron picked up his mobile and rang Stella to ask if they had anything on No 10 which they didn't, it was definitely No. 9 on all the other contracts and delivery sheets. She hadn't noticed that this one was to be delivered to No 10.

"I looked at that building," said Ron. "Looks like a warehouse, a huge one at that, with loading doors and bays along the side I could see, with a small entrance at the front. There is a fence all around, and the gate was locked. It could have been vacated since the delivery, but it definitely warrants a closer look. I'll get the guys to do some reconnaissance. "

The team leader answered his call on the second ring; Ron told him what he wanted him to do. After consulting his printouts, the leader said he thought they could get a decent view of the left side from the car park of the building next to it, and of the back from the buildings behind. Those buildings fronted the main road so they would have to go that way to remain unnoticed, as long as there was no security in or around them. Ron told him that they would be back within thirty minutes.

Two of the men walked back to the main road to have a look at the rear of No 10, whilst another went to the building next to it, to see what he could see from the side. Another slowly walked past the front a few times, leaving one to wait with the Land Rover. In forty five minutes, all seven men were gathered beside the Land Rover that Ron had just driven back.

He had parked a little further back toward the main road to avoid any undue attention. Ron's men were from X team and consisted of three SBS and two SAS troopers, he now introduced Adam to them all.

The reconnaissance had given them a good understanding of the outside of the building. Both sides had four loading bays each with roll top doors, the front, a small glazed area with double doors and another roll top door stood at either side. To the back there were four more similar doors but without loading bays. In the center was an access ladder with a hoist attached to the roof beside the ladder.

All the windows with the exception of the glazed area at the front where at a high level, so were no good to them.

But there was bound to be roof lights, judging from the size of the building so if they could get onto the roof, these may give them a decent visual inside.

The perimeter fence would not be much of an obstacle, and there didn't appear to be any surveillance, certainly no security lights were visible. The decision was to wait until it got dark and then go in for a closer look.

Until then, three of the men would continue to roam around the estate, keeping both buildings in sight at all times. They would all return to the Land Rovers fifteen minutes before they went in. At the moment, all were dressed in either casual wear or work clothes and wanted to change into their black gear just before dark.

Once the three had set off on their patrols, Ron rang Layton on his mobile. After Layton had gone home that morning to change, he had gone into Scotland Yard, waiting for their call. He picked up his mobile and told Ron that he would ring him back within ten minutes. He didn't particularly want to be overheard and decided to find a quiet corner to talk. During his return call, Ron told him what they had been up to and what they had discovered amongst the purchase orders, and about their next moves.

Layton didn't have an issue with what Ron intended to do and also thought the medical equipment was of interest, but he did ask Ron not to go until he arrived. He thought a police presence would be a wise precaution, to which Ron agreed.

Just before it got dark, two at a time they climbed into the back of one of the Land Rovers and changed into dark tops and trousers over thermal gear and climbing shoes. They were light, flexible and quiet which they preferred for this type of work. There was even clothing for Adam.

Layton arrived as Ron and Adam finished changing

and as the sun completely disappeared. As they got out of the vehicle, the team leader said,

"Did you see those two cars that just passed?"

Ron shook his head.

"Well I've been here all day and I haven't seen them before, not driving in or in any of the car parks. I'm positive I haven't missed them it's not as though there is a lot of traffic here"

"What were they?"

"Both new black Audi A6s."

"So maybe we have someone in there, or there was?"

Making their way through the fence was easy, it didn't appear to be alarmed. One man went through and across the rear yard and as no security lights came on, the rest followed leaving one man behind on the other side of the fence. Quickly they made their way to the center of the building beside the access ladder and then equally as quickly up onto the roof.

There was very little light by now. Ron held up his hand to hold the rest by the roof edge, put on his low light gear and walked gingerly to the first of the roof lights. There was a little illumination coming from inside just enough for the naked eye, so he removed his gear and peered through the roof light. As expected, it wasn't clean, years of dirt obscured much of his view and after a minute or two of watching below he wiped a section to give him a better view.

Again he waited and watched. There was enough light down there to give him the impression that somebody was indeed there, but as there seemed to be no reaction to their entry to the roof he waved over the rest of the team. When they had all arrived and removed their low light gear, which they had donned for the move across the roof, they all stood in silence watching.

There were several more roof lights spread around, but they remained by the first until they could establish if the building was definitely occupied. There were lights on below that much was obvious, suddenly a shadow appeared then disappeared, someone was definitely down there. Ron indicated to two of them to move out to others roof lights, observe, fix their mics and report back in fifteen minutes whilst he and Adam remained there.

From this vantage point, they could see that one part, almost half, had been portioned off with solid looking walls and roof. It also appeared to have some air handling units connected to it, running up to the roof. Here, it was connected to yet more air handling equipment, also appearing to be a recent installation and far larger than would normally be expected for a warehouse.

Off on another side they could see packing cases and next to them some vehicles that looked like 4x4s. There could have been a sound of a television but the air handling units were making enough noise to mask anything else.

When the two returned, one reported that he could see a bunch of army cots, perhaps fifty, all set up and that he was sure there were a few people down there watching a TV. Within a few minutes, a door opened in the parti-tioned area, and a man walked out, crossing the warehouse until he disappeared from view.

Ron whispered "You two stay here; we might get more from the recordings from the mics." He and Adam then made their way back down the building and through the fence. Ron instructed the trooper at the fence to stay there but to make sure he kept out of sight.

Once back at the Land Rovers, which were only a ten

minute walk away, they appraised Layton of what they had seen.

"OK what do you want to do now?"

"Get inside, wouldn't you?"

"Yes, I would, but we will need a search warrant first. That I can get, but it will take a few hours"

"Cool" was Ron's reply "Gives me time to get what I need here, but make sure it happens before daylight, at least two hours before."

"I think we will also need a police backup." he added.

Ron's X team members had come up with only a very basic kit. Many of them rarely travelled anywhere on duty without sidearms, so they had their Sig Sauer P226s along with their radios, Sat Com gear and low light gear but little else. The Sig only had an effective range of fifty meters or so and Ron really wanted a little more fire power just in case, along with several other pieces of kit.

He didn't fancy a four hour drive there and back to Poole, but he could get what he needed dropped off. Aldershot was only a forty five minute drive even in the Land Rover. After making a call to Poole Barracks with his shopping list, he then rang the team he had sent to Cambridge, they were the nearest.

He didn't want to go in with just the seven of them; that should have been enough, but the extra three would make him far more comfortable. He gave them the address and told them to leave immediately.

Turning to Adam he said: "Fancy a drive, mate?"

"Sure, where are we going?"

"Aldershot, I need some supplies."

"Fair enough. We should leave now, I guess."

Chapter 35

Meanwhile, the remaining Iranian scientists that left the warehouse in Wandsworth as it got dark were now sitting in the departure lounge at Heathrow airport waiting for their flight to be called.

After the forty five minutes journey, Ron pulled up at the airfield security gates; they were expected. Once Ron's ID was thoroughly checked they were admitted through the gates and pulled up five hundred meters further along the road by a hanger. As they got out of the Land Rover, they could hear the sound of a helicopter approaching. The sound grew as it appeared out of the murky sky, hovered and landed twenty meters away.

As the rotors of the Lynx slowed, Ron walked forward beckoning Adam to accompany him. They instinctively ducked as they neared the side of the Lynx and the side door slid open. The crew chief stuck out his hand, which Ron shook. Then he turned back into the cabin and began pulling out bags from the storage compartments. He placed them, one by one, beside the open door.

As the bags were placed by the door, Ron checked each carefully. Once satisfied with the contents he handed them to Adam, who put them in the back of Land Rover. Following the eight bags, came two long waterproof pelican cases. Again Ron opened each, to reveal a G3SG1 sniper rifle, complete with night sights and 7.62 NATO rounds.

Next came three smaller cases containing smoke flash bang tear gas grenades and Det-Cord. Once all was checked and stowed Ron waved off the Lynx, which took off heading back to Poole. Adam and Ron did likewise, heading back to Wandsworth.

They arrived back at the industrial estate a few minutes after the team from Cambridge arrived. It was now just past midnight and Monday morning.

As Ron began to sort through the equipment, his mobile rang It was Colonel Chandler, with whom Ron had spoken before leaving for Aldershot. After a brief conversation, he hung up, returning to the equipment. Colonel Chandler headed the SBS and had given Ron the go but only with the compliance of Assistant Deputy Commissioner Layton and the search warrant he required. In the meantime, they geared up.

He handed out body armor, tactical helmets with night vision gear to Adam and the four troopers that were not either patrolling or still on the roof of the warehouse.

He then gave a Diemaco C8 Carbine equipped with Eclan optics to two his troopers, and the cases containing the G3SG1s to the other two but said to Adam, "I'm not giving you a C8, I can't. Layton would freak, but you can have this." He handed Adam a Sig Sauer pistol and three magazines, the same as he now wore.

"But keep it under your body armor." Adam nodded in agreement.

In an instant, the six men were transformed from a bunch of ordinary looking civilians, albeit slightly dubious, dressed in dark clothing, into a deadly fighting force. Ron instructed two of the men to relieve the two on the roof, "Take the body armor and helmets in a bag but leave your C8s, we will bring them up later" he instructed as they left.

As they left he took Adam aside and asked "Are you up for this? I'm presuming you want to go in with us, but you don't have to."

"I'm good. I can't say I'm not nervous, but I want in on this."

"OK mate, just follow our lead, I will be on the roof, you will go with Simon and Bill. I've worked with them for years, and they are the best, and you'll be fine"

Now came the wait, which was probably the hardest part of the job. At the outset, it was all a rush in the need to get ready to go, adrenalin flowing, and minds on the job in hand. Then came the wait. Inevitably, waiting for permission to do what you had to do. It was 1.00 am they were ready to go, but Layton hadn't appeared and there was nothing to do but wait for him and the piece of paper they hoped he carried.

The team on the roof radioed in; all the lights had gone off, and it was all quiet with the exception of the plant on the roof, which still hummed away. They had gained nothing of use from the radio mics and were no closer to establishing the numbers inside, or what they were up to.

The only thing they were reasonably sure of was that something was going on, and they needed to find out what it was, and stop it. The cots indicated that there had been quite a lot of people there, but they didn't seem to be there anymore. So, where were they now and what were they doing?

The first hour passed slowly, the second even slower. By 3.30, they were all getting worried. But then, five minutes later, Ron's phone vibrated. When he answered he heard Layton say "We are on the way and will be there by 4.00."

"Do you have the search warrant?"

"Yes, and you can ready your team." he added before ringing off.

"Finally! I was beginning to get worried" said Ron with relief.

He called the two men who had been patrolling back to kit up. They had come up with the operational plan during the wait and were all ready to go by the time lights appeared on the road behind them. Layton's car pulled up behind the second Land Rover, out of which stepped Layton accompanied by another officer. Behind them were two Police vans, they had stopped fifty meters back along the road and out piled a dozen or more policemen.

Ron briefed Layton on the plan and asked him to block off the road and secure the perimeter but to keep out of sight until they had entered the warehouse. He also advised Layton that the Land Rover they would be leaving had weapons in it and asked that it be secured by an officer. Layton agreed with Ron's requests as well as his tactics.

His and Ron's superiors had spoken at length several times over the previous few hours, and it had been agreed that it was a counter terrorism operation with the police providing support.

Ron and another trooper climbed into one Land Rover after final instructions were given to the remaining troopers and Adam. He drove off as the six moved forward to take up stations, near the gate to the warehouse.

Not wanting to be seen walking through the streets of Wandsworth with sniper rifles over their shoulders and carbines secured to their webbing, they drove around to Armoury Way and into the car park through which they had entered the rear of the building earlier.

Parking the vehicles beside the fence, they moved through it and were quickly up the access ladder and on the roof.

Once up on the roof, Ron radioed the team by the gate with a simple go. At this, the team cut through the fence beside the gate and moved to their pre-designated positions. The glazing to the roof lights was reinforced with wires running through it, but they would easily be breached with a little fifty grain Det-Cord.

The team below split into two teams of three and applied similar cord to the roll top doors. Adam teamed up with Simon and Bill as previously instructed. Ron and another trooper attached their rappelling lines and laid them out toward one of the roof lights, to which Det-Cord had been applied. Once ready and double clicks were received from the teams below confirming their readiness, Ron gave the command, "Ready, Go".

At the go, the roof lights were blown, Stun Grenades were thrown down onto the warehouse floor from the center roof light and from the one closest to the cots below. Seconds later the doors were blown and Ron, along with another, rappelled onto the roof of the structure inside the warehouse.

As they hit the roof, the snipers above searched for targets, as did Ron and his colleague. With the two levels of high ground, they had excellent vantage points over a good portion of the warehouse floor. The two teams by the doors then entered the building also searching for hostiles with their night vision scopes. Groans could be heard coming from the cots and then motion in one corner.

One man must have been sitting there dozing. As his senses recovered from the flash bangs, he came to his feet with a MP5 in his hands. No sooner than he was on his feet, two sniper rounds took him in the chest flinging him back into the corner.

All the ingress teams had been assigned sectors to cover and search. Simon and Bill along with Adam were assigned to the cot area. There were five men there, all suffering from the effects of the flash bangs which had detonated in the middle of them. While Simon and Bill covered them, Adam took plastic cuffs and quickly secured each man's hands behind his back.

Ron, with his partner checked part of the warehouse, whilst the other three covered another. With the prisoners secured Simon and Bill moved forward to help the others, leaving Adam to cover the prisoners.

Within minutes, the majority of the warehouse was confirmed as clear, leaving only the portioned off structure to one side. Hostiles could easily be hiding in there and the structure was sizable, accounting for over a third of the total floor area. Close to one end stood a lorry trailer with a forty foot container mounted on it, which appeared to be refrigerated as a humming sound could be heard coming from a unit mounted at one end.

Satisfied that there was no one else on the main warehouse floor, they approached the portioned off area with caution. Through the intensified illumination of the night vision equipment, a large window could be seen along one side. Inside, side by side hospital type beds lay.

There seemed to be no direct entry to this section, but a set of double doors was set in the center of the wall a few meters along from the window. After a closer examination, the doors appeared to be airtight and made of metal rather than the wood they would have expected. It was the only means of entry into the structure.

With one man holding the handles of one door and another man holding the other, they pulled the doors partially open, half expecting a hail of gun fire, as a result.

When this didn't happen, Ron crouched down beside the door with his C8 at the ready, signaling for the door shielding him to be pulled fully open; revealing an empty room beyond. The room extended the full depth of the structure with glazed double doors on either side, providing access to the room they had witnessed earlier and to another room opposite the first.

At the rear of the room, they had just entered were rows of environmental suits along with other medical equipment. Both doors were similar to the first in that they were airtight, with neither room showing any light. At the sight of the environmental suits, Ron was glad he had taken his more risky route of entering the laboratory, rather than throwing in a flash bang. This may have breached the airtight doors, but he was now extremely wary of entering either room, without adequate protection.

Rather than enter the rooms he pulled his men back closing the doors behind them. They checked the rest of the warehouse again before radioing Layton asking for his presence at the breached main doors to the warehouse.

When Layton arrived, accompanied by the several offi-cers, Ron briefed him on what they had discovered and asked for thermal imaging equipment to inspect the unsearched rooms, rather than enter them directly. Layton turned to one of the accompanying officers with the request, and then entered the building with Ron.

The two of them inspected the inside of the warehouse together, whilst the SBS team secured the building entrance and maintained a guard by the clinic unit as they were now calling it. The police contingent secured the building's perimeter fence.

As they walked around Ron explained what had happened as they entered.

He described the single armed guard and why he had been shot, and the prisoners now under watch of one of the SBS team members. The lights had been switched on, and under their illumination they saw the packing cases with the 4x4s sitting next to them. Neither said much, but both wondered what they contained. Looking up they noticed Adam still in his body armor, with his Sig concealed beneath it and helmet under his arm, looking up at the refrigerated trailer unit, wondering what was inside.

The three climbed up onto the back and pulled the levers securing the doors. They opened with a blast of frigid air, followed by a white mist that seeped out spreading along the floor beneath the trailer. They entered the frigid cold, and with the light of a torch that Ron carried a haphazard stack of large dark plastic bags could be seen at the rear.

One bag lying in front of the rest was roughly two meters long with a zip running the entire length.

With dread in the pit of his stomach, Adam reached down to pull open the frozen zip. As he forced it open, the light from Ron's torch swung away from the stack of bags, to one Adam was attempting to open. Adam staggered back as Ron shouted,

"Stop, get out now!"

All three turned, ran and jumped out of the container, hurriedly closing and securing the doors behind them.

"Everyone out of the building.

"Now!"

The prisoners were pulled to their feet, and everyone retreated through the breaches made earlier in the roll top doors.

As the last of the prisoners were pulled, Layton was already on his mobile requesting the immediate attendance of HART, the Hazmat response team responsible for the securing hazardous materials, along with ambulances and the coroner.

The opening zip had revealed a ghostly face in a hideous rigor, white from frost and covered in open sores.

Ron turned to Layton and Adam.

"If that's chemical, we could all be exposed already if it's biological, then perhaps not. We obviously made the right call going in there, but what we've actually found is anybody's guess. Whatever it is, it constitutes a major threat. We have to get this place properly secured immediately."

One of the police vans had been driven into the car park, into which the prisoners were being secured. Ron had also asked for one of the Land Rovers to be brought in, in the back of which, the three now sat. They expected it would take the HART teams an hour or more to get there, and during the wait they discussed what they had discovered and what it might mean.

The first priority was to secure the building, then establish the general nature of what had killed the man. Although they thought it unlikely that the brief exposure of the body would be enough to contaminate the building, no chances could be taken. If it were biological, it was very unlikely to be airborne, considering the frozen condition of the corpse. If it were chemical, then it was anybody's guess.

They still hadn't established whether there was

anybody inside the laboratory, either alive or dead, that then constituted their second priority. Up until that point all they could do was speculate, yet again, which was exactly what they did.

They worked on the obvious assumption: that these people were terrorists and were planning a strike in the UK. Probably, in London, but there could easily be other cities being targeted, extending their threat scenario to include all the cities in which De Costa had maintenance contracts for, seemed prudent.

Then was the detail about the cots. Although nobody had yet counted them, there seemed to be at least 50, all with blankets roughly laid over them. They appeared to have been occupied until fairly recently. The conclusion they had to make was that the attack was imminent, a day or two at most.

They discussed the options until the first of the HART vehicles arrived, when Layton went out to brief them. As he did so, several more vehicles arrived.

As soon as they were all briefed, several of the HART team members put on Hazmat suits, as did two of the SBS troopers and entered the building. Others secured temporary environmental enclosures complete with self-contained chemical showers to both breaches and covered the broken sky lights on the roof.

With this complete Ron and several of his men donned all the spare suits they could lay their hands on. Armed with the thermal imaging equipment that had just arrived, they re-entered the warehouse.

Layton went to question the prisoners, but not before several phone calls to his superiors, leaving Adam alone to brood about the situation he had got himself into. Things just weren't working well for him at present; he seemed to be stumbling from disaster to catastrophe, each one worse than the last.

He thought back to several weeks ago before he had met Isobel and had been dragged into this nightmare. How, as an environmental scientist, he had worked to help provide the world with clean sustainable power, something he had always believed in. But what really was the point when the world seemed to be populated with either terrorists' intent on murdering them, or businessmen intent on making themselves rich at the expense of everything else.

And politicians; all they wanted to do was bend you over and fuck you in the arse. Was there a point in any of it? At this rate, they were all doomed anyway.

He'd told Ron he wanted to see this through but the more he found out, the more the world seemed to be completely fucked up. Maybe be he should he return to Plymouth, buy a boat and just fuck off somewhere with Isobel and Dan, leaving them all to just get on with it. But he despised people like that; those that had the know-how to do the right thing but selfishly just took care of themselves, leaving him but a single choice, to follow this through to the end.

It was after ten by the time Ron reappeared and by now the black clouds that had been overhead all night decided to shed their load the rain hammered on the roof of the Land Rover. Ron jumped inside again followed by Layton. Both of them wore the same bleak expression that he knew he held.

Ron told him what he had seen.

There were crates of weapons enough for a small army, with supplies of water, food and fuel long enough to last for weeks. And then of the lab; how it had been used to test their weapon. It now seemed to of a biological origin, but the exact nature was still unknown, and of the bodies in the refrigerated trailer, twenty eight in total.

The place seemed to be both a command post and a siege center but the nature of the weapons found in the crates indicated that they definitely had offence in mind.

There was a major terrorist campaign under way with a biological strike imminent, if not already taking place. This did nothing to lighten Adam's mood, but his rising anger did bolster his resolve to be part of the solution not play ostrich.

Chapter 36

Although they were now certain a biological attack was about to take place, the means of delivery were far from clear. Inside the laboratory area of the warehouse, equipment had been discovered which appeared to be for filling pressurised canisters. But as to what type of canisters, or how they were to be used, they had no idea.

Layton and Ron had already established their best next move. It would be to send armed police officers to each of the buildings that De Costa and Roseau's companies had maintenance contracts for. In addition, they had to search every building De Costa, rented, leased or owned.

They had no idea what they were looking for but hoped something would stick out as though it didn't belong there, from which point they could evaluate their next steps. It wasn't a great deal to go on, but they had originally worked with far less, but still trusted a lot to luck.

Both Layton and Ron had made numerous phone calls from inside the warehouse to their superiors over the preceding few hours. A full Cabinet Office Briefing Rooms (COBR) emergency meeting would be convened in conference room A in the Cabinet Office main building at 70 Whitehall, later that day. In the meantime, a truncated COBR committee had been formed, to evaluate the threat, manned by SIS and police personnel, which the Prime Minster and other senior ministers would join as soon as they were available.

COBR's decision was to send police to each building in question. In those cities where there was already a contingent of SBS members, they would support the police and enter each Town Hall with them. They thought that the Town Halls would be the most likely targets. COBR had been assured by the Palace of Westminster Protection Division of the Met that there was no possibility of any imminent threat to the Palace itself

But, it was still the Palace of Westminster, in Ron's opinion that represented the most likely target.

On any given day, there were hundreds there, from politicians to tourists, and on a day like today when the PM was due to make a major announcement concerning the Enterprise negotiations with Iran, the house would be packed to the rafters. There would be media and demonstrators everywhere, add to the guests in the newly refurbished function rooms with even more onlookers and tourists and that number could be increased tenfold.

At Ron's insistence, he, Layton and the SBS troopers with them would go to the palace, to meet members of the Special Protection division there. Hopefully a plan would materialise, but they knew there were on the back foot and time was of the essence.

It wasn't much of a plan at all, but it was they had. The HPA had been called in by the HART team's commander. They would be working as fast as they could to establish the nature of the biological threat. With Layton's car and the Land Rovers crammed to capacity, they set off toward the center of London and the Palace of Westminster.

A police car led the convoy, its blue lights flashing, and sirens howling at every intersection to speed them on their way.

The discussion in the car was that of delivery method. Layton in the front passenger seat with Ron sitting behind the driver talked about various methods whilst Adam sat quietly thinking. He thought back to the purchase order documents Stella mentioned. They had concentrated on the medical equipment, but there was something else she mentioned that was sitting on the edge of his consciousness.

There had been lots of building and cleaning materials and all manner of other supplies. He texted Stella, asking for a list of the type of things they purchased.

A few minutes later Stella replied to the text Adam sent.

"You mentioned some equipment for filling pressurised canisters, how about fire extinguishers, would that work?" He asked.

"You may be onto something there, what do you think Ron?"

"Possible" was the reply "They are pressurized, I can't see any reason you couldn't put gas in them, let me make a couple of calls. Check the type they were and how many they ordered"

Adam was on the case and had texted Stella the request already; it wasn't long before he received the reply "They were all carbon dioxide extinguishers of two different sizes, one kilo and nine kilos and they ordered one hundred of each."

He continued after looking at the next text Stella sent "They were all delivered to Armada Way. And, none were ordered for their other depots around the country either."

A few minutes later Ron, after finishing his third call said,

"This is seriously bad news; they are high pressure and are easily portable. That small one could be concealed under a jacket. The worst part about it is; a biological agent stored in carbon dioxide and kept cold would stay viable for a long time."

The convoy was making good progress despite the London traffic; they had just passed Lambeth palace. As they turned left over the bridge and through the Members Entrance, large crowds were evident in front of the palace. In Parliament Square at least one protest was going on; placards could be seen, and although not all of them could be read, there was something about human rights in Iran.

Another group congregated on the other side of green, chanting some slogan or other. There was a barricade along the opposite side of the St Margaret Street, manned by police who were trying to keep the way clear for cars entering the palace.

It was a busy day. Two major announcements planned; the first, an interim report from the Robertson Inquiry, the second, an announcement by the PM about his negotiations with the Iranians for the return of the Enterprise, and the release of her crew. This he would not delay no matter what the crisis.

On top of that the newly refurbished Westminster Hall and Parliament Terrace overlooking the River Thames were being used for the first time for corporate conferences amid the normal fanfare. As a result, there were vehicles trying to get into and out of the several gates, media vans with their satellite dishes broadcasting to the world, and possibly a thousand or more people along for their say or simply to watch the proceedings.

The cars stopped in The New Palace Yard, directly underneath Big Ben, after navigating the Members Entrance. Here, they were met by a senior member of the Palace of Westminster division of the Met. With the SBS troopers remaining by the Land Rovers, Layton, Adam and Ron were led across the yard toward the main security office on the far side.

Just as they were about to enter the office, a call of "Ron" was heard from behind them. Ron turned to see an elderly man limping towards them.

Ron walked toward the man, whom he thought he recognised. The man, as well as a pronounced limp, had his left arm in a sling. Ron put out his hand just as he thought he remembered the man's name, "Charlie, isn't it?"

"Yes" he replied taking Ron's hand.

"How are you, what are you doing here, and what on earth happened?"

"A little argument with a limo, long story, but I work here, still, just about."

"Really, they make you come to work in that condition?" Looking him up and down.

"Not quite, to be honest I came in today for the first time in a couple of weeks, so they wouldn't get rid of me any earlier than were going anyway."

"Look," said a distracted Ron "I've got to get into a meeting now, but I will try and catch up later."

"Actually," came a voice over his shoulder. "I think he should come with us," said the officer of the Palace Division. He looked at Charlie continuing, "I didn't know you were in, Charlie."

Turning to address all three he added "Charlie here

knows more about this place than anyone else alive. We may as well have his input."

Once all were seated in the security office, along with two additional senior officers on duty, Layton told them everything they knew. When he finished, the most senior of the officers said,

"I appreciate your anxiety over this, but I can't see how they can pull it off here as I've already informed COBR. A few years ago some nut job got a spray can into the House of Commons and since then, everyone and everything goes through our recently updated scanners and metal detectors as well as a physical search. There is no way a fire extinguisher, or many according to you, can be brought in today or any day for that matter."

"OK, I understand that," replied Ron "But let's say they were brought in several days ago, as part of regular maintenance schedule or something like that."

"But according to you they would need to be refrigerated for the virus to stay viable."

"Which is possible, you have to admit that."

"Well yes, but only with the collusion of people working here and they're security vetted, every one of them."

"What about all the contractors?" Put in Charlie.

"What do you mean?"

"Over the past six months there have been so many contractors, from the building and refurbishment, to works, to all the new maintenance and cleaning contractors. From what I've seen the personnel seem to change on a daily basis. You never get to know any of them as they all keep to themselves."

"Perhaps" was the officer's reply "But in that case they are still vetted through the contracting company."

"Providing the company has given you the correct info," said Adam.

"Very well," said the officer, still seemingly unconcerned. "I will call in some extra personnel and begin searching the building. If we gather all the fire extinguishers we find, that should take care of any threat."

A thoughtful Charlie then said "You know if I wanted to spread something through the entire building I wouldn't risk trying to spray it from a bunch of extinguishers. That would be far too obvious. What I'd do would be to use the air handling system; it distributes chilled air to nearly every room here."

"I know a little about them," said Adam. "They normally have plant rooms on the roof, near the external chillers, which pump air into ducts and through to the rooms via ceiling grills, is that what they have here?"

"It used to like that, but six months ago a new system was put in. There is a large plant room in the first basement area, next to all the maintenance workshops. The air is sucked in from the outside to there, along with chilled water from the chillers on the roof; the air is then chilled and distributed throughout the building"

"Can you show us that room?" Asked Ron. The officer nodded his agreement, adding he would organise his officers to search the building and would be on the radio if needed.

Chapter 37

They followed Charlie into the bowels of the building, the area they were making towards constituted part of the first basement level. There were several basement levels extending down to where Guy Fawkes attempted to blow up the old Houses of Parliament in 1600s. A fire in 1834 destroyed much of the old building with what was left demolished, to make way for a new building completed in 1870. But much of the subterranean structure remained.

Without Charlie they would have been lost within minutes passages left the main corridor to the left and right every four or five meters. After a ten minute walk, Charlie opened a door and entered a large room, the maintenance office, and storage area. He would need to talk to the engineers to get the keys to the plant room.

Layton was the second to follow him into the room as they did a man dressed in overalls rose from the desk he was sitting at. Before Charlie could say anything, Layton said walking forward past Charlie,

"I'm a police officer can I have a word please?" the man smiled reaching down under his desk, and pulled out an automatic rifle before Layton could react. The man sprayed rounds directly at him, catching him in the throat. His arterial blood sprayed high into the air. After the initial burst, he turned toward Charlie.

Ron and Adam still were standing by the door. Ron pushed Adam back through the door and grabbed Charlie by the collar, dragging him back with him, before pulling the door closed. Several rounds peppered through the door, striking the corridor wall opposite and ricocheting down the corridor.

"This thing" indicating his Sig he'd removed from its holster "is no use against that rifle. I need my men" he said as he pulled the radio that he had been given earlier from his pocket. He gave the Met officer a situation report and asked for his men to be sent immediately.

Inside the room, other similarly overall clad men came running in, all armed with H&K MP5s. Some of the MP5 armed men took positions behind cover around the room while others pushed several large filing cabinets against the main doors and disappeared through adjoining doors.

Ron asked Charlie if there were other entrances and exits the man inside could use, to which Charlie told him that there were plenty; the whole place was a maze.

"We need a map."

"Yeah," said Charlie who had already produced a sheet of paper and pencil from his pocket and was busy sketching.

Inside the main plant room, to the left of the room where Layton lay and opposite the chilled storeroom, two men were busy removing the nozzles. Then, using flexible hoses, they attached the fire extinguishers to an intricate system of pipes and valves. He called to the man next to the door to get the rest of the extinguishers in now. He disappeared to fetch them.

Ron's men were on the way, guided by three Met officers while a system of silent alarms was being triggered throughout the maze of buildings. The palace's design, had it been done today, would have been impossible with the current emergency escape regulations. There were hundreds of rooms opening onto corridors which then joined others; if it weren't such a historic building, the fire brigade would have condemned it. As it was, a system of alarms had been installed that would alert security staff, they had already begun to evacuate the building, but it would take time. Far too much time.

Charlie had finished his floor plan, indicating the various avenues that the men inside that room could escape the building, or more pointedly, avenues that Ron could use to box them in and gain access to the plant room.

With their worst fears confirmed, and far from prepared for what they had to do, Ron's men arrived and Charlie explained the layout, suggesting options.

By now the remaining extinguishers were being attached to valves. It would take a little time to transfer the carbon dioxide with the Smallpox virus it contained, to large accumulator cylinders. This reduced the pressure to five bars, about sixty PSI, without the whole system icing up. In the meantime, the rest of the men had taken up defensive positions.

. . .

Inside the Commons Chamber, David Blain had already announced his agreement with the Iranians for the return of the Enterprise and her crew. The facts amazed all that heard what he had to say. It was the general consensus that the Iranians would demand excessive terms that could never be agreed upon.

Blain told all those assembled that the Iranians would release the Enterprise with no conditions. That all they wanted was to improve relations with the West, and would release the Enterprise solely to achieve that end, at that a hushed whisper went around the chamber followed by a thunderous applause. Blain's lies had once again been successful, and he was to be the hero of the hour with this settlement.

The House had then gone on to the next large piece of business for the day. An interim report from the Robertson Inquiry had been read out. The gist of this report was that three senior executives at the International had been complicit in the phone hacking. It had also named two ministers and the PM's media secretary as those that had conspired with these executives. It had also called into question whether or not Dandelion was a fit person to be running a company of such a size and such an influence, given his supposed lack of knowledge into the endemic hacking within his company.

This caused uproar in the House; the immediate resignation of the named ministers and the secretary was demanded by the Labour MPs. They also called for the Monopolies Commission to investigate the company and recommend how to remove it from such an influential position. Heated arguments inevitably ensued, which virtually amounted to screaming matches between the parties.

There wasn't a chance in hell that the security staff,

which would soon be gathering at the doors, would be noticed, and definitely not be able clear the chamber.

The routes that the terrorists could use to escape the basement had been relayed to the palace Division, who moved to block them with armed officers. Four of Ron's men, guided by Charlie, were led through another route to the maintenance area and the rear of the room in which the terrorists were holed up.

They had decided that they had no choice but to perform two simultaneous assaults into the room and the plant room beyond. They'd heard objects being moved behind the doors to reinforce them, so decided to go through the walls.

The easiest way to do this was with a shaped charge which they didn't have. It was improvisation time. Det-Cord was all they had available.

Large metal filing cabinets were dragged out of rooms off the corridor and filled with everything they could find, then pushed tight against the wall and wedged there covering Det-Cord placed against the wall. This, they hoped would focus the explosive charge of the Det-Cord toward the brickwork of the wall.

It wasn't going to be pretty and they almost certainly were going to take casualties, but there was no other way if they were to do it before the virus was released.

Adam, with another impromptu idea, asked Charlie over the radio whether the duct leading from the room split up inside or if it passed through another area before it split. Charlie confirmed that the duct work left the room directly into a services riser adjacent and from there split up. The main section rose up the air shaft before diverting into the main ground floor area, with a smaller section remaining on the basement level, supplying that.

He quickly told Ron of his idea, asking for one of the SBS men, some Det-Cord and detonators. And, to get the remaining police who were originally searching the building to get to the basement and evacuate it.

Adam and Simon ran through the rabbit warren of corridors, and after a couple of wrong turns they found the access stairs Charlie had directed them to and burst out into the Central Hall.

The hall was packed with people. The services riser was on the opposite side of the hall; it had originally been constructed as a Mess area but had been converted years ago to be used as a riser cupboard. It took power, water and more recently air conditioning and ventilation to the floors above the basement level. There was an access door to the riser cupboard which, as they expected, was locked.

With no time to find the key or for nicety, Simon brought up his C8 selected 3 round bursts and put 3 three bursts into the door and lock.

The gun fire brought about the expected reaction, the lock and a section of the door disintegrated. But it also brought about total panic from those within the hall. Screams issued from all around them followed by running feet. That'll get them out, thought Adam, hoping that nobody would get hurt in the stampede.

One of the officers standing inside the Commons Chamber had a similar idea; he had been trying to get the attention of the speaker for several minutes but wasn't getting anywhere. He pulled his side arm and fired it into the air. To his knowledge this had never been done before, and he was sure it was a capital offence; nevertheless he could be saving hundreds of lives.

With the transfer from the extinguishers just finished, the engineer turned a system of valves allowing the gas to mix with the outgoing chilled air. It would then pass through a series of ducts before being distributed to the rest of the palace.

The SBS troopers led by Charlie had also reached their destination and were in the process of applying Det-Cord to form a breach in that wall. They radioed Ron to confirm.

The gunshot in the Commons achieved the desired result; the tumultuous noise instantly stopped, replaced by screams. As they died down, the officer shouted,

"There is a biological weapon threat. You must leave the building immediately. Please do it now in an orderly fashion", he repeated this several times before there was a reaction.

The reaction was fairly predictable, and it was far from orderly.

The riser cupboard was about five meters across, Adam could see the ductwork attached to the opposite wall; there was no way across, they couldn't even jump across, there was nothing to jump onto. The ductwork ran down about 5 meters before turning into and passing through the wall, presumably into the plant room the other side. A smaller section continued across the riser and through the opposite wall. The only option was down.

Adam went first, landing on the half meter wide duct which gave a little under the impact. Simon then threw down the Det-Cord and detonators and then his C8, all of which Adam caught, putting the sling of the C8 over his shoulder. Simon then jumped onto the duct, landing beside Adam.

"OK Adam, what's the plan?"

"We wrap the cord around the duct and blow it, the air then can't go up the duct into the rest of the building."

"But surely it will rise anyway?"

"I don't think so; carbon dioxide is heavier than air, it's only being mixed the other side of that wall, in theory, it will sink but at worst it can't spread to the rest of the building, only to the hall above, and I'll bet that's empty by now."

"And us?"

"Well, we can try to climb that electrical cable, but I don't think that's going to be much good, I reckon we jump again." Adam said peering over the side.

"How far do you reckon?" They couldn't see a thing.

"Not far, I think I'm more worried about what we land on. Sorry, guess I should have said something before we jumped."

"Don't worry mate, I'd have jumped anyway, the Det's my job. If I left it to a geek who fucked it up, Ron would castrate me. Oh yeah, one more thing, if we go down and so does the gas?"

There wasn't much point in finishing his sentence.

Adam added, "Sorry again, suppose I should have mentioned that too."

"Fuck off, lean over and grab the Det as I swing it

under the duct, we'll put one here, and one on the other side, that will do the trick."

In the Commons Chamber, the evacuation was anything but orderly; those on the benches nearest the huge double doors, by which the officers stood, ran past them. The TV crews that recorded the proceedings in the house from viewing balcony surrounding the chamber left in hurry, forgetting even to turn off the cameras. Not by conscious choice as they would claim afterwards it was purely accidental but with the cameras still running, their pictures were transmitted to the broadcast vans outside the palace, who in turn were broadcasting the scene live to the world.

There were several disabled MP's in wheelchairs in the Chamber police officers hurried forward to help. MPs fought their way past, pushing the policemen and others slower than them out of the way.

Blain, whose allotted seat was at the far end of the chamber, was desperately trying to get out, heedless of whom he pushed out of the way to do so. He elbowed his way through the bottleneck forming near the door and was nearly out, until blocked a policeman attempting to get a wheel chair and its occupant to safety.

Undeterred, he then tried to jump over the wheelchair, but collided with it, knocking the policeman, the wheelchair, and its passenger over. Stumbling forward in an attempt to regain his balance, he knocked several more of his fellow MPs to the ground.

Blain picked himself up, and without turning to help or check what he'd done, he ran out of the Chamber, all to be recorded by several TV cameras sitting on the balcony above.

. . .

Adam radioed Ron; he told him that they were about to blow the duct and that they shouldn't to go into the room, just yet.

He suggested that they blow the duct simultaneously with the walls and then throw the stuns and gas grenades into the room. He also gave Ron a quick lowdown on what it would mean to both him and Simon, Ron agreed and wished them luck.

"Ten seconds?" Simon said with a shrug.

"I guess, if we haven't stop falling by then, we'll be dead anyway."

"On three, then"

"One, two, three" both jumped.

They fell, nine perhaps ten meters before hitting the bottom, which as Adam thought was strewn with builder's rubble, fortunately nothing very sharp. As they hit, both rolled tight against the walls as the DET blew and a section of duct smashed onto the ground between them.

Both of them were stunned by the explosion and the impact of the duct work, but both were aware enough to see a thick white mist spewing from the damaged duct work above backlit by light coming from the open door of the riser cupboard. As Adam had guessed, the gas was drifting down, already enveloping them.

"Do you think we should try to get out of here?" suggested Simon.

With the ductwork out of the way, a little more light filtered through. They thought they could see an access door similar to the one they had entered through above.

Adam had almost forgotten about the C8 until jumping, when it crashed into his side breaking several ribs. He now brought it round, and as Simon had earlier, put several rounds into the door. They couldn't see a lock, so Adam switched to full auto and emptied the clip. Enough damage was done to enable Simon to kick open the door, and both stumbled through.

They found themselves in a darkened room, what little light there was came from under a door. Both men made their way toward it, falling over furniture as they did so. Simon pulled the fortunately unlocked door open. The illumination from the corridor gave them enough light to see the light switch beside the door. Turning it on illuminated the room, into which was flowing a thin white mist.

The room was some sort of storage room; empty boxes were strewn across the floor, with a desk on one side. Adam hobbled to the desk as quick as his damaged ankle would allow, and grabbed a roll of packaging tape that was on it. At the door, Adam pulled it shut after him, and began taping around the door and frame to try to seal it.

As Adam did that, Simon was on his radio. He told Ron they were out of the riser and that the gas was moving down, not up, but they still needed to shut off the pumps.

Ron had blown the wall, as had the troopers on the far side of the room, when Simon had blown the ductwork. It wasn't pretty, but it worked. The filing cabinets directed the blast into the wall, and then crashed back as the wedges gave way, followed, by a hail of gunfire from inside the room. Once the smoke and dust cleared, they had their breach, and through it, they threw flash bangs and tear gas.

Now, after hearing from Simon, they threw in more flash bangs and smoke, diving through the hole seconds later. The team on the other side did likewise.

Chapter 38

Hundreds of people were now running through the building's exits, most onto St Margaret's Street, where more TV cameras recorded the scenes accompanied by a running commentary from the reporters. Afterwards, many would liken it to the commentary during the World Trade Centre attacks; sheer disbelief that it was or even could be happening.

Whatever the commentator's perspective it was a disaster, happening right in front of them, and one if the terrorists had been entirely successful, would have cost hundreds if not thousands of lives.

Police vehicles were arriving in their droves, followed by ambulances and soon after, both HART and HPA response units. Still the cameras recorded.

Mobile screens erected beside the broadcast vans displayed the images. Some repeatedly showing David Blain knocking over a policemen and wheelchair bound MP along with several others, in his desperation to get out of the Commons Chamber.

. . .

Meanwhile, back inside the basement, Ron and his men looked around the smoke filled room for targets; most of the terrorists were still lying on the floor in very poor shape. Their ear drums ruptured, blood running freely from eyes, ears, noses and mouths, so many flash bangs in such a confined space had a devastating effect.

Despite that two did struggle to their feet, only to be cut down with 5.56 rounds from the SBS's C8s.

There was still another room to enter; the pumps that supplied the air to the ductwork were still running. More C8 volleys tore the door to shreds, followed by more flash bangs and another suicide dive into the room by the SBS team members.

This time they met more resistance.

Three terrorists were in the room, and all got off rounds with their MP5', mostly striking body armor, but it really wasn't any contest. The SBS, all marksmen, took down the terrorists in their pre-determined sectors.

Two of the SBS members received wounds, one in the arm, another to his leg, neither were life threatening if treated quickly. While two members took up station beside each of the doors, should there be any remaining terrorists Ron hustled in Charlie, asking him to figure out how to switch off the pumps and isolate the gas cylinders.

One man watching the drama unfold on TV was initially enraged then after considering it for a minute or so, he began to smile. His men at the palace must have made a mistake somewhere he thought, gaining the unwanted attention of the authorities. But, that didn't matter. With all their attention focused here, they would never discover that this was merely the opening salvo of his strike. Tomorrow's action would still go ahead successfully; they would still bring the British to their knees.

He chuckled to himself as images of the Prime Minister again hit his TV screen humiliating himself worldwide. That would show the world what cowards they were, De Costa thought as he packed his clothes in preparation for the morning's flight. It was only a short walk from his hotel to the terminal building; nothing would stop him or his countrymen tomorrow.

The remaining two terrorists were in the corridor beside the plant room door as the last of the flash bangs detonated; they decided it was time to get out. They made their way at a run to an access stairway at the northern end of the basement; they had worked here for several months and knew it well.

If they had dropped their weapons before making to the top of the stairs they might have gotten away with it, but they didn't. As they rounded the final curve of the staircase they were seen by armed police at the top, again if they had dropped their MP5's the police may not have shot them, but they hesitated. Seeing fingers near the triggers was all the policemen needed, they opened fire, sending both men tumbling down the stairs.

With the machinery shut down and the smoke clearing, Ron walked back into the adjoining room and over to Layton's body. He hadn't liked him much when they'd first met outside the Carlton Towers, but over the last few days he had grown to like the man. He knelt by his body and, heedless of the pool of blood seeping onto his knees, put his hand gently on Layton's forehead.

"Sorry mate, but without you we would never have stopped them." Rising slowly he radioed the palace policemen, whom he assumed were still on the floor above.

Ron then moved back into the plant room to check on his own men, who were being attended to by their colleagues. Satisfied with their condition he sat down at the desk, to wait. He would have liked to get all his men out. Simon had radioed that they thought they had the gas contained, he would rather not have taken the chance, but no way was he going to leave this room until it was properly secured.

Stretching and rubbing his eyes which by now were smarting from the smoke he was pleased when he opened them to see Adam and Simon enter the room.

"Not sure you guys should be here, you have to be infected but if it spreads to us that quickly, I guess we are all walking dead, already."

"Yeah, we definitely breathed it in but no virus can act that quick you should be fine, but we need to be quarantined fairly quickly."

"That was a brave thing you did Adam, I have to admit I had my doubts you were up to this, yeah you too, Simon", he directed at Simon standing behind Adam "You're brave too, but you get paid for it, he doesn't."

"As Simon said before we jumped, Fuck Off."

"Yeah, I echo that," said Simon.

"You saw Layton?"

"Yeah the poor sod. Fuck, if we could only have trusted him a week ago, none of this shit would have happened."

"Yeah, I know, but that's what it's got like, who can you trust these days."

"I need to get you two out of here and into hospital. HART must be here by now I will get two suits sent down and you out. Look. Don't worry about it, the first thing they and HPA will do is identify the virus and produce a treatment, it's not as though they don't have samples" indicating the large yellow cylinders opposite.

"The bodies in the container will probably tell them a lot as well."

Adam added "Shit, I really ought to ring Isobel, this must be all on TV and she will guess it's us."

The Palace Division officers arrived whilst they were talking, bringing white paper suits and masks for Adam and Simon to wear along with a large plastic bag each for their clothing. The officer in charge introduced himself as Chief Superintendent Isaacs as he handed the items to Ron but remained standing in the door.

"Go into the other room as far away from others as possible, put these on, your clothes in the bag and seal it, they will be contaminated. Please."

They did as requested as the officer looked at the Heath Robinson-like contraption, attached to the air handling system. Nobody had yet counted the fire extinguishers attached to it via flexible connectors. "Fifty." he said. "Quite a few, eh?"

He was about to continue as Ron interrupted "Shit there is supposed to be a hundred, we need to search this place and find the rest."

"Not until I have cleared and secured this building you don't."

"You don't have time" was all Ron got out.

"No." the man said. "You all get out now this is my building my people will take care of it."

"I don't think you understand."

"It's you that doesn't understand, you are leaving

NOW, we are securing all the entrances and have people moving in to decontaminate it. Please, all of you come with me."

"I should be removing all your weapons, but I doubt that you will oblige, so go now before I change my mind. You too Charlie, and don't come back until cleared as fit."

The SBS team along with Adam and Charlie followed two officers toward the main access staircase and into the Peer's Lobby, and from there back to New Palace Yard where they had left the Land Rovers.

As they walked Adam asked one of the officers through his mask,

"What the hell is the matter with him?"

"He's screwed up, hasn't he and he's pissed. If he can lay blame, he will, I don't suppose you guys have seen the TV have you?"

He didn't add to that statement, and didn't look as if he would welcome any more questions, so the rest of the walk was done in silence.

When they reached the yard, the SBS team where ushered into the Land Rovers, all except Simon who was helped into an ambulance along with Adam.

Ron told them that he would need to go to Thames House but would be at the hospital as soon as possible. He somehow doubted that the remaining extinguishers would be found in the palace and was extremely worried about it. With Layton dead, he needed to alert his bosses to the possibility that this still wasn't over.

Chapter 39

It was several hours later, but Ron did make good his promise to Adam and Simon. By the time he reached the hospital, it was late at night, and only a few hours before the general strike started.

On arrival, he was initially told that it was too late to see them. He was not prepared to take that.

He walked toward the isolation unit, where they were being kept with a nurse trailing behind, still trying to tell him he couldn't go in. Pushing through the doors at the entrance of the unit, he was met by two security guards and a doctor. He was again told he couldn't go in as the patients were being isolated and could be contagious.

He told the doctor that they either get him a suit or he would go in without one. One of the guards tried to put his hand on his shoulder, he didn't make it. Ron simply took his hand twisted it around and smashed the guards face into the wall.

"I was trying to be polite" he said.

The other guard was already retreating quickly down the corridor. Ron had removed his body armor and his Sig, but he was still wearing his black gear with the legs below the knees still coated in Layton's dried blood. And this guard was not about to join his colleague now groaning on the floor. Fortunately for him, a policeman that had been sitting beside the door of the room Adam and Simon were being kept in, came forward.

"Let him in"

The nurse thankfully hurried off to get Ron a suit.

Both Adam and Simon were deep asleep when Ron finally made it through the double airtight doors.

Sleeping, lucky bastards,

He momentarily thought which was quickly replaced with worry for both of his friends. They were both connected to monitoring equipment which, in his uninitiated opinion read fine, but he knew that soon both could be very sick.

What these two had done had prevented the spread of the virus throughout the palace. There was no trace of it anywhere other than in the riser shaft and the room they exited through. Both had laid their lives on the line and had saved well over a thousand in doing so.

He sat between the two beds thinking how tired he was, not being able to remember the last time he had slept, but he still had work to do and couldn't afford the luxury of sleep. After a pause, he tapped Adam on the shoulder, who moved, then groaned and finally opened his eyes. Ron had both good and bad news for him.

"You don't half look weird dressed like that, you know mate?"

"I hope it was one of those dog ugly guards that undressed you and put you to bed rather than that very pretty nurse."

"You OK, Adam?"

"Not bad mate, probably have a little cold tomorrow so

I'm told, my ribs hurt a little, my ankle is on fire, but at least I'm getting some sleep at last. You look like you could do with some."

"I could, but need to talk to you first."

"That bad?" asked Adam.

"Some."

Ron proceeded to tell Adam what he knew.

He started with something that he knew would make him laugh. The Prime Ministers public disgrace. He knew what Adam thought of the man and was rewarded with Adam's spluttering laughter.

He then went on to explain the rest.

"The good news is that you probably have Smallpox."

"If that's the good news, I don't want to hear the rest."

"Shut up and listen, it is good news.

They know what the virus is, unfortunately, it's a strain that they haven't seen before; you will understand that better than I. They tell me they are working on production of an antiviral or something like that, and have already vaccinated you and Simon, so you don't have to worry about that.

Next" he said before Adam could interrupt again.

"We think we have found all the large fire extinguishers, they were found evenly dispersed at each of the town halls. We seem to have caught a lucky break on this. Do you remember that guy throwing an extinguisher from a roof at a demonstration earlier this year?

"Well that must have rung a bell somewhere, when the buildings on Stella's list were checked, they also checked all the accessible roofs and found all of the remaining fifty stashed away.

"We are presuming that they meant to spray the people at the rally there tomorrow, from the roof. Now each site is under observation, when the terrorists return we'll have them."

"That is good news, but the small ones, I guess that's the bad news?"

"Nothing yet but they only constitute 10% of the total. Another bit of good news, is that, after what happened today a lot less people are expected to attend the demonstrations, which should make it easier to spot these terrorists" he ended, hopefully.

"So what are you going to do now?"

"I'm going to get some sleep, a couple of hours perhaps, and then we are going to Birmingham to reinforce the search teams, but first I'll tell you a bit about the warehouse while you go back to sleep.

"It looks as though they have been building up to this for about a year, not that we got anything out of the prisoners but some of the bodies in the trailer have been identified and two of them disappeared about that time.

"Apparently they volunteered for some medical research, but not quite the research that they anticipated. They had seen the ads on Facebook and thought it was a legit medical center, only to be kidnapped and brought to the warehouse in Wandsworth; the rest you can imagine. They used all of them all to test and perhaps perfect the virus and delivery method."

"Not exactly a bed time story mate."

"No, but you need to know what you've helped prevent, and in a big way, without your persistence, they would have pulled it off. In the warehouse, we found video tapes of their experiments, which have given the scientists very valuable information for treatment, and there was a little paper work, which contained a prediction.

"They estimated at least half a million deaths, anarchy across the UK and that we would be quarantined from the rest of the world. The net result, a total collapse in our society and they could have done it.

"The warehouse was to be a base to continue the attack after the initial spread of the virus. It was stacked with weapons and enough supplies to last for months, and I'll bet we find similar caches at their other depots around the country."

It may not have been a bed time story, but Adam had dropped off to sleep again.

Ron wasn't convinced he was going to make it and if the virus did take hold he was going to suffer badly despite the drips and the morphine in his arm. He deserved to know how many lives he'd saved.

As Ron arrived in Birmingham, other men were arriving at their rendezvous. It had been arranged for them all to appear in ones or twos between 3.00 and 5.00 in the morning, to be briefed and primed for the day's operation. Not an operation to them, more like a day's fun that would also be profitable.

By 5.00, the whole complement had arrived at the Birmingham rendezvous, there they were met by three of De Costa's men. Once they were all settled, one began,

"We will be accompanying you tomorrow, and this is what we want you to do."

He explained that they were to join the rest of the demonstrators at the main meeting point, close to the Edgbaston Cricket Ground. They would move out with the marchers in groups of five or six, every fifteen minutes beginning at 10.30.

At 12.00, they were to begin their work. By that time, the groups would be fairly evenly spread out over the whole march route. Their job was simple; to assault and rob as many of the marchers as possible, cause as much confusion and chaos as they could and draw the police away from the rally points at the Town Halls.

De Costa has thought long and hard about this part of the mission. He wanted to infect as many as possible, and not rely solely on the virus being sprayed from the roofs at the rally points. That is when he came up with the diversionary tactic; it was something they had used well in the Middle East.

The use of peaceful demonstrators to divert the authorities, while forces loyal to their cause planted bombs or ambushed the military had worked well in Egypt and Tunisia. It was still working in Syria, destabilising the governments for the eventual takeover by forces loyal to Iran. A variation on that theme could work as well here.

He had no religious zealots to manipulate, therefore could not play the religious card. What he could do was to use the disenfranchised of the country; every country had them the UK was no exception.

Induced by promises of rich pickings, he had assembled groups all over the country and through their leaders, organised riots at every one of the demonstrations that had taken place over the last year. Each had been a test bed for what was to come.

They had analysed police responses and times and used those to develop their strategy. Up until now, all the gangs had to do was loot and burn. As this culminating event was to be a little different, he'd added a little extra, to ensure these people remained compliant.

"We have with us something that will make the job much easier," said De Costa's man standing in front of the men in Birmingham. He produced one of the small fire extinguishers.

"In here is carbon dioxide gas mixed with Ketamine, a

tranquilizer used for horses, you will probably know it as Special K".

"Wonky Donkey in a spray can, man, a dream come true" came a cry the back of the group "Let me try it" the man pushed forward to try to take the extinguisher.

De Costa's man aimed the nozzle at him and sprayed a little; instantly the man's knees buckled and insane laughter issued from his throat.

"We have enough for everyone but only later after we've finished, you can have as much as you like when we get back tomorrow along with your very generous pay. Each group will have several of these, those you spray won't know what hit them as your friend here has just demonstrated" he said, gesturing toward the man still on his knees in front of him.

"What's in this for you?" one of the gang asked.

"Good question, my employer despises this government as much as you do. He intends to cause as much havoc as possible, sow the seeds of anarchy and one day bring them down. So we have the same goal, wouldn't you agree?"

"Good enough for me", was the reply.

"Give us a go", several then said.

The man complied spraying the gang members in front of him.

Chapter 40

Ron hadn't been 100% truthful with Adam. He had told him he was going to get a few hours rest then go to Birmingham, but the only rest he was going to get was perhaps two hours in the back of the car that had been waiting downstairs to drive him to Birmingham.

The instructions from COBR to go there had been only come just before his visit to the hospital. He was going to stay in London, with the eight squad members who were with him, to help reinforce the police action there.

But the searches of buildings in London had not shown up any fire extinguishers. And, the rally end point for London was planned at The Palace of Westminster. Nobody was going to get close to there tomorrow, so that demonstration was dead in the water.

The decision was to send the three men who had been in Cambridge back to Cambridge. Three would go to Bristol, and Ron, with the remaining two, would go to Birmingham.

For the first time through this whole debacle, they now knew what to look for.

The freezers they had seen at two of the depots run by De Costa would be perfect to keep dozens of the small fire extinguishers cold. So their targets were anybody with an extinguisher. The carbon dioxide expanded and cooled upon release and would produce condensation, in the form of a white mist. This would give a positive indicator which could be used to target the terrorists.

They knew where to look.

Amongst the crowds; gathering at the start of the march, during the march and at the rally points. Every policeman the country had available was being sent to one of the eight target areas and had been explicitly briefed.

Under the Military Aid to Civil Power act, (MACP) all available Special Forces members and several contingents of Marines would reinforce the police. During the briefings, they had all been given the Smallpox vaccine, which had been flown up overnight to the target areas.

It was anticipated that the gangs would run distractions as they had in Sloane St and with that in mind weak spots had been created to accommodate these tactics. The gangs had broken off from the organised marches at everyone that year, to go on a looting and destruction spree. So rather than trying to prevent these breakouts they would allow easy avenues for this to happen, all along the route.

It was impossible to line the routes of the marches with shoulder to shoulder policemen; there wasn't enough in the country to do that. The tactic they decided on was to have police officers, supported by service personnel manning the barricades between these avenues.

There would be fast response teams of armed officers, ready in the streets parallel to the march route and spotters and snipers in strategic positions. There would also be SBS, SAS troops and marines out of uniform, along with plain clothed officers in small groups all evenly dispersed, moving with the marchers.

Ron still had a forlorn hope that the raids on all of De Costa's buildings would be in time to stop the terrorists, before they left for their missions. That wasn't to be; the raids had been conducted in the late afternoon. Although there were still some employees at each location, and all had been detained, none, as expected owned up to being terrorists. And, more importantly no fire extinguishers, other than what would have been expected were found nor were the transport freezers.

Early the next morning, everything they could do was in place an hour or so before the marchers were due to begin to assemble.

All Ron could do now was hope they managed to stop the terrorists before too many people were infected. It was a foregone conclusion that some would be. Ron and his superiors had argued for announcements to be made on TV and radio, warning the demonstrators away from the marches, as had the police.

This had been vetoed by the powers that be, with the dual rationale that, one the virus and the terrorists would still at large, allowing them to shift venues, to shopping centers perhaps. And two, many would not believe them, believing instead that it were a government tactic to quell the demonstrations.

COBR had also been assured by the HPA, that although this was up until now an unknown strain of the Smallpox Virus resulting in a more rapid onset of symptoms, they had effective treatments. Anyone exposed to the known strain of Variola virus if given the Smallpox vaccine before the onset of symptoms, normally between five to seven days, would either not develop the disease or lessen the severity of it, making it treatable with antibiotics, intravenous fluids and medication to control the resulting fever.

The video footage discovered at the warehouse showed that this particular strain both accelerated the onset of symptoms and increased the airborne distribution of the virus. But, that still gave them a sixty hour vaccine treatment window from first exposure.

If treated within this window, only 10% of those exposed would develop the disease but in much reduced severity and most importantly the subsequent airborne stage would be nullified.

Doctor Higginson, the lead scientist from the HPA, now sitting with the full COBR committee in place in Whitehall, told those assembled that, despite the fact that the disease had all but been eradicated over the last twenty years, there were large stockpiles of the vaccine readily available. Enough to treat forty thousand people was being distributed around the country to every demonstration venue and more was being sent from several European nations. And, that the two men exposed at the Palace of Westminster had already been given the vaccine and were now under constant observation and would provide very useful test case data.

He went on to explain that for anyone that did develop full blown symptoms an experimental drug, Cidofovir, had recently been shown to be effective. And although there were complications resulting from the use of it, manufacturing large quantities of it had begun and would not take a great deal of time.

He warned COBR that the drug had to carefully administered, and in hospital conditions. It needed to be injected intravenously, but only after another drug,

Probenecid had been administered. This reduced the possibility of side effects, which could include kidney disease. COBR now could do little more but wait to see how the events would pan out over the next few hours.

By 9.00 AM, the first of the marchers began to arrive. They did so in dribs and drabs to start with but by 10.00 each of the gathering points was filling up. At 10.30, the call had been made for them to begin. Still people arrived, and the assembled throng grew.

Ron had instructed all his men, like the other leaders of the joint SBS and SAS task force had done, to wait until most had moved out before they joined, roughly between 11.00 and 11.30 they all did so. None as yet spotting any of the indicators they were looking for.

One of the few services that would not come to a complete standstill that day was the ferry companies. The companies operating ferries out of the UK were staffed with personnel from both the countries they connected with. But they were not operating normally; they were running on a much reduced schedule. When the strike was in its planning stage De Costa put forward a maneuver that would absolutely guarantee the UK's isolation from Continental Europe.

This called for a ferry to Roscoff, Santander, Amsterdam, Esbjerg and Ostend, to carry one of his men. Each would be easily able to carry several spray cans in their luggage. Roseau had objected to it as being too unpredictable and that the virus may spread to the Middle East. It was therefore vetoed by the planners in Tehran. Now, unfettered by Roseau he was free to activate it.

As the general strike would prevent the use of public transport, each of the men designated to catch the ferries had a hired car and now sat in that car in queues at each of the ferry terminals, with the exception of the man due to take the ferry from Plymouth to Roscoff.

At Portsmouth, Hull, Ramsgate and Harwich the queues extended for miles and in each queue a terrorist sat, becoming increasingly nervous with each hour that passed. The man destined for Roscoff had no such worry. He had set off earlier than the others due to the length of the drive to Plymouth. Arriving earlier than expected he was near the front of the queue for his designated ferry as it boarded.

He now sat in the main seating area of the ferry, occasionally reaching into his bag and releasing a little of the contaminated spray into the air.

In Birmingham, the planned march route began at the assembly point in Calthorpe Park. The organisers there estimated one hundred and twenty thousand people, far fewer than had been anticipated a week ago, gathered before making their way into the city center along Bristol Street.

Many had made their way using their own cars, but buses and coaches had also been laid on for those that needed them. An examination of a cross section of the crowd would have shown many walks of life represented here. As the schools were all closed, whole families joined the throng, along with doctors, nurses, public sector employees, factory and construction workers, shop keepers, firemen and ambulance drivers.

The atmosphere, despite what had occurred the day before was more one of a carnival than demonstration, much as the organisers planned. The organisers had tables arranged at the perimeter with bottled water and food, along with tee-shirts proclaiming their support for the general strike. More such tables would line the bunting lined march routes. Bands had been laid on at the rally center for entertainment later that afternoon. This was to be a day of unity. A show of strength toward the government, but it was also to be a day to remember in a good way, with no repetitions of the events earlier in the year.

The mass of bodies moved into Smallbrook, along Hill St, and past the train station, all of which had been closed to traffic and into the streets around the city center. Others joined over the mile and a half walk and by midday one hundred and fifty thousand people filled the streets and the square in front of Council House.

The square where the speeches would take place would hold no more than thirty thousand. To accommodate the anticipated turn out, alternative gathering places were set up with large screens by the Cathedral and throughout the pedestrian shopping district of New Street and the Bull Ring.

As Ron walked along with the assembled masses, he continually scanned those around him as did his men. Then at midday a radio call went out, a group somewhere behind him had been spotted spraying the crowd. They had assaulted and robbed several of the marchers, some of whom had collapsed. Then another call went out, followed by another a minute later.

Many of the attack victims seemed to have been affected by a drug but from what Ron heard over the radio this was not the virus they expected. Some merely stood or walked in a disorientated fashion, others had fallen to the ground and yet more began vomiting. Had they made a mistake with the assumption about the Variola Virus or were the terrorists using something even more deadly on the crowds?

As each group was spotted, squads of riot police held in reserve along the side streets were guided in by the spotters and snipers positioned on roof tops along the route. In teams of twenty all wearing gas masks and riot gear, they drove into the crowd, for the time being ignoring all but those armed with the extinguishers.

They knocked them to the ground, disarming and cuffing them. Once they were incapacitated, others manning the barricades sort out anyone else that had been witnessed assaulting any of the marchers. Teams of marines formed a perimeter twenty meters from each incident and paramedics treated the injured. As a semblance of order was brought to each incident, the marines then began to shepherd all those they'd contained within their perimeter, down an available side street.

A group walking together, having just completed the march route, stopped beside the Victoria Square cafe to watch and listen to an impromptu band whilst they waited for the roads to clear a little. News of the trouble was yet to spread. The crowds ahead and following around them were in a celebratory mood. Then a sharp scream pierced the festivities, followed by a raucous laugh. This caught the ears of a man within this group, turning he witnessed a young woman getting mugged. He immediately called to his friends; all work colleagues from a local distribution company, they all ran forward to assist the lady.

As they neared the mugger and his victim they were confronted by a dozen men or more, one wielding a fire extinguisher over his head with that same insane laughter cackling in his throat. As they saw the men coming to help the girl, they surged forward to intercept them.

As the two groups charged into each other, they started to fight, fists, feet, bottles, chairs anything within easy reach. Initially the gangs had the edge, not through numbers, but through delight in what they were doing, driven by the drugs following through their veins. The members of the gang were soon outnumbered as more of the peaceful marchers that had been enjoying the band playing outside the cage joined the fray.

Throughout the crowded Birmingham City Centre streets, little pockets violence erupted, in some the gang members were tackled by peaceful demonstrators, at others the police intervened. Similar scenes were repeated all over the country at every venue. And confusion reigned.

The panicking crowd, attempting to leave, ran down side streets, many of which the police had deliberately left clear, only to find themselves kettled there by more riot and mounted police.

With hundreds of people pouring onto these streets, some of their volition, others guided there by the marines, the police tried the best they could to separate victims from any gang member or terrorist, but that proved to be an impossible task. Kettling was the only answer.

Street after street was filled up and then was sealed at either end. Everyone that could be was detained, and those suffering from inhaling the gas were treated.

Medical staff from the Army, Navy and Air Force, had been busy erecting makeshift medical centers. They were simple tented structures on streets kept clear by the police.

Hundreds of people were now being ushered towards them ready to be vaccinated as printed cards were handed to each explaining that they had been contaminated by a toxin and would be vaccinated immediately.

As the authorities attempted to bring order to the chaos, and new incidents ceased a semblance of order gradually returned. The rally continued, some demonstrators, those already at the rally centers, unaware of what was transpiring around them.

Megaphones could be heard chanting slogans, and air horns blasting into the sky.

Air horns!

Ron turned; they were coming from behind him, from the direction of the rally point near the Town Hall, no more than four hundred meters away.

Ron ran followed by his men he screamed into his radio as he raced through the crowded street.

"The air horns stop them!"

One hundred meters ahead at the edge of the crowd, gathered in front of Council House, he could see or more hear an air horn being held up and blasted into the air. A faint white wisp of condensation formed then slowly sunk into the crowd with each fresh blast.

As Ron neared the man, with a backpack on his back and the air horn held high, the man turned, alerted by shouts from the crowd. The terrorist looked directly at Ron for a few seconds and then the men running up behind him, but then quickly turned and began to run through the crowd toward the center of the square.

The air horn held high in the air, as he ran, emitted a continued blast. The SBS squad pursued the terrorist as Ron followed pulling out his radio,

"The men with the air horns are the terrorists they are at the rally points at the Town Halls, and they need to be taken down now."

The terrorist stopped in the center of the crowd he pulled another canister from his backpack and attached it to the air horn head.

Holding it above his head in his left hand and a semi-automatic which had also taken from the pack in his right, he aimed in the direction of the SBS troopers closing upon him.

The crowd around the man, deafened by the air horn turned to look and, at the sight of the pistol in his hand, they moved. Some turned and ran if they could; others merely collided with the crowd behind. Cries of,

"He's got a gun!" created a wave of demonstrators pushing each other to get out of the way and the stampede they dreaded began.

A clear pocket formed into which the SBS men ran, the lead drew his weapon heedless of the rounds coming towards him unleashed by the terrorist, he calmly and carefully aimed, and fired twice, striking the man in the center of his chest.

Yet, Ron could still hear another air horn somewhere within the crowd, pinpointing it coming from the rear, he pushed through in pursuit.

Calls at each rally went out instructing the snipers at each of the Town Hall rally points to neutralise the terrorists with the air horns. At each of the locations, the spotters and their accompanying snipers searched for targets. As each was found, the telltale wisp of white condensation confirming their quarry, they took their shots.

None of the distances was more than three hundred meters, well within the range of the snipers, and each hit their intended target with the first round, sending him flying backward into the crowd. At this panic erupted once more as the crowds pushed and fought to get away.

Ron pushed through the bewildered and panicky crowd in the square in search of the terrorist armed with the air horn, which had just gone quiet. Stunned groups of protestors stood all around him, not trying to flee anymore as no escape routes presented themselves, but all were ashen faced wondering what was happening and what was going to happen next. Others were worse of being caught in the initial stampedes and now lay on the ground. Ron was torn between helping these victims and finding the terrorists but knew he had no choice; the terrorists had to be stopped before they infected any more.

Passing one such knot of protestors huddling in a doorway for protection, he spotted an air horn lying on the ground, next to which was a small rucksack. Inside were more canisters, but there was no sign of the terrorist.

"Can you see him? Ron asked of his men scanning the crowd.

"No," one replied. "Can't hear any horns either"

They stood, scanning the crowd

"Okay guys, I can't hear any, there is no point searching blindly the spotters will tell us if they see anything, we should help the injured until they do"

In the streets behind them, crowds fleeing the scene collided into other protectors still joining from the Bullring direction, unaware of the disturbance ahead of them, they blocked any escape. Shouts of shootings and fights rippled through the fleeing crowds which looked for a route to escape the madness.

The Police manning barricades at the junction of Corporation Street pulled back the barricades that had previously closed off the street allowing the panicked protesters through, only to find their escape blocked off by mounted Police and dog handlers at the end of the street.

From the rostrum in front of Council House, the organisers appealed for calm urged on by policemen that had now joined them. Some thirty thousand people were contained between the Council House Square and the Cathedral grounds but another hundred thousand now spilled out into streets around the city center. Calm slowly descended again but not before hundreds had been hurt in the stampede.

Similar scenes occurred in Bristol, Cambridge, Edinburgh, Glasgow, Liverpool, Manchester and Newcastle. The organisers and the police's appeal for calm broadcast from large screens gradually calmed the panicked crowd.

Ambulances manned by service personnel were allowed through the barricades and police lines to tend to the injured, and police prepared routes through which they would let out the kettled crowds. As each was admitted through, their names and addresses were taken, and each was given a small card informing them that there was a possibility that they had been exposed to a toxic substance and would need to attend the hospital or clinic named on the card.

Chapter 41

As day turned to night, the police managed the scenes at each incident. Those within the vicinity of a spraying incident had been immediately treated, and slowly all were being released. Schools and community centers up and down the country were taken over and kitted out as clinics and staffed by members of the military.

Despite those that had possibly been infected at the demonstrations had been told to attend the clinics named on the printed cards the next day, many had ignored the instructions, and had headed straight to the nearest A&E. These filled up fast and now queues stretched out of the front doors and into the car parks.

At 7.00, that evening the Deputy Prime Minister began his announcement to the country.

It was broadcast on every channel and repeated hourly. Initially the Prime Minister insisted he should be the one to speak to the people, but after advice from representatives of every party in the UK, he decided not to. They'd advised him that public opinion of him was so low following the broadcasts the day before from the Houses of Parliament that the announcement would be far better coming from his deputy. His resignation was already being demanded, not just from the opposition Labour Party, but from within his own.

Dick Smeg began the address by thanking the nation for its attention, and then began the onerous task of explaining that they were under a terrorist attack and the nature of that attack.

He explained that despite that the fact that the virus was of a strain that had never been seen until recently, a drug to combat the smallpox disease it caused, had been developed, as was right now being produced in huge quantities. Enough to treat the entire population of the UK, if necessary, it would be available at clinics that were being set up in schools and community centers, as well as their doctors' surgeries.

He went on to describe the signs and symptoms of the disease but assured the nation that no one would be infectious for at least forty eight hours. He asked all those that had been present at the demonstrations, who had not already received a vaccination, to attend one of the centers the next day, and that they would be listed after the broadcast.

He urged everyone else not to turn up to the centers unless they believed they had been infected, but to use the telephone numbers that also would be listed after the broadcast for further information. He advised them to make an appointment for a vaccination and promised that all who wanted the vaccination would have one by the end of the week.

He advised that all schools and universities would be closed until the end of that emergency and asked that with the exception of education all to go to work normally. In particular he asked all emergency and medical personnel even those on leave to turn up for work the next morning.

He told them that buses were being laid on, which would be manned by Territorial's to transport those that needed to attend a clinic could do so and that mobile treatment units that would be directed to remote areas.

He ended by asking the viewers not to panic and assured them that he would be moving heaven and earth to discover who was responsible for this atrocity, and to bring them to justice.

Not at any point did he speculate upon the source of the attack but as he thanked the nation and bid his good-byes, every news channel had a pundit doing just that. They also speculated on what would have happened had the terrorists been truly successful.

Sarah Jane had the dubious honor of doing so for Star. To either side of her sat experts from the medical world and bio warfare, behind her an electronic map provided the background.

They based their predictions on the numbers the organisers of the demonstrations had anticipated would turn out, estimated at two and a half million across the country. And then used a further estimation factor of 10% for those contaminated with the virus, this according to their attendant experts was a realistic number.

As they talked the electronic map filled the screen, each demonstration target was marked in red and Day One, two hundred and fifty thousand infected sat in the bottom right hand corner. The experts discussed the spread of the virus.

The map changed to reflect their predictions; it now had Day Four in the bottom right followed by two and a half million infected. The red dots had now expanded outwards to encompass a twenty five mile radius from each original infection point.

The screen then changed again, to depict a hundred mile radius, the caption the bottom now read, Day Ten, twenty five million infected.

It was debatable whether anyone at the Star or any of the news channels had actually thought through the effect their predictions might have, or even reviewed the inclusion of the graphics in the broadcast. By all estimations, their thoughts were only about capturing the biggest audience in history and besting their rivals on viewer numbers.

But the presenter's face told it all.

Whilst interviewing her experts, she looked down at a monitor in front of her, which was displaying the same prediction map that was blue screened behind her. The point of realisation was painfully obvious. Her expression turning to shock as she realised she lived within the first red circle and to horror that her mother, sister and all her family were contained within the second.

Whether it was due to the Deputy PM's announcement, the emergency radio messages, the TV news shows, or purely a natural response, was open to discussion, but the events that followed over the next two days followed very a predictable pattern.

Early the following morning there was a run on face masks, latex gloves, and anti-bacterial products of every conceivable nature.

Many that went out covered their faces with scarves; their hands were gloved and they tried their best to avoid proximity with anyone else. Despite that they had been informed that it would be several days before the virus could spread, they were not taking any chances. Supplies sold out within the first few hours and scuffles ensued as stocks ran low.

Queues of cars formed at every open supermarket and petrol station across the land. People were desperate to stock up, get home and hole up. Less than half those working in the shops and supermarkets turned up for work that morning, although they had been told there would be face masks for them to wear and antibacterial sprays to clean their hands.

As a result, the queues in them stretched throughout the shop nobody wanted to stand close to anybody else when they did more scuffles, and then fights ensued.

By late afternoon many simply picked up what they wanted and left and as the sun set, no one was bothering to pay for anything; they grabbed what they needed and ran.

Darkness only brought on more violence.

Those that had decided not to stock up during the day; did so that night. Not only were food shops broken into, but every conceivable type of shop, from electronics to pharmacies. These two days would produce the worst scenes of looting the UK had ever witnessed, whether they were armed with a plastic rubbish bag for the stolen goods or the back of a transit van, there was little to stop them.

A lone shop keeper here or there tried to protect his store but to little avail. As more joined the fray, it became easier to steal from those that had already looted the shops. Fights broke out in the streets; some involved two fighting over some item or other. Others involved much larger numbers fighting outside shops, for the right to loot the choicest locations.

As the fighting escalated so did the destruction. Those not content just to loot began to burn.

There was still a large police and service presence out

on the streets, but most were still tending the incident sites. Those that could be freed up assisted the fire brigade trying to quell the fires now raging out of control in many a city center.

At many of the fires, the fire brigade came under attack by those that had set it. Whilst waiting for the brigade to respond to the fire, ammunition was collected in the form of bottles and bricks then used as missiles to bombard the fire fighters. The looting and the violence carried on pretty much unchallenged all night and into the next day.

But that wasn't the end of the looting. Attention now turned to warehouses and distribution centers and this a more organised affair. With no security present and no one available to respond to the alarms; cars, lorries, vans and vehicles with trailers pulled into the car parks, and once through the loading doors, filled up at their leisure.

Society, already peeling at the seams, was beginning to unravel. So much so the question of martial law was now to be discussed at the next COBR.

With the rising of the sun the following day, a picture of mass destruction appeared on the streets of towns and cities, across the country.

Now, almost every town and city became a ghost town; nobody turned up for work. No buses ran or trains moved. The occasional police patrol, or a fire engine responding to yet another fire, a furtive silhouette appearing for a second in the distance or the squeak of a shopping cart trolleys wheels and plumes of smoke disappearing into the shy. Streams of soot blacked water flowed around discarded cardboard boxes or a dropped TV set, and the glass from hundreds of shop windows, littered the streets.

The only major signs of life were at hospitals, doctor surgeries and improvised clinics. Thousands of people had turned up at them during those two days. Some of those had been present at the demonstrations and had been advised to go, others just wanting the inoculation as a precaution.

Already hundreds were claiming they had caught the disease, although as yet no sign of the actual symptoms of Smallpox had actually been discovered.

Chapter 42

But then, with the dawning of the third day after the attack, a near miraculous event occurred.

People began gathering on the streets, not with the intent to loot and burn but armed with brooms, bins and bin bags in their hands. Many had received inoculations; others wore face masks, and together they began to clean up the destruction of the previous two days.

There had been no particular organisation in this; someone appeared to clean up their wrecked shop to be helped by a neighbor and then a friend of the neighbor and then a friend of the friend.

Word soon spread as social network sites gossiped. More came out to offer their assistance, shop owners opened up their shops handing out food and water to all those that wanted it. Those supermarkets that hadn't been, raided opened up and also provided food, free to those that couldn't pay.

This wave of humanitarian gestures spread and calmed descended on the UK's towns and cities, as though the eye of a hurricane had reached them. By the end of the day, thousands across the country turned out to help. Some to clean up the streets whilst others went to check on their neighbors, some to get food for those that couldn't do it themselves and yet more to ensure peace reigned. Violence and destruction would no longer be tolerated.

Day three also brought in those with the first symptoms. Not in huge numbers. No more than five hundred people were admitted to hospital, and as all hospitals had stopped routine treatments and operations except those of emergencies, they had plenty of capacity to cope. These figures would slowly rise but would never become the plague that was dreaded. Every member of every medical profession from the ambulance drivers to the surgeons had inoculations at the start of the emergency and had staff in plenty.

This wasn't the case in Continental Europe. The governments there obviously were very much aware of the situation in the UK and had taken precautions. These included the inoculation of their medical staff, but they had not considered a wholesale inoculation as they had in the UK.

When people started to turn up at hospitals in France and Germany, complaining of symptoms associated with the Smallpox disease, the realisation dawned. This attack had not been confined to the UK as they originally believed. Interpol was already working with the UK authorities investigating the terrorists' activities and had raided all the known addresses that Roseau and De Costa were known to have, spread about the continent. But the authorities were not prepared for the spread of the disease across Europe and began to make emergency plans to halt the spread of what could very easily become a plague.

Although flights in and out of the UK had been grounded for several days, a small number had taken off from Heathrow; all private flights. The passengers were either from the government or the security services and were travelling to meet their counterparts abroad. Initially the finger of blame was pointed toward Muslim radicals, but as more was discovered about the activities of Roseau and De Costa, a clearer picture began to emerge.

At a meeting in The Hague attended by senior government and security personnel of all nations of the UN, it was shown that without a doubt, that these two were Iranian and that the attack had been sponsored by the government there. Embargos were to be immediately emplaced; nothing was to go in or out of Iran.

They would give the population there the chance to rise-up against their masters, but should that not occur, there was only one solution; an invasion. The resolution passed without a single dissenting vote. A task force would be formed to ensure this represented by every nation of the globe. Every leader around the world was enraged about what the Iranians had done. They had been very close to causing a worldwide pandemic.

This was an indiscriminate killer, taking no account of color, race or creed. Those infected came from a comprehensive cross section of society, heedless of their religion. They vowed never again to let the fundamentalists, whether they were national or religious, to be able to repeat what had been done.

Repercussions were not only being planned in The Hague they were already being felt in many countries. Outside Camp Bastion in Afghanistan a lorry had stopped five hundred meters away from the gates depositing fifteen bodies into the dirt, on one was pinned a note with a single word; Terrorist. Similar events happened in Pakistan. Although alive, a dozen bloodied and bruised senior members of the military were delivered to an American base there.

For the past couple days, the whole of Europe had been holding its collective breath, waiting for the major outbreak they thought to be imminent. The source of the infection that had so far infected those in Continental Europe had been traced to a single ferry from Plymouth to Roscoff.

And yet, details discovered at the warehouse in Wandsworth indicated that the terrorists had intended to send lone terrorists to at least five ports in the UK destined for Europe. Leaders of all the European nations had broadcast emergency messages with much the same content as the Deputy PM in the UK had sent out a few days before.

Treatment centers were being set up, and drugs to treat the infection produced and shipped as they braced themselves for the onslaught that they believed to be coming.

Then a collective sigh of relief flowed like a wave across Europe as abandoned cars were discovered at Portsmouth, Hull, Ramsgate and Harwich, close to the designated ferry terminals. Each car held half a dozen spray cans of the virus.

For the next few days, inoculations and cleanups continued all over the UK. Ron and his troopers stayed at their various locations to assist with these efforts. There were no more incidents of looting or arson; the military presence now on the streets made sure of that.

Those few that had been prepared to help each other

on the third day of the riots had inspired many others. Their numbers had swelled until the streets filled with volunteers and the eye of the hurricane didn't pass. Still it would be many weeks before normality returned.

Much of De Costa and Roseau's plan was successful but not enough to say the mission was a success and definitely not enough for their masters in Tehran. Those masters were about to feel the wrath of the entire world. And, although the UK government had been both humiliated and weakened, they were far from defeated.

Some ten thousand people were estimated to be infected, and many more would receive the antidote in any case. Had it not been for the foresight of the little team around a kitchen table in Wembury, the picture would have been far different.

Adam had been lucky, only displaying mild symptoms of the disease, a severe headache, a high fever and nausea accompanied by horrendous bouts of diarrhea, which lasted for five days. And Simon fared the same. Both were used as test cases to evaluate the virus's virulence and its treatment, and were released from hospital within the week.

The data they provided helped in the treatment of all those exposed both in the UK and Continental Europe and, as a result, the mortality rate was exceedingly low. What deaths that occurred, ironically most on the continent served to spur on the anti-terrorist movements, taking hold worldwide.

Clive Gooding was sitting at his desk when the phone rang. The events of the past ten days had taken their toll on the man, as they had done to nearly everyone in the UK and around the world.

It was now universally accepted that Iranian terrorists were the culprits behind the attack and that they had been sponsored by the Iranian Government. Retributions were underway already, and what the consequences to the world would be was anybody's guess at this point.

But Clive was party to secrets discovered by Adam and his ad-hoc team; secrets that exposed levels of corruption hitherto unknown in the UK, and secrets that had ultimately allowed this terrorist strike to happen. What distressed Clive the most was that this corruption and all those involved would never be exposed.

He answered the phone and was told there was a parcel for him that had just been delivered hand delivered by a woman, would he like it brought up? He answered that he would. A few minutes later, the Desk Sergeant knocked on his door before opening it and handed Clive a large envelope. Mystified and not expecting a delivery he opened the envelope and pulled out fifty sheets of A4 paper. The top sheet said simply:

We thought you might know what to do with this. Stella.

As he turned over the page, he was greeted with lists of names, dates and numbers, followed by a few details. He couldn't help but recognise many of the names.

Yes, he knew exactly what to do with this.

As Gooding read through Stella's dossier, Adam sat on the couch watching the news. Isobel lay out next to him, her head on his knee, and Dan sat on the couch next to them. They had let him leave the hospital the night before as long as he promised to keep pumping the fluids back in, and he was very happy to be back home with his family, and in one piece.

While Adam had been in hospital, Stella had been busy. In addition to compiling the dossier that had just been delivered to Clive Gooding, she had also completed uploading all the material that she had compiled onto a website, with the help of Dan and Isobel.

Every dirty deal recorded in Jonathan's data was now available for the world to see. Stella, in addition to using computer networks to procure information, also knew how to use it to disseminate it. She designed a series of viral ads, which were then spread through social networking sites advertising the presence of the website containing all the data.

The media's concentration had been on either various events in Afghanistan, Pakistan and Indonesia as well as in the America, UK and in Europe where the attacks and the delivery of terrorist radicals to the authorities were the topics of discussion. Or with their experts discussing what could have happened if it had not been caught just in time. Experts had differing opinions about the spread and the rate of it. All had graphics depicting their predictions, but the consensus of opinion was that a significant percentage of the world's population could have been wiped out, had the terrorist plot not been discovered, right at the last minute.

Now with Stella's viral ads, a new story was breaking.

Although the details revealed hundreds of under the table deals, many of which were illegal and if not, certainly unethical, and the networks that them possible, it was one that was going to grab the world's attention and the headlines in every major newspaper in every major population center for many days to come.

This revelation concerned De Costa and Roseau, and the contributions they had made to the Conservative party. These contributions helped them secure the contracts in the Palace of Westminster and other government buildings around the country. Dandelion too, was not going escape, his organisation had been pivotal in the creation of the network that allowed this to happen.

Without the greed and complicity of these few there would have been no terrorist attack.

Adam clicked off the TV, having had enough of all of it as it possible to have.

Dan turned to his brother.

"Not too bad for a rugby playing science geek."

"Fuck off and get me a cup of tea." he earned as his reward.

De Costa stood on a balcony overlooking the city of Tehran; his penthouse flat on the top floor of the building gave an excellent view of the city. As the blood red sun set, the call to prayer rose from a dozen or so mosques that were within his hearing. With a screech of tires, two vans pulled up at the entrance of his building, disgorging their passengers onto the pavement.

He knew they would be coming for him. Not only had he let them down, but he had put them in a grave situation. The West had discovered the government's involvement in his scheme and for that, they would demand his blood.

Picking up the satellite phone he called a number and

then sent a code that would activate the bombs in the Enterprise.

He might have been Iranian by birth, but he was a true Jihadist Warrior to his core, and his mission would continue despite his death. After throwing the phone as far as he could manage into the street below, he knelt on his prayer mat, facing Mecca, put his Glock into his mouth and pulled the trigger.

Dear reader,

We hope you enjoyed reading *A Plague of Dissent*. Please take a moment to leave a review, even if it's a short one. Your opinion is important to us.

Discover more books by Nic Taylor at

https://www.nextchapter.pub/authors/nic-taylor

Want to know when one of our books is free or discounted? Join the newsletter at

http://eepurl.com/bqqB3H

Best regards,

Nic Taylor and the Next Chapter Team

About the Author

Nic grew up in Penzance, Cornwall, and spent these formative years either hanging out on the beach surfing and diving, or taking photographs. At the age of twenty he talked himself into a job as an architectural assistant with a prestigious practice in London, and spent the next seven years designing banks and partying in the city. By the age of twenty seven the wanderlust hit him, and he headed off to Montego Bay in Jamaica. Once there, he both ran a diving school and freelanced as an architect for hoteliers.

For five years he managed to keep this up, and himself narrowly out of trouble. Until after one too many close calls, he decided it was time to leave. He boarded a plane and headed for Singapore to visit a Singaporean girl he'd got to know.

Singapore, or more pointedly the Singaporean girl, managed to calm Nic down somewhat. For a dozen years he based himself in Singapore, working in various fields. He taught diving and escorted dive parties to remote locations throughout the South China Sea, the Indian Ocean and the Indonesian archipelago. He designed the odd hotel or two in the Maldives and Thailand, and expanded his photographic repertoire to become one of the foremost photographers in the region.

He also diversified into the moving picture industry, to eventually shoot several short films and documentaries, including Burning Earth for the Discovery Channel. In Burning Earth he spent many weeks camped out in the burning jungles of Borneo, hanging out of helicopters with a camera on his shoulder. He did find the time to get married to the same Singaporean girl, who later gave birth to two sons, Adam born in 1996 and Dan a year later.

In 2003 he moved back to the UK and built a house overlooking the Wye River, on the outskirts of Ross on Wye, in Herefordshire. The move back to the UK was prompted by two very different reasons.

Firstly, the events in the U.S on the 11th September 2001 changed Asia; it had always been a lively place to live and work, but the atmosphere had changed. Throughout Malaysia and Indonesia a pronounced anti-western attitude was taking hold, culminating in the Bali bombings at the Hard Rock Cafe, where Nic used to hang out along with his sons.

The second was his awakening to environmental issues. The fires he filmed in Borneo were certainly one of the catalysts; another was the visible degradation of the oceans and reefs he couldn't help but notice. The coral bleaching of the Maldivian reefs, the raw sewage pumped into the ocean by hotel developers, mangrove swamps destroyed to make way for prawn farms and the overfishing, all of them taking a horrendous toll, and plain for anybody to see. This all prompted him to be a part of the solution, rather than ignore these issues as the majority of the planet seemed to be doing.

Armed with an idea inspired by villagers growing seaweed on one of his favorite remote islands, groups Nusa Penida and Nusa Lembongan, he set about working on a concept. This concept entailed growing macro algae in marine farms along with fish and shellfish; the fish and shellfish already had a ready market and the macro algae could be processed to produce renewable fuels.

Being the foolhardy and impetuous soul that he can be

much of the time, Nic thought he could make this contribution on his own and set up a research company, Taylor Made Marine, to work on his concept. The concept was good and he is still working on it today, although no longer alone because the financing was seriously flawed. These flaws became evident in 2007, when the bank pulled the rug from beneath his property development company, developing sustainable and affordable housing which provided the funding for the research. This resulted in the collapse of the company and seizure of his assets on which loans were secured.

Nic and his wife had another child, a girl named Shakira. However, as a consequence of stress, Nic's marriage soon disintegrated and he decided to move to Plymouth. In Plymouth he joined forces with Plymouth University to continue with his research, and work towards a PhD.

Nic now spends his time equally divided between his research and the Plymstock Oaks Rugby Club, where he coaches the Under 15's. He runs several projects, including coaching rugby to the disabled and using rugby as a social inclusion vehicle to get kids off the streets. And of course his writing: you're currently reading his first book "A Plague of Dissent" and he is presently working on the sequel, Gaia's Warriors.